The
LOST
LETTERS

Sarah Mitchell

The
LOST
LETTERS

Bookouture

Published by Bookouture in 2018

An imprint of StoryFire Ltd.

Carmelite House
50 Victoria Embankment
London EC4Y 0DZ

www.bookouture.com

ISBN: 978-1-78681-453-1
eBook ISBN: 978-1-78681-452-4

In memory of my parents

'When two roads diverge, take the one that leads to the beach.'
Hannah McKinnon

CHAPTER ONE

Canadian airspace, recently

'… seven, eight, nine …' Martha Rodwell is counting under her breath. On ten she opens her eyes and her left hand – freckled, slim and workmanlike – slackens its grip on the arm of the airline chair. Little by little the slope of the gangway begins to level and the grinding whine of the engines slows to a growl.

'Well,' she murmurs, 'I guess we can all breathe again now!' The man in the seat but one from her own lifts his head from the well of a ring binder, spearing her with light blue eyes.

'I'm sorry?' he says. 'What did you say?'

'Oh!' – Martha laughs awkwardly – 'I… Well, I just… Oh, it was nothing…'

Her attention is caught by the seatbelt sign. Large, illuminated letters remind her even now the plane is climbing, climbing… She rubs a sticky palm on the denim of her skirt.

The cabin is crowded but not quite full: families with squirming children, a handful of middle-aged executives, three nuns in teal-blue habits and a few solitary travellers like herself.

'Do you know' – the words are out of her mouth before she can stop them – 'that eighty per cent of aviation accidents occur in the first ten seconds immediately after takeoff or during the last ten seconds before landing?'

Her neighbour blinks in surprise. 'If you say so.' His accent brings to mind those imported period dramas she watches at the weekend, a microwave dinner on her lap and a glass of Rita Hills red at her elbow.

He picks up his binder. He has another on his lap and has placed a stack of loose papers on the empty seat between them. They were all tied together with a pink ribbon that he pulled off as soon as Martha sat down and is now draped over his knee. In a moment it's going to fall off and work its way under the chair in front of him and he will lose it altogether. Martha thinks about mentioning this but he is already engrossed in his reading again, swiping the occasional sentence with a highlighter pen and daubing the page with yellow Post-it notes from a pad of them tucked into the palm of his other hand. His concentration is fixed and fierce and Martha sees how young he is. Not a great deal older than her own daughter, in fact.

The thought of Janey pokes her in the ribs as sharply as a pointed stick. Recently, Martha hasn't been able to shake the sense that something is wrong. Almost as soon as Janey left for England the previous fall her correspondence dwindled to minimal, dry fragments of text, the very absence of words a restatement of all the hurtful sentiments she'd yelled at Martha before she left. Now she telephones more often, but Martha has to perform a monologue just to keep the call afloat, or else ask a stream of questions that sound even to her own ears like an inquisition and are answered with merely a dead-end 'yeah' or 'fine'. It feels like struggling to lift a heavy weight while Janey watches from afar refusing to lift so much as a finger to help.

The cabin fills with the snap of metal clips, the papery rustle of clothes and the rattle of trolleys. A few moments later a young female member of the cabin crew offers her something to drink. 'Champagne, perhaps?'

'Yes,' Martha says, she would like a glass of champagne. She deserves it, after the recent, horrible weeks.

The plane is horizontal now, the hum of the engines steady and relaxed. Tentatively, she leans back in her seat and looks out of the window. The sky is a blinding, brutal blue and the carpet of rolled-up cloud so resembles snowdrifts that she idly assumes they are skimming the ice-fields of Canada and Greenland until an inner voice reminds her that the actual ground curves somewhere out of sight, far, far below. She averts her gaze and takes several quick sips of too-sweet, imitation fizz.

'Fuck!'

Martha's neighbour is brandishing a half-opened bottle of tonic water and regarding it with alarm. A stream of bubbles has burst out of the seal and is cascading onto his papers. His other hand is burrowing into the recess of a trouser pocket searching, she assumes, for a handkerchief, but the precarious organisation of his papers appears vulnerable to the smallest sideways movement.

Martha rummages in her travel bag – a small practical rucksack, the many pockets of which she has packed for just such contingencies – and presents him with a packet of paper tissues. For a minute or two he carefully dabs the page of inky blotches and then searches for somewhere to put the sodden tissues.

'Let me,' Martha says, and stuffs them into her glass, which is now conveniently empty.

'Hey. Thanks.' He has the lanky kind of build that belongs on a running track or a soccer pitch rather than a baseball field. It isn't so apparent sitting down but now she can see how he is twisted sideways by the cramped seating and how his back hunches awkwardly over the inadequate fold-down table. Despite the formality of a suit there's still the air of the college student about him. His shirt has loosened from his waistband, the knot of his tie has twisted under his collar and his fairish hair is floppy at the front in a boy-band sort of way. His eyes flick over her face and then he picks up his pen again. '*Ex parte* injunction in the QBD as soon as I get back. Sorry to be unfriendly.'

Martha says, 'Of course.' She has no idea what he's talking about.

*

An hour or so has passed. Martha's novel is open, face down over her knee. With rapturous horror she's watching the outside light deepen to velvet indigo as they hurtle towards the enveloping night. Before long she hears clinks and chinks and snatches of conversation from the galley and the hot smell of food begins to waft through the cabin. The drinks trolley clatters around and when Martha asks for a French red (she's en route to Europe, after all) the young hostess hands her two miniature bottles of Merlot. Shortly after that comes a tray piled with an assortment of foil cartons and cellophane packages. Once or twice she casts a glance at her neighbour but he continues to read as he forks chunks of chicken into his mouth, the binder jammed uncomfortably between his lap and the table.

Soon Martha can barely feel the forward motion of the plane. Since her father died just under a month ago she's felt a crushing physical fatigue, as if she has to drag her grief around like ankle chains. He was found on the porch, surrounded by sheets of writing paper skimming over the lawn and skewered to the rose bushes. Six months previously he had stepped down from the municipal council to write his memoirs. Elizabeth, her sister, had offered to proofread them but she told Martha that he refused point-blank to let her see them.

'Not until they're finished,' he said. And then he mentioned, casually, as if it were of no import at all, that in order to finish them he would need to go back to England.

'Why,' Elizabeth asked Martha on the telephone that evening, 'does he want to go back now, when he hasn't set foot on British soil for seventy years?' Martha didn't know. But when he died they discovered he had booked a hotel and rented a beach hut in a small English coastal town, called Wells-next-the-Sea, for the whole of May.

Martha thinks she ought to be dealing with the bereavement better; she's a forty-four year-old schoolteacher, for heaven's sake – she has said this to herself, scrabbling for a tissue at the lights or hijacked by tears at the checkout packing groceries into a box – but she feels older, exposed. As if mortality is tapping at the window. A week ago she dreamed of him. He was crouched with a group of boys in the bottom of a wooden boat that was pitching and tossing in a grey, biblical sea. While Martha watched, a thin mist of music rose from the water as the children began to sing, oblivious to the foam-tipped waves that slopped over their shoes. She woke feeling wretched and confused. Her father had never once wanted to talk about his evacuation, so why was she dreaming of it now?

She and Elizabeth spent the week after the funeral clearing out his house. On the first morning Elizabeth found the printout of their father's memoirs in his study and spent the afternoon meticulously putting in order all the papers that had been scattered so carelessly around his porch. Over tacos for dinner, both of them too drained for anything but comfort food, her brow furrowed as she spoke to Martha about it. 'The strange thing is,' Elizabeth said, 'the story only starts when Dad turned twenty and he met Mum at the benefit dance.' (Over the years they had both been told the story countless times of how their mother's date had gotten too drunk to walk her home and their father had stepped up to the moment and into his future.) 'There's no mention of anything before then at all.'

'Maybe there's some stuff on his computer he hadn't printed out?'

Elizabeth shook her head, taco dangling from one hand. 'The version on the computer is no different from the one in the study. I already checked.' Late into the following night, sustained by a combination of Haagen Dazs, tea and Amaretto, Martha read the printout herself. She found that her sister was right; the first twenty years of their father's life were missing entirely.

The empty trays have acquired a sluttish appearance, overflowing with discarded packaging, half-eaten food, and empty bottles.

Martha frees her flight blanket from its cellophane sleeve, tucks it over her legs and all the way to her chin. Presently, the lights dim and a fragile hush descends on the cabin, broken only by the distant wail of a baby. Perhaps there's nothing to flying after all. The sky, she sees, is now a fathomless black. Martha stares at it for a second, and then snaps down the shutter.

She must have fallen asleep because her body reacts even before she is conscious of processing the words. She feels winded, the air knocked from her lungs, her stomach gripped by a sick and panicked cramp. She opens her eyes. The cabin is bright as day, both the overhead and window lights blazing at full intensity. A recorded voice, loud and compelling, floods the tannoy system.

'EMERGENCY. EMERGENCY. PUT THE MASK OVER YOUR NOSE AND MOUTH AND BREATHE NORMALLY. EMERGENCY. EMERGENCY...'

Martha gasps, 'Oh... Oh!' *This is it*, she thinks. *This is it.* Any second, any instant, the plane will fall away beneath them. A vision of the stricken aircraft tumbling and turning through layer upon layer of cloud appears before her eyes. Or instead a gaping crack will open and she will be sucked from her seat, shrieking and grabbing at nothing, into the freezing, unbreathable air. *Will I die*, she wonders wildly, *before or after I hit the sea?* And then she notices the pink ribbon curled on the floor. And then a thought hits her as if a brick has fallen into her lap.

Janey.

Janey doesn't know where she is. Janey will hear of the plane crash on the radio while she's eating breakfast. Her spoon will hover, dripping milk, and she'll pull the sad, respectful face that people make when they learn of a tragedy that doesn't concern them. Later in the day Elizabeth will call her.

'What do you mean?' Janey will say, not understanding at first, winding a clump of butter-coloured hair around her index finger in that last blissful moment before her life switches course. 'What do you mean my mother was on the plane? She can't have been. Why would she be coming to England?'

'EMERGENCY. EMERGENCY. PUT THE MASK OVER YOUR NOSE AND MOUTH AND BREATHE NORMALLY…'

'Oh!' Martha says again. There's something dangling in front of her face on a long string. The cabin is full of yellow plastic masks and wide, frightened eyes shining over the top of them. It's eerily calm, nobody is screaming or shouting, even the baby has stopped crying, although one of the nuns is crossing herself and chanting under her breath.

Martha reaches for her mask but her arms feel numb and heavy. Finally her fingers close around the elastic and she tugs the yellow cone towards her and puts it over her face. She glances across the seats next to her. The guy with the ring binders is jerking his cord, but the mask is stuck about six inches from his face and his blue eyes are manically ablaze. Tremulously, Martha lifts her own mask away so that she can see better what's happened. Her mind is racing. Any second, the cabin oxygen will run out and she'll suffocate. Any second, the plane will fall from the sky or burst into a million pieces. She's about to die and now she's not wearing the one thing that might possibly save her. The young man is yanking hopelessly at his useless contraption as Martha unclips her seatbelt and staggers upright.

'Let go,' she says. 'It's knotted.' He drops his hand, and Martha twists and threads the string back on itself until it releases. She places the cup over his nose and mouth, adjusts the strap around his stubbled neck, and sinks into her seat again.

Her relief is short-lived. There's no oxygen coming through her mask, none at all. Perhaps she's doing it wrong? She should never have taken it off. She sucks hard at the inside of the plastic but it's dry and airless and smells of rubbery chemicals and a sickly trace of her own perfume. She jabs at the cord but it makes no difference. Her neighbour seems to be in a similar position because he lifts up his own yellow cup and takes a breath from the cabin before settling it back over his face again. Martha does the same thing. It strikes her that the plane is still horizontal. The emergency announcement has stopped and the unruffled drone of the engines fills her ears. She sees that some of the passengers have taken their masks off altogether and are looking along the gangway to where the young flight attendant has got out of her seat and is making her way to the cockpit.

A moment later there's a buzzing on the tannoy system followed by the pilot's voice. Martha listens to a rich blur of words she ought to understand but they are somehow indistinct and incomprehensible. Several times she hears 'mistake' and 'unfortunate' and 'apology', but her brain seems unable to construct a sensible sentence from them. What kind of mistake is he talking about? She remembers vanished aircrafts plunging into oceans thousands of miles off-course. Is it that kind of mistake?

The young man grabs her arm. 'What did he say? What's gone wrong?'

Martha shakes her head in confusion.

A few rows ahead of them an older flight attendant is trying to push some of the masks back into their compartments but they continue to bob and dangle about people's heads like a swarm of yellow jellyfish. The tension in the cabin appears to be dissipating. A woman in the row ahead has even picked up her book again. A minute later the older hostess bustles by their seats. The young man catches her elbow. 'What the hell was that all about?'

The air hostess stops. Her face is white but smudged with sharp spots of embarrassed pink. She leans across them as she speaks, lowering her voice. 'A gentleman in first class was taken ill. He needed to use an oxygen mask and the captain activated the whole emergency system by mistake. He turned it off again but now we can't get the masks to go back up.'

'Is that all it was?' Martha asks weakly. 'There's nothing wrong with the plane?' She frees her arm from her neighbour's clutch but a part of her is still braced, waiting for a sudden, disintegrating lurch.

The air hostess grimaces. 'Gave us all a bit of fright, didn't it?'

'Fright?' repeats Martha's neighbour as though that hardly covered it. He looks at Martha and then at the flight attendant. 'Well we both need a fucking drink!'

He runs his fingers through his front lock of hair and then holds his hand out to Martha. 'Raymond – Ras. Ras Alby.' He pauses. 'Thank Christ we didn't need those masks.'

'Martha,' Martha says. 'Martha Rodwell.' A second later. 'Did you think we were going to crash?'

'Yup, part of the twenty per cent. So much for your fucking statistics.' His voice is saltier now, as if the stress has stripped away some of its polish. When the air hostess returns with four small bottles and two plastic tumblers he pours a brandy and gives it to Martha with a trembling hand.

'Twenty per cent...? Oh!' – Martha laughs – 'I see what you mean.' She takes several gulps in quick succession, pauses and then has another one. The kick of it burns a path through her stomach and ignites a wild and growing euphoria. She isn't about to die! Ras smiles at her. Definitely a boy-band smile. He's very attractive, she sees. And far, far too young, she sternly reminds herself.

'So, Martha,' Ras says, emptying two bottles at once into his own tumbler, 'what takes you to London?'

'My daughter for one thing.' Martha looks down into the amber pool of alcohol. 'My daughter, Janey. She's studying in England. At Cambridge University.' She can't stop a note of pride from creeping into her voice.

'Nice!' Ras says approvingly, and tips a long draught of brandy down his throat. 'She'll be pleased to see you then.'

'Well,' Martha says. Her voice dips. 'I hope so.' She opens her mouth, and then shuts it again while she finds the best way of putting it; how does she describe the weekly battles and the slammed doors, the sheer energy her daughter expends keeping her mother as far out of her life as possible? 'As it happens Janey's going through an independent phase right now.'

'An independent phase.' Ras swills the sentence around his mouth. He looks amused at something. 'Right. So where will you stay?'

'Well, I shall see Janey, of course, but I plan to stay in Norfolk. My hotel is booked for the next four weeks.'

'Norfolk?' Ras' eyebrows shoot upwards.

Martha starts to say that her father hired a beach hut for the whole of May, only he died, he died a month ago, and now she is going to use it herself, but her voice tails away before she can describe the situation properly. She sees her father shuffling around his redundant study, tidying his few remaining council papers, straightening picture frames, breathing hard on a photograph and then rubbing the glass with the sleeve of that raggedy blue coat he still wore as a kind of bathrobe, the one with his name, *Lewis Rodwell,* sewn into the collar with cotton tape. She hears his voice, confident and crusty, dismissing concerns for his health with the same impatience he showed to any insinuation of frailty – to most things in fact. She feels a pull in her chest, like a thread tugging loose, there's a hot, pinching sensation across the bridge of her nose and her eyes begin to pool.

Ras shifts uncomfortably and transfers his gaze from her face to the seat back in front of him. Martha pulls a tissue from her sleeve and blows her nose. Eventually, she asks with a forced, brittle breeziness, 'Do you know Norfolk, Ras?'

'Nope. Live in London. Born and raised in the Cornish metropolis of Shag Rock.' He looks at her sideways, twisting his lips in delight.

Martha splutters a mouthful of drink. 'Shag Rock! Is that actually a place?'

'Yeah, it actually is. Well, it's a part of a place called Downderry, but Downderry doesn't sound like nearly so much of a good time.'

Martha laughs and Ras sits back in his chair again with an expression of relief. He pauses and then cocks his head. 'So! The whole of May on an English beach? That's pretty bold.'

'Bold in a good way?'

Ras shrugs. 'Well, I guess that depends on Norfolk. A Spanish beach would make more sense to me. Or France. Anywhere else in Europe, really. Since you've come all this way.'

'Elizabeth thinks it's crazy too.'

'Elizabeth?'

'My sister.'

'Ah.'

Ras is looking down at his binder. Martha suspects he's lost interest. She closes her eyes and Elizabeth comes to mind, as she always does – click, click – heels first. They trip briskly from one engagement to the next, drawing attention to the apple of her calves, the bustle of her hips. The whole time she talks she never keeps still. Even when Elizabeth telephones she's either in transit or switched to speakerphone so she can combine the conversation with another, more productive activity. Everything she does, even the way she speaks, is a lesson in efficiency. 'Well!' she might say, or 'Fine!' A whole army of other words will be jostling behind the front man but she never has to utter one of them to make their meaning felt.

'Right!' was all Elizabeth said when Martha announced that she had negotiated four weeks' leave and was going to England. Martha was about to explain that she badly needed to see the Norfolk coast for herself and discover why their father had chosen such an odd location to finish his book, but Elizabeth snapped shut her purse, pecked Martha on the cheek and left for her Pilates' class. Martha knows Elizabeth's lack of enthusiasm about the trip is due, at least in part, to the number of their father's possessions still to be disposed of; some of the more personal ones they haven't yet been able to bring themselves to give or throw away, others, such as his computer, require – according to Elizabeth – hours of painstaking attention.

'You can't just trash a computer, Martha! It has to be cleaned up first.' In their rush to clear the house the items have been stacked in Elizabeth's spare room.

It is highly likely Elizabeth also suspects that Martha's other, unstated, reason for taking such a lengthy vacation is to spend time with Janey. Martha is reluctant to admit the strength of that desire even to herself, let alone Elizabeth; the last time Martha confided to Elizabeth the problems she'd been having with Janey, Elizabeth's only, rather hurtful, response was to say, 'It's been the two of you for so long, Martha. It's not surprising you're having such a hard job letting go.'

The silence swells and Ras picks up the binder with an apologetic shake of his head.

Martha is disorientated. She seems to have been sitting here forever, the whole world shrunk into the capsule of the plane. They could be anywhere. They could be travelling at hundreds of miles an hour or going nowhere at all, without a fixed point to measure against it's impossible to tell. And what time is it? Presumably there's a proper answer to that question, depending on their longitude and speed – really, she ought to know – but the query feels man-made, like the shiniest of polyesters. She swallows the last of her brandy, leans her head against the chair-wing and lifts the edge of the window flap.

'Oh, Ras look!'

It seems they've flown right through the night and out the other side. The golden disc of the sun is clipping the horizon. The eastern sky is a dazzling lapis blue and brushstrokes of pink and tangerine paint the blanket of clouds below. 'Oh do look!' Martha says again and pushes the flap completely open so that Ras, when he lifts his head from the page, can see it too.

When she wakes, an ordinary light fills the cabin. There's the smell of coffee and the young flight attendant is handing out more plastic trays. Martha's head is throbbing slightly and her mouth is dry. She drinks a small tub of juice without pausing for breath and asks for water. The mood is businesslike and expectant. Breakfast is whipped away before she has even finished eating and she takes the chance to lever herself into the gangway and join the queues to the restrooms.

The light inside the cubicle shines cold and unforgiving. Traces of grey fleck her curls where the auburn has begun to drain over the past few years and papery fork marks imprint the fine skin around her eyes. She finds tinted moisturiser, mascara and a peachy lipstick, brushes the life back into her hair and hoiks up her skirt so she can pull her shirt down more snugly over her bust. Finally, she fishes further into her make-up bag and takes out a pair of earrings. As she threads the silver hooks through her earlobes, small squares of translucent blue glint back at her in the mirror. Something about their colour and simplicity is reminiscent of her truncated youth, that brief period before she rated careers based upon their daycare and health insurance.

By the time she returns passengers are gathering belongings, checking their watches and filling in landing cards. Only the yellow field of nodding masks lets slip that the flight has been different from any other. As she squeezes past Ras his eyes seem to graze her face and then slide downwards to her chest, but she's too surprised to register the moment and a second later he's reverted to his papers.

The plane tilts downward and Martha's ears begin to hurt. A fog of a rubbed-out white swirls forever beyond the window and then all at once they break into an earthy palette of greens and browns, the colours of solid things, of fields and roads and Monopoly houses sprawled beneath the weak English sun. The young flight attendant arrives looking agitated and gestures that Ras must pack up his papers and fold his table away. He says something to Martha but she can't hear a thing.

'My ears are blocked,' she says, shaking her head. Her voice sounds hollow and far away.

All at once the wing below her disappears and the plane banks. The airport is underneath them now, the spidery outline of gates and terminals, the tarmac grids and orderly rows of shiny planes. As the world straightens again, a river of grey rises to meet them. Martha has a sudden sensation of tremendous speed, there is a jarring thump and then the engines scream manically backwards until the plane abruptly capitulates and they are pottering down the runway as if out for a Sunday drive. It is only once the captain has welcomed everyone to London and informed them the weather is damp with scattered cloud – which she can see for herself anyway – it occurs to Martha that she forgot to count to ten as they landed.

With a wave of his hand Ras jumps into the gangway and then there's a surge of families hell-bent on getting out as quickly as possible before Martha can gather her coat, her bags and edge into line. She steps out of the tunnel and into the terminal. *English soil!* But there's nothing remarkable about it: an endless walk through corridors echoing with footsteps and the rumble of suitcase wheels, a ride on a conveyor belt between a plethora of billboards advertising banks, and the light, constant patter of rain on the windows.

In the immigration hall she makes her way towards the desks amongst a mass of sleep-deprived faces. While she's waiting in line she switches on her phone. It bleeps and blusters as it scrabbles to get its bearings. A little girl with brown-button eyes watches her over the top of a shoulder draped in gold cloth. Martha holds up the screensaver to show a cute Dalmatian puppy (taken at the 'bring your pet to school' day) but the little girl looks away and her mother edges a few steps further forwards, although the queue hasn't actually moved. Martha puts the phone in her jacket pocket. How she would like to call Janey – for Janey to be expecting that call.

'I've arrived!' she would say. 'But you'll never guess what happened on the flight!'

Martha sighs. It feels impossible to call Janey.

By the time her passport has been checked, she's hauled her enormous suitcase from the baggage reclaim and wheeled it under the noses of two vicious-looking Alsatians her spirits are sinking further.

In the arrivals hall there are hugs and tears and home-made placards everywhere she looks. One banner reads, '*Welcome home Auntie Linda*', another, '*Great job Twickenham ladies!*' Small arms encircle adult necks, elderly spouses are holding hands like teenagers, and one young couple is brazenly entwined in the middle of the walkway so that Martha has to manoeuvre her suitcase around them. It should be heart-warming but instead she feels her heart is breaking. The people she loves aren't here. And there seem so few of them anyway; the crucial members of her little family – Janey, Elizabeth, her father – are dreadfully depleted. Who would come to meet her at an airport now?

She stops and the crowds swarm past like water round a stone. She has to find a route to central London. It occurs to her that she should have arranged for a cab. If she saw a scrap of paper with *Martha Rodwell* written in wonky capitals she would at least feel awaited – not entirely alone, not completely invisible. She eases the rucksack from her shoulders and balances it on top of her suitcase while she grapples with arrows and outlines of trains and buses.

'Martha!'

It takes a moment for the voice to penetrate her concentration.

'Martha!'

She looks up. Ras is striding across the floor towards her, his cell phone in one hand, the other dragging a large black bag that makes him look like a doctor even though Martha knows it's actually just full of paper.

'My case settled!' He waggles the phone in a hot-off-the-press sort of way. 'No need to rush to work after all.'

'Oh.' Martha blinks. She's unsure of the relevance of this development to her, but it's good to see him. It's good to see someone.

'So…' – Ras bites his lip – and there's something deliberately coquettish about it – 'I thought I might go and grab a coffee, freshen up at the airport hotel.' He's looking straight at her with his take-me-or-leave-me blue eyes and time appears to slow right down as Martha tells herself that it's very important she doesn't misunderstand him, that she doesn't get hold of the wrong idea. But then the lovely Ras leans forward, lifts a clump of her auburn curls and removes all possible doubt by whispering in her ear, 'How about a welcome-to-England shag? To remind me of home.'

She's appalled, of course she is, but nevertheless a small flame of triumph erupts. Her ego is running up and down the arrivals halls with a new lease of life and a placard of its own that says, *Martha Rodwell – not invisible after all!* Goddamnit! When did she last do anything reckless, any one thing that crept even remotely close to the concept of recklessness? Martha moves a fraction and for an astonishing, liberating moment it seems she's about to accept the invitation, but then her chin makes a redactive, semi-circular motion and she finds herself shaking her head, unable to utter a word.

Ras shrugs. 'Shame.' He grins at her again; obviously, he's not exactly heartbroken. 'Well, enjoy your Norfolk beach.' And a second later Martha is watching his cute butt disappear through the slowly revolving terminal door.

It's several minutes before Martha gathers up her luggage and begins to steer a path towards a different exit. The rucksack feels heavier than it did before, while her brain seems to be engaged in a heated internal debate; although her sensible and entirely predictable decision has met with approval, a little voice off-stage keeps shouting something about wasted opportunities, about regret, about the need to *live a little, Martha.*

CHAPTER TWO

As Martha passes the taxi stand her phone vibrates. There's a message from her network provider, a welcome to the UK that tells her to click on a link to discover the exorbitant cost of using her phone abroad. And there's also a record of two missed calls, both from Janey, both of them made some time before Martha went into battle with a yellow mask midway over the Atlantic.

Once clear of the idling engines and thumping doors she stops beside an enormous sign stating No Pick Up Or Set Down and listens to Janey's number ring and ring until it gives way to Janey's voice asking the caller to be sure to leave a message. When three more attempts produce the same result, Martha glares at the phone as if it bears personal responsibility for the failure to connect her and stuffs it into her coat pocket. A moment later she hears the magical sound of the opening bars of her own ringtone and, stabbing at the buttons, sees the identity of the caller too late.

'Hey, Martha! How's it going? How was your flight?' Elizabeth sounds like she's making a public address. Martha guesses she's driving and using the speakerphone. She does some quick mental arithmetic.

'Elizabeth! My God, what time is it? What are you doing up at this hour?'

Elizabeth sighs. 'My meetings are scheduled *before* the TSX opens. I'm *always* one of the early birds.' In Martha's mind, Elizabeth lifts her hand from the leather-clad steering wheel of her silver Buick and makes an impatient gesture towards the breaking dawn. 'I thought you'd know that by now.'

Martha examines the nails of her left hand; it seems the wash of her sister's success can even cross the Atlantic. She wills a searching question on the state of the Toronto Stock Exchange to materialise in her head but it remains obstinately jet-lagged.

'So – how was the flight?' Elizabeth repeats into the silence.

Before Martha can reply there is roar like a rush of approaching water and the belly of a plane hangs briefly over the beetle-busy cabs before it pulls up and into the sky.

'What in God's name was that?' Elizabeth says. 'Are you actually standing on the runway?'

'No, I'm just outside…'

Elizabeth cuts across her. 'Hey,' she says, and her voice sounds different, 'I had another look at Dad's computer, to test out what needs to be deleted before we get rid of it.'

'Did you find some more of his book?'

'No.' There's a gap, as if Elizabeth is negotiating lights or a junction. Then, 'Martha, do you know anyone called Catkins?'

'Catkins? Is that even a name?' When Elizabeth doesn't respond immediately she adds, 'Why are you asking?'

'There's a folder with the tag name *Catkins*. And it seems to contain all kinds of stuff, but mainly letters. Letter to Catkins on this date. Letter to Catkins on that date.'

'You accessed one of his folders?' Martha thinks of her father's obsession with privacy. Everything under lock and key. She's not sure he would be comfortable with even his daughters trawling his hard drive.

'I had to, Martha. There might be anything on it. Financial stuff, personal data…'

'Okay, okay, I get it. Well, don't the files explain the tag name?'

'I expect they do.' There's a crease in Elizabeth's voice.

'And?'

Another pause, although this one doesn't appear to be traffic related.

'The files are password protected. They're all password protected.'

'Oh.' Martha lowers herself down on top of her suitcase. 'Maybe Catkins is a company name…?' Her voice tails off; why in heaven would her father keep on writing to the same company and lock away the files?

'I don't think so.'

Neither of them says anything. Martha imagines she is probably thinking the same thing as Elizabeth, that Catkins sounds like a pet name, a term of endearment – *my cutest Catkins, Catkins my honeybun* – but she can't bring herself to tackle this directly. Instead she mumbles, 'I guess it could be short for Catherine.'

'Right.' It's clear Elizabeth has already considered this. 'But I don't know any Catherines. Not family friends.'

Martha racks her brain but the only Catherine she can think of is the Vice-Principal at her school who has no connection with her father at all. 'So,' she says at last, 'I suppose it looks like he might have had…' – she pauses because the word seems absurd in the context of her father – 'a girlfriend.'

Silence.

Martha waits but when Elizabeth still doesn't speak, she says, 'It's okay isn't it, that he had someone? I mean it's better than him being lonely, even if he didn't want to tell us.'

'No Martha,' – her sister's voice has an odd, stretched out quality that suggests she's on the verge of tears – 'it isn't okay. The dates on the Catkins files, they go back forever. To before Mum died.'

Martha shivers. The English drizzle is starting to seep into the gap between the collar of her mac and her neck. Her first thought is that they will have to ask their father about it because it's not the kind of thing that can be left just hanging, and then she realises with a thud of emotion that is closer to anger than grief that they will never be able to ask him about it.

'What should we do?'

Martha can't remember Elizabeth asking her that before. She stands up and looks out over the grey concrete of the terminal buildings. Memories arrive like a flock of homecoming starlings: their parents in evening dress, young, glamorous and doubled up with laughter; the four of them – her father, mother, Elizabeth and herself – toasting s'mores in the garden beside a bank of Moonflowers; their mother in bed, pale and sick and brave, their father reading aloud to her from the newspaper.

'Martha?'

The expanse of airport seems grimmer and colder. She feels her jaw tense. 'I guess we find out who Catkins is.'

'How are we going to do that?'

'Just now I have no idea, but I'll think of something when I get to Norfolk.'

It takes nearly three hours to do it, but once Martha's navigated a route through the complexity of the London subway map, thrown her first English pound coin into the saxophone case of a busker playing 'Baker Street' and nursed a coffee for fifty minutes at the railway station, she's finally on her way to King's Lynn, which appears to be the closest destination to her hotel in Wells-next-the-Sea.

The train is surprisingly small and crowded. Being first in the carriage she grabs a spot by the window, but a stream of commuters follow hot on her heels and soon the surrounding seats become occupied by soft-bellied executives who slump beyond their share of the stained cushions and claim the table with laptops, phones, Styrofoam cups and, in one case, a four-pack of beer. Two of them fall asleep while the other types feverishly on a computer. Martha stares out of the window at the monotony of suburbia that gradually gives way to a semi-rural sprawl of wire-fenced paddocks and functional farm buildings. It's lulling her to sleep when she realises that her phone is bleeping. A message from Clem is pasted across the middle of her screen.

'*Hi M hope all gd with u*', it begins neutrally enough, and Martha snatches up her phone. She scans it quickly. He's a little worried about Janey. He's sure it's nothing. But could she call him sometime?

He doesn't know, of course, that she's in England. She's had no need to keep him informed of her vacation plans for almost sixteen years. The only communication they have concerns Janey. She corrects herself. Most of their communication concerns Janey. Absurdly they still send each other birthday cards. (Is it crazy to send your ex a birthday card? She can never make up her mind, though she wishes she could forget about his birthday altogether. But she never does, each year a little alarm goes off on 19 May. Only two days until Clem's birthday! And then not sending him a card for the very first time in twenty years… Well, she hasn't been able to do it yet.) Not long after they separated she and Janey got sick at the same time and he came home to spend two days making chicken soup and dosing them with sachets of adult and infant Tylenol. Naturally he slept on the couch, though since Martha was running a temperature of 102 at the time the arrangement wasn't much of a statement.

'Why, for Chrissake, did you ever split up?' Elizabeth asked her afterwards, for about the hundredth time.

Martha shook her head. 'We got together far too young,' she replied, as she always did. There was no point trying to explain the agony she knew they had both felt watching their relationship, like a thing apart from them both, turn septic under their noses. The joy, even the smugness of having found each other so soon, had soured under the pressure of bills and a baby. She reproached Clem for wanting to be out, partying with the rest of their friends, while he claimed she resented the loss of her college place; shortly after Janey's second birthday Clem spent the night with an ex-girlfriend called Taylor and his speedy, abject confession was not enough to dampen the destructive force of Martha's hurt.

Nearly two years ago now, in the November of Janey's senior year, Martha took a call from Clem's wife, Christabel, who, to Martha's annoyance, never seemed to be the slightest concerned that Martha and Clem have once been married. 'Wouldn't it be nice,' she said, 'for Janey to have both of her birth parents together around the same Thanksgiving table for once?' Stunned into acquiescence Martha and Janey drove through the darkening afternoon along roads covered with slush and lined by walls of early snow. At the door of their ranch-style house Christabel greeted them with hugs, her hair, skin and clothes all shades of honey, vanilla and taupe. Clem stood uneasily some distance behind. The table was set with a white cloth and matching napkins, white scalloped-edge plates and two tall, white candles. Even the eight-year-old twins – Clem's sons, she had to keep telling herself – wore white, immaculate shirts. Every time Martha lifted her head the glare from it all made her drop her gaze again and she spent the meal adjusting her napkin or re-positioning her water glass.

When at last they came to leave, Christabel scooped the twins back into the house and let Clem see them to the car. Janey climbed into the passenger seat and immediately jammed a set of headphones into her ears. Martha turned to say goodbye to Clem and found he was a step closer than she expected. His face bore a twisted expression and when he opened his mouth for a hiccup of a moment, Martha thought he was about to say something important. The expression passed, he kissed her on the cheek and said, 'Well, you be sure to drive safely.'

And Martha said, 'Well, you be sure to thank Christabel for a wonderful meal.'

Clem said, 'I certainly will.'

As Martha started the engine, he stepped around to the passenger side, rapped on Janey's window and pulled a silly face when she looked up from her iPod.

Martha sees with a start that not only has the train stopped at a station but also the sign on the platform bears the name CAMBRIDGE. She hasn't checked the stops between London and King's Lynn and it feels like an unexpected gift, almost an omen, to suddenly find herself in Janey's university town.

She presses her nose to the glass and finds herself scanning the concourse for Janey's elfin face, her long, silken ponytail or the wilted-wallflower stoop to her shoulders. Of course, there's just a swirling mass of strangers lugging bags and bicycles and an elderly lady tugging at a small, white dog that is refusing to get off his backside. Even so, she's this near to Janey! Somewhere, just beyond the coffee booths and ticket gates, Janey is studying in her college, or punting on the river, or... Martha's imagination fails. She realises that she has only the vaguest idea of how her daughter passes her days. She stares with renewed intensity through the window, as if clues to Janey's life are planted in the flowerbeds bordering the station railings. Perhaps she should go in search of Janey now? Yet when she pictures Janey's reaction it's not one of amazed delight that comes to mind, but shock that quickly turns to horror plastered with a sheen of cold disdain. Whatever Martha tried to tell her about the beach-hut booking, and the curious missing parts of her grandfather's memoirs, Janey would be certain to believe her mother had come to England purely to keep tabs on her daughter.

'Can you not leave me alone?' Janey would say. 'Did you really have to follow me all the way to Cambridge?'

Martha resolves to be patient. She has four weeks in Norfolk; she will make herself wait out two of them before she tells Janey where she is. By then, with luck, she will have discovered why this remote patch of England exerted such a pull on her father and be able to satisfy her daughter that she really did have her own, non-maternal reasons for the trip.

After Cambridge the carriage feels quite empty. Martha has the table to herself, layered in rattling cans and empty chip packets. The train rumbles to the next station, and then the next, and then the one after that, and on each occasion a few more people spill out into places that seem to be the middle of nowhere: a small ticket office, a

smattering of parked cars and an insular huddle of rooftops. In between
the land rolls towards them, and then, green and flat, vanishes behind.
Martha takes up her phone to message Clem that she'll call just as soon
as she can, but the signal is gone, swallowed, it seems, by the never-
ending stretch of rain-clouded fields that extend as far as she can see.

By the time the train pulls into King's Lynn the only people who
disembark with Martha are a woman pushing a sleeping toddler in a
stroller, an elderly man who seems none too steady on his feet, and
two teenage girls, linked at the elbow and screaming with a kind of
boisterous hilarity. Within moments they all disappear. Martha looks
around. There's one other platform, which is empty, and beyond
it a covered walkway onto a nondescript street that has a constant
line of one-way traffic. Martha has a sudden lurch of doubt. Why
on earth did her father want to come here? And, more to the point,
what's *she* doing here?

Passing the ticket barrier she notices a café. Peering in, Martha
can make out a panelled counter, some lacquered pine furniture
and a number of wooden ceiling fans that resemble old-fashioned
airplane propellers. She presses open the door.

A woman is wiping the counter top with vigorous, circular sweeps
as if preparing to close up. At first Martha thinks she's the only
customer, but then she sees a man in the corner. He has a wide face
that sprouts patchy blonde stubble and is wearing a Metallica T-shirt.
From his doorstop of a sandwich a slice of bacon dangles fatly over
the newspaper spread on the table in front of him. Immediately the
smell of it penetrates Martha's stomach and she realises how mas-
sively, urgently hungry she is. She parks her suitcase and hurries to
the counter. The woman sighs but writes Martha's order on a pad,
tears off the page and without speaking shoves it through a hatchway.

A minute or two passes. Martha isn't sure what to do. Should she
sit down and expect the food to be brought to her? She opts to wait,
shifting from one foot to the other and watching the woman tighten
sheets of cling-film over dishes of crumbled tuna and egg mayonnaise.

Beside squidgy bottles of ketchup and yellow mustard she spies a Perspex box containing a stack of small cards. Idly she picks one up: *Colin's Cars*, it says, and gives a cell phone number underneath.

'It's for taxicabs, right?'

The woman nods her head. For a second her features sharpen as if she's about to say something, but then she dips sideways to retrieve the plate that has been placed on the hatchway and by the time she hands it to Martha her face has closed up again.

Martha sits with her elbows propped on the table and bites into the sandwich. It tastes so good that for a while she can't think of anything else. The bacon is thick and pink with golden, crispy edges and the bread leaves a powdery trace of flour on her fingers. While she eats she examines the card. She needs a cab and this option seems as good as any other. She digs out her phone and dials the number. From the corner the posturing twang of an electric guitar explodes into the room and all at once Martha knows exactly what's going to happen a split second before it actually does.

'Colin's cars.' The eyes of the man in the Metallica T-shirt don't move from his newspaper and after speaking he takes another bite of his sandwich.

'Hi,' Martha says. 'I need to get a ride to Wells. Wells next-the-Sea,' she adds, in case there is more than one Wells, pronouncing the full name of the place with self-conscious care. The man slowly raises his shaggy head. On meeting Martha's hesitant smile he gradually stops chewing and swallows.

'What time do you want it for?' Although his gaze has switched to Martha the phone still hovers a little below his chin.

Martha gestures at her plate. 'I should be good to go in five. How about you?'

In ten minutes' time she's settling in to the passenger seat of Colin's blue Ford Mondeo engulfed by a scent that is the chemical approximation of something floral but doesn't quite mask the underlying smell of nicotine. By the stick-shift is a multipack of gum. After wedging his newspaper under the windscreen, Colin wrenches open a packet and offers a foil-wrapped oblong to Martha. She declines. It feels a tiny bit odd to be sitting next to Colin, as if they were friends or even a regular couple, but as they approached the car Colin surprised her by asking, 'front or back?' and in the time it took Martha to process what he meant, and then wonder whether electing for the back would sound rude, he opened the front passenger door and transferred both her rucksack and suitcase into the trunk.

As they head across town Martha lowers the window a surreptitious inch to let in a breath of fresh air. A polka-dot rain is falling, plinking on the glass in tadpole-shaped rivulets. The urban contours have a melancholy look: narrow roads, modest buildings and dinky cars create the impression that someone has pushed the edges of the town closer together to make it fit into a smaller space. Then all at once Colin turns onto an open road that seems to stretch ahead of them for miles. There's no clue as to where it leads, just a sense of man-made structures falling away and the expansion in all directions of steely clouds and dyke-edged fields. Forty minutes later, Colin breaks off mid-sentence and points out of the window. 'Here we are,' he says. 'This is Wells.'

A moment later the car has slowed to a crawl to avoid running into the many groups of people filling the busy high street. Some are holding boxes of fish and chips, which they're eating with their fingers as they walk or perch on top of a low wall that separates the road from a narrow parking lot abutting a harbour. Although it has stopped raining a lot of them are still dressed in bright cagoules or transparent ponchos. Small children dangle from adults' arms, or dart about their parents' legs waving ice-cream cones and poking each other. On the inland side, snack bars and take-out restaurants line the pavement. There's a gift shop too, its windows full of postcards and pottery, and even an open-fronted amusement arcade with neon signage over the entrance.

Martha's gaze is diverted from the crowd. A bottle-green engine shed, or something just like it, is suspended high over the traffic, jutting from the wall of a stern-faced building towards the port. 'What in heaven's name is *that*?'

'It's a gantry,' Colin says. 'For loading grain from the granary into ships.' It sounds like he's explained this several times before.

'For loading grain?' Martha is ready to be enchanted. She cranes her neck as they pass underneath it. 'But no… wait' – she points upwards – 'there are curtains!'

Colin shrugs. 'It *was* a granary. It's flats now.'

'Oh.'

A second later the road loops sharply inland. As Martha realises that they've now driven the entire length of the seafront something troublesome occurs to her. 'Stop!' She touches Colin's arm in consternation. 'Please can you stop!'

Colin swings into the driveway of a guesthouse and Martha pivots in her seat to look behind them. Milky sunlight is lifting off the waterfront, showcasing the fishing trawlers and the spent nets heaped on the quay, the cobweb rigging of the yachts and the small, perky motor boats squeezed in between them. She frowns and turns anxiously to Colin. 'I thought there was a beach?'

To her great relief, Colin nods. 'There is a beach.' He gestures towards the western end of the harbour where Martha can just make out the beginnings of a channel to the open sea. 'It's bit of a hike but worth it when you get there.'

'Oh!' Martha says. 'I should like to see it.' She cranes her neck pointlessly. 'If I can figure how to find it, that is.'

There is a short expectant silence before Colin snaps the car into gear and turns it back the way they came.

The route from the seafront is unexpectedly long, running ruler straight between a high embankment and an endless stretch of emerald marsh. On the way they pass a stream of oncoming traffic and weary pedestrians weighed down by bags with bits of plastic sticking out and armfuls of wet-weather clothing. It seems everyone else is calling it a day.

After pulling up alongside a shuttered café, Colin gestures at the handful of pines scattered over the dunes in front of them. 'You can head in that direction. Or' – he points to the far end of the emptying parking lot where a track leads into a copse – 'you could walk through the woods and *then* onto the beach.'

Martha nods. She already has the door half-open and can almost taste the spacey freshness outside. 'What will you do?'

Colin reaches for the gum and his newspaper. 'I'll be all right.'

Halfway up the nearest dunes, Martha pauses and takes off her sandals, wobbling on alternate legs while she releases the buckles. She wriggles her toes and buries them in the sand. It's warmer than she expected, finer too, a silken, sifting blanket. She can feel it bunch under her arches as she walks, the muscles of her feet stretching and working. She's so wrapped up in the moment that when the beach opens before her she's formed no real notion of what to expect.

She stops in her tracks at the sight. Before the day seemed plain, with dull, moderate weather, but here the light is washed with golden splinters, making a lens of hazy yellow through which the shoreline glows and shimmers. In the middle distance the tide is in retreat and the blue-grey band of sea has left mirror-like lakes where gulls are strutting in the shallows and pecking at trailing strands of seaweed. The last families are packing up; shaking blankets, gathering hoodies and scattered shoes.

Skirting the water, Martha heads towards a mound that occupies the centre of the beach. Climbing it requires more effort than she anticipated and at the top she crumples gracelessly onto the sand. Now she can see the whole length of the coastline and the row of beach huts that hug the ridge between the beach and the pinewoods like a necklace. They stand cheek by jowl – different colours, different heights – hooded by the darkness of the trees behind. For the next four weeks, she thinks, one of them is mine. The wonder of it fills her with a jolt of unexpected joy. Sitting sideways, she gets a vista of the sea too; the channel leading to the harbour and straight ahead a sweep of open ocean that shifts and breaks in front of her as if it is a living thing.

For a while she tries to count the huts but her mind won't focus on the numbers. It's as restless as the sea she can't stop watching. She always thought their family had such well-delineated roles: her mother the dedicated homemaker; she, Martha, the romantic who messed up; Elizabeth, the gifted mathematician, the economist and triumphant careerist. While her father's story, his adult story at least, was familiar to them all: the scholarship he won to college, the position he took as an articled clerk, only to ditch it within six months and start his own business selling log cabins for vacation homes. And then his decision to give it all up and apply himself to politics instead; local causes and disputes that used to bring constituents knocking on their door just, it always seemed, as they were sitting down to dinner – Martha can still hear her mother's sigh as she deposited her napkin on the table and headed back towards the kitchen to make coffee. Now the images are blurring, the soundtrack distorting, it feels as though her father's life has taken place behind a fogged-up window and that some of it – important, personal parts – his daughters failed to spot at all.

She scoops up a handful of sand and lets it trickle through her fingers. The silence is unlike any other she can think of; it's different from the tense empty silence when she switches off the TV at night, or the holes of agonising silence that wreck her conversations with Janey, or even the occasional, precarious silence of her classroom. Instead there's a vast bank of it, a pillow into which she could sink her head. Some way off she can hear a man calling a dog's name, but his voice is thin and tinny and no match at all for the strong, certain calm of the beach.

She could sit here for hours, she muses, before realising that of course she can't do anything of the sort because Colin won't chew gum and read the newspaper indefinitely and might anytime soon decide to cut his losses and leave her here. It's then that it occurs to her that she has left all of her luggage – her clothes, her phone, *her credit cards and passport* – in the possession of a person she only met this same afternoon. She doesn't even know his full name.

She jumps to her feet, heart drumming, swipes the sand from her dress with a single stroke and forces herself into a ragged jog towards the distant line of trees.

CHAPTER THREE

Norfolk, May 1939

Sylvie was watching her daughter dribble a golden E across the top of her porridge in thick syrup, knowing it would never get eaten. It was far too warm for food like that. Sunshine was bouncing white and clean from the damask cloth – striking the tunnels of dust motes floating by the French windows that had been flung wide to catch the laundry-fresh air sweeping in from the North Sea.

It was their third day at Headlands; the brick and flint house with yew trees stationed on both sides of the gateposts and the rusting weathervane on the roof, where Sylvie had lived with her parents until she married Howard. She had brought the children back for her aunt's funeral, but Howard had stayed in Norwich. Sylvie didn't mind about that. It was like shutting a door on a dirty, disordered room, for a few days at least she could pretend the problem wasn't there.

Next to Esther, Lewis had pushed back his chair, swinging his legs with a sullen expression that soured the still-soft lines of his ten-year-old face. His looks were Sylvie's, for the most part at least: the heart-shaped face, the sandstorm of freckles across the bridge of his nose and the stretched-out limbs that seemed to grow visible inches night after night. But whereas Sylvie's eyes were Serpentine grey, his own were a darker, unsettling blue.

Sylvie was sitting in the exact same place she used to sit as a child, her father at one end of the table, her mother at the other, facing the bay window with its three pairs of blood-red curtains and the lawn beyond. Dishes of marmalade and butter dotted the table, along with a toast rack and a cut-glass bowl of grapefruit. A plate smeared with egg and the silver filigree of herring bones rested by her father's elbow. For as long as Sylvie could remember he had eaten the same breakfast every Saturday, his appetite undaunted by either funerals or warm weather. Now, dressed in shirt, tie and a sleeveless pullover he was using an ivory knife to open the mail. As he slit the last of the envelopes something solid fell onto a willow-pattern saucer, and the high-pitched chime of it ricocheted through the dining room and made them all jump.

Her father picked up a small brass key, turned it over with a puzzled expression and put it down beside his plate. Then he unfolded a letter typed on creamy vellum. 'It's from Ginger's solicitor,' he said scanning the page. 'He says it's been sent to me because he doesn't have Sylvie's address.'

'My address?' Sylvie said.

Her father didn't reply. He moved the paper closer to his face and carried on reading for a while. Finally he lowered it again. 'Well, Sylvie,' he said, his voice tight with surprise. 'I'm told your aunt owned a beach hut. It seems she's left it to you in her will.'

There was a moment of silence. Her father swallowed a mouthful of tea, still holding the letter in his other hand as if there was something unfinished about it.

'A beach hut?' Sylvie repeated. 'Ginger's left me a beach hut?' She wasn't sure she'd understood him correctly. 'What do you mean? Where is it?'

'It's here in Wells. On the beach near us.' Her father put down his cup, staring the length of the table at Sylvie's mother. In a different, sharper tone he said, 'You didn't tell me that Ginger had bought a beach hut. Here.'

Sylvie's mother fiddled with her napkin. 'Oh,' she said. "Didn't I mention it?' She gave him a vague smile. 'It must have slipped my mind.'

'Why has she left it to me?' Sylvie looked from one parent to the other. Both appeared to have forgotten she was there. It reminded her of childhood mealtimes. The heavy, underwater feeling while she listened to her father relate the details of his day's research, and her mother's bland, regular prompts of, 'Yes, dear,' and 'How very interesting,' and, 'Did he really think his book would be finished before Christmas?' The notion of a beach hut floated in front of her like a trick or an apparition that couldn't be trusted and made no sense at all. 'Hello!' she wanted to shout, 'Hello!' Instead she said, more loudly, 'Why did Ginger leave me her beach hut?'

'You'd better ask your mother,' her father replied.

There was a pause before her mother cleared her throat. 'Well,' she said carefully, 'perhaps she thought you might enjoy a little retreat of your own.'

'A little retreat!' At the other end of the table her father practically spat the words onto the table. 'What on earth does Sylvie need to retreat from?'

Sylvie glanced at her mother but she had scooped up a spoonful of porridge and was trying to persuade Esther to eat it.

'Not retreat, exactly' – her mother continued to cluck encouragingly at Esther – 'I meant somewhere that she can take the children. When she comes to visit us.' She put down the spoon and smiled, as if this was a perfectly satisfactory answer. Next she began to serve herself some grapefruit, although Sylvie knew she didn't really care for it at all.

Her father watched for a moment and then his gaze dropped, as if defeated by the illogicality of it all. He gathered up the key and handed it to Sylvie.

'Suffice to say,' he said, drily, 'your aunt has not lost her capacity to astound me, even from beyond the grave.'

Esther, who had abandoned any pretence of eating, was staring at her grandfather as if he might next produce a rabbit from a hat.

'What is it, Mummy?'

'It's a secret,' Sylvie said. 'For later on today. A secret from Ginger.' She was pleased to see Esther's eyes widen as she digested this astonishing piece of news but the effect was spoiled when Lewis nudged her hard with his elbow.

'Don't be silly,' he said. 'Ginger's dead. It can't be a secret from her.'

'Well it is!' Sylvie frowned at him. 'When people die they can leave you special things. And this is something that Ginger has left for me.' She gazed down at the cool weight of the key. The possibility of something new, something more than the dusty claustrophobia of her own home glinted back from the palm of her hand.

'But why,' Lewis persisted, 'has she left you something? You didn't even know her.' He was six years older than Esther and seemed intent on widening the gap, as if childhood was something to be got out of the way as quickly as possible.

'Well, that's not quite true,' Sylvie said, but she let her voice taper to nothing because it was so close to being true that she couldn't honestly contest the point. When her father had telephoned one dismal Sunday evening to tell her Ginger had died she had very nearly asked who Ginger was, before remembering Ginger was her mother's sister. After that she had made an effort to feel sad but managed only a remote sort of proxy grief on behalf of her mother who had, apparently, taken it very badly.

'I suppose you'll go to the beach today?' her mother interjected. 'The weather couldn't be better.'

Sylvie nodded. A nub of excitement had lodged in her stomach. She pushed back her chair, scraping it over the parquet floor.

Her father picked up the *Daily Express* and opened it wide with an airy crack. A moment later his face appeared over the top of it. 'I nearly forgot' – he tipped his head towards the envelope containing the solicitor's letter – 'there's a map in there that tells you which hut it is.'

Sylvie extracted a sheet of notepaper and flattened it out on the table. In slanting blue ink someone had written '*sea*' at the top of the page and '*woods*' at the bottom. A row of small crosses ran across the middle that were also marked in blue, apart from one towards the left-hand edge which was large and crimson with the number '*23*' beside it.

'You'd better make the most of that hut,' her father said suddenly from behind the screen of his newspaper, 'before somebody requisitions it for ten evacuees.' Sylvie felt the temperature dip several degrees. Her father's grim prognosis about the prospect of war was becoming alarming. Her mother must have felt the same way because she made a sharp clicking noise with her tongue and said briskly,

'Really Philip, not more gloomy talk. The last few days have been bad enough without that.'

Sylvie thought her father was about to lecture them about the threat of the German-Italian alliance but instead he announced he was going to finish his tea in the library and read. Ten minutes later Sylvie caught sight of him through the half-open door, smoking his pipe and gazing out of the leaded window over the lawn towards the Gardenia roses. The *Daily Express* was neatly folded at his elbow.

In the murky coolness of the larder Sylvie cut some bread and laid it on the marble slab her mother used for storing meat when the refrigerator was full or – as seemed to happen with tiresome regularity – not working properly. She was making a picnic for the beach. She liked the larder, the quiet closed-off feeling and the rough irregularity of the pamment tiles under her feet. Taking a fork, she spread out mottled wedges of corned beef and sliced garlands of tomatoes. She put one tomato aside for Lewis. He loved to eat them like an apple, wiping the juice with the back of his hand as it dripped down his chin.

Lewis. Sylvie sighed. Three weeks earlier she had breezed into his bedroom with a pile of clean laundry to find him sitting with his back against the headboard of the bed, turning something in his hands.

From the tender way in which his fingers skated over its surface, at first she thought it was some kind of creature he had captured in the garden, but then she saw four black hooves, its dappled back and tightly coiled tail and realised it was the little cast-iron bull that Howard used as a paperweight.

'Where did you get that from?' she said, although she knew he must have removed it from the top of Howard's marking pile.

He drew it closer to his chest. 'Daddy gave it to me.'

So badly did she want this to be true that for a second Sylvie almost believed him. It couldn't be, of course. 'Don't tell fibs, Lewis Rodwell, you've taken it out of the study!'

There was silence. Sylvie held out her hand and waited.

'I just wanted…' Lewis said and stopped. He looked down at his hands. Sylvie could see the effort it took him not to blink, trying to keep the tears in. She felt her own throat constrict. She knew what he wanted.

'Give it to me,' she said more gently. 'I'll put it back before Daddy gets home.'

She had practically forgotten the incident when almost the same thing happened two weeks later. She had just come out of Esther's room when the briefest flicker of light from the far side of Lewis' door caught her eye. Quietly, she pushed it open. The floor was awash with soldier figurines: Highlanders in glossy red coats and ebony kilts lay scattered between cowboys, Indians and an assortment of artillery guns, wagons and carts. But Lewis seemed to have tired of the game. Cross-legged amongst the mess, he was clutching Howard's cigarette lighter, transfixed by the spurt of flame that flared and died as he pressed and released the thumb-lever.

'Lewis!'

He jumped, and then looked up at her guiltily, but before she could say anything else they heard the unmistakable clunk of the front door opening and then the echo of Howard's footsteps in the hallway.

Lewis' eyes widened. Sylvie grabbed the lighter and dropped it into her pocket. On hearing the bolt of the lavatory door she took her chance, hurried downstairs and slipped the lighter back into its usual position next to the anglepoise lamp on Howard's desk.

Sylvie placed the sandwiches on top of each other and cut them into triangles with a bread knife. It wasn't something that could be resolved by talking to Howard. She didn't need to try to know that for a fact. Lewis was like a patch of quicksand in the middle of their marriage from which they both had to keep as far back as possible. She could speak to Lewis, of course, but what to say? He saw the intensity with which Howard doted on Esther, the way she lit up his face while he, Lewis, turned it flat and cold, and there was nothing Sylvie could say to make things better, to let him know the fault was hers and not his. An all-too familiar surge of guilt made the look and smell of the sandwiches suddenly unbearable. She let go of the knife with a clatter. From the kitchen came the sound of voices, the clink of crockery and a gush of water as someone turned a tap. Sylvie stood for a moment in the gloom, pressing the heels of her palms into her eyes, then she let her hands fall to her skirt, rearranged her face and pushed open the door.

She found her mother filling the kettle, talking to Lewis over her shoulder about bicycles. Sylvie hadn't brought any, of course. Visiting by bus meant she could only carry with them the crammed contents of one small suitcase, but outside the kitchen window the last whispers of cloud had burned away and she could see the walk to the beach would be long and hot. Hunting in the garden shed, she unearthed her old bicycle, which she thought would do for Lewis, and a clanky old contraption with a basket on the front and a child's seat on the mudguard that her mother had used when Sylvie was small, and still did when the mood took her.

Eventually they were ready to leave. Lewis set off easily, but Sylvie's bike was heavy and to begin with she struggled to control it. Esther barely fitted onto the back; the dense pink of her thighs was squashed against the iron frame and her weight made them sway in sudden, sideways lurches. Before they reached the end of the road Sylvie's foot slid from the pedal causing it to whip round and sting her calf, and when her mother called to ask if she was all right she didn't dare turn her head but simply shouted as loudly as she could over the handlebars.

She steered cautiously around the lime trees that ringed the green in front of the house and then, with increasing confidence, turned onto the broad curve of Station Road. She had forgotten how thrilling it was to cycle, free from the stop and start of the city, the rhythm and spin of the wheels, the wash of the wind on her face, and the power to go just where she wanted. It made it easier to see things, even Howard, in a more positive light.

He hadn't wanted to come to the funeral. Sylvie had stood beside the door of his study while they discussed it, mindful of the invisible line that prevented her from stepping into the circle of light bathing his desk. Howard lifted his head from the pile of exercise books in front of him but didn't pause his marking. On the wall behind, Sylvie's fingernails were buried into the flock of the wallpaper. It was unbearably quiet, apart from the relentless ticking of the Chester clock, which seemed to grow louder or softer just by her thinking it, and Howard's pen scratching like a needle on a stuck gramophone record. In the end she said that if he wasn't going to come back with her she might as well make a trip of it, and stay with her parents over the Whitsun weekend. Howard had only mumbled a reply and carried on making swift, deft marks on the paper in front of him.

When Sylvie and the children arrived at her parents' house, her mother opened the door and held out her arms. 'No Howard,' she said, glancing behind them, but she managed not to turn it into a question and Sylvie, grateful, hugged her tightly.

*

Now, with the touch of the sun hot between her shoulder blades and the hum of the tyres in her ears she could almost put the episode down to tiredness and the incessant demands of school. And wasn't it awfully difficult to take a day off during the busiest term of the year?

On turning north a wedge of sea glittered in front of them. Sylvie pointed it out to the children and Lewis began to cycle faster, his thin white legs pumping the pedals. The road bent and flattened against the water's edge. As they sped under the arm of a gantry, Sylvie shivered – the echo of cascading grain and the roar of muslin dust had been stamped on her when she was Esther's age, transfixed and terrified by the loading of the ships. Beside them sprawled the seafront: a jumble of whelk boats, trawlers and greasy ropes, the sound of gulls and the rocking clink of the halliards. Currents of air licked Sylvie's bare arms. She could smell chips and sugar and the reek of fish from the sprat boxes piled on the quay.

To get to the beach they had to take a shingle track that followed the tidal creek, heading straight out towards a wood at the point where the coast road bent inland again. At first the distant trees were only a curdled mush of colour and the path ahead so featureless that they seemed to make no progress; on one side the relentless edge of the harbour wall and on the other unfenced fields of corn and barley reaching to the marshes. It was further than Sylvie remembered and she could feel her muscles protesting at the effort of propelling both her and Esther against the breeze lifting off the sea. Gradually all the shades of green became a wood, and then it became a heap of familiar, ragged pines, and then thankfully they arrived at the rutted area of bare land in front of the trees themselves.

Breathing hard, Sylvie propped her bike against a salted trunk and lifted Esther from the back of it. Esther immediately dropped to her knees and began to examine the dirt by her feet, picking up bark and rubbery fringes of green. Sylvie gazed around at the peeling trunks and the long, bright spaces between them, watching the light pool at her feet.

Lewis came up beside her. He wasn't out of breath at all. 'Look!' he said, pulling her arm and pointing to the track. 'Look over there!'

A boy of about his own age was emerging from the shadows, followed by a woman with a patterned scarf around her head carrying a large wicker basket in one hand and a windbreak in the other.

The boy ran towards them before abruptly stopping about ten feet away. Dressed in shorts and a white vest, he had muddy smears across his knees and a blunt, uneven fringe as if it had been cut with the kitchen scissors. But his hair glowed the colour of caramel and his nose and chin turned upwards in a defiant, spirited tilt. Just as he opened his mouth, the woman with the windbreak – his mother, Sylvie supposed – called out sharply, 'Charlie! Whatever are you doing? Get back here at once!'

It occurred to Sylvie the children could play together, but just at the second the woman glanced across, Sylvie's nerve shrank and she dropped her head, pretending to examine the pale green buds on the bushes alongside the path. When she looked up again both the boy and the woman had disappeared. After waiting another minute she pulled Esther to her feet, slapping the worst of the dirt and twigs from her knees, and then she spent more time than necessary fiddling with the bags and finding something for each of the children to carry, so that when they finally left the bicycles to the dappled custody of the pines the other family was nowhere in sight.

Sylvie knew not to take the immediate opening onto the beach, having seen from the map they should walk as far as they could through the woods first. To the seaward side the ground was steep, sloping up over the dunes. Inland, the path was bordered by a lake where some tired-looking rowing boats were tied like a camel train in bunchy, complicated knots. The air was hot and still and the children had fallen silent, as if the quiet of the place had slipped under their skin. When the track eventually exhausted itself before a thicket of brambles they scrambled up the ridge at last, Sylvie towing Esther over the crest and into a sudden infinity of blue and gold.

The tide was out and the shoreline stretched away to a strip of sea that was barely distinguishable from the expanse of sky curving to the tips of the horizon. Directly in front of them a string of wooden beach huts, painted in sweet-shop colours of lemon yellows, sugar pinks and summer blues, stared out towards the ocean over clusters of families settled on blankets and towels. Between the beach huts and the sea, a sandbank made for climbing stood as the only barricade from the waves and winds of distant Norway.

'Remember we're looking for number 23,' Sylvie reminded the children. Her cheeks felt hot and red and her dress was sticking under her arms and across the top of her back. Lewis spurted ahead while she and Esther walked more slowly, counting out loud the figure painted on the side of each hut until they arrived in front of the right one.

It was forget-me-not blue with a grey, pitched roof trimmed in white. Sand spilled over the bottom treads of a staircase that led to a veranda edged with railings where a pair of double doors occupied nearly the whole of the front facade. 'Here we are,' she said with relief, and they all let the bags fall in a soft heap at the foot of the steps. Sylvie climbed up with the children close behind and put the key in the lock. At first it wouldn't move to either the left or the right, and for a moment she feared the wrong key, the wrong hut, a dismal, defeated, untimely return. She pulled the door hard towards her, willing the lock with her fingers, and grittily, grudgingly, the key turned.

'Are you ready?' Her heart was beating hard. She held the door close and then let it swing triumphantly.

CHAPTER FOUR

Inside the air was warm and stale and smelled as if it had been baked in an oven with a strip of sawn pinewood.

'Is this it?' Lewis asked. It was tiny, a cupboard on legs; the contents could be fitted into a garden wheelbarrow and carted off the beach again in just one trip, had Sylvie a mind to do it. Already she knew she never would. To her it was perfect just the way it was.

Two canvas deckchairs with broad stripes of cream and fuchsia leaned against one side. A box seat was built along the length of the back wall and three cushions with water-stained crochet covers were strewn across the top of it, together with four tin mugs and a bottle of Plymouth Gin. Sylvie lifted the stoppered glass up to the light; there were still a good few fingers in the bottom of it.

'Was that Ginger's?' Lewis sounded rather disapproving.

Sylvie put it down. 'I expect it was for emergencies. Why don't you go and play with Esther?'

She shooed them out of the door and sank onto one of the cushions. Something was different. She took a breath and realised the shadow that normally accompanied her everywhere, that slow-burning sense of dismay, was gone. A marvellous, ridiculous phrase came to mind: a woman of property! It was silly of her, really, since she and Howard had a fine home in Norwich. When they initially moved in she had been so proud of the house, a central property near the Cathedral, but how quickly that novelty had worn thin. Now it felt like a stage set, a place where she performed the role of a married woman to an audience of one. Of course, the wedding should never have happened in the first place. A friend had introduced her to Howard when she was at her lowest – soon after Kennie had left her shocked and heartbroken. Howard was so persistent, appearing uninvited on her parents' doorstep and wooing her with flowers and little gifts. He was hard to ignore. And he was older too; his job, his status, gave him a gravitas, an aura of security that finally persuaded her that if she couldn't be with Kennie she might as well be safe. She warned Howard, told him quite explicitly she was still in love with somebody else, but instead of putting him off it seemed to make him all the more anxious to marry her, as if he wanted to claim her quickly, in case Kennie should return and take her back. If only she had waited, instead of allowing herself to be swept along by Howard, how differently it might all have turned out.

She inhaled the pinesap and surveyed the four walls of her castle. Two photographs pinned next to her head were partly obscured by a paisley shawl hanging from a nail, its tassels stiff and clumped with sand. Pushing it aside she saw a portrait of a man, a very handsome man. Sylvie stared. He looked vaguely familiar. He had black hair and a black moustache but it was his eyes that dominated the picture, they shone with such purpose and anticipation he might have been watching a woman undress right in front of him. In the other photograph Sylvie's mother was sitting on one of the striped deckchairs next to a woman who had to be Ginger. Sylvie recognised her mother's dress from just the previous summer. Ginger was wearing a halterneck bathing suit, the paisley shawl draped around her shoulders. They were both laughing and each holding one of the tin mugs, raising them towards the mystery photographer in an extravagant toast.

'Mummy! Mummy! Come outside!' Lewis' voice disrupted her trance. As Sylvie hurried out of the hut, he pointed down the shoreline. 'Look, it's the same people again!' he said.

'Which people?' Sylvie had to shield her eyes from the glare of the sun. But he didn't need to answer as she could see both of them now, picking a way through pockets of children crouched over buckets, mothers in bathers and fathers stripped to their braces with rolled-up trousers. They must, Sylvie realised, have taken the first set of steps and walked the whole, exhausting length of the beach. For a while they seemed stuck in the distance like a scene from a postcard and then all at once they were nearly in front of her. The woman was wearing a gingham dress that had the ordinary, almost dowdy, look of something home-made, and lace-up shoes that were quite hopeless for the beach. A brick-coloured cardigan was knotted around her waist, the windbreak that Sylvie remembered from earlier was tucked under one arm and the heavy-seeming wicker basket was hooked over the other. The long struggle across the sand had made the woman red-faced but the boy bobbed effortlessly about her legs as if tied by invisible kite strings.

Surely they must recognise us, thought Sylvie, but the woman was staring straight ahead with a fixed expression. Sylvie hesitated and then, to make up for her unfriendliness in the woods, waved her hand. When the woman still didn't turn her head she leaned a little way over the veranda railing. 'I say,' she called, 'it's a marvellous day, isn't it?'

The woman stopped and looked at her. For a second Sylvie had the peculiar sensation of seeing herself as the woman must; her freckled, triangular face, her pale blue eyes, her hair she had put up carefully and tied with a bandeau, and her rather exotic beach pyjamas that weren't new, but might have looked as if they were, because she had kept them nicely laundered and mended a tear with such excruciatingly tiny stitches it hardly showed.

'Oh yes, quite marvellous,' the woman answered. But it didn't sound as though she thought the day was marvellous at all. Her voice was flat and the way she spoke suggested Sylvie had said something upper class and condescending. For a second Sylvie was speechless and then in a loud voice she told Lewis she needed to fetch something from one of the bags. Inside the hut, she leaned against the door and closed her eyes, feeling the wood warm and coarse against her shoulders. She told herself how silly it was to let an absolute stranger spoil her mood and began to search for her bathing costume.

Her spirits rose when she pulled it out. It was terribly modern; two separate pieces in a splotchy sort of animal print that left a section of her stomach quite daringly bare. She had bought it only the week before and had thrown away the receipt and tissue paper before Howard could find it. She always worried how he would react to her shopping trips. Sometimes it seemed he liked to see her in new things. He would ask her to put the latest dress on for him, touch her hand or her cheek, say how pretty she looked and tell her to make sure she wore it the next time they went out. Yet at other, unpredictable, times all their unsaid business seemed to burst to the surface like an underground river, pitching them onto opposing banks. Howard would accuse her of wasting money, even threaten to reduce her housekeeping, although both of them knew money wasn't the problem at all.

Sylvie pulled up the edge of her top and pinched the roll of flesh that had never quite disappeared after her pregnancy with Esther, worried, now the moment had come, that perhaps the costume wasn't suitable after all. Just as she had decided there was nothing for it but take the plunge, she heard footsteps on the staircase, a brief shuffling on the veranda outside and then the crescendo of a child's voice, immediately hushed. Startled, she smoothed her clothes and opened the door. Before she had time to register anything at all, something – a key – was thrust towards her face.

'Excuse me, but you're in *our* beach hut!'

Sylvie gaped in astonishment. It was the woman with the windbreak. Close up, she looked younger than Sylvie, and whereas Sylvie's locks were fair and long and – without the help of rollers and heating tongs – unforgivably straight, the woman was a brunette and her hair made a wonderful, wavy shape, although it had been cut short and fell only just below her ears.

'Look, it says here 23. And this is number 23, isn't it?' The woman jabbed at a small square of cardboard attached to the key where a number was scrawled in black ink. Although her face was wide and lovely with deep brown eyes the expression on it was tight with accusation.

'Yes,' Sylvie said, 'this is number 23.' The wonderful, peaceful feeling from only minutes earlier had now dissolved entirely. The woman appeared so sure of herself that Sylvie supposed she must be in the wrong, but couldn't think how. Perhaps she ought to have brought the solicitor's letter, but it was still lying on the breakfast table with the rest of the morning post. She supposed she would have to move their belongings and find the hut they were meant to be in, if she really did have one at all.

Without knowing quite what to do next, she turned the cardboard between her fingers. A lumpy crease ran through the middle of the number 3. She studied it in an absent sort of a way and then with increasing concentration. 'Wait a moment,' she said, smoothing the wrinkle with her thumb. 'This actually says 25. Not 23. I think you've made a mistake.' It was hard to keep a note of triumph from her voice.

The woman examined the cardboard for a long time. When she looked up her cheeks were crimson and all at once she seemed to be only about seventeen. 'The boarding house said the key was for this one. They should have got it right. For the amount it's cost to rent.' There was a pause – an ungracious pause, Sylvie thought – before she finally added, 'I'm sorry for the disturbance.'

'Well,' Sylvie said, 'no harm done. Number 25 must be close by.' The sense of relief made her generous. 'My name is Sylvia – Sylvie,' she added, and held out her hand. After a moment the girl took it.

'Connie.' There was a flicker of a smile before her face sprung shut again. She turned and began to walk stiffly down the steps, the wood vibrating under her shoes.

'Charlie,' she shouted. 'It's not this one. It's further along. Get your Queen Mum off the sand!'

*

An hour later, Sylvie's whole attention was taken up with not noticing Connie and Charlie. The huts were so close together that number 25 was barely any distance away and yet the space between them seemed so unbreachable they might have been in different counties. Sylvie had watched Connie unfurl the windbreak and use one of her shoes to knock the posts into the sand. Afterwards Connie and Charlie had disappeared into their hut and returned wearing black woollen bathing suits.

Now all Sylvie could see were Connie's head and shoulders when she bobbed above the top of the windbreak. So actually there was nothing to look at, and yet her eyes kept wandering in that direction. At the same time, as their disembodied voices floated back, she found herself gripped by their accents: the dropped 't's and 'h's, the slur to their words, and the unfamiliar timbre that managed to sound both tough and oddly soothing.

Exasperated with herself, she picked up a magazine and thumbed the pages. It was the latest edition of *Vogue* and entirely focused on Ascot, to which she knew Howard would never agree to take her in a million years. 'The greenest turf; the greyest toppers; the loveliest and best dressed women,' she read, without interest, her ears tense with the effort of listening.

'Do you want to make a sandcastle?'

Sylvie risked a glance. Charlie had approached Lewis, who was in the process of making a wicket. He was trying to balance a length of bark on top of three sticks, his profile concealed by a screen of fine, barley-coloured hair. Facially he was the spitting image of Sylvie – everyone always remarked upon it – his father's genes appeared to have left no impression at all.

'No.' Lewis didn't look up.

'There's a competition today. Best castle wins a shilling.'

Lewis' hand froze in mid air, but then he shook his head.

'Why not?' Charlie seemed curious, rather than snubbed.

'I'm too old for sandcastles.'

'How old are you then?' Charlie pushed his face closer. 'You don't look too old.'

Sylvie heard the hesitation. 'Eleven.' She smiled at the added year. 'That's not too old.'

Lewis turned his head and glared at him. Charlie didn't move. 'I don't like sandcastles anyway,' Lewis said, and throwing the bark down, walked towards Esther who was busily occupied with a collection of pebbles.

Sylvie watched Lewis for a moment and then put down her magazine. Creeping up behind him, she touched his shoulder. When he spun around she pointed at the big sandbank. 'Race you to the top!'

Without hesitation, he propelled himself forward in one fluid movement. Sylvie followed him. At first the ground was soft and deep and seemed almost to suck her backwards, but as they neared the dune it became flat and hard and she began to run properly. She felt her breath fast and ragged, the slap of their feet flecking her legs with wet sand. The sense of freedom fired her blood and for a moment she felt she might, after all, become the person she wanted; a person who didn't wake each morning full of doubt and self-recrimination. Yet by the time they reached the foot of the dune she had been forced to slow to a walk. At the summit she doubled over, palms pushed against her thighs while the breeze whipped the hair from her bandana and blew it across her face. As soon as she had got her breath she grabbed Lewis, wrapping her arms so tightly about his chest she could feel the pounding of his heart inches from her own. Ahead of them the sea was infinite; humanity compressed into a small, irrelevant hinterland.

By mid-afternoon the tide was coming in. Sylvie was sitting in one of the striped deckchairs with her face turned to the sun. Lewis was sitting a few feet away, scraping at the struts of a wooden glider with a penknife. Esther was asleep, curled on a towel at Sylvie's feet. Sylvie had draped another one across Esther's legs and arms, and now Esther's hair clung to her brow in sweat-drenched clumps.

It was still very warm. While Sylvie watched, the sea remained stationary between the expanse of sky and the irregular sweep of yellow, but if she closed her eyes then, like a game of Grandmother's Footsteps, the water would dart forward so that when she opened them again she found the waves had captured the next stretch of sand. Gradually the sea was creeping around the central dune. It was forming a lake in the basin of beach directly in front of the beach huts where differently shaped sandcastles peppered the ground like a selection of discarded hats. Charlie had built a fort and decorated the turrets with feathers and stones. Although he had spent a lot of time on it he hadn't won anything. Earlier, a reporter from the local paper had come around and taken pictures of the first-placed entry and afterwards Sylvie heard Charlie complaining to Connie the judging hadn't been fair. Now, most of the creations were about to be washed away and a number of people were packing up their bags to go home.

Sylvie stretched out her toes. She wished there was a way to say thank you to Ginger, or at least that she had more memories of Ginger to call upon. They had probably met several times but she could only recall one occasion, the last of them, in any detail.

It was late summer, a few years after the end of the Great War, when she must have been quite little. One morning without warning her mother ushered her into the back of the Crossley and Buck drove them to the railway station, an astonishing, gaping structure that smelled of soot and smoke, with a distant glass roof suspended on iron pillars. She sat opposite her mother, perched on the edge of a creaking seat, as the train ate its way through the countryside, belching trails of steam over cattle and sheep.

They crossed town in a hackney carriage and stepped from the glare of the London pavements into a room painted the colour of river water. Chandeliers held by long, slender chains hovered above tables draped in linen, and in the far corner a pianist was playing 'Clair de Lune'. Sylvie recognised it, the melody familiar from the obligatory piano lessons, and pulled on her mother's arm to tell her so, but at that moment Ginger swept towards them.

She was wearing a single row of pearls and a white dress in floaty silk, printed with pale green, exotic-looking plants. Her face was bright with rouge and lipstick and over her big grey eyes were penciled two such perfect arches they might have been drawn with a compass. But in one respect, she was quite a disappointment. After a minute or two, Sylvie could bear the confusion no longer. 'Why are you called Ginger,' she burst out, 'when your hair isn't ginger at all?'

Her aunt threw her head back and laughed, her glassy blonde bob catching the wavering light. Then she leaned forward and took Sylvie's hand across the table.

'Just because I like it, darling,' she whispered, although it didn't seem to Sylvie something that needed to be kept a secret.

Sitting next to Ginger her mother didn't look the same. She was older, duller, than she had been on the train and dressed in far too many clothes. Sylvie tried not to notice the difference. Yet it was difficult not to see how the waiters clustered at the back of Ginger's chair. How a man on the far side of the room with golden sideburns kept glancing across in Ginger's direction. Her aunt was like the new shoes sitting under her bedroom chair. When her mother had unwrapped the tissue and put them in the wardrobe they had made her old shoes look so shabby that Sylvie had taken them straight out again. She slipped her hand into her mother's palm, and asked when it would be time to go.

'We haven't even had tea yet, darling,' was her mother's bemused response.

A waiter did eventually bring tea. It came in a silver teapot together with a cake stand wonderfully arranged with tiny triangular sandwiches, finger-sized chocolate éclairs and miniature strawberry tarts. Sylvie was so hungry – breakfast had been such a very long time ago – that she piled several things onto her plate all at once, then stopped, expecting to hear her mother say something about good manners and being out in public. But her mother wasn't taking any notice of her at all.

'How is The Spoiler?' Ginger asked a little later. As she spoke she was licking the cream off her fingers. 'Did you have to get written permission to come and visit me?' She paused and glanced up. 'Oh, come on, don't look like that. I know he hasn't approved of me for years.'

'Nobody approves of you, darling,' her mother said. 'It doesn't mean they don't like you.'

'Still,' Ginger persisted, 'has he relented, just a tinsy bit? Is he going to let you come and visit your big sister more than once? Or am I still the big bad wolf that might gobble up his adorable little pussycat?'

She was laughing again, as though it was all terribly amusing, but her mother said nothing and began to slice her crust-less sandwich into even smaller pieces. After a moment Ginger fell silent and stared at her with a look of astonishment.

'Oh my God!' she said, leaving a slow, affected, space between each word. 'You didn't ask him did you, darling? You snuck out! Like a pussycat! A pussycat sneaking into the night with its baby kitten!'

'Oh for goodness sake, Ginny, it was broad daylight. There was no sneaking about and certainly no pussycats. I didn't trouble Philip about it because… well, because it was easier that way. And now I really need to keep an eye on the time because we absolutely must be home in time for dinner or else I shall be in trouble for keeping Sylvie out so late.' Her eyes swept around the room as if to locate a clock, and she began to smooth her skirt vigorously, looking for all the world as though she were about to stand up and go that very moment.

'Nonsense, darling!' Ginger's eyes were shining. 'You cannot possibly come all the way to London and then leave again five minutes later. And if you dare to go now, I shall have to keep your little kitten hostage!'

She wrapped both her arms around Sylvie and pulled her so close Sylvie could see the beads of perspiration sitting on Ginger's cleavage and a dusty trace of talcum powder somewhere in the darkness below.

'Besides,' Ginger cried, 'I'm certainly not going to let you go before we toast The Spoiler with something suitable for the occasion.' Still pressing Sylvie against her she grasped the arm of a passing waiter and with a spectacular smile ordered two of something called 'Gin and It'.

At first her mother shook her head decisively. No, she couldn't possibly drink it. Not in the afternoon. Not when they really had to be leaving at any moment. But Ginger was insistent, raising her glass and crying, 'Hoorah for The Pussycat! And to The Spoiler, who didn't manage to spoil this afternoon!'

Or perhaps her mother hadn't protested that much after all, because quite soon afterwards Ginger was ordering two more, saying, 'Oh do come on darling! Don't be boring. You've broken all the rules and now you must jolly well enjoy it while you can.' And soon enough her mother's napkin had slid unnoticed onto the carpet and she was throwing back her head and laughing like Ginger, so that Sylvie didn't know whether to feel proud or embarrassed at being at the loudest, funniest table in the room.

At one point, Ginger leant across and cupped Sylvie's chin in her hand. 'Do you know,' she said dreamily, her gaze tight on Sylvie's face. 'I think she's the image of me!' Sylvie gazed back into Ginger's opulent eyes and squirmed with pleasure.

When they finally left the daylight had softened. The London evening was filled with the bustle of women in long beaded dresses and fox-fur; men with gleaming shoes and groomed moustaches; the smell of petrol and sugared peanuts. Although nothing was said, Sylvie knew they had missed their train, and they had to take a much later one, rattling them uncompromisingly back home through the tawny countryside. Once, when they stopped in the middle of nowhere, she saw a barn owl. For a second or two it flew ghostlike alongside the carriage before it banked and swooped out of sight over the sepia fields. Her mother fell asleep, crumpled in the corner, her mouth slightly open and leaking a tiny tributary of pink lipstick. Sylvie had to wake her when they got to the right stop, flattening against the cold glass to read the station name above the platform in the near dark, shaking her mother's shoulder until she roused herself with a start.

Buck was waiting for them. He was leaning over the bonnet of the Crossley smoking a cigarette, a diminutive glow of orange in the night. He made an exaggerated display of stamping it out under his boots as they drew near, slammed both the doors, and barely said a word to them all the way back home. At last she heard the familiar crunch of rubber on the gravel drive and through the steady yellow squares of the downstairs window she saw her father stop his pacing of the hallway, lift his head and move towards the front door. A few moments later, scooted up to bed against the nap of a nanny's skirt, she could hear her father shouting from the far side of the library doors.

Afterwards, she never saw Ginger again. Once or twice she thought she caught her name, but only at the edges of heated conversations that died with the abruptness of a felled tree as soon as she stepped into the room. Yet the day in London had kept like amber, a forgotten thing, she'd had no call to think of until her father telephoned, breaking the brittle silence of her evening with Howard, to say that Ginger had died.

Sylvie's thoughts were interrupted by a cry from behind the windbreak. Connie's head and shoulders appeared briefly. Sylvie saw her raise a hand to her face and then she disappeared from sight again. A few seconds later there was another low moaning sound. Presently, Charlie stopped his game and ran over to her. Lewis put down his glider and came to stand by Sylvie. As they watched, Charlie's feet and shins emerged from behind the canvas, as if he was lying on his stomach or knees.

'What are they doing?' Lewis asked.

'I don't know,' Sylvie said. She touched his arm. 'Why don't you run over and see if everything is all right?' Lewis looked appalled but she gave him an encouraging nod and a light push in the direction of Charlie's legs. He came sprinting back a few minutes later.

'They're hunting for a ring. The lady put it down but she doesn't know where.'

'Oh, how sad!' Sylvie said. She gazed at the hundreds of acres of dimpled sand. 'They'll never find it. Perhaps I should go and look too?' She remembered Connie's fierceness and hesitated.

As she dithered, Esther stirred and then kicked off the towels and sat up. Her face was a bright, boiled red. With a regretful glance at the windbreak, Sylvie fetched the remains of their picnic lunch. They had eaten the boiled eggs, the corned-beef rolls and the apples, but there was still lemonade and she had deliberately kept back slices of ginger loaf wrapped in waxed paper.

As they ate they couldn't help but watch the other family. They were still crawling about, although now the search area had widened. Every so often Connie would stop her frantic scrabbling to stand and look at the sea. It was getting much nearer. Soon, Sylvie thought, everyone would have to move closer to the beach huts and the ring would be lost for certain.

Getting to her feet, she brushed the cake crumbs from her lap and walked over to the windbreak. 'Can I help?'

Connie sat back on her heels. Silvery snail tracks shone through her face powder. She wiped a cheek with her wrist. 'I've lost a ring,' she said. 'A wedding ring. I took it off in case we went for a paddle and it came off in the water. I was certain I put it in my shoe but I can't have done after all.'

'Your wedding ring? I say, that is bad luck!'

Connie's face twitched. She broke eye contact and gazed instead at her lap. 'I've got to find it. I've just got to.'

'Does it matter so terribly much?' Sylvie asked gently. 'Only' – she made a vague gesture with her arms – 'only, you'll be lucky to find it in all this sand.' When Connie didn't answer, she added. 'Will your husband be angry if you don't find it?'

Connie didn't look up. 'No,' she said in a flat voice. 'He won't be angry.'

'Well, that's one good thing.' Sylvie smiled. 'I think mine would be. Awfully angry.' Her voice faded as it struck her with chilling certainty how Howard's rage would be fuelled by the irrational belief that losing her wedding ring was the final, definitive proof of her treachery. She brought her attention back to Connie. 'He might buy you another one,' she said brightly. 'If you manage to play your cards right!' As soon as she had spoken she knew by the mask-like set of Connie's face she had said something terribly wrong.

Connie's face twisted. Then she said, 'I don't have a husband.'

Sylvie stared, not understanding.

A shudder seemed to pass from Connie's hips through to her shoulders. 'It's not my ring.' She took a breath. 'It belonged to my mother.'

There was a painful silence. Sylvie took a step backwards. 'I'm so sorry,' she stammered. She watched, horrified, as Connie rubbed her face again.

For a second Connie looked defeated, but then she tilted her chin and said in a tight voice, 'Now you see why I've got to find it.'

Despairingly, they both gazed at the sand.

'Could you have dropped it in the beach hut?' Sylvie said at last. 'When you were changing, perhaps?'

Connie shook her head. 'No. I would have noticed. It would have made a noise when it fell. It's somewhere around here.'

'Well, in that case…' Sylvie said. Her brow furrowed. 'I have an idea. Wait just a moment.'

She hurried to where her own belongings were scattered around the deckchair and fetched a spade. While they watched she placed herself at one end of the windbreak and then began to walk backwards, dragging a corner of the spade through the sand to cut an incision that extended beyond the edge of the canvas. Next, she executed a sharp right angle and scored another line that ran perpendicular. Eventually she turned again to mark a track parallel with the first, and finally she swung back in the direction of the windbreak. By the time she straightened up, pink and a little out of breath, she had drawn a rectangle about the size of a tennis court snug against the length of the windbreak.

'Now,' she said, 'we must all line up along one side as if we're about to have a race and then we must each search the strip of sand immediately in front of us.'

Connie looked doubtful. 'But supposing I didn't lose it there?'

'The chances are you did because you haven't moved far from the windbreak all day.'

Connie gaped at her.

'Well' – Sylvie rushed on – 'we can't possibly search the whole beach and this is the best way of doing the most important part of it properly.' Since Connie still seemed unsure, she added, 'I saw something like it in a film.'

'You saw a film about someone losing a ring at the seaside?'

'Not exactly,' Sylvie admitted. 'They were actually looking for a murder weapon. And it wasn't on a beach. But I don't see why it wouldn't work the same. It's just a way of making sure we don't search the same area twice and miss out other places altogether.' Connie looked across the demarcated piece of sand, as if seeing it with fresh eyes.

Sylvie called the children over. With a rather heady sensation of being in charge, she explained what they were going to do. Esther, now fully awake and racing in circles, had to be bribed with the promise of a Snofruit at the quay before they went home. 'It won't take long,' Sylvie vowed, grabbing her arm. 'Not if we all do it together.'

But it did. The hopelessness of the task confronted her as soon as she sank onto her knees. Close up, the sand was such a fusion of every shade of gold that it might have been designed for the very purpose of hiding a small piece of jewellery. Some was pale and blond as ash, some of it a vivid, primrose yellow and yet other grains were shades of black and brown and quite volcanic looking. There were bits too, hundreds of bits of things in every square foot; pieces of driftwood, fragments of shattered shells, and broken feathers – all perfectly able to conceal a wedding ring within their chinks and shadows. Feeling the silky wash of it through her fingers, Sylvie wondered whether she should tell Connie they were wasting their time, that the idea might work if you were looking for a knife or a pistol but not when you were searching for an object smaller than a hatpin that by now had probably burrowed below the surface.

She sat back on her calves and cleared her throat. 'I say, Connie.' Saying her name out loud felt bold and a little peculiar. Connie didn't respond. She was bent low, her face rigid with concentration. It reminded Sylvie of the foxhounds at a Boxing Day meet, noses pressed to the ground, desperate to unearth a scent. 'Connie!' she said again, louder this time.

Connie lifted her head, but instead of waiting for Sylvie to speak, she began to talk herself, as if she hadn't heard Sylvie at all. 'I'm sorry about earlier, for being so rude. I thought in the woods you didn't want to know Charlie and me, and then what I said, about the key, it came out all wrong.' She flashed Sylvie a sudden lovely smile before dropping her gaze again.

Speechless, Sylvie watched her for a moment; then she sighed and settled back into the sand. She tried to focus on the very smallest of patches and scour it methodically before moving onto the next, but inevitably she would glimpse something that dragged her eyes further away and when it turned out only to be a particular sort of stone, or a shard of old glass, or a top from a beer bottle, she had to guess at where she had last been looking which meant that she must be leaving gaps in her search big enough to hide hundreds of rings.

Although the sun had slipped a little in the sky the temperature had hardly dropped and before long the children lost heart and drifted away. In the corner of her eye Sylvie could see Lewis and Charlie scratching out a game of noughts and crosses with the spade, but she didn't have the heart to call them back. She was in the process of discarding a honey-coloured pebble when the fingers of her right hand brushed against something small and solid. It lay half-buried, catching the lengthening rays, and caused her heart to leap so hard that at first she couldn't bear to touch it and suffer the inevitable disappointment. When a moment later it lay in her palm, she could only stare at the roughened gold, the engraved lettering on the inside of the band, shocked into silence by the trouncing of statistics, the triumph over probability, the purity of her luck.

It took Lewis to break the spell. He must have noticed her sit up and come over to see why. As he peered over her shoulder, his face lit up, 'Mummy's found it!' he yelled. 'Mummy's found the ring!'

The moments immediately after that were a blur. All she remembered was holding out the ring to Connie while the children jumped around her legs, seeing Connie's face quiver and then crumble as she jammed it back onto her finger, and then eventually hearing her own voice above all the hullabaloo. 'Well, all I can say is for goodness sake don't lose it again. I don't fancy our chances of finding it a second time!'

When the excitement had died down nobody seemed to know what to do next. Sylvie turned to Lewis and Esther. 'I suppose we ought to pack up and go home.' But of course it wasn't her own home they were going to and she felt too full of success to face the smell of furniture cream and lavender, and the rather queer atmosphere that Ginger's death had induced. Besides, the day was mellowing into a beautiful evening. The beach was nearly empty now, the tide was in, and the thickening light had softened and intensified the reach of water and sky. 'Actually,' she said with a rush of impulsiveness, 'why don't we have a game of something together first?'

Half an hour later Sylvie was standing in the beach hut waiting for Connie to pass up the bat and ball. Now she was even hotter than before, but in a relaxed kind of way rather than the tight, itchy heat she had felt kneeling on the sand. As she came out of the hut she gathered up two bottles and the enamel mugs. After she had given some lemonade to the children she turned to Connie. 'What do you think?' She shook the bottle of Plymouth Gin so that it sloshed against the glass. 'I rather fancy a drop.'

Connie's eyes widened. 'Where did you get that?'

'I found it when we arrived. I've just inherited the beach hut from my aunt. Actually, I think she might have got up to all sorts of things here, but nobody's telling me very much.'

'You're the lucky one!' Connie stared wistfully across the beach. 'Two more days and we're back in the smoke.'

Sylvie jiggled the bottle again.

'Go on then,' Connie said. 'That little drop there can't do us much harm.' But there was more than they expected and not much lemonade left to dilute it with. They sat together on the steps watching the children stamp about in the water. Almost immediately Sylvie felt the bite and then the glow of the gin spread through her limbs. She and Connie were sitting close together, their thighs almost touching. It was hard to remember Connie was the same woman who had challenged her in the beach-hut doorway earlier that morning.

Sylvie had closed her eyes, almost dozing, when Connie said suddenly, 'Just in case you're wondering, Charlie's my little brother.'

Sylvie snapped awake. She *had* wondered, but in the end decided that Connie was too young for Charlie to be her son. Although Connie's face often had an older, almost matronly composure, at unexpected moments she looked exactly like a schoolgirl. Sylvie hesitated and then asked the real question that had been playing on her mind. 'Where's your father? Did he…? I mean… Is he still alive?'

Connie took a while to reply. 'He's in London,' she said finally. 'He's busy. He… he has these ideas. Political ideas.' She drank a slurp of gin. 'He's gone a bit mad since Mum died. There's nobody can talk any sense into him now.'

'What sort of ideas?'

'Have you heard of…?' Connie began, but she stopped and lifted her cup again. 'I'd best not say too much.' She glanced at Sylvie, saw her expression, and added, all in a rush, 'It's not like he does anything. Most of the time he only goes to meetings. He just wanted me and Charlie off his hands for a few days, that's all.'

Sylvie was still goggling at her when a male voice interrupted them. 'Celebrating something, are we ladies?'

It was the reporter from earlier, the one who had taken the picture of the winning sandcastle. He was dressed in a suit, or what remained of it; trousers rolled to his calf, shirtsleeves to his elbow. He was still wearing a waistcoat and tie, however, and the camera slung round his neck gave him a dashing, professional air.

Sylvie looked guiltily into her mug, but Connie stuck out her chin. 'So what if we are?' she said. 'What's it to you?'

'Me? Oh, I'm naturally curious.' The reporter patted the side of the camera. 'Goes with the job.' He crinkled his eyes at Connie and waited.

'Well, if you must know, we have got something to celebrate.' She paused theatrically and the reporter raised his eyebrows in an exaggerated show of anticipation. 'I lost my ring in the sand' – Connie flashed her hand towards him – 'but my friend here found it. Now,' she said triumphantly, poking Sylvie hard in the ribs, 'what are the chances of that happening? Doesn't it make a better story than a silly old one about sandcastles?'

The reporter laughed. 'Do you know,' he said, 'I think it might. Come on ladies, let's have you down here, standing in front of the beach hut.'

Connie jumped up, but Sylvie stayed sitting. 'I'm not sure we should,' she murmured.

'Oh come on!' Connie pulled her forwards.

They stood side by side while the reporter wrote down Connie's spirited account and made a note of their names and addresses. The children stopped their game to watch, until Charlie splashed Lewis from behind and they started chasing each other again.

'It sounds like you were quite the heroine,' the reporter said to Sylvie.

Despite herself, Sylvie blushed with pleasure. She linked her arm through Connie's arm, and when the reporter pressed the button she cheered. Almost immediately, however, a tide of melancholy swept over her. The image of her mother and Ginger in almost the exact same spot came to mind. Perhaps it was the suddenness of the gin. She remembered vaguely that gin was supposed to make you cry and all at once she wanted to cry now. The day was nearly finished, the earth tipping away from the sun, just as every perfect moment tipped unstoppably away, even as the shutter of a camera came down.

As soon as the reporter had left, she sank down on the beach. Connie's earlier bravado seemed to have disappeared too. She settled herself next to Sylvie, and after a while her voice broke into Sylvie's thoughts. 'I say,' she said, quietly. 'Do you think there's going to be a war?'

'I don't know,' Sylvie said, pushing the emotion back down her throat. 'Let's hope not.' There had been an article in the newspaper the day before by someone who said that he was quite sure there wouldn't be. The piece in the *Daily Express* had been quite cheering, until her father had looked over shoulder and snorted derisively. She drew a circle in the sand. 'At least Lewis and Charlie are far too young to fight.'

Connie gave her a sideways look. 'But what about your husband?'

Sylvie studied the shape she had made. 'Yes, I suppose he might have to.' She hadn't really thought about the impact of a war on Howard. 'What about you?' she asked, after a second, keen to move the conversation somewhere else. 'Is there anyone in particular you would worry about?'

'Well,' Connie hesitated, 'I suppose I am stepping out with someone, if that's what you mean. At least we've been to the pictures a few times…' She let the sentence trail to nothing but then, as if sensing Sylvie's expectation, added, 'His name is Ted. It's not serious between us, not' – she pulled a quick face – 'not on my side, anyway. But I would worry about him; I don't like the thought of him being in danger. Though if there's a war I suppose we'll all be in danger. Everyone says London is going to be flattened and we shall have to evacuate.' She shuddered.

'And will you?' Sylvie turned to look at the children. Charlie was giving Esther a piggyback and Lewis was flicking water at Charlie's legs.

'No!' Connie followed Sylvie's gaze. 'I can't leave Dad. And I don't want to send Charlie on his own to a lot of strangers.'

Sylvie nodded emphatically. 'I couldn't do it either. Not know where they're going. Not know who's going to look after them.' She shuddered. 'Suppose they never came home again?'

They sat for a while staring out over the sea, as if the German fleet might materialise in front of their eyes at any moment.

'A man came round last week with a gas mask,' Connie said eventually. 'He wanted me to try it on so I'd be certain to know how to fit it. It squashed my hair and he seemed quite sorry about it and said that it might melt my mascara as well! I told him I couldn't imagine bothering to wear mascara, if there's a war going on.'

'I shall,' Sylvie said grimly. 'I don't see why the Germans should stop me from looking my best.' She shivered and rubbed her arms. The sun was beginning to dip behind the top of the pine trees and they were sitting now in the lengthening shadows cast by the beach huts. 'I suppose I'd better take the children home.' The long cycle ride back was unappealing. So too, the disapproval her late, dishevelled return would almost certainly provoke. And now her breath probably smelt of gin. She sighed and turned to Connie. 'You will be here tomorrow, won't you?'

'Well, we've nowhere else to go.' It sounded, thought Sylvie, a little grudging but then Connie laughed and took hold of Sylvie's elbow. Sylvie could feel the sandy friction of her fingers, the latent heat beneath them.

Connie glanced at the sky. 'Do you think it will be nice again?'

'Yes,' Sylvie said firmly, although she knew the forecast was quite unsettled.

CHAPTER FIVE

Norfolk, recently

Cresting the ridge of pines, Martha braces herself for the sight of an empty parking lot, a Ford Mondeo-shaped hole in the place where Colin's car should be. The relief of seeing it there, blue and solitary, floods her with affection for Colin, for the beach, for Norfolk, for the whole of wonderful, rainy England. She picks her way over the stone-spattered sand to allow her breathing to return to a calmer rhythm, but Colin is too preoccupied to notice her arrival anyway. He's hunched over the steering wheel, phone flat to cheek, but he terminates the call as soon as Martha climbs in and remains oddly quiet for the rest of the journey. Outside their destination he rouses himself, fetches her luggage from the boot and insists on lugging it through the door and into the foyer. By this time Martha feels so bad she believed him capable of stealing her things she tips him more than she can sensibly afford. Colin holds out an enormous, ham-like hand. 'Any time you need a cab,' he tells her solemnly, 'call Colin's Cars.'

The hotel is not what she was expecting. The hallway has pale green walls hung with oil paintings in cracked-gold frames and rubber plants flank a staircase carpeted in red tartan. Martha was, she realises, hoping for something more *seaside*, a jollier decor of stripes, or nautical whites and navy, enlivened by the impatient clamour of small children hopping about with buckets and spades. A three-course dinner menu displayed by the entrance to a dining room reveals the evening specials to be Sea Trout en Papillote and Fillet of Beef Niçoise. It reminds Martha she hasn't had a proper meal in a long while, but the wave of emptiness she feels is not confined to her stomach. As she gathers up her bags she hears the Mondeo's engine start up and then its tapering rumble as Colin heads for home.

Behind the reception desk a woman with blonde-grey hair is jotting numbers on a piece of paper, lips moving silently. Seeing Martha, her pen freezes and a flash of irritation crosses her face before she arranges it into a smile. As she records Martha's passport number and fetches a room key a river of bracelets rustle up and down her forearm as if someone is shaking a beaker of sand. A man is summoned to help lug the suitcase to the top of the tartan stairs and on reaching her room, Martha's unsteadiness is dispelled by a burst of accomplishment. *Here she is at last!* In England, in Wells, at the very hotel her father planned to visit! Immediately after the door closes behind her the sense of achievement dulls and then disintegrates altogether.

She drops on top of the bed, shucks off her shoes and a puddle of beach cascades onto the carpet. All at once the idea of venturing downstairs for dinner seems beyond her. It doesn't help that somebody has already turned down the bedcovers and drawn the curtains, giving the room a muted, night-time mood. I'll lie down for just a moment, she thinks, but once horizontal her eyelids drop like shutters and there is no realistic alternative to pulling off her clothes and sliding in. Yet, perversely, in the matter of seconds it takes Martha to peel off her dress and settle beneath the covers her mind determines not to let go of the day after all. She's increasingly conscious of the small-town noises outside the window and the occasional passage of voices and creak of floorboards along the landing. Pretty soon she's too hot. And then she's too cold. At some later point she becomes aware of a person in the adjacent room: the rough clumping of a drawer wrestled shut, a spark of radio immediately extinguished, a toilet flushing and then, eventually – infuriatingly – a steady progression of nasal grunts on just the other side of the wall.

To pass the minutes she scrolls through the names of everyone she can think of to locate a possible Catkins, or even a Catherine. At first it's by way of distraction from the neighbourly snoring, but soon she's sifting systematically through lists of her parents' friends and acquaintances, even characters from when she was small and the evening drift of adult laughter and her father's cigar smoke would curl as far as her own bedroom. Not once does she encounter a likely candidate. Finally, perplexed and frustrated, she reaches for a book and clicks the bedside lamp. By the time she turns it off again, the dark bulk of the bedroom furniture is visible in the ash-grey light and the first strands of birdsong are trailing the start of the new day. Relieved it won't be long before she can go in search of breakfast, she sinks back against the pillows.

*

The airplane is plunging into the sea. Lurching uncontrollably from side to side, the overhead lockers are wide-open, luggage sailing through the cabin. Yet it's not bags and briefcases careering past Martha's head, but the forgotten contents of Janey's toy box: the real china tea set painted with sugar-brown teddies, cheerleader Cindy waving a spangly baton and a pair of roller skates with Velcro straps that date from when Janey passed her first piano exam. Martha is ducking and dodging the flying items as peals of music come over the tannoy system. She's expecting the pilot's voice to follow, telling everyone to retrieve their life vests from under the seats and adopt the brace position, but instead the song gets louder and then, somehow, she's in the water, floating upwards, and almost of its own accord her arm stretches out and makes contact with her cell phone.

'Mom?'

Martha hauls herself into a semi-sitting position, blinking at the daylight pooling on the carpet and a picture above the bureau of cows grazing placidly in a long-grassed meadow. She tries to remember where in heaven's name she is.

'Mom? Did I wake you?'

'Uh huh.' Martha can only croak; her tongue is clamped to the roof of her mouth. With an effort, she pushes herself further up the headboard. 'Janey,' she manages, finally. By her elbow, the red of a radio alarm is flashing 14.30. Half past two in the afternoon? That can't be right. Someone is vacuuming next door, pounding against the skirting board, and the noise is making it difficult to string her thoughts together.

'I waited until nine thirty.' Janey's tone is thin and pinched, like she's squeezing her voice through an old-fashioned washing mangle. 'You're normally up by now.'

'It's okay. Really, I'm good.' At last, Martha's vocal chords spring to life. She wiggles herself more comfortable on the mattress and smiles happily into the phone. 'It's so lovely to hear from you, honey! How are things?' Too late she hears her own eager intensity and in the heartbeat that follows she senses Janey, deer-like, back away.

'I'm just fine.'

'And the course?'

Slight pause.

'Fine.'

Martha racks her brain for a question requiring more than a one-word answer. How many times since Janey turned fifteen has she played this particular game, desperate to fan a tiny flame of communication into an actual conversation? After a moment she says with determined brightness, 'Well, what are you doing this weekend?' When Janey doesn't answer immediately, she adds without thinking, 'Have you made any plans?' *Damn!*

'No. Not really.'

Martha twists the bedspread around the fingers of her free hand. It's a plain, startling white. All of the bed linen is white – which strikes Martha as an ambitious colour for a hotel.

Then Janey says, 'I tried to phone you yesterday. Twice. And couldn't get through.' After a moment she adds, 'So I called Auntie Elizabeth instead.'

Martha swallows in disbelief at the monumental unfairness of parenting. Janey can be out of contact for days – once for almost two weeks during which time she must have seen, for goodness sake, the number of occasions her mother tried to get in touch. Yet she has to be available whenever her daughter chooses to make contact. This time, however, her irritation is tempered by guilt; not only has she not answered Janey's calls, Janey hasn't the slightest idea where she is. Unless, of course, Elizabeth has told her. This would be ironic, since it is Elizabeth who always insists Martha should stop monitoring Janey so closely.

'What did Auntie Elizabeth say?' Martha asks, warily. Although Janey has given no sign she knows her mother is only a train journey away it's hard to envision Elizabeth covering for her, much easier to imagine her practical and professional, telling Janey the truth.

'She said you'd probably gone to a movie, switched off your phone and forgotten to turn it on again.'

'Oh!' Martha unspools the pristine bedspread.

'So did you?'

'Did I what?'

'Go to a movie and switch off your phone.'

'Mm… sort of,' Martha mumbles. The last part at least is true. 'I guess your exams must be soon?' she asks, partly to change the subject and partly because at one point in the night it occurred to her that Janey had said nothing about them.

'I've finished them. They were last week.'

'Last week!' Why didn't you tell me?' Martha rocks fully upright, an irrational panic blooming in her stomach. She has never quite managed to suppress the notion that Janey's academic success might be influenced by, might actually depend upon, a good-luck text or willed prayer of support at the appointed hour, some silent communion between herself and kismet to shift the cosmic energy patterns and realign the stars in Janey's favour. Perhaps it's a side-effect of the fact that in the distant past, she, Martha was always so good at exams – the challenge, the focus, the simple strategy of working out what the examiners wanted and then providing them with it. A similar strategy, she realised years later, to the one she had followed with Clem; which resulted in getting pregnant, dropping out of her final year and being married at twenty-two.

'You'd only have fussed, Mom.'

'I would not have done!' Martha cries, wishing this were true.

'Anyhow,' Janey says, 'they went fine.' And then in a smaller voice. 'I think they went fine.'

Martha is seized by a violent desire to rip the word 'fine' from every dictionary in existence and build a towering funeral pyre of the word 'Well, then,' she says, keeping her voice even, 'will you go out to celebrate?'

'I guess,' Janey says. 'Maybe.'

Silence latches onto the sentence and expands, lake-like, into the seconds that follow. Martha clamps the phone more closely to her ear, listening to the feather trace of Janey's breathing, willing herself to find the key, the code, the stepping stones of words across the void.

The feeling is not a new one. The first time Martha experienced the same sense of helplessness, Janey was aged about five. She began to throw tantrums, terrible sobbing rages of the kind that made other mothers steer their own children clear of such a spectacle and run Martha up and down with worried eyes. That Janey should possess such a temper was unsettling enough – Martha didn't regard either herself or Clem as the kind of person who made a public exhibition of their feelings – but the most troubling aspect of the matter was the outbursts seemed to come from nowhere, never remotely related to what was happening at the time. They might be in a shopping mall or at the grocery store and all at once Janey would refuse to take another step, would plop onto her backside, and scream her face the other side of beetroot to a drained and tear-stained white. Martha would watch, helpless and embarrassed, by turns angry and cajoling, waiting for the storm to pass. Of course, she put it down to Clem, rather, the absence of Clem. But plenty of Janey's classmates had parents who separated with far greater acrimony and yet those children seemed relentlessly content, cooperative and sunny. What was Martha doing wrong?

One afternoon Martha came across a parenting book at the library. The author suggested that when trouble struck she should try saying something along the lines of, '*It sounds like* you're mighty angry about life today.' Or, '*It sounds like* someone has made you real upset.' And so on. When the demons next appeared Martha made herself listen hard. Then she said, 'It sounds like you're feeling pretty…' She was right on the cusp of saying, 'mad' but, at the very last second, switched to, 'sad,' instead. 'You sound like such an unhappy girl this morning,' she added. Janey's crying hiccupped to a halt. Nodding slowly she held out a damp hand and let Martha pull her to her feet.

'Janey?' Martha grips the phone a little tighter. She stops. 'Janey,' she says again, 'it sounds like…' But the sentence falters and dies in her throat.

'Mom, I have to go.'

'Janey, wait a second!'

What it really sounds like, Martha has realised, is that her daughter is frightened – scared out of her wits – and won't tell her mother a thing about it.

'Janey!' she calls.

'Bye, Mom. Speak soon.'

And the line goes dead.

Martha drops back on the pillows. A moment later she's sitting again. She tests out possible sentences in her head: 'Janey, it sounds like something's wrong and I'd like for us to have a proper talk. Janey, you sure don't sound happy and I'm starting to worry. Janey, honey, you won't believe this, but it just so happens I'm in England!' But hovering over the redial option she remembers the promise she made to herself on the train – *wait, for just two weeks* – and flings the cell across the snowy mound of bedspread.

*

Downstairs the hotel is eerily quiet apart from the bluebottle drone of the vacuum, which is still faintly audible on the floors above. In the restaurant deserted tables are cluttered with smeared plates, pink-tinged wine glasses and scrunched-up napkins. *Where is everyone?* It's like arriving at a theatre after the performance has ended, the props scattered over the stage but the actors and audience long gone. From the door to the kitchen a waiter appears with a plate of sandwiches and bustles away from her in beetle-black trousers. Following behind, Martha comes to a bar where a sober-looking crowd is quietly occupied with drinks and magazines. A couple of table lamps have already been lit and a Labrador is sprawled over the floor, tracking the waiter with mournful devotion. Martha takes a menu from a pile on the counter. She's in no hurry to leave the hotel. Outside the window the sky is a watery pewter and a woman is marching fast along the pavement wearing tights and a body warmer. With Ras' words ringing in her ears – 'The whole of May on an English beach!' – Martha steps carefully over the Labrador and lowers herself into a leather-studded armchair. Perhaps some food will lift her mood.

A moment later she becomes aware of someone at her shoulder. An elderly woman is standing beside her, balanced on crutches and dressed in a billowing kaftan of red-and-black African print. A bushel of silver hair is clasped at her neck and a box is wedged under one arm.

'That's where I normally sit!'

To Martha's relief the woman's gaze is fixed not on Martha but a couch where a young couple are perched so close together their faces are practically touching. Without warning she wobbles alarmingly and Martha sees her right leg is encased foot to knee in plaster. Quickly, Martha gestures at the empty seat beside her own. 'Well heavens! Why don't you sit here instead?'

The woman's face might have been drawn with a sharpened pencil, but the cinnamon gold of her irises is filmed with milky vagueness. Nevertheless, she throws Martha an arched look of surprise as if to indicate that Martha's presence has only that very second come to her notice. 'How kind, although,' she adds with emphasis, 'I prefer the couch.' With a final glare at the preoccupied couple she starts manoeuvring towards the empty cushion. Martha jumps up but her offer of help is brushed away. She's still poised in an indecisive, semi-upright position when the battered-looking box begins to slip and then, in leisurely fashion, pivots into the emptiness and falls. As Martha grabs at air, the lid detaches and half of the contents cascade onto the floor in a confetti of paper and plastic.

'Oh!'

The anguished gasp leaves Martha no alternative but to crawl around on her hands and knees, gathering up wafts of pastel-coloured money and little green-and-red houses that have bounced ridiculous distances over the slate tiles. Straightening eventually, she rubs her kneecaps, slides back into her chair and lifts the board out of the box so she can return the items to their slots.

Her companion leans forward. 'Are we having a game?'

'Well, no,' Martha begins, 'I was just…' But her voice tails away as she sees the woman unfold the furred Monopoly board and begin to organise the cards and counters. Martha is still transfixed when the waiter appears.

'Hello Mrs Gretchen, I can get you something?'

Mrs Gretchen shakes her head. She's bent low over a stack of money from which she's deftly creating two smaller piles. Martha and the waiter both study her in silence. After a moment, Martha touches the waiter's sleeve. 'I'd like a long black coffee and a tuna-fish sandwich.'

As the waiter turns to go he stumbles over the crutches that are lying by the table. Rubbing his ankle, he mutters something that Martha understands to be both foreign and rude, places his foot back down with the air of an injured racehorse and leans over to pick up the poles. Before he can unbend himself, Gretchen's fingers close over his forearm. 'I'll have a whisky and water. But' – releasing her grip, she holds up her thumb and forefinger to create a gap of less than an inch – 'only this much water.'

'Gretchen!' Martha says as the waiter limps away. 'My, that's a pretty name!'

'I'm Gretchen Clarke.' She scrutinizes Martha expectantly. 'Have you heard of me?'

'Why no,' Martha says slowly. 'I don't believe I have.' When Gretchen's expression slumps, Martha adds, 'I'm Canadian, you see. I expect that explains it.'

Forty minutes later Gretchen has not only acquired most of the available properties but also added such clusters of development that even the very cheapest squares extract a hefty price every time Martha lands on them. Naturally Martha knows what's happening, but that hasn't made it easier to do anything about it. The first time she saw Gretchen help herself to the cash reserve in the bank, Martha ignored her. On the second occasion she gave a small cough of reproof, but Gretchen gazed back with such guileless innocence that Martha wasn't able to say any more and had to busy herself with her sandwich.

While Martha is contemplating whether it's even possible to circumvent the board in a way that avoids her opponent, a young woman strides purposefully into the bar. She's dressed in a mustard cotton skirt, green shirt and pixie boots, and her bare legs are the same colour as her chestnut flock of hair. She squats beside Gretchen and plants a kiss on her cheek. 'Are you cheating again, mother?'

Gretchen looks aghast. 'I never cheat!' She looks at Martha. 'I didn't cheat, did I?'

Martha manages a neutral expression. 'Not that I noticed.'

'See!' Gretchen says triumphantly.

'Okay, have it your way! You never cheat.' The girl raises dense brown eyebrows at Martha. Martha smiles back.

Gretchen peers from one to the other and her face puckers. 'This,' she says a trifle stiffly, 'is my daughter Epiphany.'

The girl pulls a face. 'Pip,' she says, and Gretchen's face furrows some more. Pip gazes at the crowded Monopoly board. 'I hope you haven't had a wasted afternoon,' she says to Martha. 'Since mother broke her ankle, she stops here while I'm at work and always ropes some poor unsuspecting guest into a game. Nobody stands an earthly, do they, mother?' Pip squeezes Gretchen's arm, as if to neutralise the sting of her words. 'She used to be an actress and has perfected the role of batty old lady down to a T. You should count yourself lucky she didn't suggest playing for money.'

'Well, I didn't mind one bit. It's been an entertainment.' Martha turns to Gretchen who is gazing over the top of Pip's head with a chilly expression 'Actress!' Martha says in an upbeat voice. 'I'll bet that was an exciting life.'

Gretchen's face unfreezes a little. 'My father bought a theatre. Right here in Wells. I was practically born on the stage!'

'Come on mother' – Pip stands up – 'we need to get you home and let—'

'Martha.'

'… Martha, get on with her day. Not,' she says consulting her watch, 'that there's a great deal left of it.'

After they've gone the bar deflates like a day-old balloon. Martha packs the Monopoly set away and takes it to a shelf stacked with similar tatty boxes. When she returns two men with knee-length socks and binoculars strung around their necks are already settling at her table. She looks through the window at the marly weather, hesitates for just a moment and then walks straight past them, out of the bar. Upstairs she strips off her summer skirt and hauls her jeans, trainers and a thick, wine-coloured hoodie out of her suitcase, leaving a trail of clothes sprawled across the floor. Just as she's about to leave the room, she doubles back and collects her rain jacket.

A vase of lilies has been placed on the reception desk. When Martha asks the blonde-grey woman about the key to the beach hut she regards her with surprise from behind their huge velvet heads. 'It was booked with the room so I suppose there's no reason why you can't take it.' She runs her eyes over Martha's sturdy, beach-ready outfit before adding, 'But there's no point going out now. You'll no sooner get there than you'll need to come back.'

'I don't mind,' Martha says. For some reason, the urge to go to the beach has become overwhelming. She has never suffered from claustrophobia before but something similar is making her practically jig on the spot, even the scent of the lilies is suffocating. She holds out her hand.

With a resigned sort of detachment, the blonde-grey woman searches in a desk drawer and retrieves a small key. 'The beach shuts at dusk.'

Martha nods reassuringly, although she doesn't understand what the woman means. Beaches in England didn't shut, surely? The key is attached to a plastic fob on which the number 25 is written in marker pen. Heart quickening, she zips it deep inside the pocket of her jacket and hurries to the door.

CHAPTER SIX

Instinctively, she heads towards a narrow lane that leads north. A sharp breeze is lifting off the sea, whipping the upper reaches of the tallest trees and rustling the garden hedges, but after the hotel bar the wash of oxygen tastes as rich as cream. The buildings that border the pavement are built from egg-shaped flints or mellow red bricks, their surfaces made cracked and tactile by years of grainy, coastal winds. Martha trails her hand along the walls, feeling the rub of age and inhaling the salt-flecked air and hum of fish.

Before long she passes under an archway and finds herself crossing the coast road at the western end of the port, close to the channel and the route to the beach. The seafront is transitioning from afternoon to evening. Teenagers attached to phones loiter behind parents, a thudding bass leaks from a stationary car, and the neon signage above the arcade radiates pinkly over the curtain of voices and the beeps and thumps of the games machines.

A footpath runs along the ridge between the long, straight road to the beach and the sea. Climbing up, Martha sees a cluster of boats wedged into a sludgy bank that shelves into the water below her feet. Most have ropes coiled between the seats and a soft mesh of nets bundled into the bow. Beyond the mud a line of smarter yachts are moored nose to tail along a jetty, and the flurries of wind are causing their hulls to dip and bob like marionettes, or ghosts even, clinking and rattling their chains. Pulling up the zipper of her jacket, Martha begins to stride along the track. She tells herself it's not cold, but there's something about the pale olive marshes and cement-coloured sky that makes her bunch her shoulders and quicken her pace.

Soon the path thins of company. She passes a woman in a felt hat painting on an easel, and then a couple of dog walkers striding head-down back towards town. After that she can't see anyone ahead at all. The pine trees that mark the ridge of the beach are still a good way off and it occurs to her that it's the perfect time to call Clem.

She pulls out her mobile and moments later, from a distance of three-and-a-half-thousand miles, she hears his familiar voice say, 'Hi there!' in that slightly surprised, rather guarded tone he seems to adopt whenever she catches him at home.

'Hi,' she says back. 'How's it going?'

'Oh fine, I guess. Just fine. How are you?'

'Me? I'm good.' A small pause. 'And Christabel?'

'She's doing great.'

'And the boys?'

'Yup, they're good too.'

'Well, tell them hi. From me.'

Every time they go through the same routine. Martha has come to think of it as the opposite of a courtship dance. Instead of a beckoning or invitation it's an acknowledgment of their separateness, of other relationships more important than their own – Clem's other relationships anyway, their *lack* of relationship – a reassertion, a pegging out, of the space between them.

Clem coughs and then sneezes loudly into the phone. 'Are you okay?' Martha says. 'Do you have a cold?'

'No,' he sniffs audibly down the line, 'hay fever.'

'Oh my! May was always so bad for that. You should get some of those—'

'I will. I have…' Clem says, cutting across her. There's another pause before he says, 'So, I left you a message about Janey, remember?'

'Right.'

Martha senses Clem take a breath.

'Do you think there's something going on there?'

'How do you mean?' Martha's tone is careful. Although some-thing most certainly is *going on*, she badly wants to know what Janey has said to make him think it.

'She hardly calls. She hardly talks.' Clem sneezes again. 'And for the last month or two she's stopped Skyping Christie.'

'She used to Skype Christabel?' A pain shoots through Martha equivalent to knocking the tender spot on her elbow or ankle.

'Well, Christie *and* the boys. The boys mainly. Come to think of it.' Clem's tone is smooth. Too smooth.

'Oh,' Martha says. 'I didn't know that.'

There's a silence. Martha experiments with her zipper, but the jacket won't do up any further than she has pulled it already.

Finally Clem says, 'Well, the point is she doesn't any more. The boys don't understand why. Do you think something is wrong?'

'Maybe,' Martha says vaguely. Her head is taken up with images of Janey having cosy Skype chats with Christabel while she – *Janey's own mother* – is delighted with a text, treasures an actual conversation much as she would a plate of beluga caviar. She forces herself back to the issue. 'Maybe,' she says again, more firmly this time. 'To tell the truth, I've noticed it too. When she calls me, it's hard to get more than a word or two out of her.'

'Well we need to find out what's wrong,' Clem says, in a way that suggests this is an insightful observation.

'Well, I know,' Martha says steadily, 'but it's not so easy—'

'… when she's in England.'

'I wasn't going to say that. I was going to say…' – Martha gazes at the empty track, the approaching woods – 'Oh, never mind!'

'But you'll get to the bottom of it, right?'

'I guess… I hope… Actually, Clem' – Martha clears her throat – 'I'm in England right now.'

'England? Did I hear you right? You're in England?' He sounds so dumbfounded she might have said she was on Mars. 'Well, that's great!' He rushes on before Martha can respond. 'I knew you'd sort it!' She hears the relief cascade through his voice, senses him relegate the problem of Janey to the bottom of his agenda. 'She's got a great mom! You're a great mom, Martha!'

Clem, it occurs to her, has always treated parenting like a form of management; happy to delegate the groundwork to somebody else, but with regular checks to be certain the staff come up to standard. 'Well, I haven't told Janey—'

'You know that, don't you, Martha?'

'What?'

'That you're a great mom!'

'Clem, Janey doesn't have any idea—'

'Now be sure to keep me in the loop, won't you? I'd better shoot. Twins have got softball practice and Christie's off to Bikram.'

'Okay,' Martha says faintly.

'You will keep me posted, right?'

'Right.'

'Bye.'

'Bye.'

As the call disconnects, the spectre of Clem – the broad-shouldered, smokey-eyed bulk of him – evaporates from the basin of blue-grey sky and water. Instinctively, Martha braces herself, waiting for his departure to do its normal destructive thing, to rake up the old, painful memories and raise a condemnatory mirror to her Clem-less life. She sweeps her gaze over the landscape. It stares implacably back. In the middle distance a pair of lily-white egrets lift themselves from the scrub, float briefly above the path and then disappear over the marshes. After a moment Martha tucks the phone away and carries on walking.

There have been other men since Clem, of course. Early after the split, boyfriends were not merely a distraction from the hurt but also something of a novelty; at times it was even fun to be 'out there' again, having gotten together with Clem so early. The first of them, a curly-haired chef of Italian extraction, used to head to Martha's apartment at the end of a shift, his fingernails smelling of onions and garlic. Sometimes he would cook in her tiny kitchen, breaking eggs with one hand to make them both omelets at four in the morning. After that relationship ran its course she briefly hooked up with a librarian from Detroit; a pale, earnest man who always insisted on getting stoned before they went to bed. That didn't work, of course, not with little Janey in the very next room requiring a functioning parent on hand throughout the night. For a while Martha stayed single, and then, just around the period that Christabel fell pregnant, she finally acquired a serious, grown-up relationship.

Michael was the Head of Theatre Studies at the Junior High where Martha had taken a position teaching English to grades seven and eight. At the outset she found his attentions flattering, and then, after a colleague's exuberant leaving party hastened matters along, there was the illicit, childish thrill of keeping their liaison secret. The shared glance, the surreptitious squeeze under the canteen table and the casual brush of his hand as they passed in the corridor added a rosy fraughtness to the school timetable, not to mention a welcome distraction from the bulletins on Christabel's growing bump that Janey delivered every Sunday evening. Martha and Michael had barely been together eight weeks when, without saying a word beforehand to Martha, Michael resigned. Afterwards he informed Martha it was time their *status* became public and he had therefore taken the post of Deputy Head of Dramatic Art at a larger school in a different part of the city.

The difficulty was that Michael seemed to think being a recognised couple meant Martha would want to spend her every spare second with him. It turned out he didn't like sharing her with anyone at all. At first, Martha used to joke that if she wanted to see her friends – attend an exercise class, visit her father, take a walk, go to a bookstore – she needed his written permission a month in advance. Very quickly it changed to something she didn't find funny in the slightest. If she resisted, Michael's face would fold into a kicked puppy expression and he would start referring to the many sacrifices he had already made for her. The first time he did this Martha couldn't think what he meant, but then it dawned on her that he had in mind his change of employment.

'What sacrifice?' she stormed. 'It's a bigger department! You're earning more now than you did before!'

After that outburst Michael fell into a silence that lasted for three days, at the end of which he began to talk about the need for them to move in together so the same misunderstandings wouldn't arise in the future. Unbelievably, it was still a further two years before she finally summoned the will to finish with Michael for good.

Taking a gulp of sea-infused air, Martha sees she has reached the parking lot. A notice on the gatepost reads, THIS CAR PARK IS LOCKED EACH DAY AT DUSK. That must have been what the woman at reception meant about the beach closing. But when is dusk? As an instruction or warning it seems unhelpfully imprecise. On an ordinary spring day she would expect dusk to be late, but this particular evening has an autumnal feel; the very last of the cars are being loaded with children and dogs and they all appear keen to be leaving as soon as possible.

To get onto the beach Martha follows the same route as she did before but once over the dunes she turns left and makes straight for the row of wooden huts. The tide is fully out and the carpet of wide-angle yellow glimmers as if the sun is lighting it from beneath. With the helmet of grey above and the luminous sand below, it's like the world has flipped, spun through 180°, and she's walking across the sky with the earth moulded over her head. This strange sensation is exacerbated by the fact that in the whole panorama she can't see another single living soul: not one.

Close up, the huts are not quite so uniform or picturesque as they appear from a distance. Some are tall and freshly painted; others have a sunken, forlorn look, their steps practically buried with sand crowding the doors and windows. Number 25 is a brownish colour

– who paints a beach hut *brown*? Martha wonders – and a good deal stubbier than its swankier neighbours. Nevertheless, Martha climbs the steps with a quickening sense of anticipation. After all, this is just what her father planned to do; for some reason this musty little structure held sufficient attraction to entice him all the way across the Atlantic.

Yet opening the door reveals nothing of note. Deckchairs are stacked against the back wall, a child's bucket with a broken handle has been left in the middle of the floor and an ancient torch dangles from a string hooked around a nail. The only embellishment to the shed-like design is a hatch next to the door, hinged to open downwards and form a glassless window. Martha stands for a moment, regarding the bare, highly unremarkable walls with disappointment and frustration. How and why could this have been of any interest to her father? There's no clue here at all. And as for her rash promise to Elizabeth on the telephone, *I'll think of something when I get to Norfolk...* Martha sighs. Well, she hasn't yet so much as identified a starting point for figuring out who Catkins might be.

Returning to the small veranda, she consults her watch. It's barely eight thirty and yet a powdery gloom is spilling over the beach like coal dust. She ought to head back, but the thought of the interminable walk isn't appealing and, besides, she feels cheated of the day, as if it's slipping, unlived, through her fingers and with it the chance of some vital, fated occurrence.

She fetches a deckchair and sits on it. Now the only sounds are her breathing and the occasional light snap of a bough or twig in the pinewoods behind. Hoping to recapture the serenity of the previous day she leans back into the canvas. Yet she can't seem to settle, her mind keeps straying to the parking lot, which by now is presumably locked and empty, and the long, unpeopled road towards town. A sudden quiver of anxiety makes her touch the reassuring bulge of cell phone in her pocket. Perhaps she ought to head back, before it gets too dark? But as she stands up a sliver of light appears on the horizon and by the time she's stashed the chair inside and locked the door it's begun to prise apart the seamless joinder of sea and sky. Martha leans on the balustrade to watch. Gradually, as if an awning is being cranked, the clouds roll back to expose a freshly minted coin of a moon, suspended over the water.

She's so entranced that at first she doesn't notice the noises coming from the woods behind. Then all at once a loud crack makes her jump and immediately freeze, straining her senses into the murkiness. Now she's listening properly, she can hear, unmistakably, the sound of footsteps. Some are louder than others, as a branch or stick gives way, but their slow, steady rhythm is mounting persistently.

Martha tells herself not to be paranoid. Someone is obviously taking an end of day stroll. But the location feels uneasily remote. She could have been followed all the way from the town. Suppose she's been shadowed by a madman or a rapist? She tries to recall the details of the walk, whether anyone was behind her, but the exercise is pointless – she was much too preoccupied by her conversation with Clem to notice.

The footfall ceases. Martha waits, and when it doesn't resume she unclenches her fists from the balcony railing, gives herself a little shake and makes to leave. She gets as far as lowering one leg to the first of the steps before stopping again. A dark shadow is moving silently along the sand, a hulking outline clearly visible in the silvered moonlight. Martha's heart leaps and then begins to hammer so hard she has the impression it's jumped outside of her chest and is trying to beat its way back inside. It strikes her that the phone in her pocket is actually as good as useless. *Who would she call? And how long would it take them to reach her here?*

As she watches the figure draws closer. She can see the shape of it now, disconcertingly wide as if something of size is being concealed beneath a coat or cloak. She wills herself to think of a sensible explanation, a convincing one that will carry her down the staircase and calmly past the stranger on the beach. But her head has other ideas, ones that feature bodies and blood and all the psychopathic murderers she has ever encountered in late-night cop shows. Her heart and mind begin to race; if she can see *him* – she's convinced the silhouette is masculine – then surely just as soon as he turns this way he'll be able to see *her* too?

Moving quickly from the edge of the veranda, she feels in her jeans pocket for the hut key, eases open the door and slips inside. A perfect black engulfs her. She waits for her eyes to adjust but the inky void remains impenetrable. At first she can't hear anything at all, but gradually she starts to make out sounds: a slight rubbing, that might be trees blowing in the wind, but could be someone striding over the sand; a series of creaks – rhythmical, scale-like – that might be pure imagination, but could be wooden boards, surrendering to the tread of a boot; a dry rustle that might be her arm, catching on the nylon of her jacket, but could, alternatively, be a bag opening, an implement being extracted.

You're being ridiculous, Martha scolds herself. She should turn on the torch and calm her nerves. But suppose, she worries, it seeps through the gaps in the wood and signals her presence? Instead, she turns around, fumbles for the keyhole, and with a shaking hand secures the lock. Dropping onto the floor, she tucks up her legs and rests her head on her knees.

It's hard to retain any sense of time. The darkness is oceanic. Presently, she reaches for her phone, careful to cup her hand around the glare from the screen.

21.34

The cheerful glow is reassuring. So too the reminder it's not the middle of the night, that somewhere she can picture, people are eating and talking and going about their evening. Gradually, her breathing settles into a less frenzied rhythm and her thoughts begin to spin around more familiar worries: Whatever is the matter with Janey? And, Skyping Christie! How often, did *that* happen, for heaven's sake? It's hard – crouched on the floor of a beachside shed, unable to see a thing – not to question what she's doing with her life.

Eventually, Martha checks her phone again.

21.59

The instant it flips to ten she straightens up and uses the light from the screen to locate the bolts of the shutter. Rusted and stiff, they have to be jiggled a bit before they ease into the sockets and the panel releases. As it swings down, Martha has a fleeting vision of a psycho standing on the balcony, brandishing a machete, but her fears evaporate into the emptiness beyond the window.

Sticking her head further out, Martha drinks a lungful of the soft night air. At first she thinks there's nothing to see apart from the pale stretch of beach and the hovering moon. It's only as she's drawing back, about to close up and depart, that she spots something which fills her with giddy, helium-like relief. Directly to her right, two beach huts away from her own, a man is squatting on a fold-out stool. He's wearing a waxed jacket and baggy, probably tracksuit, pants tucked into rain boots. In the space between his knees, three long tapering legs create a tripod on the top of which a telescope is fixed, pointing out towards the sea. The man is leaning forwards, attentive, his right eye pressed against viewfinder, and he appears to be entirely unaware of Martha.

After Martha has vacated the hut she stands for a moment at the foot of the steps fidgeting with the key. Still the man seems oblivious to her presence. She walks closer, dropping to a dawdle as she passes in front of him; for some reason she doesn't want to leave without an acknowledgement of each other's presence. *Hey, look at us rule-breakers! Still here on the beach after dusk!*

'Hi!' Martha hasn't spoken for so long that it's hard to judge the volume right.

The telescope man springs back on his stool and peers over his balustrade. Martha waves. Slowly, the man raises his palm, hinging it at the wrist and keeping it waist level. Martha can't tell how old

he is, but the gesture, somehow, appears quite youthful. She steps
forwards to get a better view and senses, rather than sees, a look
of alarm bloom on his face. 'Hi!' she says again. 'I... er... was just
taking a walk. I guess I must have lost track of the time.'

The telescope man stares at her. She appreciates only too well how
hard it is to come up with a rational explanation as for why anyone
might be alone out here so late. Maybe he thinks she's broken-hearted
or suicidal. Or an alcoholic; perhaps he imagines she's been hiding
out on the dunes downing cider.

She tries again. 'To tell the truth, I saw you walking along the
sand. I was in that hut over there' – she motions vaguely behind
her – 'and you looked' – she hesitates – 'very bulky. Unusually
bulky, I thought.' She stops and smiles, but there's no response.
Clearing her throat, Martha ploughs on. 'I wondered, you know,
what you might be carrying and then my imagination got a little
carried away and I thought I might as well wait a while. To make
sure you'd gone. In case, you know—'

'It was only my telescope.' The man's voice is surprisingly deep
and clear.

'Well, of course, I realise that *now*.' Martha shifts her weight from
one foot to another. 'I'm feeling a little foolish, to be honest with you.'

There's a gap of maybe two seconds before the man says, 'Would
you like to come and take a look?'

'Well...' Martha wavers. She glances over her shoulder at the
darkening heavens and then up at the arthropod-like instrument.
'Why not?' she says to herself. 'Thank you,' she says out loud. A trifle
self-consciously she scales his set of steps. As she reaches the top the
man gets up and inclines his head.

'I'm Henry.' He towers over her by a good six inches.

'Martha,' Martha says.

Henry gestures at the stool. 'Be my guest.'

Martha sits. For what seems an age Henry fiddles with the
tripod, adjusting its height and angle. After that he spends even

longer fine-tuning the focus of the viewfinder, leaning across Martha to check and then correct it, the cedar-like smell of his jacket sleeve brushing against her cheek. While he works to perfect the arrangement Martha gazes out at a sky that's now liquid navy and erupting with stars.

At last she feels a gentle pressure on her shoulder guiding her forwards. She has the impression of being ushered into a secret place, given a pass to an inner sanctum, and when her face makes contact with the telescope she lets out an involuntary gasp.

The lens is pointing directly at the moon, but it's not a moon she recognises. Or rather, she recognises it, of course, but it's not remotely like the moon she knows. Until that moment it had been merely a circle or crescent, a simple shape in the sky to which she paid little more regard than the furniture in her own home. This moon is an orb, a sphere, its silver curves falling away to the blurred, penumbral edges of its visible surface. As Martha stares, bewitched, a kaleidoscope of other moons come to mind: Janey's crayoned moons in flaking, canary wax; shiny, school-made moons of foil-wrapped cardboard dangling from coat-hangers; and calendar moons, full and cloud-bedecked, printed onto glossy paper. But somehow the solid, three-dimensional actuality of it moving through the sky had escaped her comprehension, even her notice. And in a surge of understanding it hits Martha that if the moon is true, then everything else must be true as well; the planets, the stars, the rest of the universe into which the tiny telescope is pointing, are all really, really out there.

She draws her eye away from the viewfinder. She's shivering, she realises, and also a little dizzy. She wonders if Henry has any inkling of her thoughts.

'It's awesome, isn't it?' he says, and she knows he's using the word not as one of her eighth-graders would use it, but literally.

'Awesome,' she agrees. Standing up she folds her arms, searching for warmth in the shell of her rain jacket. They look at each other, and then at the same instant they both look away. 'I'd better get going,' Martha says. 'I'm here on vacation and my hotel might lock me out. I didn't expect to be this long.'

'Will you be all right,' asks Henry, 'walking back on your own?'

Martha glances across the vista of sand. The ambiguity of evening is over. Despite a wash of moonlight, the pine trees behind the huts are a dense, lightless mass.

'Sure. I have a torch. See?' Martha flourishes the battery-powered monstrosity she scooped off the nail as she was leaving her hut, but when she switches it on the beam is barely powerful enough to illuminate the toe of her own sneaker. 'Oh!' They both regard the feeble glimmer with dismay.

There's a moment of silent contemplation before Henry says, 'Don't worry, I'll come with you. We can use mine.'

'Really?' Martha wrestles briefly with her sense of guilt. 'I don't want to spoil your evening,' she adds a little lamely.

'Not a problem.' Henry is already releasing the telescope with one hand and collapsing the tripod with the other. It's too gloomy to see his expression but as he dismantles the apparatus his movements are calm and unflustered. When he is finished he passes Martha his phone. 'Would you mind shining this inside the hut, so I can find the torch?'

She holds the screen high and steady until a flag of proper light billows through the doorway. Henry comes out carrying a camping lantern and rests it on the ground. As he kneels to pack the equipment into some kind of case the bulb illuminates his face and for the first time Martha can see him properly. A steady, weathered expression gives his brown eyes an anchored look, while his skin has the worn appearance of something that's been crumpled for a long time at the bottom of a wardrobe. Tellingly, the harsh, bright glare reveals no sign of swagger that would once have made a face like that good looking.

Henry picks up his telescope bag. 'Shall we go?' he says, and holds up the lamp.

They don't speak, but walk side by side, the night encircling their pod of yellow. Sometime earlier the tide must have turned because the rise and drag of the waves is now clearly audible. Martha tips back her head to look at the stars. As she gazes upwards, more and more of them appear, as if responding to a question.

'Watch yourself!'

Henry catches Martha's elbow to stop her from tripping over something. They've reached the bottom tread of the steps into the pines. He leads the way over the ridge, holding out the lantern so that it shines on Martha's side of the path. On the other side he stops and waits for her to fall into place again.

After the open space of the beach the woods seem disconcertingly watchful. Trees loom in spidery bluffs and brambles grab at Martha's hair and jacket. Every so often she stumbles over a root and has to grab at Henry's arm. 'Do you live here, Henry?' she asks conversationally, keen to normalise the intense quiet.

He nods.

'What is it you do? For a living, I mean.'

'A bit of decorating, gardening…'

Something tells her it's not the whole story and she waits for him to say more, but after a few more paces it becomes obvious that he's not going to oblige. 'I'm an English teacher,' Martha volunteers. 'For seventh and eighth graders. In Canada that means eleven and twelve-year-olds.'

'Then it sounds like you're doing something worthwhile.'

Surprised, but pleased, Martha considers this. Teaching seventh and eighth graders had never been the plan.

As the woods thin the sky unfurls in front of them again. They make rapid progress across the deserted parking lot and come to a halt beside the gated entrance. A chain is looped around the post and secured with a padlock.

'Do you ever wish you'd done a different job, Henry?' Martha asks.

Henry turns to face her. The creases between his eyebrows deepen further. 'No,' he says, slowly, 'I don't.' Then he says, returning to his normal pace, 'Are you okay to climb over it?' It takes Martha a moment to understand he's talking about the gate.

Henry goes first and Martha passes him the bag before she clambers onto the top bar and manoeuvres herself into a sitting position. As Henry helps her down his hands feel rough and warm, like the texture of the bricks on her way to the seafront. Immediately she's on the ground, Henry releases his grip, puts the lamp on the grass and begins to fiddle with a cable of some kind. At first Martha thinks it's something to do with the gate but then she sees he's releasing a bicycle. Once he's done he packs the lantern in the bag, slings the strap onto his shoulder and swings the handlebars around to face Martha. When he makes no move to get on board, she realises that he intends to wheel the bike all the way back.

'Look,' she says. 'There's no need to accompany me. I'm okay now.' She means it; the lights of the harbour, the cafes and take-outs, bob cheerily in view and their promise of people, of Saturday-night verve and bustle make the loneliness of the woods and huts seem very far removed.

'Are you sure?' Henry sounds neither relieved nor disappointed.

'Yes,' Martha says with conviction. She has surely disrupted his evening enough. 'I'll be walking through that hotel door before I know it! Thanks for… well, for the rescue, I guess.' She smiles but can't see whether Henry's expression changes. 'Maybe I'll see you again on the beach?' She meant it as a throwaway remark but somehow it comes out a question.

'Maybe you will.' For just a second Henry appears to hesitate and then he swings his leg over the saddle. 'Are you certain…?'

'I'm just fine.' When he still doesn't move she flaps her hand good-naturedly. 'Go!'

As he pedals away, the backlight of his bicycle glows a round, comforting red. Martha watches until it shrinks to a pinprick.

'Goodbye,' she calls out suddenly, and she thinks she sees Henry raise his palm before, a second later, he disappears.

As she walks into the foyer, laughter gusts from the bar. 'It's a club night,' the girl in reception informs Martha – she's not the grey-blonde woman from before but a young brunette with green nails and a copy of *Hello* on her lap. 'A cricket club for middle-aged men,' she adds, answering Martha's unasked query. 'They're worse than all the young ones put together.'

Martha is tempted to take a peek, but she's grubby and wind-swept, hands slick with grease from the fish and chips she ate out of a polystyrene box on the last lap back to the hotel. Back in her room she kicks off her shoes, sits on the bed and massages her toes with relief. The trek has given her sore feet, but her adventure has imbued the room with a homely feel. She pads into the bathroom and begins to run a bath, tipping in bubbles, watching the steam and anticipating the pleasure of sinking into the water.

She's in the process of undressing, wriggling out of her jeans, when someone whistles. Martha freezes in mid-movement. Ears tense, she can hear nothing except the steady gush of the running water. She wonders if someone from the middle-aged cricket club could have followed her upstairs for a joke or dare. She pulls up her jeans again, fingers resting uncertainly on the zipper.

And then the whistle comes again.

It's a cheap, brazen, flaunting of a sound, but this time she spies the flickering that accompanies it from beneath her rain jacket. Martha stretches towards it and her hands closes around the cigarette-case slimness of a cell phone. Plastered across the front is a text message.

CD CU 2MORO CM Helen

Martha gapes at it uncomprehendingly. Who is Helen? And why is she asking Martha to call her about tomorrow?

But wait! This isn't even her mobile! Just as her scattered strands of thought reassemble to reach the single, awful, logical explanation, the screen goes blank before a little dial of white petals appears only to vanish a second later.

Martha stares in disbelief as the phone – *Henry's phone* – dies in her palm.

CHAPTER SEVEN

Norfolk, July 1940

Sylvie and her mother were in the kitchen making jam. The daily help had left the previous week to nurse an injured nephew, forcing Sylvie's mother to do everything around the house herself. She had even managed to acquire some preserving sugar from someone whose name apparently now escaped her and was boiling it up with gooseberries, of which the two spindly bushes in the garden had supplied an astonishing number. Red and rumpled from the belching heat of the Aga, she was folded over a Maslin pan, dressed in the help's apron with her hair pinned severely back. It was not yet midday but already a syrupy, botanical fug clung to the room.

Sylvie was pulling stalks from yet more fruit heaped untidily on the table like an upturned box of marbles. Her movements were mechanical and tense and every so often she paused and gazed at her hands as if to remind herself what she was doing.

'Any word from Howard yet?'

Sylvie started, although she had been expecting her mother's question ever since she and the children had arrived at her parents' house that morning. Sylvie brought them to visit most weekends taking advantage of the fact they woke so early to catch the first Saturday bus from the city. Each time her mother asked the same thing, although Sylvie had told her more than once that Howard was sailing around the Cape of Good Hope to Africa and probably wouldn't be able to write again for weeks.

On this occasion Sylvie hesitated before she replied. An envelope lay deep inside the right-hand pocket of her dress. It rustled every time she moved, making her constantly aware of it, like toothache or a sore ankle. She hadn't been able to think of anything else since it came two days earlier, written on paper so thin and shiny it might have been an onion skin.

'Actually,' she said, 'I had a letter last Thursday.'

She was glad her mother couldn't see her face. The dimpled oak table with the piles of gooseberries was positioned at the opposite end of the kitchen from the range. Along the adjoining wall an enormous dresser displayed the kitchen crockery, a stash of *Good Housekeeping* magazines and a copper kettle that had once belonged to Sylvie's grandmother. Beyond the kitchen there was a scullery with a brick floor covered by coconut matting that opened onto a small yard and the outside lavatory. Her mother had propped open both the kitchen and the scullery door to coax a breeze inside, but the air was still and thick with the threat of impending thunder.

'Well, how is he then?' Her mother took a teaspoon from a drawer of the dresser and dropped a bead of jam onto a saucer. She prodded it anxiously a couple of times and then continued stirring.

'Howard is fine,' Sylvie said carefully.

'All this time and that's all he's got to say for himself?'

'He said the journey was uneventful' – Sylvie articulated the last word with deliberate emphasis to show that she was quoting it directly from Howard's letter – 'and now they're living in a camp.'

'I suppose he can't tell you too much.'

'No, but at least he's still alive. Or he was four weeks ago anyway.'

It had been disturbing to read the letter and imagine him writing from an African tent. Even more upsetting had been the thought he might already be lying dead in the desert, or horribly injured in a makeshift hospital. She wondered if she would know, deep in her bones, if something happened to him. Kit Parker had said that when her husband's ship was torpedoed she knew right away something terrible had happened, even though it was broad daylight and she was queuing in the butchers at the time. Sylvie didn't think it would be – could be – the same with Howard. Yet their writing had acquired a stoic sort of joviality, something that had been almost entirely missing from Dorset House, and, remarkably, Howard seemed almost to approve of her again. Digging over the flowerbeds to plant potatoes, carrots and marrows – which she had managed herself with the heavy old Skelton – and joining the Women's Voluntary Service to help with the war effort had induced him to write in his second letter, '*I can't tell you how cheered I was to hear about all you are doing at home. Well done, darling!*'

But then this most recent one. In his closing paragraph, almost, it seemed, as an afterthought, he had dropped a bombshell as dreadful as any German one might be. '*I'm sure you will understand why I am quite certain that this is the best course of action for Lewis, however difficult it may be for you*', he had closed in his regular, compact hand.

Of course she understood, and the previous night she had lain awake while her conversation on the beach with Connie spun round in her head until it became an unbreakable loop, mocking and taunting her fears in the style of an omen or prophecy.

'Sylvie?'

Sylvie turned around.

Her mother had stepped away from the stove and was frowning. 'What's the matter?'

Sylvie touched her pocket. She took a breath. 'Howard says that we should evacuate Lewis to America.' The sentence seemed to flutter from the ceiling and settle like a lace cloth over a dining table.

'America?'

'Yes. Or Canada perhaps.'

'Oh!' Her mother's hand shot to her throat. 'But isn't it much too late for that? I thought all the Government boats were full up.'

'Howard says he knows someone on the Reception Board. Somebody who owes him a favour and would find a space for Lewis.'

Newspaper reports had written of hundreds of people swarming the Reception Board's office on Berkeley Street and the lines along the pavement snaking down into Piccadilly. There had been pushing and arguments and apparently two fathers had come to fisticuffs. It was just like Howard, Sylvie thought bitterly, to find a way to jump in front of them all. She waited for her mother to see – willed her to see – the impossibility of the situation.

Her mother lowered her hand. Sylvie watched her digesting the news, adjusting.

'Now that France has fallen they say we could be invaded any day. And if that happens the coast will get the worst of it. Perhaps Lewis *would* be better off sent abroad.' Her mother's voice was neutral. Beige. Sylvie wanted red, purple, orange.

'We don't – I don't – live by the coast. Not really.'

'But it's not safe in the city either, is it? Nowhere is safe now…' Her mother's voice trailed away; she was gazing out into the garden. There was a crumpled, worn look to her that was more pronounced than even the Sunday before, when Sylvie had seen her visibly pale as they listened to the prime minister telling the country to fight street by street, if it came to it.

There had been two raids on the city in the past few weeks and both of them had been without warnings. Sylvie hadn't been to see the bomb damage, which was mainly on the outskirts of town near the mustard factory. Some of the girls leaving work had been killed as they pushed their bicycles up the hill. Sylvie didn't want think about it, but she did. It played in her mind as if she had watched it happening on a newsreel. One minute having a laugh about that supervisor who fancied himself as the next James Stewart, or wondering if the hot water would hold for a bath, the next the faint drone of an aircraft, someone pointing to the sky, the unbelievable, intensifying roar, the panic, grabbing one another, someone shouting, 'Get down!' and then all of them torn into pieces and hurled into craters of shattered concrete.

But that, Sylvie told herself, must have been just dreadful bad luck, a solitary bomber clearing his load on the way back home; surely London was the real target? She shook her head to clear the terrible images from her mind.

'America is so far away. He'll be with strangers. In a foreign country. Supposing…' She stopped – hearing again her words to Connie on the beach – then made herself go on. 'Supposing he doesn't come home again?'

Her mother stared. 'Of course he'll come home again! Why on earth wouldn't he?'

Sylvie looked back across a kitchen floor that seemed as wide as the Atlantic.

'Why, he'll probably be back by Christmas!' Her mother lowered herself down on the pamment tiles, placed a folded tea towel under her knees, and began to rummage in the far reaches of a corner cupboard.

Sylvie opened her mouth. *I could tell her*, she thought. *This very instant.*

From inside the cupboard came something indistinct and hollow about not spending too long on the jam and needing to get dinner for Sylvie's father. Her mother's backside was square and solid and covered with the same floral print that she was wearing in the beach hut photograph with Ginger, though faded now and with a neatly mended tear along the hem. Tears pressed against Sylvie's eyes and she closed her mouth again.

Her mother reversed slowly out of the cupboard, fingers hooked into several glass jars, and struggled to her feet. Some of her hair had fallen out of its pins and was hanging limply down her cheeks. It was starting to go almost white in places.

Seeing Sylvie's face, she let the jars clatter on top of the counter. She came across the kitchen and put her arms around Sylvie's waist. 'Oh Sylvie! Of course it's hard, but perhaps it's for the best. It's only because Howard loves Lewis that he wants him out of harm's way.'

Sylvie gazed helplessly at her mother. Eventually she whispered, 'He doesn't want Esther to be evacuated.'

'I expect that's because he thinks Esther is too young. Anyway' – her mother's brow furrowed – 'you don't want Esther to go as well, do you?'

Sylvie shook her head.

'Well, then.' Her mother patted her shoulder and returned to the jam. Sylvie hovered over the bowl of gooseberries but couldn't bring herself to pick one up. After a moment her mother cleared her throat. 'Do you remember Mary Baxter?'

'Of course,' Sylvie said absently. 'We were at school together for fourteen years.' And then more sharply, 'Why do you ask?'

'I ran into Mrs Baxter at the bank. It seems Mary's brother got caught up at Dunkirk.'

Sylvie's stomach fell away. Immediately the kitchen felt icy cold. 'Do you mean Kennie?'

'Yes,' said her mother, nodding. 'Kenneth Baxter.'

For a second Sylvie thought she must have said something after all, conjured the past like a monster from a swamp. Her hands shook as she picked at one of the husks. She put it down again and gripped, instead, the edge of the table, as if the kitchen walls were crumbling around her. Ashes to ashes. Dust to dust. Before Ginger died she had only been to two funerals, both of them for grandparents; there had been weeping of course, but the civilised kind, easily contained with murmured condolences and freshly pressed handkerchiefs. And at Ginger's funeral the only person visibly upset had been her mother.

She pressed shut her eyelids. 'Was he killed?' From the hallway she heard the grandfather clock strike the three-quarter hour.

'No. Thank goodness. But injured, quite badly it seems. He took a piece of shrapnel in his chest. From what his mother told me it sounds as though he was lucky to get out of it alive.'

She opened her eyes. 'Where is he now?'

'Living back home again these last six weeks, ever since he came out of hospital.' Her mother heaved the jam off the stove using both hands. She paused for a moment as if remembering something. 'Weren't you and Kenneth sweet on each other once?' She smiled at Sylvie, oblivious, Sylvie realised, that the sentiment was so inadequate it might as well have been a lie. 'Why don't you pay him a visit? I can mind the children this afternoon and it might do him good to see an old friend from the past. I don't suppose Mrs Baxter will mind. You can take her a jar of jam.'

'I might,' Sylvie said.

'It's a fifteen-minute walk at most.'

'I know,' Sylvie said.

As they spoke the light drained from the kitchen making it suddenly sullen and shadowed. There was a crack as if someone had dropped a tin tray on the floor, followed by a long, low rumble, and then within seconds the fat clatter of raindrops on the outhouse roof.

'Thank heavens for that! It's been building for days.' Her mother flicked a light switch and began to ladle jam into the first of the glass jars, wiping the spills with a dishcloth. After a moment she stopped and put it down. 'Goodness, the washing is still on the line!' She turned to Sylvie. 'Be a dear and fetch it in.'

Outside, a slate-grey sky hung low over the outhouse and the yard was lacquered black with rain. For a while Sylvie stood motionless beside the washing line. Droplets ran in tributaries down her face and arms, soaking into the fabric of her dress. In the same way a bath can be so hot it tricks the senses into seeming, for a second, almost cool, the prospect of seeing Kennie again had stunned her to a point where she couldn't function properly. The last time she had gone to his mother's house was more than eleven years ago. Yet she could remember standing outside the door on a dull spring evening as clearly as if he had happened the previous week.

The glow from the kitchen window seemed a long way distant. Sylvie saw her mother take the saucepan to the sink and fill it from the tap, pause, arching her back as if to ease an ache, and then begin to scrub with the wire wool scourer. A moment later she looked up, rapped on the glass and gestured vigorously at the line. Slowly, Sylvie reached up to unclip the pegs and began to gather the wet washing over the crook of her arm.

Peering around the corner of North Street, Sylvie saw Mrs Baxter put down her shopping basket and say something to a Boy Scout collecting paper in a wooden barrow. It was just gone three o'clock. Her mother had bundled her out of the house twenty minutes earlier insisting the timing was perfect, dinner would be finished and supper not yet started. There was no need to worry about afternoon tea either because Mrs Baxter wasn't the type to bother with that kind of nicety. Sylvie had intended to walk straight up to the door and knock, just as any other visitor would do, but had fled at the sight of Kennie's mother on the step.

She made herself count to sixty before she peeked again. This time there was nobody about apart from the scout and some girls of about ten or eleven who were playing with a skipping rope on the pavement that ran the length of the terraced houses. They looked quite normal, thought Sylvie, happy even, as if there wasn't a war happening at all. Their voices rang out tonelessly in time with the scuffed double beat of the jumping girl and the smack of the rope:

> Sweetheart, sweetheart, will you marry me?
> Yes love, yes love, at half-past three.
> Ice-cakes, spice-cakes, all for tea.
> And we'll have a wedding at half past three.

As she walked passed them Sylvie slapped at the brick dust that clung to the back of her dress from where she had cowered by the wall. The storm had passed and her heels sounded sharp and clear in the quiet afternoon. She let the words of the ditty fill her head and their rhythm propelled her all the way to number 47. But once outside the door she nearly lost her nerve again. How many times had she stood here? Looking at the peeling paint and the brass knocker shaped like a lion's face, a fierce-looking lion that had always seemed just right for Mrs Baxter's house.

It had started at the age of thirteen or fourteen, the rippling awareness of Mary's big brother, that thrill of anxiety whenever they passed on the stairs or she happened to glimpse his lanky, shifting presence in another room. Sometimes he would actually sit with them – to hang about and cause trouble Mary said – and then Sylvie would hear the lilt of the accent he had inherited from their father who had gone back to Ireland for reasons nobody spoke about. It was not the only thing Kennie must have got from his father; looking at Mrs Baxter it was hard to believe such a conspicuous combination of swan-white skin and blue-black hair could have come from his mother.

Before long Sylvie began to call on Mary every weekend, pausing at the door to adjust her clothes and apply the tiniest smear of 'Pale Rose' lipstick from the stub she had discovered in the pocket of her mother's housecoat. And then, just when the disappointment had become so familiar it had dulled to a blunt kind of ache, one perfect, golden evening Kennie asked her to go to the pictures. In the sweetness of the days and weeks that followed Sylvie used to skip all the way to the front door and never had to wait for it to open because Kennie would be watching from the window. She was so certain of him, so certain they were meant to be together, that her future seemed to have been rolled out in front of her like an unfurled carpet she only had to walk across, hand-in-hand with Kennie.

But less than a year after they started courting came the memories she didn't care to think about at all.

The perfectly normal evening when Mrs Baxter informed her – cold as stone – Kennie wasn't there, that he had gone to Ireland to be with his father and wouldn't be back for at least a year. At first, Sylvie wouldn't believe her. Then she began to cry right out in the street and Mrs Baxter hurried her inside and made them both a cup of tea. At the time she thought Mrs Baxter was being kind, but afterwards she realised Mrs Baxter had wanted her to see for herself that Kennie had really and truly gone. The very next day she asked Mary, begged to know, what had happened. Although Mary didn't want to talk about it, she eventually told Sylvie that Kennie and his mother had argued so dreadfully Kennie had left straight away, taking a suitcase of all his clothes along with the jar of shillings put aside for the gas meter. 'He'll come home soon, won't he?' Sylvie pleaded. 'He'll come back for me?' But Mary had only given her a queer, pitying look that turned Sylvie to ice.

And then the terrible day Kennie did come back from Ireland, and found Sylvie married, washing dishes in an empty house while Howard was at work. She had yelled at him, ranted and wailed, for leaving it too late, until he pulled her close and held her long and tight against the cloth of his coat before slowly, deliberately, reaching behind her back to release the bow of her apron string, murmuring her name, how much he had missed her; Sylvie was lost.

Finally, the most painful memory of all, the night six months later, when she had stood in front of Mrs Baxter's house gazing at the almond glow around the sitting room curtains, listening in the darkness to catch the sound of voices, laughter, then Kennie whistling as he ran up the stairs, before she belted her coat over the bulge of her stomach, picked up a small, brown suitcase and walked away, back to Howard and the marriage to which she should never have agreed.

Now Sylvie closed her hand around the striker and knocked before she could change her mind. There was nothing, and then a moment later footsteps on a tiled hallway, the muffled effort of the door sticking slightly, and then he was there, standing right in front of her. He was wearing grey trousers that were so loose the belt made folds in the waistband and a white vest with a pale brown stain on the front of it. His face was grey and unshaven, the stubble the same charcoal as the shadows under his eyes. Sylvie had a tight, burning sensation in her chest. It's all right, she thought, it's different, he's different, the war has changed him, taken away his charm and made him the same as everyone else.

Kennie leaned against the wall, holding the door only half-open. On the side of his right shoulder Sylvie could see the end of a bright red weal that disappeared under the cotton of the vest. For a long moment he stared at her without speaking, and then,

'Sylvia.' The way he said it made a little humpbacked bridge of a word, lyrical, yet serious at the same time. She remembered how she used to repeat it to herself at night, to try to recreate the way it made her feel to hear it spoken like that.

'I came to see how you are, Kennie.' She kept her voice bright. 'My mother told me you were injured getting out of France and back at home to recuperate.'

He hesitated, then spoke, 'Well in that case you'd best come in.'

He let the door swing wide. Sylvie wondered whether to kiss him on the cheek, like she might a cousin or an uncle, but he had already turned to lead her down the passage.

The parlour at the back of the house was a small, murky room adjacent to the kitchen. A wing chair stood at an angle in front of the fireplace and four spindle chairs encircled a wooden table where a dirty dinner plate and a bottle of Pale Ale were sitting on a tablecloth printed with yellow flowers. Sylvie placed herself by the mantelpiece, holding her handbag in front of her like she was waiting for a bus or a train. By her head the wireless was tuned to a soft, ragged kind of jazz. The music and the green-grey light so unhooked the room from the summer afternoon that it felt as though the street and skipping girls belonged to a different time and place altogether.

'Shall I make you some tea?'

Sylvie shook her head. Her throat had closed up and she didn't think she would be able to eat or drink anything. Neither of them seemed to know what to say.

Kennie reached across and turned off the wireless. Sylvie wished that he hadn't. Without it, the silence seemed too much for the room to accommodate. Kennie seemed to think the same thing because after a moment he switched it back on.

'It's been a while,' he said at last. He was standing in front of the armchair, but he didn't sit down.

Sylvie nodded.

'You must have kiddies by now?'

Sylvie flinched. 'Two,' she said after a second. 'A boy and a girl. Esther is six and Lewis' – she broke off – 'Lewis has turned eleven.' An abyss opened beneath her feet, but Kennie didn't seem to be listening. He was staring at her in a way that glued her feet to the carpet.

'You're looking grand.' His gaze was intense but it had a dulled, dead aspect to it.

Sylvie gulped and nodded. 'You look' – she hesitated – 'good too,' she made herself say, although she thought he looked terrible.

'I look good?' He made noise like a short, dry bark. 'I must have aged ten years on that beach. Waiting to get out.'

Sylvie's chest constricted. She was flooded with guilt for what he must have seen and done while she had been planting in the garden, and knitting, and playing with the children, things which were normal and safe but which she had taken for granted and let her unhappiness spoil.

'Was it very awful?'

His pupils opened wide and black, as if he were watching something private inside his head. 'The smell was the worst of it. The stink of the sand covered in' – he stopped himself – 'covered in mess.' He stepped closer. 'Do you know what I thought of,' he said, 'trapped like a rat in a cage; waiting for my chance in the water?'

Sylvie shook her head. She was looking at the angry red tip of his scar. She wanted to trace the line of it with her fingertip. At the same time she wished she hadn't come.

'I thought of you. What you would be doing. Where you would be going. Who you would be seeing.'

Sylvie felt her skin retract, like she was teetering on the edge of a cliff. 'You didn't know what I was doing,' she whispered uselessly.

His eyes were fixed on her face as if it was the only light in a dark place. He walked forwards until there was barely space to slide a cigarette paper between the flannel of his trousers and the cotton of her dress. He waited a moment and then slowly began to caress the base of her neck with his thumb.

An electric dart of panic rocked her backwards. It was the same Kennie after all, thinner, greyer, but nevertheless the very same person who made her raw and naked simply by being in the room, and by saying her name, which he was repeating now, over and over again. This, she thought frantically, must be what it's like for a drunk, believing one drink will be perfectly fine and then finding themselves seized by something feverish and uncontrollable, wondering how they were deceived, at what point they crossed the line.

'Stop it, Kennie,' she said. 'This isn't why I came.' But her voice was quiet and the words might have been anything at all. His tongue was now around her ear and she noticed she was holding her breath, as if this could stop the jumping and twitching.

'And, of all the things I thought, Sylvia, on that beach' – Kennie's hand slid underneath her dress and touched the back of her thigh, between the top of her stockings and the silk of her knickers – 'I had one regret. Do you know what it was?'

He paused, as if it was a proper question that deserved a reply, but she could only shake her head, dumbly.

'That I didn't marry you, when I had the chance. Why didn't we get married, Sylvia?'

She started to say, *because you left me; you left me and I thought I would die*, but before she could get the words out he pressed his mouth onto hers. The smell of him was both shocking and wonderfully familiar. A voice, small and anxious, was telling her to leave, but it was obliterated by a louder, more urgent one. *Why stop*, it asked, *if we all might die tomorrow in this dreadful war?* She heard a thud and realised her handbag had dropped to the floor.

Somehow the sound of it brought her back to herself. She leaned away from him, and when he didn't release her shoulders she pulled backwards until his hands dropped. 'I have to go, Kennie,' she said. 'We can't do this. I'm married to Howard.'

'But you should be married to me. You're mine, Sylvia. You always have been.' His eyes were searching her face like spider silk. She could feel the ropes of it tangling her thoughts, her reasoning, and reducing them to the solitary fact of Kennie being there, wanting her again. Without a word, she wrenched herself free and headed blindly for the hallway. Nothing had changed, she saw that now, the narrow shapes and spaces of the place were just the same as they had been when she used to visit as a girl, and she was just the same too, the intervening years seemed to have vanished, a house of playing cards collapsed to nothing.

Her fingers were upon the cold brass of the front door handle when she realised with a jolt that she didn't have her handbag. For a period she stood quite still, not knowing what to do. The idea of returning to the parlour was a terrible one but at the same time it felt like a gift fallen into her lap, something she was required to do, for which she couldn't, afterwards, be blamed. Even as it occurred to her that she could come back later, when Mrs Baxter would be home and fetch the bag while she waited on the step, she had already turned around.

Kennie didn't seem to have moved, waiting in the exact same spot she had left him. 'I forgot my handbag,' Sylvie said. At the sight of him her heart had leapt to her throat again.

'You'd best come and get it then.'

She hesitated a moment and then walked across the room, deliberately avoiding his gaze. Although the leather strap was lying by his feet, he made no move to pick it up or move aside. The distance to where he was standing wasn't far at all but it seemed to take minutes to cross. Finally she bent down, reaching for the bag, but as she did so he hooked it with his heel and pushed it behind his legs. Sylvie froze, staring at the carpet. It was the dull red colour of rust or dried blood, smattered with some crumbs that Mrs Baxter must have missed when the room was last cleaned. Slowly, she stood up, straightening, as she knew she would, into the lee of Kennie's chest. His arms circled around her waist making a tight, compelling hoop. When he leaned forwards to kiss her, Sylvie lifted her head and opened her mouth.

This time there were no voices at all; Howard, her mother, even the children, all belonged in somebody else's life. She traced the taste of beer and cigarettes on his tongue and pushed her hips against him. For a while they swayed together, moving their hands over each other, plucking at the fabric of their clothes. Then Kennie pulled her down towards the floor. 'Here?' Sylvie said, suddenly doubtful, but he was already urging her back against the carpet, his torso rising and falling above her. The wool under her head felt rough and had a stale, sour odour. She went to touch the angry tip of his scar but Kennie caught her wrist with his left hand and held it away, his face pale, almost grim. His right hand unfastened the front of her dress and slid the straps of her bra over her shoulders. Next he reached under her thighs, cupping the cheek of her buttock, and began to probe and rub the space between her legs, making her breaths turn into short, quick gasps. He seemed to press down more and more of his weight, as if fusing the bones and the cords of them together, and then he lifted his head and started to rake the stubble of his face against the skin of her breasts until Sylvie cried out and reached and fumbled at the buckle of his belt. As she drew him inside, it felt to her like falling; falling and believing you were never going to land.

Afterwards they sat together on the floor. Kennie's back was against the seat of the chair, his legs outstretched. Sylvie was curled up beside him, her head resting on his vest.

'I meant it,' Kennie murmured, 'when I said I should have married you.' He was holding a cigarette, blowing the smoke over the top of her hair.

Sylvie closed her eyes. He had said it once before, of course, and the waste was almost too much to bear; the effort of life with Howard, the pretence and inexpressible complexity of it all, made her suddenly exhausted. There is nobody, she thought, who really knows who I am and it seemed incredible that this should be true of someone so ordinary. From a lifetime ago the soothing nonsense of the skipping jingle floated into her head.

> Sweetheart, sweetheart, will you marry me?
> Yes love, yes love, at half-past three.

She found herself intoning the words into Kennie's chest. He tipped her chin up towards his face and looked at her uncomprehendingly, but she carried on with the rhyme, tapping the floor with the palm of her hand to accentuate the pulse of it.

Kennie kissed her again. Gently at first, but then he ground out his cigarette and pulled her towards him, reaching immediately under her dress. Surprised, Sylvie went to push him away but Kennie's grip locked around her ribs and he began to lever her backwards onto the carpet.

'Wait!' she said.

For a ridiculous moment she thought he wasn't going to stop, but then he suddenly relaxed his hold on her, sat up and reached instead for his Chesterfields. 'My mother could be home at any minute.'

Sylvie nodded. She felt a little dizzy. She also wanted to tell him about Lewis, that Howard had decided to send him to America. In a peculiar sort of way she thought he should know about it.

Kennie took a cigarette and knocked it against the side of the packet. He lit it before tucking his arm around her again. 'I'm moving up to the city for a while,' he said. He drew on the cigarette and offered it to Sylvie.

Sylvie shook her head. 'Why's that?'

'To be closer to you, of course.' He gave her waist a little squeeze. Sylvie's eyes widened. Then he said, 'Don't be daft. How could I know you'd come today?' He kissed the top of her head. 'I can't tell you why. I need to speak to somebody about a special kind of recruitment, that's all.'

'But you were injured, Kennie,' Sylvie said anxiously. 'Haven't you done your share?'

'I may not be good enough for the army but I can still do my bit. And the good thing is' – his hand skated over her right breast – 'while I'm staying in the city you can come and see me.'

Sylvie couldn't reply. The awful reality of what she'd done, of what she might continue to do, swelled inside her like a balloon.

The scratching sound of a key, the rustle of bags and then the slam of the front door made them both scramble to their feet. Kennie sat down in the armchair just as his mother came into the parlour.

'Hello, Mrs Baxter,' Sylvie said. Her voice was too loud and as she thought it her cheeks began to flush pink.

'Sylvia.' Mrs Baxter's eyes ran down to Sylvie's ankles and back up to the collar of her dress. 'I hope you haven't worn him out?' she said, looking at Kennie and then back at Sylvie. 'He still gets very tired you know.'

'Don't worry, Mother,' Kennie said easily. 'She's been very well behaved.'

Sylvie clamped her jaw. She thought she would laugh from sheer nerves, and then what would Mrs Baxter think?

'I'd best be going, my mother will be wanting me back.' Sylvie flicked her head towards Kennie but daren't meet his eyes. 'I'll be seeing you, Kenneth.'

'Wait a moment.' Kennie stood up. 'That book I told you about, I'll write it down for you, if you like?'

Sylvie swallowed. Her mouth was dry. 'All right.'

Kennie fetched a notebook and scribbled something. Then he tore out the page, folded it in half, folded it again, and held it out to her. He took his time, his movements slow and liquid smooth. Sylvie put the paper in her handbag and snapped it shut. She was conscious that all the while Mrs Baxter's eyes were following them both. *In a moment*, thought Sylvie, *she'll ask me for the name of the book and I shan't be able to think of anything at all.*

As Sylvie walked to the front door her heart was thudding. Mrs Baxter followed behind down the hall, as if Sylvie couldn't be trusted not to double back, but she didn't ask any questions.

Outside the street was empty. Although it was still warm the sky was the colour of chalk, as if the pigment had been leeched from the day and left it flat and listless. Sylvie knew that she ought to hurry. Her mother would want to be getting on with some chore or other and by now Lewis and Esther would be hanging about the kitchen, pestering her to play cards or asking for pieces of malt-loaf and margarine. Nevertheless, as Sylvie crossed the small park that marked the halfway point between North Street and her parents' house she dropped onto a wooden bench next to some swings. Her head was full of fuzz, like static on the wireless. The smell of Kennie lingered on her fingers.

She opened her bag and pulled out the paper he had given her. It simply said '*12 Victoria Terrace*'. She let it fall into her lap. *I mustn't see him again*, she thought, and was immediately engulfed by a hopeless, caved-in feeling that made her quite unable to move.

As she tried to gather herself, a newspaper someone had left further along the seat caught her eye. Sylvie reached over and slowly picked it up. The headlines reported yet another torpedoed ship, hundreds of sailors still to be accounted for. In her mind appeared images of the smoke and blood behind the small black print, the screams and explosions and the heaving weight of water. She remembered Kit Parker, who knew the moment her husband had been lost at sea, and a new rush of guilt and fear washed over her. *Hundreds dying every day. Her own husband away fighting.*

She put the newspaper down and with trembling fingers ripped the address Kennie had given her in half, then tore it again until it was nothing but strips of white confetti. She scrunched the pieces into a tight ball, dropped them into her handbag and stood up. As she did so her fingers brushed against something hard and cold. It was a jar of gooseberry jam.

CHAPTER EIGHT

Norfolk, recently

There's a convivial lunchtime feel to the hotel bar. Well-dressed families have come to eat in batches that appear to span eighty years or more. Nursing a large gin and tonic, Martha counts three toddlers make a grab for the chalk left foolishly beside the menu blackboard and twice hears the list of Sunday roasts repeated at volume to elderly relatives. On the table in front of her is Henry's mobile; somehow Martha managed not to give it back to him at the beach, and somehow he failed to notice. They must both have had their minds elsewhere. Obviously she now has to return the item, but how?

The best and simplest course of action, she decides, is to take the item with her every time she goes to the beach. One of her trips is bound to coincide with one of Henry's visits; since he must know she has the phone maybe the same idea will occur to him, and he will head to his hut as often as possible with the hope of running into *her*. The notion they might both be making the same plan is pleasing in a way that is hard to put a finger on. Draining her glass, Martha tries to picture Henry's face or remember what they talked about. She realises that apart, presumably, from wanting his little computer back, she has no idea if he would be pleased to see her again or not, all she can remember is the deep-water look of his eyes and his steady, even-tempered way of speaking. She can't even tell if he would have retained that same equanimity on his cycle ride home or let rip a flurry of soft curses as soon as she was out of earshot because his evening had been spoiled.

After lunch she considers heading directly to the coast – she might as well put the strategy into action straight away – but it's wet again, a persistent curtain of rain, and besides, Martha can't help but remember the text message that flashed briefly on the screen before it died. Today Henry could well be occupied with Helen. Whoever Helen might be. Eventually she decides to pass the afternoon exploring the glut of pipe-narrow, cottage-lined alleys that run inland from the harbour.

She almost doesn't spot the old theatre at all and stops only because the volume of people filing in and out of an enormous plate-glass door piques her curiosity. Wide sash windows and stone pillars flank the incongruous modern entrance, while attached to the brickwork, beside the left-hand column, a chrome sign testifies that she's standing by the OLD THEATRE GALLERY. Inside the lobby a student-age guy with no hair and a gold stud embedded in his lower lip is doling out exhibition guides and price lists. Behind him double doors open onto a large, light-filled room where a murmuring crowd is shuffling around the perimeter, relieved, it would seem, to be out of the damp.

Martha tacks on the back of the line. The paintings appear to be by local artists, all of who have tried in different ways to capture the beauty of the coastline. Standing in front of a canvas baring one single sweep of yellow paint it occurs to her that the building was probably Gretchen's theatre – or rather, her father's theatre – although there's now no remnant of a stage, or the heavy velvet curtains she pictures sweeping down as Gretchen, hair aflame, took her bow in the spotlight.

Preoccupied, Martha automatically moves to the front of the last item before she sees the picture in question isn't part of the exhibition at all. It isn't even a painting. Rather it's a black-and-white photograph of a man. His face is pale and grave with a formidable forehead and hair slicked sideways, but the feature that jumps out is the lapel of his suit, which is practically sagging under the weight of medals.

Casually, Martha glances at the brass plaque underneath. And then she does a double take as stagey and dramatic as anything Gretchen herself might have done. The inscription states, *Local celebrity, Howard Rodwell, CBE, opened this theatre on 24 January 1946.*

Rodwell! It's like touching an electric fence. Martha's mind begins to fizz. It doesn't take a genius to work out Howard Rodwell is likely to be a relation, but what relation exactly? The man in the photograph has to be at least thirty-five. That means he could easily be the father of her father, Lewis, and Martha's paternal grandfather. It would make perfect sense; it might even explain her father's mysterious decision to complete his memoirs here, the home of his own father. Apart, that is, from two inconvenient facts. The first being he couldn't possibly have entertained any realistic notion that Howard might still be alive. The second problem is that she has always believed her father was an orphan when he was evacuated. Had she and Elizabeth been told that explicitly? She tries to recall her father's occasional war references but the harder she presses herself to remember the more intangible the memories become.

She takes a step closer to the wall, as if Howard Rodwell might be tempted to whisper the answer. Predictably, he stares sadly, and silently, back. Perhaps the picture was taken soon after the armistice, thinks Martha, when he was still burdened by the war. She hopes so. He has such an unhappy demeanour that she doesn't care to think of it lasting for long.

Outside, a wan sunlight is forcing a path through the slowing drizzle. She wanders aimlessly for a while, her thoughts jumping unhappily from one uncertainty to the next; instead of answers she seems only to be finding questions, all the gaps held together, lace-like, by the barest threads of what she knows – or thinks she knows, she's beginning to wonder if she understands anything about her father's past at all. Eventually, she heads into a cafe where a woman in a headband and tracksuit is trying to speak to a male colleague over the violent grind of a juicer. When Martha asks for a cappuccino she smiles to show a row of tiny teeth behind a neon-green brace.

Settled at a table covered by a plastic cloth Martha plants her elbows and raises the cup to her lips. The froth is dense as cotton wool and sprinkled with bright, bitter chocolate. Then her brow puckers and she puts the china down again. Why on earth had she and Elizabeth never asked their father about his childhood during the war? Now, it seems such a flagrant omission, but she supposes the truth is that growing up she didn't think much about her parents' lives beyond their obviously central purpose of – well – being her parents. And once she reached an age when her focus might naturally have broadened, a series of overwhelming events intervened.

Only a few days after Martha had enrolled on the English Lit program at McGill her mother fell ill. To begin with both parents maintained the diagnosis was no more than a hiccup, a mere disruption to their busy schedules, which would be behind them and forgotten about in a matter of months. So convincing was their performance that the increasingly dark hints in Elizabeth's letters from home didn't prepare Martha for the truth of the matter. Coming back for Thanksgiving she was deeply shocked to find a hospital-style bed in the old TV room and the house seeped in a mist of disinfectant that couldn't quite conceal the underlying stench of decay and fecal waste. Several times during the course of the next forty-eight hours her sunken-faced mother grasped Martha's hand and made a point of telling Martha how much she loved her, how proud she was; topics that as a family they had always been too squeamish to speak about before. Martha listened with disbelief and horror; unable to stop hoping for the miracle she now saw was needed.

Her mother died before that first semester was out. At the funeral Martha held Elizabeth's hand as they walked behind the coffin and put her arm around Elizabeth's shaking shoulders as the eulogies were read. Whenever she looked back, it always seemed to be the last occasion she could remember feeling like the older sister.

Immediately afterwards she met Clem. Predictably, everyone blamed the relationship – or its doomed trajectory, at least – on the death of her mother. If Martha hadn't been defenseless with grief, or in search of security, then surely she would never have got so involved with Clem, certainly she wouldn't have got pregnant and never in a millennium would she have married and dropped out of college. It made no difference, Martha considered these theories a load of baloney and said as much a number of times over the years. Clem, she reckoned, had been like an avalanche, the momentum gathering from the point on an inauspicious Tuesday afternoon that Martha happened to pick the same library table as the one on which Clem had just left his thesis notes. When she caught up with him by the vending machine, the fix of his grey-eyed gaze felt much as she imagined a tonne of snow emptying over her head would feel. Its unstoppable force obliterated her hitherto neat and studious existence, changing her landscape in an instant. Even now it can seem like she's still digging herself out.

Martha exhales so hard flecks of milk foam blow into the saucer. Whatever her reasons or excuses might be they don't change the fact she knows next to nothing about her father's life in England. For example, she definitely doesn't know whether or not his father was called Howard. She scoops her hands around the coffee cup, which is now lukewarm, and drinks it quickly. From somewhere behind her, a jazzy ringtone pings across the cafe. As it is silenced Martha considers her own phone, the ease with which it finds the answers to most of her questions: timetables, route maps, a recipe for banoffee pie. A sign propped on a ledge above the deafening juicer offers customers free Wi-Fi. Martha digs out her cell and logs on. She plugs the name *Howard Rodwell* into Google. It's pointless, of course. Twitter and Facebook are chock-a-block with Howard Rodwells, all of whom are very much alive and far too young to be the tragic-looking person in the photograph. After a moment, Martha types *Evacuation to Canada Second World War*. Immediately, a number of links jump onto the screen. She clicks on the first and up pops a page of Wikipedia; a section entitled the Children's Overseas Reception Board, which appears to be the official title of the body in charge of the Government's evacuation program. She blinks, draws the screen close to her face and begins to read.

It turns out that precisely 2664 children were evacuated between July and September 1940, and sent to places like Halifax, Brisbane and Sydney. This was a critical period in British history, the authors state, when the Battle of Britain was raging and German invasion forces were massing across the English Channel. Martha raises her eyes to the chatter and sunshine now pouring carelessly through the cafe door, the sea and the solid bulk of Europe not much further beyond. My father lived through this, she wonders, trying to conceive of the dread and uncertainty, but it's hard to comprehend. It feels like something just around a corner – unknowable, untouchable, but closer than she has ever before realised.

The Wikipedia entry finishes by naming the ships that were used in the scheme, the dates they sailed and their destinations. It occurs to Martha that if she can find the passenger lists for those bound for Canada the records might include the name and address of each evacuee's next of kin, which would throw some light on her father's parentage. She scrolls to the bottom of the piece to examine the references. The first is described as *The National Archives Children Overseas Reception Board*. Without expectation, Martha copies the exact same phrase into Google. Again a link appears. This one takes her to a web page of the National Archives and invites her to browse the 113 files comprising the records of the Children Overseas Reception Board.

It's like dropping a ball of string and watching it roll across the floor.

'I say, is anyone sitting here?'

Martha turns towards the voice and starts in shock. For a slow, unfathomable second the couple beside her are both wearing military uniform, and then the boy melts into a person dressed in an ordinary camouflage jacket, jeans and sneakers, and his companion into a girl with a petrol-blue blazer unzipped over a crop top. Each of them is carrying a tall glass of psychedelic juice and a piece of carrot cake.

Martha makes a vague, uninterested gesture towards the empty chairs, her attention back on her phone. The dossiers of the National Archives appear to be in chronological order. The first is headed *Press Announcement,* the next, more evocatively, *Broadcast Talk*. Martha closes her eyes. It's almost possible to recreate that broadcast; the crackle of an ancient wireless and a voice in clipped English, a chance of escape from the firestorm and the promise of safety. But the price, how terribly, agonisingly high the price of it was. She opens her eyes and sees the boy feeding a spoonful of cream frosting to the girl. Could she have evacuated Janey? In the normality of thriving England it feels unthinkable, but how can she ever know for sure?

The entries that follow the *Broadcast Talk* heading are mainly minutes or statistics but a few of them refer to individual problems: a late addition of an evacuee to one of the ships, a sudden withdrawal, an illness, a request to delay... Martha is searching for mention of the passenger lists, passing quickly through the files, when she stops and stares at the screen in disbelief. She has reached entry DO 251. It's one of the personal records. And on this occasion it's personal, in particular, to herself. The descriptive caption is short and to the point, RODWELL, LEWIS: EVACUATED TO CANADA: CLAIM BY FATHER FOR HIS RETURN: 1945.

Trembling a little, Martha clicks again, but the magic has broken, the ball of string has come to a halt. A message informs her the file is not digitised and can't be downloaded. However, it is available to view at the National Archives itself, in Kew.

'You don't like this cappuccino?'

Martha looks up blindly. Somebody must have asked her if she wanted more coffee, because there is another at her elbow, thick and velvet – and stone cold. The male waiter is regarding it sadly. Martha shakes her head apologetically. As he lifts it away, she touches his arm. 'Excuse me,' she says, 'how far away from here is Kew?'

The boy in the camouflage jacket answers before the waiter does. 'Kew is in London, south-west London.' He sounds vaguely curious.

Back at the hotel Martha digs Colin's card out of her purse and dials his number. It takes a while for anyone to answer. The first thing she hears is a distant, agitated bark, like the dying syllable of a shouted word, before, in a worn-out sort of tone, Colin finally says hello. When Martha asks for a ride to the station the following morning, he doesn't attempt to disguise his surprise. 'You want to go to the station again?'

'I have to go back to London.'

'Already? But you only just got here.'

Colin sounds exhausted, she thinks. Exhausted and drained by the fickle behaviour of his fellow man.

'Something has come up. Is ten o'clock too early? Should I call somebody else?'

'Nah,' Colin says. 'I'll be there.'

CHAPTER NINE

Norfolk, July 1940

'Now who has hidden away my bag of scraps?' The question ricocheted around the walls of the church hall like a matins bell. Elsie's voice had that indefinable classroom quality, Sylvie thought, which wasn't surprising, since she used to teach somewhere in Kent and still spoke fondly of 'her girls', although by this time most of them must have grown-up children of their own. The room let in just enough natural light to prevent the copper-topped ceiling lamps from having much impact so that even in summer it could seem dreary as an autumn afternoon. Before the war it had been used by a group called the Mackintosh Players – once Elsie had found a cast list for 'Cinderella, A Pantomime', a wig of tangled silver and a wand wrapped in tinfoil behind a cardboard cutout of a fir tree – but now the stage was occupied by trestle tables covered with patchwork blankets and banks of wool sorted into different colours.

Sylvie was perched on a metal-framed canvas chair; a group of them had been placed in a semi-circle under a casement window that badly needed a wash. She reached behind her seat and hauled forwards a bulging pillowcase out of which spilled a bright confetti of cottons and flannel. When she joined the WVS Sylvie had wondered at the point of collecting such tiny offcuts, now she was used to seeing them assembled into baby-sized bed coats and mattress covers.

'I say' – Elsie leaned close to Sylvie as she reached for the pillowcase – 'has Sheila had any news?' She jerked her tight, white curls in the direction of the woman who was sitting opposite Sylvie, staring into her lap and knitting with robotic monotony. Sylvie shrugged and quickly shook her head; she could tell the woman was listening from the way her shoulders had stiffened. Besides, her misery was obvious; although dressed smartly in a twinset and a single string of pearls she had the winded, desolate air of someone shipwrecked.

Elsie touched the woman's knee. 'Don't give up hope, my dear. No news is good news.' She spoke a lot more loudly than necessary, as if talking to a naughty child, or someone hard of hearing. The woman made a little shuddering movement, but didn't lift her head. After a moment Elsie pulled a despairing face at Sylvie and walked away.

The platitudes must kill you, Sylvie thought. The determination to stay positive when everyone knew that missing in action almost always meant dead. Yet what was the alternative? Some mornings the only things that got her out of bed were Lewis and Esther – their touch, their smell and their routines, which she clung to now like the rungs of a rope ladder – and the unexpected comfort of this dowdy hall.

She hadn't set foot in the place before the war but during the terrible, floating grey of February, when all the talk was of stricken ships and rationing, she had put her head round the door on her way to the library, hijacked by the unusual sound of women laughing. Now she came every Monday and Tuesday without fail. She had feared the school holidays would thwart her routine but Evelyn from The Close agreed to mind Lewis and Esther at the beginning of the week and in return she looked after Evelyn's little girl on Wednesdays and Thursdays.

Presently the new, rather brash brunette sitting beside Sylvie got up and announced she was going outside for a smoke. Sylvie took her chance.

'Sheila, is there really no word about Frank?'

The whey-faced woman hesitated before she lowered her needles and blew her nose. 'No,' she said. 'Nothing.' She paused another moment before adding, 'It was his brother's birthday at the weekend.' She sounded oddly bitter about it, and began to wind the loop of pearls round and around the fingers of her right hand.

Sylvie watched, not understanding. 'Did you manage to celebrate?'

Sheila didn't seem to hear the question. 'Richard turned eighteen. All he wants to do is play cricket or chase pretty girls, and now, any day' – the strain on her necklace threatened to snap it – 'he'll probably get his call-up papers too.' She stared at Sylvie with a sudden, dreadful intensity. 'I'm going to lose both of them, aren't I?' Her eyes were disconcertingly dry, but Sylvie felt her own begin to prick. She gazed back, helplessly.

'You mustn't say that. Frank may yet turn up right as rain and Richard hasn't gone anywhere yet.' Hating the false, bright sound to her voice she added in a softer tone, 'You must just carry on as best you can, and try not to think the worst.'

There was a shout from the other end of the room.

'Teatime, ladies!' A head of wiry brown hair appeared through the kitchen hatch. 'Don't all rush at once, but there's a packet of Garibaldis today!'

Sylvie got up. 'I'll go and fetch us both a cup.'

A woman called Marjorie was pouring tea in the small kitchen next to the stage. Tall and sturdy-boned, Sylvie considered her surprisingly handsome, despite the fact she never wore make-up and didn't seem to care much for her own appearance, often turning up in a pair of trousers and a plain white shirt she wore open at the collar. As Sylvie was searching out a plate for the biscuits, Elsie bustled into the kitchen brandishing a pencil and notebook. 'I've decided to organise a door-to-door collection,' she said. 'To boost the scraps supply. I expect most people would be only too pleased to give up a few straggly odds and ends for a good cause like ours. Now, what about this Saturday morning? Can I put you both on the list?'

The biscuit plate slipped from Sylvie's grasp, clattering onto the counter. As Elsie and Marjorie turned in surprise she felt suddenly cornered. Daisy was having a birthday party on Saturday afternoon, which, if they didn't go to Wells, would give her almost two hours without the children. When Evelyn had told Sylvie that morning, such a perfect opportunity to see Kennie seemed almost like fate, as if it were something that was meant to be and not so very terrible after all. However she hadn't expected to have to face the dilemma of it so soon. 'I usually stay with my parents at the weekend…' she began. Although her handbag still contained the shreds of Kennie's note, she knew she wouldn't need to piece them together, the address he had written, 12 Victoria Terrace, was locked in her memory. 'But…' – she regained momentum – 'I might not be visiting them this weekend after all.' Glancing at the others she flushed unexpectedly.

Elsie gave her a curious look. 'I'll put you down with a question mark.' She made to leave and spotted the biscuits. 'Garibaldi!'

'Just one each mind!' Marjorie wagged her finger good-humouredly.

'Absolutely! What a treat! I'll come back for mine when I've spoken to the others about the collection.'

Marjorie waved her cup towards Elsie's departing back. 'You know,' she said to Sylvie, 'I've never seen her so happy.'

It was true, mused Sylvia, while the rest of them were becoming increasingly tired and wan, Elsie was blooming. She had to be seventy, sixty-five at the very least, but the speed and purpose in her step could make her seem almost youthful at times. In fact, Sylvie realised, while so much of the war was ghastly beyond belief at least these days when she wrote to Connie even she felt that she had something to say for herself. By comparison, the years beforehand sometimes seemed bland and indistinguishable, as if they hadn't contained any purpose of their own, but had merely been the waiting, the preparation, for this part of their lives, the real and testing part, to begin.

Her correspondence with Connie had quickly settled into a regular pattern and had continued now for over a year. Sylvie had written first, soon after Connie returned to London, uncertain as to whether she would get a reply. But the response had come by return of post. Reading Connie's large and careful handwriting, Sylvie could hear the familiar voice jumping from the page as clearly as if they were in a room together, and penned her own answer as soon as possible. Once the war started the frequency of their communication slowed, but to compensate the letters gradually became lengthier and more serious.

In September Connie wrote that children from London were being evacuated to the country, but immediately added *'Charlie isn't going anywhere. I'm not going to be waiting on some stranger's telegram to tell me where he is.'* The word 'anywhere' had been underlined, but whether this merely signified Connie was fed up defending her decision or that she wanted to convince herself she was doing the right thing, Sylvie couldn't tell. At Christmas Sylvie made her a present of some torch batteries because Connie had mentioned they were harder to find in London *'than a black cat in a coal cellar',* and in January gave her the news that Howard had joined the army, although she hadn't tried to explain the complicated mix of sentiments his decision had provoked, pride and worry, of course, but guilt too, that she didn't feel as stricken as the other wives whose husbands had done the same thing. When she asked Connie if her beau had signed up as well, Connie replied to say that Ted had failed the medical because of his flat feet and that she couldn't help being glad about it although she knew it was *'wrong and selfish'* of her.

At Whitsun, when the wireless was filled with the invasion of the lowlands and Chamberlain resigning, Connie sent Sylvie a card with a picture of a cottage by the sea. *'Doesn't it seem longer ago than a year that we met? I wish we were on the beach together now.'* Sylvie knew Connie meant to cheer her up, but holding the drawing, knowing the place where they had made sandcastles and drunk gin and lemonade was blocked now by landmines and barbed wire, she felt that same unravelling – the same sense of falling uncontrollably forwards – as the instant when the reporter had taken their photograph.

Soon afterwards, as the news grew worse, the tone of Connie's scripts became less chatty and acquired a kind of dogged melancholy. *'It's never quiet here, but it is today'*, she wrote when France was lost. *'Everyone is too upset to speak, even the paperboys and the bus conductors have stopped talking. How wide is the Channel, do you know? Sometimes I imagine it like the Thames and think of Hitler popping across whenever he fancies, but then I remember Norfolk, how the sea went on forever, and I feel better again.'*

Marjorie interrupted her thoughts. 'Shall I take Sheila some tea?'

Sylvie reached hurriedly for a clean cup and saucer. 'I'd better do it. I promised her one ages ago.'

'Has she heard anything about Frank?'

'No, and now Richard's turned eighteen, she's terrified that he'll be off soon too.'

Marjorie glanced through the open hatchway. 'God, how awful! This war has made me glad I haven't got kids. Or a husband. I never thought I'd say it, but there it is. I've got nobody to worry about and if I go there'll be nobody to worry about me.'

'Don't be silly, Marjorie,' Sylvia said, shocked. 'We'd worry about you. We'd all worry about you dreadfully.'

'Still,' Marjorie persisted, 'people like her have it the worst' – she nodded in Sheila's direction again – 'mothers of sons old enough to fight.'

'And mothers of children who have to be evacuated,' Sylvie added without thinking.

'Oh?'

Sylvie hadn't told anyone but her parents about Howard's letter; she pressed on before Marjorie could ask any questions. 'If they put all the mothers in a room together they'd have a peace deal worked out before the kettle boiled.' The instant the words were out of her mouth she realised that it was not only true but also unutterably sad; everywhere she turned there was waste. 'I'd really better take that tea out to Sheila,' she said. 'Before the pot goes stone cold.'

She carried out the cup and put it at the foot of Sheila's chair. After a minute, when Sheila had taken no notice of it, Sylvie said to break the silence, 'Will you come again tomorrow?'

'Yes,' Sheila replied. 'I can't bear being in the house. All I do is sit and think and it's making me quite ill.' She had stopped knitting and was sitting now, perfectly still, with both hands resting on her knees.

'Perhaps,' Sylvie said, a little desperately, 'you could help me with this week's wool raffle? We haven't sold many tickets yet.'

'I'll buy one.'

Sylvie twisted around to see that the voice belonged to Rosemary Dawes. *Lucky Rosemary.* A baby with corkscrew curls and fists like miniature peaches and married to the manager at the waterworks who, according to Rosemary, had been told the closest he would get to seeing action was when his men found out that they weren't going to be paid for any shift time spent in the air-raid shelter.

'Are you sure?' Sylvie cast a look towards a trestle table bearing a jar of piccalilli and a plate of broad beans. 'We're still waiting for most people to bring in a donation for a prize.'

'That's all right.' As Rosemary fumbled for her purse a flyer fell out of her handbag and fluttered to the ground. Sylvie bent down to pick it up. The photograph of the man on the front of it, the brazen fix of his stare, seemed familiar. To her surprise, as she was still gazing at it, Rosemary rolled her eyes in an oddly exaggerated fashion and gave a little shimmy with her hips. 'Montgomery Clarke!' I just adore him, don't you? Fancy him coming here!'

'Did you say Montgomery Clarke?' Sheila's eyes flickered from her chair. 'He used to be my absolute favourite too. Can I see?'

Rosemary tweaked the flyer from Sylvie's grasp and passed it to Sheila. 'Look,' she said. 'His new play opens tonight at the Theatre Royal.'

Clutching the paper, Sheila stood up. She seemed nearly to be smiling.

All at once Sylvie realised where she had seen the man before. The picture on the flyer was considerably more recent than the photograph in her beach hut, but it was unmistakably the same person. She considered Sheila's animated face. 'Perhaps we should all go and see him?'

'What, today?' Rosemary asked.

'I don't see why not. If I can find someone to mind the children.'

'Oh, I don't think I can do that. Not tonight.' Rosemary appeared quite alarmed at the idea. She took the flyer back from Sheila and put it back inside her handbag. Her earlier gaiety had vanished entirely. 'I've got a husband and baby to think of.'

'What about you, Sheila?' Sylvie asked. 'Would you like to go?'

'I don't know.' Sheila's hand went to her pearls and then she glanced down at her knitting. 'I suppose it would be nice to get out. And I don't believe Alan would mind. He thinks it's best for me to keep busy.'

'Well, that's settled then,' Sylvie said quickly. 'Let's meet by the theatre at seven o'clock. If we're feeling really risqué we might get a drink at the bar first. Assuming they have anything to sell us.' She picked up a dirty teacup and headed back to the kitchen before Sheila could change her mind.

Elsie was standing at the sink, elbow-deep in soapy water. Sylvie slid the crockery into the sea-foam of suds. 'I'm going with Sheila to the theatre tonight,' she announced.

Elsie beamed. 'That's quite an achievement, I must say.'

Sylvie wrinkled her brow. 'Assuming I can find someone to mind Lewis and Esther.'

'Well I can help with that.' Elsie began to rinse the china under the hot tap, propping the saucers against up-turned cups.

'Oh,' Sylvie said, 'I didn't mean…'

'An evening out would make a nice change.'

'It's hardly an evening out,' Sylvie protested. 'Looking after two children.'

'I shall enjoy it. I quite miss the company of children. They rather keep your spirits up. And I can hardly say the same of my poor sister.'

She sighed. It was on the tip of Sylvie's tongue to ask Elsie about her sister, but something in the dismal set of Elsie's mouth changed her mind. Instead she picked up a tea towel.

'Where do you live, Elsie? I don't like the idea of you walking too far at night?'

'Victoria Terrace, number 4. It isn't very far at all. Not if you cut across Chapelfield Gardens.'

'Victoria Terrace?' Sylvie felt a little rush of energy, as if she had accidentally brushed against something hot.

'Yes.' Elsie shook the water from her hands and dried them on the end of Sylvie's cloth. 'Why? Do you know it?'

'No' – Sylvie tried to flatten her voice, dampen the buzz in her stomach – 'I just know someone who's staying there temporarily, that's all.'

It had started to rain; the fine, summer kind that seemed simply to hang in the air, and the theatre foyer was already filling up as people hurried inside, heads bent, holding the collars of their coats. Sylvie had arrived early to buy the tickets. She told herself these days nobody thought much of a woman going out alone, but nevertheless she felt conspicuous queuing at the box office and made her request for two tickets in a deliberately big voice. She had decided to dress up a little – it was the theatre after all – and had chosen a crimson dress with organdie puffed sleeves and a wrap-around bodice. It was a long time since she had worn anything so nice and she had forgotten the sculpted feel of stiff fabric against her skin. Too sculpted, perhaps. It pulled a little across her stomach and the neckline was deeper than she remembered – or perhaps she had expanded in that department as well? She would have buttoned up her coat, so she didn't feel quite as exposed, but the skies had been clear when she left home and recently the weather had been so hot that she hadn't thought to bring it.

There was still no sign of Sheila. As she waited she became aware of someone's gaze from behind her left shoulder. Instinctively, she shifted further away and for the sake of something to occupy her hands, found a handkerchief in her handbag and pressed it briefly to her nose. As she folded it away again, a young man stepped right in front of her. He was shorter than her with gingery hair and the beginnings of a moustache on his upper lip. Although he was wearing army khakis, under the jacket his right arm was strapped across his stomach in a grubby-looking sling.

'Hello,' he said. 'Out on the town by yourself?' Despite his appearance, he sounded very sure of himself.

Sylvie took a step backwards. 'No, I'm waiting for a friend.' She peeked anxiously over his shoulder but there was only an elderly couple struggling with an umbrella in the doorway.

'She's leaving it a bit late, don't you think?' The man's eyebrows flicked upwards and he moved closer to her again. His pale, almost colourless eyes were rimmed with red and Sylvie caught a sour smell of sweat and beer.

She folded her arms across her chest. 'I expect she's been delayed. I'm certain she'll be here any minute.'

The man reached inside his jacket pocket with his left hand and brought out a packet of cigarettes. He flipped open the top with his thumb and held it out towards her. 'Would you mind?'

Sylvie stared at him. 'Would I mind, what?'

He jostled the packet impatiently.

'Oh, I see.' Gingerly, she extracted a cigarette.

He tucked the packet away, plucked the cigarette from her fingers and put it slowly between his lips. Then he reached in his trouser pocket for a box of matches and handed them to her, watching her closely. At first Sylvie fumbled with the match but finally it struck the box cleanly and the tip flared. Bending towards him she felt his eyes travel up and down the contours of her dress.

'I say,' he said, taking a pull from his cigarette, 'If your – friend – doesn't turn up, how about a little drinkies with me instead?' It was the way he paused before he said the word 'friend' that made Sylvie understand he didn't think she was waiting for anyone at all.

'No!' The word shot away from her as she looked wildly around for Sheila. 'Certainly not.'

At that moment there was a sharp cough and then an assertive voice spoke from the back of the foyer. 'Could everyone please take their seats. This evening's performance of *Hay Fever* will begin in precisely two minutes.'

'Excuse me,' Sylvie said. 'I have to go into the theatre now.' She drew herself up to walk past him with as much dignity as she could muster, but he stuck out his good arm so that the stubby fingertips of his left hand pressed lightly against her dress. As he leaned close she could taste, rather than smell, the acrid odour of alcohol and dirt.

'Think I'm not good enough for you?' he hissed. 'I fought for King and country. And girls like you ought to appreciate that.' He searched her face with a reptilian glare. 'Because I know your type. I can spot them a mile away.'

In the interval Sylvie stayed in her seat. She could have done with a drink, a proper one with ice that clinked against the glass, but she daren't move in case the ginger-haired man was lingering somewhere. On her left was the couple she had seen coming into the theatre. As they stood up to go to the bar, the elderly gentleman gestured at the empty space beside Sylvie and then at the umbrella and coats heaped around his feet. 'Would you mind awfully if we use that chair to put our things on?'

Sylvie glanced towards the door as if Sheila might yet appear, but of course it was futile. She felt a rush of irritation. It wasn't so much the money she had wasted on the unused ticket, but the rather childish sense of having been abandoned. With Sheila beside her she would have enjoyed the wave of expectant rustling as the audience adjusted and settled itself for the performance, the sudden surge of darkness before the blaze of honey-coloured lights and the stage sprang into life. As it was she had spent most of the first half unable to think of anything but her encounter in the foyer. She seemed to see the man's peculiar eyes and the streak of shaving rash along his chin more clearly now than she had at the time. *I know your type.* Perhaps he was right. She shivered. Perhaps it was obvious to every man who laid eyes on her. She thought about Kennie and her stomach crawled with a sick kind of yearning. Of course she shouldn't see him again, and yet it was hopeless. She was hopeless.

The elderly couple returned; the man clutching his wife's arm for support, though they both made a good show of disguising it. He lowered himself slowly back down beside Sylvie. He was wearing a three-piece suit, the waistcoat a dashing and rather surprising shade of blue. 'It's awfully good, don't you think?' he said pleasantly.

'Oh, yes,' Sylvie said, although she had barely followed it.

'And marvellous to see Montgomery Clarke in the flesh, so to speak.'

'Oh yes,' Sylvie said again.

'A treat for the ladies, I imagine!' He gave a friendly little laugh.

Sylvie smiled politely, although in fact Montgomery Clarke had been quite a disappointment. At first she had assumed he was playing the handsome young son but discovered during the second act that he actually took the role of the novelist father. She supposed even the photograph on the flyer had been taken several years ago and wondered what he had been to Aunt Ginger – a pin-up, an unrequited crush or somebody more substantial than that?

'A night at the theatre helps to take one's mind off things, doesn't it?' As he spoke, a trace of pain washed across the elderly man's face. He glanced at his wife, patted her arm and turned back to the stage with resolution.

After the curtain fell, all Sylvie could think of was whether the ginger-haired man might still be about. Of course there was no reason why he should be, unless he had actually watched the play himself. Or had nothing better to do than wait to bother her again. She let herself be swept with the crowd out of the auditorium, but just before the foyer she slipped into the pink and cream of the ladies' powder room. Once inside the furthest cubicle she lowered the lid of the lavatory and sat down.

Presently, a door creaked, the distant hum became briefly loud and then two sets of footsteps approached on the tiled floor. A strong, confident voice said, 'No, I shan't bother with an autograph after all. I actually preferred the one who played Simon. Monty's getting on a bit now don't you think?' A pause then, 'Wait here, won't you?' There was rattle to the door of Sylvie's cubicle. Sylvie froze, but the same voice called out gaily, 'Oh excuse me!'

The bolt to another lavatory slapped into place, followed by the rustle of fabric and then the clear, hard sound of someone peeing. A minute later, Sylvie heard the lock once more followed by a rush of tap water. Another, gentler, voice spoke, 'I say, nobody has come out of that end cubicle yet. Do you think she's all right?'

'Oh, I expect the lavatory is out of order. They really ought to put a notice on it.'

There was the swing of a shutting door, and an abrupt return to silence.

CHAPTER TEN

Sylvie remained where she was for another thirty minutes. She passed the time imagining the story she would be able to tell Connie in her next letter. However funny she tried to make the episode sound she knew Connie would see through the pretence straight away and that her reply would burst with concerned outrage. Just picturing Connie's reaction to the ginger-haired man made Sylvie feel better and eventually she decided it must be safe to leave. It occurred to her then that perhaps they would soon lock the theatre, and she might be trapped all night, but although she hurried into the foyer with a new sense of anxiety, a boy with a weary droop to his shoulders was still sweeping up discarded tickets and cigarette stubs. He didn't bother to lift his head but merely murmured, 'Night, Miss,' as she walked past.

Outside, the rain had stopped and an eerie, expectant quiet reverberated through the streets. Sylvie dug a torch out of her bag. Its beam was fainter than the glow of the moon, which was hanging, yellow and swollen above the cathedral spire. *A bomber's moon*, she thought and shivered. She had heard the expression the previous weekend when her father used it as they stood in the garden together, and it seemed another perversion of the war, that something as beautiful as moonlight should now be the harbinger of death and destruction.

Devoid of street lamps and lit-up windows the city felt darkly alien. She followed the whitened curb, but without being able to see the outlines of shops and offices it was like navigating through sea fog. Eventually she found the wide thoroughfare of Castle

Meadow, the great bulk of the castle itself rising on the far side of the road. She must have passed it a hundred times before but now it loomed against the sky like a giant or an ogre from a childhood nightmare that might at any moment start to shift and move. She turned away and quickened her pace. The street was nearly empty, only the occasional couple scuttled past, arms locked together, heads down, and once a car crawled by, its hooded headlights picking out a meagre path through the night.

Closer to Chestnut Place the road narrowed and houses seemed to press on her from both sides. Although she knew that behind the walls families were sleeping or reading or making bedtime drinks, the blackout boards made the windows blank and sinister, as if nobody was there and all the world had upped and gone, or rather that something frightful was there, hiding in the shadows, and she might any minute hear footsteps behind her. She was scolding herself for being so foolish when her torch alighted on a mound of earth, with the glint of a spade leaning against it, and her composure fell apart like wet newspaper. She broke into a ragged, breathless trot and arrived at her own garden gate stumbling and hot.

The silliness left her as soon as she opened the front door. The hall was warm and calm. A stack of comics and a set of Meccano were sitting on the bottom stair while Elsie's pack of Happy Families had been left on the shelf above the radiator. Checking herself in the mirror, she tucked away a loose lock of hair while her pulse continued to jump and dart under her ribs. As her panting receded she became aware of another noise, a rhythmical nasal throb coming from the sitting room. She eased open the door. Elsie was asleep in an armchair, her stockinged legs propped on a footstool; without her shoes Elsie's feet looked tiny, but then so did Elsie, lost in the contours of the upholstery. Her wrists were clasped in her lap and she was sitting with her head tipped back, mouth slightly open.

Sylvie lingered in the doorway, uncertain what to do. She didn't want Elsie to walk home at this time of night but if Sylvie roused her to offer the spare bedroom then Elsie might feel duty-bound to return to her sister. Deciding it was best to leave her where she was, Sylvie fetched a tartan car blanket from the landing cupboard and tucked it loosely over Elsie's chest and shoulders. After that, she tiptoed from the room, turned out the light and went to bed.

Six hours later Sylvie woke to the sound of falling concrete. A building was disintegrating, bricks were bouncing off the pavement as she tried to gather the children into the shelter of her body, but Esther was crying – a desperate cry of terror – and then Esther had gone and Sylvie was shouting her name above the crump and blast of toppling stone.

She opened her eyes and her mind groped upwards out of sleep. The room was dark but a thin band of pre-dawn twilight outlined the edges of the blackout curtains. Esther *was* crying, she realised, and calling out too, although there were shuddering gaps between her wails. Esther must have had a nightmare, she thought, and was swinging her legs out of the bed when an explosion seemed to burst from inside her own skull. For a second, she watched transfixed as the room about her shook and the bedroom window bowed towards her like a fat man puffing out his chest. From somewhere close – *my God, how close?* – she heard the casual acceleration of a collapsing wall.

She ran into Esther's room where Esther was standing on her bed clutching a teddy bear, hysterical sobs convulsing her chest. Sylvie scooped her into her arms. The previous weekend Sylvie had struggled to lift her out of a swing, now she felt she could carry her to Scotland.

'Get up, Lewis! Get up! Now!'

He was lying, rigid, on his back; eyes wide open. Sylvie was shouting at him from the doorway and then miraculously he was right in front of her and she was touching both of them. They looked at her with such trust it was almost crippling, the panic she wouldn't be able to keep them safe, that she would fail the most basic duty of all. Pulling Lewis down the stairs, she thought of the grave-like pile of earth that had given her such a turn. It was a shelter, of course; she should have dug one herself, or bought an indoor kind. There was an advert for an Anderson shelter lying on the kitchen table, but hardly anyone she knew had got one yet. London was supposed to be bombed first, not Norfolk. She pushed the children in front of her into the cupboard under the stairs and on impulse grabbed the pack of Happy Families from the radiator shelf. Closing the door behind her, she switched on the light. Two milk-white faces gazed up at her.

'All right,' she said, and tried to hold her voice steady. 'Now we're quite safe in here but we must stay in the cupboard until the German planes have gone.'

'Are they trying to kill us?' Lewis whispered. Sylvie looked into his bewildered eyes. They were all crouched together under the sloping ceiling that followed the slant of the staircase. The ironing board leant against the wall behind her head and a number of cleaning utensils were hanging on a row of nails – a dustpan and brush with a loop of string through the eye of the pan-handle, two yellow dusters, and a gingham drawstring bag which contained tins of shoe polish and two black brushes. In that fleeting moment she had the oddest sense everything that had ever mattered was compressed inside their tiny room.

Sylvie put her palm on Lewis' head. 'Not exactly,' she said. 'It's not that they want to kill us. But it's the pilot's job to try and win the war for Germany.' Lewis looked at her blankly. 'There's no need to worry.' She managed a smile. 'We're quite safe in here.' Neither of the children said anything. 'I tell you what,' Sylvie said, 'why don't we have a game of Happy Families, while we wait for the Germans to go away?' Her voice sounded like it belonged to somebody on the wireless talking about Wimbledon or the weather. The children didn't move.

'Sit down,' she said more firmly. She reached for the ironing board and manoeuvered it across their laps to create a kind of tabletop. She could feel the cold heaviness of metal legs through the thinness of her nightdress. As she dealt out the cards a vague mechanical whine, like a gnat or mosquito, permeated the cupboard walls and she slowed her counting, making it louder. Then she looked briefly at her hand and turned to Esther. 'Have you got,' she said, 'Mr Bun, the baker?'

There was a distant, hollow crack. The cupboard shuddered and the light bulb swayed. Esther gasped, but didn't drop her cards.

'Have you got Mr Bun the baker?' Sylvie repeated. Esther shook her head, staring at Sylvie with wide blue eyes. Sylvie looked at Lewis. 'Do *you* have,' she said in a singsong voice, 'Mr Bun the Baker?'

Lewis shook his head slowly. 'You don't play it like that,' he said thickly. 'Elsie taught us how to play it properly. If Esther doesn't have the card you've asked for then you must pick one up from the pile. You can't ask me.'

'All right.' Sylvie took a card. 'We'll play it properly. Now it's your go, Lewis.' She saw a muscle on his jawbone twitch, but he nudged Esther with his elbow.

'Do you have Mrs Chop the butcher's wife?'

Esther nodded – a quick, shallow gesture as if she was afraid a bigger movement would be all it took to bring the walls down – but continued to clutch her cards.

'Well give it to me then.'

Tentatively, Esther held out a card.

'Good,' Sylvie said. 'Now it's your go Esther.'

'No it's not,' Lewis said. 'Because Esther had the card I asked for, it means I get another go.' They could all hear the moan of an aircraft again. Louder now. Intensifying. Lewis swallowed, 'Mummy,' he said, 'do you have Master Chop, the butcher's son?'

Sylvie paused, pretending to consider. 'No, I don't think I do. So that must mean it's your go, Esther. Why don't you ask if I have Mr Green, the greengrocer?'

There was an appalling shriek followed by a deep rumble and the sound of breaking glass. The light bulb jerked above them and then

the air went black. Esther screamed and flung herself onto Sylvie's
lap. Sylvie held her close, inhaling the hay-like smell of her hair while
her other arm reached for Lewis. All at once she remembered Elsie
in the sitting room. Elsie was all alone and too terrified to move, no
doubt. She ought to go and get her. She began to peel Esther from
her chest, murmuring about the need to fetch Elsie, but Esther yelled
and clung to her so tightly she couldn't move.

'Shall I go?' She felt the ironing board shift as Lewis moved to
stand up.

'No! You must stay here.' She stuck out her hand to restrain him
and then closed her eyes, resting her head against the cupboard wall.
God forgive me, she thought, if something should happen to Elsie.

But it was growing quieter again. The growl of the engines faded
until all she could hear was a ringing in her ears like echoes of planes
and falling bombs until eventually that dwindled too. They must
have all dozed a little because when she opened her eyes a bead of
light was seeping under the door and she could make out the fluted
song of blackbirds. The children were slumped together, Esther's
head lolling across Lewis' chest.

Tentatively she pushed open the door. The blacked-out windows
meant it was still quite dark but the ink of night had lifted to
pigeon grey.

Sylvie hurried to the sitting room. Elsie was fast asleep. She had
slid further down the chair and twisted to one side, her cheek against
the wingback, fingers flattened over her exposed ear. The patch of
upholstery next to her mouth was damp. Sylvie lifted the boards
from the window and let the daybreak flood the room. Streamers
of pink and gold graced the eastern sky while further up the street
a woman in a man's dressing gown was sweeping up broken glass.

Elsie stirred, struggled to raise herself from the cushions and
reached for her spectacles on the adjacent lamp table. Sylvie pulled
out a chair from the writing bureau and came to sit next to her. 'I'm
so sorry,' she began.

Elsie was looking around the room as if she had never seen it before. 'I must have fallen asleep.' She sounded as though she was talking to herself.

Sylvie placed her palm on Esther's knee. 'Yes, you did. I was late home, much later than I expected.' She hesitated. She could hardly say she had hidden in the lavatory to avoid the advances of a one-armed soldier. Besides, after the last few hours it hardly seemed real any more.

'What time is it?' Elsie asked. She didn't seem to be listening to Sylvie.

'It's early, I think. Not yet six. Shall I make us some tea?'

Elsie shook her head. 'I must get back to my sister.' She gazed at Sylvie as though she knew something was terribly amiss but couldn't quite put her finger on it. 'Was there a dreadful storm?'

Sylvie kept her hand on Elsie's leg. 'It wasn't a storm. It was bombs. There was another raid. A longer one than before, I think.' She would have said more, about the noise and how the house had shuddered and shook and how it felt as if the bombs were falling only a street or two away. She wanted to tell somebody and for that somebody to tell her back how it probably sounded worse than it was and that since the house was still standing and they were all perfectly all right there was nothing to worry about, but she stopped herself because Elsie looked so stricken that Sylvie couldn't go on. And because nobody could say anything like that anyway, since as soon as they ventured outside they would know it wasn't true. Sylvie watched Elsie's face absorb the news, the shock and then the effort to gather herself as she felt under the seat for her shoes.

'Bombs?' Elsie was trembling as she pulled at her laces. 'Oh my Lord, my poor sister. She'll be in such a state. I should never have fallen asleep like that. Whatever was I thinking?'

'It was my fault,' Sylvie said, mortified. 'For not coming back when I said I would.' But Elsie had already stood up. She clasped Sylvie briefly and hurried out of the room. A moment later Sylvie heard the empty thud of the front door. Before she could move,

Esther appeared unsteadily in the entrance to the sitting room. She was trailing her teddy by one of his paws and carrying something in her other hand.

'Will you play Happy Families with me?'

'Now?' Sylvie said.

Esther nodded.

CHAPTER ELEVEN

Norfolk, recently

The London train has barely left King's Lynn when an announcement that it is terminating in Cambridge generates a collective groan. Nevertheless, Martha is unprepared for the stampede that follows their arrival in Cambridge, the reason for which becomes clear only after she has boarded the replacement waiting on the opposite side of the platform and discovered there are no available places.

She wriggles through several carriages stuffed with disgruntled passengers, their laps loaded with bags and briefcases, before miraculously finding herself in a pocket of peace with a surprising number of empty seats. Settling with relief opposite a cool-looking guy wearing a suede jacket and shades, she gazes out of the window over the Cambridge concourse. Then she sighs, ten more days of her self-imposed embargo on calling Janey still to go. That same morning she had taken an early trip to the beach hut; sitting on the veranda, the sea crackling with the eight o'clock sun, how she had longed for her daughter to be there too.

'Hello again.'

As if in slow motion Martha turns from the glass. Somehow, the person facing her across the table, without baggy clothes or a telescope, and looking utterly unlike the person she met on the beach, has turned into Henry.

Before she can think of a word to say the calm ruptures. A band of women – eight, ten, it's hard to tell – burst into the carriage. Dressed in headbands decked with animal ears most are brandishing a plastic glass in one hand and a bulging carrier bag in the other.

'We can sit here!' The woman at the front is wearing donkey ears that quiver with energy as she shouts over her shoulder to the others.

'Isn't this first class…?'

'We had seats together before, didn't we? Until they turfed us off that train.' Donkey Ears plops down next to Henry. 'You don't mind, do you?'

'Not at all.'

A large woman with cat, or possibly fox, ears squeezes in beside Martha. Henry smiles at Martha and raises his eyebrows. Martha stares transfixed as the surrounding places are rapidly filled. Once sorted, the group start to unload the contents of their carriers; cans, bottles and packets sail onto every available surface. Amongst the Prosecco and tubes of Pringles are a selection of ready mixed cocktails, gin and tonics, tins of Baileys, and a large packet of Tesco raspberries. A cork shoots over the table with a satisfying pop, Donkey Ears showers the cluster of waiting cups with bubbles while Fox Ears chucks a raspberry or two into each of them.

'Do you realise some of us are trying to work?' A disembodied male voice floats from the back of the carriage over the shrieks and giggles and nobody takes any notice. Moments later 'Get the Party Started' begins to blast from a phone, although judging by the speed and gusto with which the refrain is taken up Martha suspects the party started back in Kings Lynn.

She's feeling increasingly uncomfortable. It's not so much the bedlam erupting around her but the realisation that she's sitting in a first-class compartment without a proper ticket. Yet leaving now would look like she's objecting to the ruckus, and to where, exactly, would she move? Besides, it would be such a shame to leave Henry.

She gives him a shy smile. He looks into her eyes and smiles back, but the moment is broken by the same venomous male voice as before, which now emanates from just behind Martha's chair.

'I'd like to see your first-class ticket. I don't believe you have one.'

Martha's stomach lurches in panic before she understands the words are directed at Donkey Ears.

The music stops abruptly and an anxious quiet descends on the carriage.

'You see some of us paid for first-class tickets so we could work, not to be forced to watch a group of drunken, middle-aged women behave worse than teenagers.'

Donkey Ears swallows. 'It's Carol's birthday,' she whispers, nodding towards a younger woman on the opposite side of the gangway. 'We wanted to give her a good time.'

'Where is your first-class ticket?' The man comes a step closer. Martha can see gold oval cufflinks peeping out from the sleeve of his jacket. Her heart is thudding in time to the beat of the train. She can't bring herself to turn and look at his face.

Henry clears his throat. 'I think you dropped the ticket on the floor,' he says to Donkey Ears. 'When you were pouring the... er... wine. I noticed it fall out of your bag. I probably should have said something at the time.'

Donkey Ears blinks at him.

'I'll get it for you, shall I? I saw where it went.'

Henry manoeuvres himself beneath the table so that only his back and the top of his head remain visible. A flurry of huffing and grunting follow before he rises waving the fruits of his search. 'Here it is,' he says, and calmly places a first-class ticket down beside the Pringle packets. Martha knows the ticket belongs to Henry and considers it highly likely that everyone else knows too.

The silence teeters, as if on a knife-edge. Only Henry appears unconcerned.

The complexion of the cufflinks man deepens slowly from red to purple. A hundred accusations appear to be on the tip of his tongue before, eventually, without saying a word, he stalks back to his seat, picks up his briefcase and storms out of the carriage.

As soon as he's gone Martha says, 'I don't have a first-class ticket either.' She feels the need to confess immediately.

'I wouldn't worry about it,' Henry says placidly. 'The trains are all up the creek today. Nobody is going to check.'

Donkey Ears pushes a large plastic cup of Prosecco at Henry. 'Here you go; you deserve that!'

'Oh,' Henry says, 'no thank you.' He seems quite troubled by the gesture. 'I'm on my way to a meeting.'

'You have it then.' Donkey Ears nudges the cup towards Martha before turning towards her friends. Gradually the music and conversation starts up again, although perhaps a little less loudly than before.

Martha takes a sip from her Prosecco and sees that Henry is watching her. 'If you can't beat them...'

He laughs.

Emboldened she asks, 'So what's your meeting about?'

'Oh... Well...' – his eyes flick down and back to her face – 'It's actually with my agent...'

'Your *agent*? You told me you were a decorator!'

Henry laughs again. 'Okay, I'm also a musician – a drummer. I used to be in a band.' Reacting to her expression he adds quickly, 'It's not like we were famous. We did weddings, birthday parties, that kind of thing.'

'Used to be?'

'The band split up a few years ago. I've taken a bit of a break since then. Done other things.' He pauses, becoming suddenly awkward. 'I want to get back into it now but I'll start off with session work for other bands, until...'

'You start one of your own again?'

'Maybe.' He grins at her.

'Henry,' Martha says suddenly, remembering, 'I've still got your cell phone.'

'I thought you would have it. I was about to ask.'

'I'm so sorry. When you were packing up your telescope at the beach, I must have put it in my coat pocket without thinking…'

'It doesn't matter. I suppose I could pick it up from your hotel tomorrow? Or the day after, if tomorrow isn't…?'

'Well yes… I mean no… I mean tomorrow would be just fine…'

A trill from Martha's own phone interrupts her. 'Wait… What is this?' She draws the screen closer. 'Oh…'

Elizabeth has sent her a photograph of a woman via WhatsApp. The subject of the picture is probably in her late thirties or early forties and dressed in a bathing costume; lying on sand, propped on her elbows, she is gazing into the camera with beautiful, wide, candid eyes. The caption reads, 'Found this inside one of Dad's books, E.'

Martha is still gaping at the woman when her cell pings again. The second image appears to be the back of the same snap on which somebody has written in blue biro, *2 June 64*. This time Elizabeth's caption reads, 'Catkins???'

'Oh,' Martha says again, before her voice dries up completely. She lets her phone drop and turns to the glass with pooling eyes.

'Is anything wrong?'

'No…' Martha takes a gulp of Prosecco. Then, 'Well, yes I suppose it is.' Right at this moment she feels her family doesn't deserve any discretion, none at all. 'It seems,' she says, attempting to sound casual, 'that my father may well have loved a woman other than my mother. Perhaps for most of his married life.' Opening her purse, she roots around for a Kleenex.

Henry doesn't say anything, but a moment later Martha feels his fingers rest gently over hers. When, after some time, he releases them Martha makes a point of scratching her nose and picking up her Prosecco again. Once the cup is empty, however, she lets her hand lie casually between them on the table until the train begins to slow and the vast edifice of King's Cross station glides into view.

*

The National Archives in Kew is an imposing, fort-like structure, fronted by an artificial lake where people are sitting on benches, lunchboxes on laps and faces tilted up towards the sunshine. However, immediately as Martha steps inside the brightness falls away and she is swallowed by an echoing cool with the gravity of a museum or even a mausoleum. Orientating herself in the sombre entrance hall, it's easy to imagine the corridors of paper that must stretch deep into the bowels of the building, recording the minutiae of past lives, like fossilised footprints studied by scientists trying to piece together an animal from a handful of random steps.

Finding the cloakroom, she stuffs her purse and jacket into a locker. She keeps out her phone and a pen, but on seeing a notice pinned to the wall puts the pen back. Only pencils are allowed in the reading rooms. This takes her by surprise until it strikes her she's going to handle the actual dossier itself, the pages created over half a century earlier.

'I get to see the real file?' Martha checks at the on-site shop, putting two new, pleasingly pristine, pencils inside one of the plastic bags that are provided in the locker room. It doesn't seem feasible that she has not only discovered papers linking her father with Howard Rodwell while idling the time away in a seaside juice bar, but that these same pieces of writing might be made available to her with less fuss than it takes to borrow a library book. It's so astonishing that at every stage of the process she expects to hit an obstacle: she needs to make an appointment; the file she wants is not available; she has to be a member of a particular society or club… The last possibility turns out to be almost true. In order to request a file from the online archives, Martha needs, she's told, something called a Reader's Ticket. But – hey – one of those can be manufactured on the spot! She fills in an online form, gazes into a tiny camera and two minutes later is handed a red plastic card with a passport-sized picture of herself in the middle of it. She knows better than to scrutinise it closely – when has anyone ever looked anything but dreadful in that kind of photo? But she can't help from taking a quick peek as she makes to tuck it in her pocket. Instantaneously, her hand freezes. The electric flash has reduced her hair to a monk-like hood and her eyes to the colour of pond life, while the recent excess of travel and jet lag appears to have turned her complexion to porridge. She hides the card away, quickly.

Once installed at a computer terminal in the research area, Martha meticulously types into the search engine the exact same phrase she used in Frederico's: '*Evacuation to Canada Second World War*'. All the while she worries the magic won't, can't, work a second time, that having glimpsed the file once, it will now be lost amid vast forests of online data. But when she follows the same links as she did before, dossier DO 251 pops easily onto the screen. Do you want to view this file? The computer asks. *Yes*. She does. With a shaking finger, Martha touches the request tab. A moment later an automated message appears informing her that the documents will be ready to view in forty minutes. Martha stares at the matter-of-fact sentence, her stomach a mixture of churning disbelief and triumph. When she gets up from the chair she sees her legs were wrapped around it so tightly that there are pink indents across her shins.

She sits out the forty-minute wait in the ground-floor café, picking at a baguette filled with crimped lettuce and mayonnaise-coated chicken. The words '*claim by father for his return*' chase around her head like a dog in pursuit of its tail. All at once she wishes Elizabeth was there too, a double espresso at one elbow and a glass of iced water at the other. I had *no* idea about any of this, Martha would say. Neither did I! Elizabeth would cry. And they would look at each other with wonder and confusion, finding a new togetherness in the strangeness of it all. One time Martha reaches for her phone but then she thinks better of it. She can actually hear Elizabeth, impatient and perplexed. 'So you haven't actually found out what happened yet, Martha? Call me when you know something!'

After forty minutes finally crawl by, Martha asks directions to the document collection point and a minute later finds herself in front of a small backless cupboard with a red Perspex front. A lot of similarly styled cubicles are stacked together locker-room fashion, each with a number printed on the front. Martha's file has been placed in cubicle thirty-seven, which, with beautiful efficiency, tallies with the place number she has been allocated in the reading room.

It's obvious immediately as she opens the red door that the dossier is not bulky, and when she picks it up she sees it is a buff-coloured folder containing no more than a handful of sheets. She carries it into the reading room as if transporting spun glass and locates the seat numbered thirty-seven. The places either side are occupied by a woman with a seal-grey bob and a man wearing a checked shirt and woollen tie. Both of them have several files spread in front of them and a small stack of books on researching family trees. As Martha lifts the front cover of her own file she has the sense of leaping into water, that same mid-air moment of thrill and trepidation.

The papers are held together with a tag in the left corner. Each sheet is so thin it's practically translucent and the typing is in a sparse, old-fashioned font. Gently, Martha leafs through the entirety of the file. The first document is obviously an application of some kind but the rest appear to be letters, written in 1945 shortly after the end of hostilities. She imagines them being dictated from a heavy desk somewhere in war-damaged London and then taken to the clatter of the typing pool, the zip and thump of the carriages, the women eager to be finished, slipping on cardigans and coats, stairwells filling with laughter and the snap of heels.

She turns the pages back again and begins to read slowly from the beginning.

Authority for the Return to the United Kingdom of child under 18 years of age and Declaration in Support of Application for Advance Towards Costs of Return Passage of Family Evacuated Overseas.

We/I the undersigned being the parent(s)/ guardian(s) of the under mentioned child/ children apply for arrangements to be made if possible for the return to the United Kingdom of Lewis Rodwell (date of birth 28 June 1928).

Howard Rodwell
dated 20 October 1945

23 October 1945

PAS. 6674
Despatch No. 272

Dear Sir,

I have received your form of authority for the
return of Lewis Rodwell. Our representative in
Halifax, Mrs Hinkler, has been advised that you
have signed this document and will contact the
foster family to make arrangements for passage.

    Yours faithfully
    Miss E.G. Nicholas
    Deputy Director C.O.R.B.

8 November 1945

PAS. 6674
Despatch No. 131

Dear Miss Nicholas,

Thank you for your despatch No. 271 (C.O.R.B. No. PAS. 6674) of 23 October 1945 informing me that you have received a form of authority for the return of Lewis Rodwell, a matter of which I informed the foster family, Reverend Chester A Simmons, without delay.

Reverend Simmons has however now telephoned me of his own accord. The purpose of his contact was to notify me that he had heard nothing from the boy's father for the duration of his stay, which is now a period of over five years. He has asked me to take steps to verify that the child's welfare will be assured on his return to the United Kingdom. He has also raised a query regarding the fact that the form of authority seeking the child's return is signed only by the father and not the mother.

> Yours faithfully
> Mrs Katherine Hinkler
> British Consulate-General
> [Ottawa]

19 November 1945

PAS. 6674
Despatch No. 281

Dear Sir,

Our representative in Canada, Mrs Hinkler, has been in contact to inform me that she has received a telephone call from Reverend Simmons, the foster parent of your son, Lewis Rodwell. Reverend Simmons has expressed concern that he never had contact from you during the child's stay and seeks reassurance with respect to the child's welfare on his return. He also expressed surprise at the fact that the form of authority for the return passage is signed only by yourself and not by Mrs Rodwell.

I would be grateful for an explanation of these matters so that the same may be conveyed to Reverend Simmons and arrangements for the passage of Lewis may be progressed without delay.

Yours faithfully
Miss E.G. Nicholas
Deputy Director C.O.R.B.

22 November 1945

Dear Miss Nicholas,

I am in receipt of your letter of 19 November 1945 and beg to confirm the fact that I am now the sole guardian of my son, Lewis Rodwell, since his mother was killed in Norwich during the Baedeker raids of April 1942.

I was unable to maintain contact with Lewis during the period of his evacuation as I was serving in Her Majesty's Armed Forces and posted to Africa until an injury during the Tunisian campaign required a lengthy period of hospitalisation. I am now returned to the United Kingdom and to my former occupation of School Master of Mathematics. I most urgently request you to inform your Mrs Hinkler that I am anxious for my son's return, as are his grandparents and his younger sister. I am now waiting word to say he is on board ship en route for this country.

    I remain
    Yours faithfully
    Howard Rodwell C.B.E.

3 December 1945

PAS. 6673
Despatch No. 142
Dear Miss Nicholas,

Thank you for your despatch No. 282 (C.O.R.B. No. PAS. 6674) of 24 November 1945 informing me that you have received satisfactory assurance as to the welfare of Lewis Rodwell on his return to the United Kingdom. I communicated the same to the Reverend Chester A Simmons. However, on 30 November 1945 I received from Reverend Simmons a letter informing me that Lewis Rodwell would much rather remain in Canada and not return to the United Kingdom. The terms in which the letter from Reverend Simmons is written leave no room for doubt on the matter. I understand that Lewis Rodwell has settled well in Canada and is very happy here. He is now seventeen years old and is contemplating joining the Canadian Military Forces when he becomes of age. In these circumstances Reverend Simmons is unwilling to complete the necessary applications to authorise passage.

    Yours faithfully
    Mrs Katherine Hinkler
    British Consulate-General
    [Ottawa]

10 December 1945

PAS. 6674
Despatch 291

Dear Mrs Hinkler,

Thank you for your despatch No. 142 (C.O.R.B. No. PAS. 6674). I have today informed Mr Howard Rodwell of the contents of your letter by telephone. He expressed regret at his son's position but he told me that he intended to respect the boy's wishes and would not pursue the matter further.

    Yours faithfully
    Miss E.G. Nicholas
    Deputy Director C.O.R.B.

Martha draws a long breath. So, Howard Rodwell *was* her grand-father, in title at least. She closes the file and leans back in the chair. A phrase sticks in her head like a tapping woodpecker: *He expressed regret at the position.* Did that, she wonders, come remotely close to covering it? How would she feel if tomorrow Janey announced she was staying in England? And yet that would be a different, lesser, thing altogether, only Janey deciding, as any grown person might, she wanted to live in a different country. Not a statement Janey would never again come home; that she was making a life in which her mother played no part at all. No wonder, Martha thinks unhappily, that Howard Rodwell appears so wretched in the gallery photograph.

And yet – she fingers the cover – there is something strange about Howard's behaviour. Opening the folder again, she leafs through the letters until she reaches the one from *our representative in Canada, Mrs Hinkler,* of 1 December 1945. It appears Howard made no contact with his son at all, even after the death of his own wife. Even if he had been away fighting, and then incapacitated by injury, surely he would have told his son that his mother had been killed, and offered some sympathy, some softness, however bad he was feeling himself? Was this, she muses, why her father always gave the impression he was an orphan? Did he consider himself abandoned; did he *feel* like an orphan? Or was it guilt? Had he come round to thinking that he should, at the very least, have stayed in touch with his father? Now she and Elizabeth would never know. But it might explain the puzzle of why he had decided to come back; perhaps he was hoping to find some kind of closure.

On the way out of the building, from the depths of her purse, her phone pings. A message from Elizabeth.

How r u? Did you get the photos? Anything 2 tell me?

Eagerly, Martha begins to type. She gets as far as, '*Hi, you'll never guess…*' then stops, and after a moment deletes what she's written. It's too complicated to explain by text. She needs to talk to her sister. But there's no urgency. Her discovery has brought her to a dead, disorientating end. And she's not the slightest bit nearer to identifying Catkins; maybe they would have to accept the possibility they would never find out who she was? She remembers the airport, hearing the choke in Elizabeth's voice: *The dates on the Catkins folders. They go back forever. To before Mum died.*

Sitting on one of the benches, Martha stares blindly into the depths of the artificial lake. Sadness close to anger gnaws the edges of her mind. She keeps remembering Howard's jacket, pinned full of medals. Her father, presumably, never knew about them. All that bravery, and Howard never even got to tell his stories to his son – if he had been the kind to tell, that is; he hadn't looked like the type to talk much about himself. She sighs so audibly the other occupants of her bench briefly look up.

How much it seems her father hadn't known about his father. And how much, it turns out, she didn't know about her own.

CHAPTER TWELVE

Norfolk, July 1940

By ten o'clock none of them had got dressed. Sylvie was sitting with Esther, curled under the tartan rug she had fetched for Elsie, and pondering whether the queue at the butchers would be better or worse than usual, if everyone would be out – desperate to talk about the raid – or shut away indoors, wanting to stay where it felt the safest, when it occurred to her she was supposed to be at the WVS and the children at Evelyn's house. For a moment she dithered, and then pulled off the rug.

A slim-fitting skirt and pleated blouse from the previous day were still draped over her bedroom chair. She put them on and sat down at the dressing table to do her face, elbows planted, staring at the giltwood mirror as she penciled her eyebrows and rouged her cheeks. On finishing the job she sat back with satisfaction. Her reflection looked the same as it normally did; from her appearance, at least, nobody would know a kernel of fear, as proximate and stubborn as a trailing coat-tail, kept reigniting the creeping wail of the planes and the explosions of brick. She shook her head, as if to clear the noise from her ears, made a final, decisive scan of the glass and went in search of the children.

Outside, the heat was slinking back. A summer warmth rose from the pavement, the sky a hesitant, wrung-out blue with puffed ridges of cloud banked in the north. Nothing nearby appeared to have been hit but the air was laced with the same smoky charge Sylvie associated with autumn, with Bonfire Night. It didn't seem possible part of the town might be lying in ruins, that it might be necessary to endure the same brutality night after night, and yet, at the same time, she couldn't now imagine going to bed with ordinary fears, the kind that melted away as soon as the sun came up.

They crossed The Close without speaking. Esther trotted at Sylvie's side while Lewis dawdled, stopping occasionally to gaze behind them or peer around corners. Sylvie told him to hurry up – rather sharply, because they were late – before she realised he was checking for bomb damage. She saw his face fall and immediately she wished she had spoken more gently, she forgot, sometimes, how he hated to displease her; she knew she was his rock, the bond between them amplified by Howard's absence, both now and long before the war had ever started. 'It's all right,' she called, 'I'm not cross.' As soon as he was within reach she looped her arm around his shoulders and the three of them walked on as a single unit.

Evelyn opened the door wiping floury hands on a floral apron. Her face was pale, without lipstick or powder, and Sylvie was immediately conscious of her own made-up one. In front of the bedroom mirror she had felt almost defiant, remembering her boast to Connie on the empty beach, the gin and the rub of the sand on the wooden steps, but now she wondered whether it was bad form to bother about her appearance when there was so much else to worry about.

'We're baking,' Evelyn said. 'Daisy and I decided you weren't coming this morning.' As the children wriggled past she ruffled Esther's hair and then turned back to Sylvie. 'Did the bombs wake you up? The worst of it happens before it gets light.' The way she spoke she might have been referring to a barking dog or a tiresome neighbour.

Sylvie nodded. 'We camped under the stairs.' She twitched, recalling the instant when the light went out, the smell of Esther's hair. 'They seemed so close.'

Evelyn shook her head. 'Apparently, the south of the city took the brunt of it, along the river, mostly. And they also hit the bus station.'

'The bus station? How dreadful! I suppose they got lucky then. That's how they'd see it.'

'I don't expect it was a question of luck.' Evelyn sounded matter of fact. 'I should think the station was targeted deliberately.'

'Oh!' Sylvie's chest tightened. 'Somehow that makes it even worse.'

'Does it?' Evelyn said, frowning. 'Why?'

Sylvie remembered Lewis' question when they were huddled in the cupboard. 'It's knowing, I suppose, that somebody planned it,' she said carefully. 'Someone in Germany looked at a map of our city and decided, "That's where we should drop the bombs. There! And there! And there!"' She jabbed at the empty air as she spoke. 'And then that's just what they did.' Her hand fell to her side and she shivered.

'Well, I imagine our boys are doing the same to them.'

'I know,' Sylvie said. 'I know. But still…' The reality of it, that someone was willing to kill her and everyone she knew, was so grotesque it filled her with the same sense of unreality she had felt crossing The Close. Pulling herself together, she leaned forward to peck Evelyn's cheek. 'Thank you for having the children. Tell them I'll be back about teatime.'

It was not far from Evelyn's house to the church hall. The quickest route took her along the eastern edge of The Close, by the Bishop's House, but on impulse she swung left along a beech-lined alley in the direction of the cathedral itself. The size of it always took her by surprise, its silvery grey enormity and the curious way it somehow stayed hidden by trees and much smaller buildings until she was practically in front of it.

To find the imposing west door meant circumventing two sides of the vaulted cloisters. The walkways were deserted; a thousand years of footfall had worn them smooth as butter and the smack of Sylvie's shoes echoed loudly down the passages. From the cloisters she took the gravel path that led to the arch of the main entrance and stopped just outside the porch. The inner door had been left ajar, allowing the closing words of a lesson to float back to her from the greenish depths. It was followed by the rustling of clothes and paper and, after the briefest moment, the rich, summoning chord of an organ.

She leaned against the stone, closing her eyes. The congregation was singing 'Oh God Our Help in Ages Past' and for a minute or two she was able to drift on the swell of the music and think of nothing at all. After the hymn had finished she opened her eyes, blinked at the brightness, and then reluctantly eased herself away from the wall.

When she finally reached the WVS her spirits rose in anticipation of the thrum of warmth and chitchat, but to her surprise the place was deserted and the lights switched off. The only sound was a steady clip and chafe of crockery coming from the kitchen.

She found Marjorie by the sink with her arms in a bowl of water. All around the room the cupboard doors were wide open and the shelves behind them bare; a gleaming stack of cups, saucers and plates spilled over the draining board and, as she watched, Marjorie pulled another plate from the soapsuds, rinsed it under the cold tap and added it to the pile. She didn't seem aware of Sylvie's presence so after a second Sylvie coughed.

'Marjorie! Hello! Where is everyone?'

Marjorie jumped and Sylvie saw her drag the dry part of her wrists over her face before turning around. 'Sylvie! I'd given up on you!'

Sylvie peered at her. She was struck by Marjorie's blotched complexion but wasn't sure what to make of it. 'I'm sorry to be so late. What with the theatre last night, and then the raid this morning' – she made an effort to sound casual about it, like Evelyn had done – 'I completely forgot what day it was.' She looked around at the empty kitchen. 'Where *is* everyone else?' There was a space, like the one it could take the operator to connect a long-distance telephone call, before Marjorie spoke.

'The others have gone over to the streets that were hit last night. They've taken the tea-urn and some of the cups.' She gestured at the empty cupboards with a wet hand. 'I thought I might as well give all the things they didn't take a good wash while I was waiting for them to come back.' There was something odd and strained about her voice and then all at once she let the dishcloth fall into the bowl and took hold of the edge of the sink.

'Marjorie, whatever is the matter? Is it the raid? Have you had bad news?' Sylvie walked forwards and put her arm around Marjorie's shoulders.

'You haven't heard, have you?' Marjorie whispered, and a stab of alarm jabbed Sylvie's stomach.

'Heard what?'

'About… about Elsie.'

'Elsie? What do you mean? What's happened to Elsie?' The sudden notion that Elsie must have had an accident on her way home flashed into Sylvie's mind with such completeness that she felt she knew about it already.

'The raid last night…' Marjorie stopped again.

'What about it?'

'Elsie's house, it took a direct hit.' Marjorie drew a quivering breath. 'They say it was totally destroyed. That Elsie and her sister stood no chance at all.'

Sylvie stood very still. Her head was spinning. For a moment she couldn't be certain what was true and what wasn't. Then she said, slowly, 'But Elsie wasn't there.'

'What do you mean, she wasn't there?'

'Last night, Elsie slept at my house. She only went home this morning. She wasn't there during the raid.'

Marjorie stared at Sylvie and then began to run her hands through her hair as if they had taken on a life of their own. 'What? Oh my goodness, that's wonderful news! Are you quite sure? Did you really see her this morning?'

'Yes,' Sylvie said. 'Of course I'm sure. Elsie didn't leave until after the raid was over.' But her thoughts had already turned somewhere else and a fresh panic began to rise in her throat.

Marjorie grabbed her arm. Her face had darkened again. 'But what about Elsie's sister? She would have been in the house, wouldn't she?'

Sylvie swallowed and nodded, although it wasn't Elsie's sister she was thinking about. 'I have to go,' she said abruptly.

'Now?' Marjorie looked like she might start crying again. 'Where are you going?'

'I have to see Victoria Terrace for myself.'

And before Marjorie could stop her, or say that she wanted to come too, Sylvie spun on her heel and bolted out of the door.

She charged down Tombland, turned into Queen Street and then into London Street, and kept on running. The narrow cut of her skirt forced her to take small, peck-like steps and she longed to rip it off, along with her shoes and stockings, so that she could sprint properly, like a man would do. Crossing the junction at London Street she nearly got hit by a delivery boy on a bicycle; he had to swerve at the last minute to avoid her and called out over the jiggling handlebars, 'Whoa there, Miss. You nearly had us both on the floor.'

Sylvie raised a hand in apology, but didn't stop. It occurred to her how the previous night she had raced through the blackout, her heart and blood pumping almost as badly as they were now. How absurd she had been and how she wished she were living that fright again now, fleeing from some ridiculous, imagined awfulness rather than rushing towards a real one.

By the time she reached Castle Meadow her chest was tight and raw and she had a stitch in her side. She leant with one hand against the window of Hepworths, her thoughts racing around the slip of paper Kennie had pressed into her hand. The address he had given her was 12, Victoria Terrace, she was positive of that. *But just because Elsie's house had been bombed didn't mean that his had been as well.* The road facing Hepworths was busy with a steady stream of cars and buses sweeping around the castle mound. It was soothing, somehow, to see them carrying on just like normal. She tried to calm her breathing and tucked her shirt back into the top of the skirt where it had pulled loose. She would probably find him, shaken and dishevelled, a cigarette hanging out of his mouth and cursing Jerry. She made herself believe it and smiled. She would have to be careful not to show how relieved she was to see him in front of other people. At that second an ambulance weaved past, drowning out the traffic, and the metallic taste of fear stirred in her mouth again.

At the top of Timber Hill she had a better view across the city. Towards the southwest she could see the tops of smoke pyramids rising into the sky, although the ground wasn't high enough to tell where they were coming from. Outside a church a man in a warden's uniform was resting by the wall, one knee bent, his foot against the flint. A helmet was lodged under his arm and he was rolling a cigarette. A woman just ahead of Sylvie stopped beside him and Sylvie heard her ask if he knew what the damage was like around Victoria Station. That was where the goods trains came in and out, and Sylvie guessed Victoria Terrace ran close by. But she didn't wait to listen to the man's answer, she could guess well enough what it would be by the flat stamp of exhaustion on his face and the way his hands were shaking as he held the cigarette paper to his lips.

When she rounded the corner the sight of the bus depot brought her up short. A charred and twisted double-decker blocked the entrance as if it had been caught trying to escape. The roof and two of its wheels had been blown off, the sides were bent and buckled like twisted strips of plasticine and glass from the windows lay scattered over the road. The buildings behind the bus, the ticket office and the rain shelters, had collapsed inwards; the furnace that must have engulfed them had left the remains ruptured and black, and a stretch of tarpaulin had been laid over the place where the timetables used to be pinned on a brass-framed notice board. Surely, nobody would have been there, thought Sylvie, at that time? She averted her gaze, but her head buzzed uncontrollably with the notion that they might have been.

As she approached the goods station, the air became noticeably denser. Fumes from the trains were thick with burning from somewhere beyond the platforms. Victoria Terrace was reeling her in, and the closer she got, the stronger the pull of it.

It was the smell of fried onions that drew her attention first. It took a moment to place it and then she saw a table with tea-urns and familiar-looking blue cups and saucers. A woman with her hair in a spotted scarf was cooking sausages on a camping stove and another was passing tea to a group of men who had formed a ramshackle line. Their clothes and faces were veiled with dust and most sucked silently at cigarettes while they waited their turn, axes and shovels left in a pile at one side. The woman handing out the tea lifted her head and Sylvie realised it was Rosemary. She raised her hand, ready to call out, when she saw the slump of bricks flooding the pavement on the far side of the table. It was, or had once been, the corner wall of the next left turning. As Sylvie walked towards it her feet seemed to disconnect from the ground. The earlier hot, sticky feeling had gone and instead a heavy coldness was seeping through her legs, as if she was wading into a mountain lake.

She reached the bricks and looked down the length of road beside them. The sign on the last piece of wall told her what she already knew: Victoria Terrace. On one side of it, the roofs sagged in the middle like an over-loaded washing line, the windows gaped black and ugly and the chimneys leaned at crazy angles as if put that way for a joke. But the other side was worse. There were holes where there should have been homes; scorched, yawning gaps in which rubble and timber lay beneath wigwams of girders and beams. She could pick out items of furniture: a brass bed-head, table legs, the floral pattern of something that might have been curtains or a chair-cover; and smaller, more intimate pieces: a gramophone, a china doll, shoes, a hairbrush with a comb stuck in the middle of it. There was heat too, rising from the burned and broken things, the smell of cordite and the sear-marks of recent flames. Demolition workers were standing on the wreckage, swinging picks at fragments of wall and ceiling and in the middle of the street an oily lake was spreading where water seeped from a shattered pipe.

Sylvie's mouth filled with bile. She clapped a hand over her lips, but she could taste it, thin and bitter, oozing through her fingers. She became aware of footsteps, a shadowing in the corner of her eye, and then an arm about her waist. A man's voice, kind and steady said, 'Here, Miss, I think you should sit down.' He pressed a handkerchief into her palm and steered her towards an upturned crate. Sylvie pointed at the closest cavity. Tendrils of smoke still trailed above it.

'Which number was that?' she asked. As she looked into his face she realised he wasn't a man at all, but a boy – sixteen or so – his clothes and face spattered with grime.

'That was number 4, Miss,' he said.

Elsie's house. Thank heavens Elsie had spent the night in Sylvie's armchair, but Elsie's sister hadn't. Sylvie closed her eyes. Keeping them shut, she asked, 'Was anyone killed?' As if a building might be razed to the ground and the occupants walk away without a scratch.

Sylvie heard his pause, the sound of picks and sifting stones in the distance, and then he said, 'There wasn't a warning, Miss. Them ones that were hit, they didn't stand a chance.'

Sylvie felt his words lodge in her stomach. After a moment she opened her eyes and made herself count the numbers up the street. *Please God, let his house be standing.* If it was, then he was probably alive. Yet she couldn't focus, her thoughts rolled around like marbles loose inside her head and all the debris and destruction made it impossible to be certain where one home had ended and another had begun. She turned in desperation to the boy beside her and tugged at his jacket.

'The other houses that were hit, do you know their numbers?'

The boy shifted his feet and his gaze flicked between Sylvie's face and a point over her left shoulder.

'I'm not certain, Miss. I'd rather not say, in case—'

Sylvie interrupted him. 'I need to know, you see. I need to find out about someone in particular, and I don't know who else to ask.'

She waited for a long, long time before the boy cleared this throat. 'I think it was numbers 6 and 12, Miss, and maybe…' but his voice dwindled as Sylvie doubled over, her arms across her middle, the agony as hot and fierce as childbirth. A surge of vomit bulged on her tongue and she spat it onto the ground beside her. The edge of the brown-specked pool had caught the hem of her skirt and she stared at it blankly. I don't care anymore, she thought, what anyone thinks. Wanting to scream, she opened her mouth but the sound wouldn't come, and then she heard herself begin to moan, a low wailing cry that rose and fell as she rocked back and forth.

Sometime later she became aware of brown shoes in the dust beside her own. Her gaze travelled upwards again and she realised with surprise the boy was still there. He looked worried. Under the dirt he was handsome with nice, even features and sandy hair. Somebody's sweetheart.

'How old are you?'

'Fifteen, Miss.' He was obviously surprised at the question.

'It might be over then. Before you're old enough to fight.' She must sound, she realised, incredibly old.

The boy gave a half-smile. 'Let's hope so, Miss.' And then, 'Shall I get you a cup of tea?' He pointed towards the table where Rosemary and the woman in the spotted scarf were still busy serving. Sylvie nodded, although she didn't care about the tea one way or the other, she felt spent, as if she had poured all there was of her onto the earth surrounding the packing crate. Just as he turned, an urgent thought occurred.

'I say,' she said, 'Please don't tell…' but he was already hurrying across the uneven ground towards the table. She watched him queue patiently with the other men and, when it was his turn to take a mug, hesitate before stirring a rounded spoonful of sugar into it. He took a careful step towards her again, holding the cup with a child's concentration, but then, at the last moment, seemed to think better of it, doubled back and said something to Rosemary who was pouring tea for the next man in line.

To Sylvie's horror Rosemary turned her head towards the packing crate. Sylvie shifted position so her back and shoulders faced the table, and dropped her head. If Rosemary saw her she was bound to come straight over and ask what was wrong. For a giddy moment Sylvie considered actually telling her. She could envisage the shock – that lovely face contorted with the effort of concealing her distaste – but she couldn't imagine what might possibly happen after that.

Putting her hand on the packing crate, she stood up, staggered a little with the newness of the sensation, and then gathered herself and moved stiffly away.

She walked without purpose or direction, her legs numb and mechanical. She felt neither hot nor cold, but hollow like an outline of a person. She would never see him again; wherever she went, whatever she did, that truth would haunt her every second. She had missed him in the past, a constant, toothache kind of hurt with sudden, unexpected darts of pain, but at least she had been able to look up at the sun, or the moon, or the trees, or the sky, and think that Kennie was breathing the very same air, and it had been a comfort, the notion he was there and somehow they were joined together if only by the fact of being human and alive.

She found that she had nearly reached the market square and halted, uncertain what to do next. Dimly she wondered if she ought to fetch Lewis and Esther from Evelyn's house, or go to the butchers and try to buy something for dinner, but the darkness in her head made the energy required for even ordinary things remote and unattainable.

Across the street there was a cafe. Red-and-white checked oilcloths and polished brown chairs were visible through the steamed-up windows. She would sit and have a cup of tea after all. Perhaps she would ask someone for a cigarette; she hadn't smoked for years, now all at once she longed to hold one in her fingers and feel the rough crawl of nicotine in her lungs.

Her hand was already on the door handle when a tap on the glass made her stop. She peered inside, but the table by the window was occupied by two young women in gloves and hats who didn't appear the least bit interested in Sylvie. The rapping came again, sharper this time. She glanced about the street and then, in the next-door shopfront, she spied a familiar pair of lace-up shoes and stockinged legs.

Elsie was sitting on a fold-out chair, a large paper bag on her lap and another one at her feet. She smiled at Sylvie, a wide smile of delighted relief, and Sylvie saw how grubby and tired she looked. Patches of dust spattered her face and a long streak of dirt ran the length of her sleeve. A bandage was wrapped around her wrist, the white of it conspicuous against the grime. She beckoned to Sylvie, mouthing words that Sylvie couldn't hear but could only have been, 'Come in,' or something very much like it.

The room was jam-packed. There was a line of chairs next to the window, but most people were swarming in front of a large wooden desk, waiting to speak to the girl behind it who was holding a telephone receiver away from her ear and asking in a harassed voice if everyone wouldn't please mind forming a queue. On the wall above the desk there was a poster of two efficient-looking Air Raid Wardens on a bright yellow background bearing the words BOMBED OUT? IF YOU HAVE NO FRIENDS TO GO TO, ASK A POLICEMAN OR YOUR WARDEN WHERE TO FIND YOUR NEAREST REST CENTRE. Another one simply said BLACK OUT MEANS BLACK!

Sylvie edged her way towards the row of chairs. Elsie was sandwiched between a woman with a baby on her lap and an elderly man who was sleeping with his chin on his chest and folded arms. The woman was bouncing the baby continuously on her knee, saying,

'There, there; there, there,' although the baby was laughing and dribbling and seemed to be the least upset of everyone.

Sylvie squatted in front of Elsie, bottom on her heels. Elsie's eyes pooled as she seized Sylvie's hand, and Sylvie could see her making an effort not to blink.

'I'm so sorry,' Sylvie said, 'about your sister.'

Elsie's grasp tightened. 'There was nothing I could have done. Nothing at all. If I'd been there, I wouldn't have saved her, it would have been the two of us instead.' The way she spoke sounded like a recitation of somebody else's words; somebody who had been there when Elsie had encountered the devastation and realised what had happened. Sylvie thought of the sandy-haired boy and wondered if it had been him. She imagined him steering Elsie to a crate and fetching her tea, just as he had for her. She ought to have said goodbye to him.

She squeezed Elsie's fingers. 'Of course you couldn't have done anything. Nobody could have done. There wasn't any warning.'

'It's gone, you know. Completely gone.' Elsie plucked at the paper on her lap. 'I found some of my things under the rubble. I wanted to keep on searching but they wouldn't let me. They said it was too dangerous. They thought another wall might fall.' Her features trembled. 'But I shall have to go back and look again. It's all I've got.'

'Is that a photograph?' Sylvie motioned at the top of an oval frame poking from the bag. 'May I see?' Gently, she pulled it out, holding the edge so it was visible to both of them. Two little girls in white ruffle dresses were perched on a couch between a woman in a high-necked black gown and a man with a styled moustache. The glass was cracked but otherwise still intact.

'I can remember that picture being taken. Mother was fussing because I'd tripped and torn my skirt just before the photographer arrived.' Sylvie brought the image closer and saw how Elsie's skirt had been folded over and tucked under her legs.

She slid the frame back into the bag. 'I think you should come home with me, Elsie.'

Elsie shook her head. 'I couldn't put you to that trouble. I'm sure they'll manage to sort something out for me here.'

They both glanced at the queue that had formed. The line wound back on itself several times and didn't appear to be moving.

'Stay with me, for tonight at least. Otherwise I think you could be waiting an awfully long time.' As if objecting to Sylvie's words, the baby on the woman's lap leaned forward and clamped his fist around a lock of Sylvie's hair. Her thighs ached from the awkwardness of her position and she was desperate, suddenly, to be anywhere but there. She extracted her hair from the baby's clutch and put her hand on Elsie's arm. 'Come on. You need a bath and a hot meal.' She struggled to her feet and picked up the bag on the floor.

They crossed the city side-by-side. It seemed astonishing that she was functioning – breathing, talking, putting one foot in front of the other – in a world without Kennie. And soon, she thought wretchedly, she was bound to lose Lewis too. Nobody would listen to her now; after the raid everyone would say that any woman in her right mind would fight to get a child on board one of those ships. She looked at Elsie glad, suddenly, of the company. Elsie took her arm and the contact reminded her of Connie, the hot beach and the triumph of the returned ring. *I'll find a solution somehow*, she told herself, *a way to bring him home again after the war.*

CHAPTER THIRTEEN

Norfolk, recently

Martha has parked on the edge of a field to call Elizabeth while enjoying the sunset. She has finally hired a car. The white Ford Fiesta is not fitted with satnav and, after some consideration, she has not bought a map either. Maps, she reasoned, require a person – a capable, patient, humorous person, preferably with map-reading skills – sitting in the passenger seat. The only other occupants of Martha's car are her travel rucksack, a bottle of water and a tin of boiled sweets purchased from a garage that envelopes her in a cloud of icing sugar every time she manages to prise off the lid. Sometimes a particular destination catches her fancy – Little Snoring, Great Walsingham, North Creake – but on each occasion she tries to locate one of these appealing names the signposts inevitably disappear, or lead her somewhere entirely different.

The places she does find invariably contain flint cottages, converted barns, and churches big enough to house the entire village; and between them, swathes of open countryside. Martha can be focused on the tightness of a twisting road, tucked into a hedge to coax an oncoming caravan through an impossible gap, and a second later a bolt of brilliant yellow will appear in the windscreen and she will be gazing over meadows and canola fields. Even on the coast road the sea is rarely visible across the deep buffer of salt marsh and shingle but the mineral edge to the air is like the steady breath of the distant ocean. All the trips finish at Wells on the veranda of the beach hut, Martha's legs propped on the balustrade while she squints into the ripe afternoon sun. Frequently she finds herself glancing at Henry's hut, but it remains empty and shuttered.

He collected his phone the day after they met on the train, but appeared to be on edge throughout the entire, frustratingly short encounter. Having readily accepted Martha's offer of a drink in the hotel bar he stood up before it was finished and tipped his head apologetically. 'I really have to go. It's my mother, she's not very well and I can't leave her on her own for very long at all.'

'Well, of course…'

'You see the person who normally helps me has been called away and—'

'I quite understand.' Martha kept smiling, although her insides seemed to be collapsing like a badly erected tent.

Henry was almost out of the room before he rushed forward and kissed her cheek. 'I'll be in touch,' he said. 'As soon as I've sorted things out at home.' After he had gone Martha stood for at least a minute watching the empty doorway, her hand raised to the transitory imprint of his lips.

That was nearly a week ago and she still hasn't heard any more from him. She tells herself it hasn't been long, but she can't help wonder if perhaps the real reason that Henry hasn't contacted her is something to do with Helen, the mystery sender of the text she spotted on his dying phone.

'It sounds quaint,' Elizabeth says, when the call finally connects and Martha attempts to describe the vista of the setting sun igniting the upturned bowl of sky. She has climbed out of the car to absorb the full impact of the orange flames, and is leaning back against the still-warm hood.

'Not quaint, exactly.'

'Hmm. Sorry, what did you say?'

'I said it isn't really quaint. It's too' – Martha pauses – 'elemental.'

There's no response. Martha can hear her sister's fingers on a keyboard, the pace of them has slowed but not stopped completely. She hasn't yet shared with Elizabeth her discovery of Howard, his existence and his rejection by their father, but listening to the gentle, Morse-like tapping, she wonders whether it would be better to wait until she gets home, when she will be able to speak with Elizabeth face to face. Assuming, that is, a slot can be found between her sister's back-to-back appointments.

'Monumental?' Elizabeth says, finally.

'No! *Elemental*. Like... Oh never mind. Look, I'll call again later.'

'Wait!' The pitter-patter stops. 'Tell me,' Elizabeth says, 'what have you discovered?'

Martha finds herself spilling out everything, from the photograph in the gallery to the letter in the National Archives seeking their father's return.

'I suppose,' Elizabeth says slowly, when Martha comes to a halt, 'that's why he never talked to us about it. He didn't want us to judge him for it, for not going back to England I mean.'

'I guess.' Martha doesn't add that she's having a hard time not judging him for it now.

'And it explains why he found it so hard to write the first part of his book.'

'I guess,' Martha says again.

'And Catkins? Have you found...'

'No. Nothing. Not yet.'

Both of them are quiet. Martha knows she and Elizabeth are looking at same thing, a photograph of woman on a beach kept secret for more than fifty years.

After a while, Elizabeth says, as if to change the subject, 'What about Janey?'

'What do you mean?' Martha says, although she knows full well what Elizabeth means.

'Have you spoken to her yet?'

'Of course I've spoken to her.'

'But does she know you're in England?'

Martha watches the light begin to dwindle below the lifting horizon. 'Not exactly.'

'Not exactly?'

'I haven't told her yet. But I will' – Martha counts silently – 'in five days' time.'

'*Five days' time?* What's stopping you from telling her now?'

This is a good question. So good, in fact, that when Martha tries to explain her thinking to Elizabeth she can't understand why she imposed such a rigid plan on herself in the first place.

When Martha returns to her hotel room she immediately calls Janey. Her heart soars when Janey picks up, but the relief is short-lived. Their entire dialogue lasts less than two minutes in the course of which Martha establishes that while Janey is far too busy to speak to her mother she is – apparently – just fine.

The following day Martha jogs down the now familiar tartan staircase jangling her car keys. At the bottom she finds Pip enticing Gretchen into a wheelchair. Martha draws to a halt. 'Oh dear,' she says. 'What happened?'

Pip's jawline is rigid and battle-weary. 'Mum keeps trying to do too much when I'm not in the room. Yesterday morning she tripped and her ankle had to be reset. The doctor says she must keep her weight off it, but she can't help getting rather impatient.' Pip's voice rises unsteadily towards the end of the sentence. She pauses and inhales. 'Anyhow, Mum is spending another Saturday here. I *have* to go to work because I spent *all* of yesterday up at the hospital. Now then mother,' – as Pip directs her voice towards the wheelchair it becomes noticeably clipped – 'just sit quietly and read a book or something. Promise me you won't bother Martha to play Monopoly with you. Or anyone else for that matter.'

Gretchen is glaring at the cream-green walls, lips pursed. As tactfully as possible, Martha says, 'I wouldn't have minded a game, but you see I won't be here. I was just about to go for a drive.' She sees Gretchen's chin sink ever so slightly. After a respectful pause Martha edges around the back of the wheelchair. She gets two paces through the front door before she turns around. 'I have an idea,' she says, making sure to address Gretchen rather than Pip. 'Maybe you'd like to come with me? For a ride out, I mean.'

'That's very kind of you,' Pip begins, 'but I don't think—'

'I would like that, Epiphany.' Gretchen's spine stiffens and she gives her daughter an imperious stare. 'I would like it very much.'

A short while later, Gretchen's chair has been stashed in the trunk and Gretchen herself in the passenger seat of the Fiesta. They haven't been driving for many minutes before Gretchen starts to hum, quietly at first but before long loudly enough for Martha to pick out snatches of showtime musicals. Her thoughts roam to her father, his prized collection of Broadway soundtracks and Verdi operas – the sight of him easing the records from their psychedelic sleeves, the crackled thump of needle on vinyl, but oddly, she feels fine about it; listening to Gretchen, driving alongside fields, the windscreen full of sky.

When they return to Wells it's not yet three o'clock. At the last minute Martha directs the car away from the hotel and towards the area of town where she stumbled on the gallery. She parks beneath a cherry tree and cuts the ignition.

Gretchen stops singing. 'Where are we going?'

'It's a surprise,' Martha says. Her voice is deliberately upbeat but Gretchen eyes her suspiciously. Martha retrieves the wheelchair from the trunk and helps Gretchen into the chair. Underfoot, the carpet of fallen blossom is oyster white and skin-soft. Martha leans forward and murmurs. 'Do you know where we are?'

Gretchen shakes her head, but as they approach the gallery she flings out her arm. 'This is where my father's theatre used to be!'

'That's right.' Martha halts the chair besides the wheelchair ramp. 'I thought you might like to see it.' When Gretchen doesn't respond Martha is struck with misgivings. *Suppose this is a bad idea? Suppose it upsets Gretchen to see the theatre again?* For a while they stand in silence, Martha feeling more anxious by the second. There's no sign of the previous crowds or the student with the pierced lip; Martha presumes the exhibition has been on for a while and has lost its allure. Just as retreat is seeming inevitable, Gretchen reaches for the chrome sign. Her fingers trace the groove of each letter individually, as if she's reading braille. 'Old Theatre Gallery,' she says out loud, and a tawny flame lights her eyes.

'When were you last here?' Martha asks cautiously.

'1975.'

'1975!' – Martha does the math – 'That's over forty years ago!'

'It's when my father sold the theatre. A new one had opened on the quay and he decided to call it a day. He was older then than I am now and I think he'd had enough.' More quietly she adds, 'It wasn't his first career, you know.'

'Really?'

'He was an actor when he was young. He used to be quite famous but he gave it all up after I was born and we moved here when the war finished.'

'Why did he do that?'

'Well' – Gretchen's voice drops still further – 'reading between the lines, I think he may have had an affair. My mother always used to say how glad she was he had stopped acting. Less temptation, you see. But I never did find out how he came to know of Wells.'

A voice at Martha's shoulder – pleasant, polite, but slightly impatient – interrupts them. 'Excuse me. Are you going into the exhibition or not? Only I can't quite get my pushchair past...' A woman gestures at a stroller where a flaxen-haired toddler is sleeping with his thumb hooked in his mouth.

'Do you want to go inside?' Martha asks Gretchen. By way of answer, Gretchen takes hold of the wheels and begins to propel herself up the ramp.

Only a handful of vacationers are meandering around the exhibition, pausing dutifully in front of each picture before hurrying onto the next. A man in a floppy sun hat is eating an ice cream, apparently oblivious to the NO FOOD OR DRINK sign in the doorway or the trail of sugary drips following behind him.

Naturally, Gretchen doesn't show the slightest interest in the paintings. Martha watches as she manoeuvres herself around the edge of the room, halting every so often to run her hand over the brickwork or stare fixedly at the back wall, where Martha assumes the stage used to be. She tries to picture what Gretchen is seeing – or hearing perhaps – the audience, the applause, the buttercup lighting, the director striding about with a script in his hand. She has no idea, of course, whether her imaginings come even close; that's the trouble with trying to picture the past, you might want to reconstruct it, you might think you're pretty close, but actually you never have the slightest idea what it was like to really live it.

After a while Gretchen stops in front of Howard's photograph. A few minutes later she's still there. Martha wanders over and stands beside her chair.

'I remember when he came to open the theatre,' Gretchen says without turning round.

Martha blinks. 'Do you?'

'I was five years old. He was wearing those medals and I asked if I could look at them.'

'Really?' Martha steps forwards so she can view Gretchen's face. 'What did he say?'

'He crouched down to let me see them. Although I wasn't allowed to touch.'

'Is that what he said?'

'That's what *my mother* said. She told me my fingers were too dirty and I'd put marks all over the metal. Mr Rodwell offered to clean my fingers with his handkerchief but my mother said she didn't want his nice white handkerchief to be spoiled either. After he cut a ribbon I had to present him with a bottle of whisky. I asked him if he liked whisky because whenever my father drank it I thought it smelled horrible. He laughed and said most men liked whisky and he liked his best with a little bit of ginger ale.' Gretchen takes a suck of air. It's the longest speech Martha has heard her make.

'Do you remember anything else about him?'

'When I was quite a lot older I remember his daughter came to teach at my school.'

'His daughter…?' The wording of Howard's letter in the National Archives acquires a sudden resonance: '*I am now anxious for my son's return, as are his grandparents and his younger sister.*' Why hasn't she picked up on the significance of this before? Perhaps, subconsciously, she dismissed the chances of the sister – her *aunt* – being traceable. But thinking about it now, isn't it more likely that as the only remaining child she would have kept living somewhere close to her widowed father?

With a rush of excitement, Martha turns to Gretchen. 'Do you remember her name?'

'Why we called her Miss Rodwell, until she got married…'

'Were you ever told her first name? Could it have been… Was it…' – a wild, sideways flash of hope – 'Catherine? Or just Cat. Catkins, even?' Martha can tell her tone has an unsettling urgency.

'Well, I don't know. I don't think so. No, not Catherine. I'm sure it wasn't Catherine…' Gretchen begins to pick at the padding on the arm of the wheelchair.

Martha's excitement ebbs, just a little. 'What about her married name?'

Gretchen gapes at Martha with unhappy eyes. Her lips move silently as if she's trying out different shapes of air. Eventually she says, 'It might have been Peel. Or Beale. Something like that. It was so long ago.' She adds tremulously, 'I only remembered Rodwell because the name is written on the plaque.'

'That's okay,' Martha says. Disappointment is threatening to reveal itself on her face. With an effort she rearranges her expression. 'It doesn't matter.'

'Can we go now?' Gretchen is examining her closely.

'Of course.' They exit the gallery without speaking. As they pass through the fallen cherry blossom, one last question occurs to her. 'I don't suppose you know,' she says, her voice moth-light, 'whether or not Miss Rodwell was married locally?'

'Yes,' Gretchen says. 'She was married right here in Wells. A group of us from school went to see them come out of the church after the service. We all cheered and she gave us a wave.' After a moment, she adds uncertainly. 'Is that what you needed to know?'

Martha beams as she opens the passenger door. 'Yes,' she says. 'That's just what I needed to know.'

*

The clergyman isn't the proper one, only vacation cover for Reverend Hopkins. He tells Martha this immediately as she approaches him after the Sunday service. He seems anxious to clarify his position from the outset, as if some sixth sense has warned him that she's about to pose a difficult question. He is disconcertingly young, with unruly ginger hair and wire-framed glasses, and when she voices her request to view the marriage register his eyes cloud unhappily. Eventually he says, 'I thought that sort of thing was available online nowadays?'

'Not these records,' Martha says; she has checked already. 'I'm interested in the marriage entries during the 1950s and the information online stops in about 1940.'

'Well I don't know if the registers kept here will go back to 1950.' The vicar runs a hand through his hair, which makes him seem younger than ever. 'The ones you need might be stored at County Hall.'

'But could I look?' Martha persists. 'It won't take long,' she adds. 'And you could stay with me while I do it. If you're worried I might damage them.'

The vicar shuffles his feet and pushes his glasses up his nose in a pantomime of indecision. 'I ought to speak to Reverend Hopkins about it first.'

'That's okay.' Martha plops down on the nearest pew. 'I can wait.'

'He's in a boat, somewhere off the west coast of Scotland. The chances are he won't answer his phone. It might be better to come back another day.'

'But could you try?' Martha smiles. 'Please.' She folds her hands in her lap.

The vicar regards her for a moment and then his shoulders sag. 'I'll be as quick as I can—'

'Thank you…'

'…but I'm not promising anything.'

Before long, the clunk of a latch reverberates off the walls and the young vicar comes scurrying over the flagstones.

'Does it ever fill up?' Martha gestures at the rows of pews.

'Only at Christmas, I think.' He stops a pace or two in front of her. 'I've brought the key to the safe. I couldn't get hold of Reverend Hopkins, but I don't suppose he would object to letting you see the marriage registers.' Fresh doubt creases his face. 'I'll go and get them.' He hurries away, as if nervous of changing his mind. A few minutes later he returns bearing two enormous, leather-bound books. 'These are the only registers we have,' he says. 'You can look at them in the vestry.'

Martha follows him into a small, plain room on the left of the chancel. Just inside the door she nearly trips over an electric fire. It's switched off, presumably because the nip in the air is nothing compared to the winter temperatures. A rail of black cassocks and other priestly garments occupies most of the space but there's also a table with an electric kettle, a jar of Nescafé, a solitary mug holding a solitary teaspoon, and an open packet of Ginger Nuts.

Using his elbow, the vicar pushes the coffee things to one side and carefully lowers the books. The first one is quite modern looking and still has a thick inch of clean pages. The second register is plainly older. Its leather binding has faded unevenly and the gold lettering on the front is cracked and splintered. For a moment they both look at it, the vicar's hands resting lightly on its cover.

'May I?' Martha edges forward. She's desperate to turn the pages. Reluctantly, it seems, the vicar removes his hands and steps towards the door.

'If you want me, I'll be sorting out the toys in the children's corner.'

Martha spied the cluster of small red chairs and the box of teddies and books on her way in. 'I'll be careful,' she says, 'I promise.'

The marriage entries are inked onto wide sheets of creamy vellum that buckle under their own weight and are infused with a grass-like, vanilla scent. Running her finger through the long list of weddings, Martha can't help but wonder what became of all these couples, whether their lives turned out happily or not. It feels like being shown the first line of a book, '*Once upon a time there lived a man and a woman who fell in love and got married…*' and then having no clue what happened after that. Somewhere in Halifax is the record of her marriage to Clem. Like these entries, it contains only their names and addresses and the date of the happy day. It doesn't mention the lace wedding dress she bought from a small ad in the paper, or the riotous bunch of wild flowers that covered her pregnant bump. And nobody who happened across the listing now would guess the relationship imploded only three years later, and that for the last eight years Clem has lived with his yoga-trendy second wife and squeaky clean blonde sons.

With a sigh, Martha begins her search for a Rodwell wedding. The old-fashioned names are lovely, all the flowers: Daisy, Rose, Violet and Iris; and their beaux, the Johns and the Billies, the Franks and the Walters, all sporting waistcoats, slicked-back hair and scarlet carnations with foil-wrapped stems. In her absorption, Martha forgets the cold.

She finds the entry on the sixth page; the curly flourish of a feminine hand infusing the capital *R* with definite artistry. Martha puts her finger on the paper, as if her eyes alone can't be trusted. But there it is. Esther Rodwell married Aiden O'Neil on 20 July 1954. And Esther must be Lewis' sister because the neat, compact signature of Howard Rodwell occupies the column labelled *Father of the Bride*. It occurs to Martha that her own father would not even have been aware the marriage was taking place, let alone sent the couple a gift or greeting. She pushes that unwelcome thought aside. Now, at least, she has a name. If Esther O'Neil is still alive it ought to be easy to find her. The question is, does she want to?

She closes the cover and carries both registers to the end of the church. They are heavier and dustier than she expected. She discovers the vicar kneeling behind the last pew, although on this occasion busily separating blocks of Lego.

'Did you find what you were looking for?' he asks, struggling to his feet.

'Yes,' Martha says. 'Thank you.' She holds out the books and the vicar embraces them with the air of somebody retrieving a baby from a particularly flighty relative.

'Perhaps I'll see you again next Sunday?' he says, rather pointedly.

'Sunday? Oh…' – for the first time since she arrived at the church Martha experiences a sensation of warmth – 'I… Well, you never know.'

On her way back, Martha reflects on the many good reasons *not* to locate Esther. First, there could still be resentment, even anger, at the fact her brother never came home, and then possibly grief when she discovers he's dead and now she will certainly never see him again. More realistically, perhaps, Esther will probably not be the slightest bit interested to meet the daughter of her long-forgotten brother; a relation in name, in blood, but not in heart or soul. And since what Martha wants most of all is to identify the mysterious Catkins, and there's nothing to indicate Esther can help with that, is there any real point in tracking Esther down? To top it all, she's blithely assuming that Esther is still alive…

Nevertheless. As she walks, Martha rubs at the imprint of dust the marriage registers left on her jeans, but it sticks stubbornly to the denim. Surely, she cannot *not* try to trace Esther? How can she open a door and not step through it? Why else, for heaven's sake, did she go to the church?

Before going up to her room she stops by reception to ask if they keep a copy of the White Pages. The receptionist meets her request with a bemused stare. 'The White Pages,' Martha repeats. 'For addresses and telephone numbers.'

The girl's perplexity intensifies. It's the brunette again, now with silver, rather than green, nails. 'Why don't you look online?' she says. 'Just google BT phone lists.'

'Right,' Martha says. 'Of course.' She feels a little ridiculous. Somehow her visit to the church with its stained glass and scented vellum has managed to throw her back twenty years, to a world where information was a physical thing.

'Look here,' the girl says, 'if you like, I'll do it on my computer.' She clearly believes Martha is a dinosaur.

'It's okay, I can…'

Silver bullets dart over the keyboard. 'What's the name?'

'O'Neil, but I can…'

'And the place?'

The chances that Esther stayed in Wells after her marriage are good, surely? 'Here. Wells-next-the-sea, but I…'

A tiny pause. Then, 'So, there are two entries. Do you know the initial?'

It's like being the passenger in a too-fast car. 'A, I think,' Martha supplies weakly, 'or possibly E.'

'I have a Mrs E O'Neil at 3, Boatman's Lane. And there's also a telephone number.'

Slow down, Martha wants to say. *Slow down!*

With a flourish of accomplishment the girl swivels the console around to face Martha and picks up a yellow pad. 'Shall I write it down for you?'

Back in her room, Martha sits on the bed holding the yellow Post-it note and fanning herself with the room-service menu. The weather seems to be shifting very quickly from early-summer fine to Riviera hot and the bedroom is stifling. She knows she will never bring herself to call Esther's number. How would she start a conversation like that over the telephone? And she doesn't need a memo to remember the address, Boatman's Lane sounds like it belongs in a nursery rhyme. Still, Martha can't take her eyes from the scrawl of information, even as the writing blurs in the grip of her stare. Eventually she gets to her feet, brushes her hair, applies some lipstick and fetches sunglasses. Ten minutes later she's setting off yet again from the hotel.

Google Maps routes her along a road that links the highway with the seafront. She turns uphill away from the coast, passing the churchyard, and then a school – the playground empty, the buildings slumbering. Soon after that she reaches a short cul-de-sac of terraced cottages. Why it was named Boatman's Lane is anyone's guess, since the only remaining hint of a harbour is the telltale lingering tang in the air. Before the doubt gnawing her insides can send her scurrying back down the hill she rings the bell of the third cottage. The clarity of it, reverberating through the rooms inside, blasts all of her tentative introductions and explanations to the four winds. She's still scrabbling to construct an appropriate sentence as footsteps approach and the door opens.

As it happens, her lack of planning makes no difference at all. There is no appropriate sentence, no natural place to start; she was always doomed to stand there slack-jawed and speechless, because the person before her, filling the whole of the entrance with his weather-beaten frame, is Henry.

CHAPTER FOURTEEN

London, August 1940

At Liverpool Street station they boarded a double-decker bus. After Norfolk, the air seemed stifling, a muggy soup of fumes and perspiration, and as they got out at Oxford Circus Sylvie's flesh peeled from the seat like a sticking plaster. She wanted to go the rest of the way on foot, thinking the shops might be a distraction for them both, but it turned out the best ones were boarded up, or criss-crossed with strips of brown paper, and she could only squint at the displays of jewellery and handbags through the gaps.

Lewis had never been to London before. Sylvie offered to take him to Hamleys but he shook his head in such a definitive way it suggested he had grown out of toys altogether. The further they progressed along Oxford Street the more he became lost in his own thoughts. He barely responded to Sylvie's questions, his gaze continuously snagged by the groups of men in military uniform they encountered every hundred yards or so. A lot of the soldiers were clad in tunics and breeches with slouch hats that were almost cowboy in style. They dropped their voices as she and Lewis passed but Sylvie was still able to catch the drawl and twang in their accents, aware of their eyes on the back of her skirt.

'Where are they from?' Lewis asked. One of the men overheard him and replied before Sylvie could, 'Australia, sonny. Ten thousand miles in *that* direction.' He jerked a thumb vertically down at the pavement and then, with an extravagant swoop, tipped his hat at Sylvie.

At Marble Arch they turned left beside the green of Hyde Park. In the distance a line of steam shovels were just visible, biting out lumps of earth, while closer by a man was standing on a platform addressing a handful of spectators. He was shouting and waving his arms, and whenever he paused the gap was filled by a smattering of cheers and clapping. For a moment they stopped to listen, and Sylvie heard, 'War won't stop until men refuse to fight! What are *you* going to do about it?' before she hurried Lewis onwards.

The brickwork of the Grosvenor House Hotel was so concealed by the vast number of sandbags stacked against its walls they nearly walked straight past. There must be hundreds of them wondered Sylvie and then, gazing at the towering piles of hessian sacks, she realised even that estimate was woefully inadequate. She was about to step inside when she saw Lewis hanging back. 'Lewis, come on!' she gestured impatiently, but he didn't move. After a second he lifted his chin.

'Why do I have to be evacuated? I want to stay with you and Esther.' His hands were balled into fists at his side. 'Why can't you tell Daddy I don't want to go?'

For a moment Sylvie was too stunned to speak. 'Daddy is away fighting,' she said at last. 'And we have to do what he thinks is best.' Her voice was low and sounded, she thought, surprisingly firm. Then she added, her tone slightly different and laced with possibility, 'At least for now.'

Reluctantly, Lewis inched forwards. Sylvie kissed him on the top of his head before she manoeuvred him into the revolving door, squashing behind him in the same compartment, and they shuffled into the atrium.

Inside there was an intense, quiet bustle about the place; like discovering a film star with her sleeves rolled up doing the dishes, it conveyed a curious combination of glamour and workmanlike practicality. Two armchairs positioned next to an empty fireplace were occupied by men in khaki, clipboards on their knees, and other military personnel were traversing the foyer in sharp, quick strides, heads dipped in conversation. Glittering chandeliers spilled raindrops onto the marble floor, but the windows were swathed in reams of blackout fabric and in the middle of the walkway an easel made a crude-looking noticeboard. CORB INTERVIEWS: BALLROOM 09.00 – 17.00 HRS, had been chalked across the front of it.

Sylvie stood uncertainly, searching for someone who might be able to give them directions. Instinctively she reached for Lewis' hand. To her surprise he didn't pull away. After a couple of moments she spotted a woman dressed in a tweed skirt, lisle stockings and brogues. She was talking to another mother in a way that suggested an official capacity of some kind, and when they were finished Sylvie asked her where she could find the ballroom.

'CORB candidate?' The woman's tone implied the status was something of a privilege.

Sylvie nodded. She was fighting the urge to pull Lewis away, out of the door, straight across Hyde Park, and back to the freedom and space of Norfolk. She tried to bury the feeling somewhere deep, out of sight, and made a tense effort to smile.

'Go left at the end of the hall and follow the signs to the ballroom. Not the Great Room, don't get confused. I hope you're not in a hurry?' She was studying Sylvie's face, as if trying to fathom the reason for Sylvie's anxiety. 'You might have a bit of a wait, I'm afraid. There's rather a lot of children to see.' She beamed bracingly at Lewis. 'Well, young man, are you excited at the prospect of your big adventure?'

'No.' Lewis was focused on his shoes. 'I don't want to go.'

'Lewis!' Sylvie shook his arm. She said to the woman, 'I'm sorry, he's nervous, that's all. About the interview.'

The woman didn't look persuaded. 'A word of advice,' she said to Sylvie through thin lips, 'when they ask him questions in there, he'd better sound excited. Otherwise he'll stand no chance of getting on a ship. None at all. There's plenty who would give their right arm to be where you're standing.' The woman fixed her with an uncompromising stare before marching off.

Sylvie waited until the woman had disappeared before she tugged Lewis' sleeve. He followed her across the hall a little sheepishly. How she wished a bad interview performance would be enough to sabotage Howard's intentions, but she understood Lewis' passage was as good as guaranteed. Several weeks earlier she had read an article in the newspaper that implied the government was hoping the children evacuated to Canada would stay permanently; apparently it had been trying to encourage people to emigrate over there for years. A day or two later she received another letter from Howard. '*As long as you put Canada on the application form,*', she read with a terrible, cold inevitability, '*I've been assured a place will be found for Lewis.*'

Afterwards she considered listing every country other than Canada, or not sending in a form at all. But she guessed word would get to Howard and, besides, Howard could probably wrangle Lewis a space even without the wretched form. If she was going to disobey Howard, the only way to do it, she decided, was to play along with the process. She knew that when word came through of the sailing, notice was likely to be short, only a matter of days. She and Lewis could simply not turn up to the embarkation point. There wouldn't be time for Howard to do anything about it and once Sylvie had let one place go, Howard's friend would surely not go to the bother of finding Lewis another?

Still, a fault line of uncertainty threatened to undermine her plan. When the hour arrived would she actually dare to flout Howard so utterly? She told herself nothing could be harder than sending Lewis away, but now it wasn't only Howard she had to contend with. Since the Norwich raid her mother had taken to saying on regular occasions what a blessing it was that Lewis, at least, would be safely out of it, and the general view at the WVS was that Sylvie had received a stroke of luck equivalent to winning the first prize in a tremendous raffle. They were all so convincing she had even pondered whether her mother could be right, if Howard might, after all, want to keep Lewis safe, whether it was her own reluctance to let him go that was mistaken, selfish even. But then she remembered the lonely formality of her marriage, Howard's antipathy to Lewis, and her spirits plummeted again.

Sometimes in the middle of the night she fantasised about telling her mother why she didn't want Lewis to go abroad. 'The thing is,' she would say, in a calm, matter-of-fact tone, 'Lewis is probably not Howard's son. I had a very brief affair with another man soon after I married. Howard has always suspected it, although it's not something we've ever talked about, and now I think he's taking the opportunity to send Lewis away for good.' She imagined the frozen quality of the silence that would follow, like the instant after a stone strikes a window, before the glass cracks and splinters and disintegrates into a thousand broken pieces.

In some ways it was surprising that nobody noticed her despair; she supposed it to be as conspicuous as a broken limb or an unsightly rash, but then of course everyone was worried sick and trying to put the bravest face on things they could. Insomnia and nerves were commonplace, mollified by aspirin or chewing gum or breathing deep and counting. What, Sylvie scolded herself, were her own problems compared to the horrors that were happening on the other side of the Channel? Yet, it didn't help to think to like that. Lewis was going, might never come back, and the wider context of the war didn't lessen the pain. Instead, she sensed, as if beyond an open window, the crushing misery of it all and had to slam the window shut to prevent it from overwhelming her completely.

The floor of the ballroom was set up with four trestle tables, each with a single chair on one side and two the other. Scraps of earnest discussions trickled back to her. Without meaning to listen, Sylvie caught, 'Would you say William is of robust character?' And, 'Has Gillian ever been to sea before? Now did she suffer from seasickness?' Around the edges of the room mothers were perched on benches, offspring by their side or hovering close by. One boy of about nine, clothed in grey shorts and a blazer, was crying bitterly. Sylvie heard him sob, 'But why can't I go, Mother? Why aren't I suitable?' His mother, dabbing his cheeks with a handkerchief, looked close to tears herself and Sylvie felt an awkward stab of guilt.

She chose a bench as far away from the desolate child as possible. It was narrow and low, as if borrowed from a school gymnasium. At the other end of it a ruddy-cheeked woman was squashed between two little girls with long blonde plaits. The woman had obviously gone to some trouble with their appearance since the children's shoes and cheeks gleamed like apples. As Sylvie and Lewis sat down, she nodded at them. 'Come far have you?'

'Norfolk.' And then because Sylvie felt obliged to reciprocate. 'What about you?'

'Yorkshire. We spent last night with my sister in Clapham. Still'– the woman cocked her head – 'it's nice to come to London and get a proper night's sleep. Not be running to the shelter all the time.'

Sylvie smiled obediently. The relative calm of the city compared to provincial towns seemed to be a common joke; on the bus she'd overheard someone saying practically the exact same thing. 'But it hasn't got going properly yet, has it? Not over here.' The woman's voice turned sour. 'Which is why we've come all this way. I want these two' – she pointed at her fair-haired daughters – 'out of the picture before the trouble really starts.' Her eyes flicked to Lewis and back. 'Just the one, have you?'

'No.' Sylvie was slightly taken aback at the question. 'I have a daughter too. But she's much younger: too young to go away. I've left her at home with…' – it was hard to think of quite the right word for Elsie, who had slotted into the household like a member of the family – 'with a friend.'

The woman wasn't listening anyway. She leaned towards Sylvie, her gaze becoming intent. 'What do you think of our chances?'

'Sorry?'

'Our chances of getting on a ship.'

'Oh.' Sylvie plucked at her skirt. 'It's hard to say.' She shifted uneasily on the bench, partly because of another nudge of guilt and partly because she was aware of Lewis listening beside her. She had presented the prospect of evacuation to him in a way that made it sound close to certain. She hadn't seen any point in doing otherwise – she didn't want to give him false hope it might not happen.

She had first spoken to him about it two weeks earlier, when they were working in the vegetable garden. It was easier to broach the subject side by side on the tatty old kneelers, their hands occupied with the final sow of beetroot and runner beans. She tried hard to keep her voice neutral, and present it as a chance to go abroad, an opportunity, an adventure, but she may not have succeeded as well as she thought, because Lewis immediately said, 'It's Daddy that's wants me to go, isn't it?'

Caught by surprise, it took Sylvie one heartbeat too many to formulate her response. 'No,' she said. And then, 'Only because he thinks it's for the best. That you'll be safe.'

'Supposing,' Lewis said steadily, 'I don't want to?' They were watching each other over the broken chocolate soil.

Sylvie wondered if the fear she detected in his eyes was merely a reflection of her own. After a moment she said, 'Daddy is quite certain you should go, and I…' – she made an almighty effort – 'I think he's probably right.' She put down her trowel and made to put her arms around him, but he leaned backwards, out of her reach. 'It won't be for long,' she said. 'A year or two at most.' A tear hovered on his cheek and he brushed it away before it could fall.

Sylvie waited a little while and then she reached for him again. This time he let her hug him. At first he was merely passive in her arms but then she felt his grip strengthen. They stayed like that for a minute or two before Sylvie pushed him gently away. She tried to meet his gaze but he kept it directed on the ground. 'Now look!' she said, with forced lightness, 'I've made muddy marks all down the back of your shirt!' She slapped the worst of the dirt away, trying to make a joke of it. Then she wiped her streaming nose with the back of her hand and returned to the job of slotting the diaphanous plant stems in between the clods of earth. A second or two later, Lewis began to do the same. Afterwards he didn't talk about the evacuation other than to raise practical queries about the length of the voyage and where he would go and who would he stay with; questions to which Sylvie didn't have the answers. She noticed, however, that he never took another thing from Howard's study.

'Mrs Rodwell?' A man with a feather-grey moustache and watery blue eyes appeared in front of her. 'Would you both come this way, please?' He was wearing a dogtooth jacket and trousers and leaning heavily on a stout-looking walking stick. There was an appealingly rumpled air to him, accentuated by the fact his left leg sagged slightly every time he took a step. As they approached an empty table, he gave Sylvie the warmest smile she'd seen in a long while. 'Dreadful business, isn't it? I'm sure the mothers feel it the most.' Sylvie couldn't reply. Somehow his kindness was worse than the haughtiness of the woman in the lisle stockings, it stripped away the last pretence that there was anything normal or even bearable about sending your children across an ocean to be looked after by strangers for an indefinite period.

The interviewer pulled a pair of spectacles from his top pocket and opened a buff-coloured folder. Sylvie glimpsed the application form it had taken her a whole evening to complete: details about Lewis' medical history, his academic abilities, their religious affiliation – Church of England, which felt newly meaningful since they now went to church most Sundays. Sylvie wondered if there was any mention of the favour Howard was owed, or whether Lewis appeared to be in the same position as all the other applicants.

Presently the interviewer lowered the file. 'Now, young man,' – he took off his spectacles and dangled them between his thumb and forefinger – 'you say you want to go to Canada.' It wasn't a question exactly, but the interviewer paused as though it had been, smiling encouragingly first at Sylvie and then at Lewis. Sylvie noticed the pupil of his left eye was slightly more dilated than that of his right one; it gave the unnerving impression he could focus on both her and Lewis at the same time.

Lewis faltered. 'I…' he began, but he ran aground almost immediately and a flush spread from the edge of his shirt collar.

'We chose Canada because it's part of the Commonwealth but not so terribly far as Australia,' Sylvie interjected. Although part of her didn't want to cooperate at all, there was something about the interviewer's dignified and fatherly manner that made it impossible to do anything but oblige him as best she could.

'What about you, young man? What do you think of Canada? Do you like fishing and shooting?'

Lewis shook his head. He was staring at his knees.

'Is that what they do in Canada,' Sylvie said, 'shoot and fish? How do you know?'

The interviewer appeared taken aback; Sylvie couldn't tell whether it was the nature of the question or the fact she had asked one at all. He put his spectacles back on and consulted the folder again. She wasn't sure if he was searching for an answer to her question or avoiding it.

As he was flicking through the pages, Lewis spoke up. 'I like being outside. And…' – he offered unexpectedly – 'I like making things.'

'Do you now? Well that sounds very promising.' The interviewer peered over the top of the papers. 'I see here that your school report is good. And there's nothing of concern in the medical records.' There was something changed about his manner, it had become quite relaxed and at the same time more perfunctory. Sylvie guessed he had found some reference to Howard. He seemed to confirm as much, by saying to her, 'Your husband's profession is teaching, I see?'

'Yes,' Sylvie said. 'He was head of the history department at a boys' school in Norwich, but he signed up as soon as war broke out. He didn't apply for an exemption. He said there was nothing special about his job, nothing someone else couldn't do if he wasn't there.' It occurred to her that when she was describing Howard to another person he always sounded much nicer than the impression of him she carried around in her head.

The interviewer closed the file. 'I think that will do. You'll be informed of the sailing date in due course. Start making your preparations now because the notification could come any day.'

'So Lewis has a place then?' The question was pointless, since she had known this all along. The interviewer scrutinised her with his uneven eyes. She had the strong impression he saw something of the divide between Howard and herself.

'It could be over by Christmas, Mrs Rodwell. Hitler will soon find he's bitten off more than he bargained for. His pilots aren't a match for our boys, but be grateful your lad has only got to get on a ship, not go up in the air and fight them.'

As they left the table, the ruddy-cheeked woman called them over. She was busy reworking one of her daughter's plaits, twisting the hair into a slick, neat rope. 'That was quick,' she said. 'Are you in?'

Sylvie nodded.

The woman sucked a breath admiringly. 'Whatever did you say?'

'I don't know.' Sylvie's jaw tensed with the lie. The two little girls were staring up at her with shiny, hopeful expressions. 'But,' she added, remembering the woman in the lisle stockings, 'I think it's important to sound enthusiastic.'

The woman seemed unimpressed by this piece of advice. 'Where did you put down for?'

'Canada,' Sylvie said.

'Canada?' The woman pulled a face. 'These two don't want to go to Canada. They want New York!' She examined her daughter's reworked hair. 'There now,' she said with satisfaction, 'fit for an interview by the king himself.'

Sylvie put an arm around Lewis, steering him towards the door. 'Well, goodbye,' she said over her shoulder. 'And good luck.'

After leaving the hotel they made their way to Marble Arch and waited for another bus. They needed to get the number 8, which Connie had said would take them all the way to Bethnal Green.

About three weeks earlier Sylvie had received another letter. '*Something's happened*', Connie had written. '*I can't bring myself to tell you what it is without being able to see your face and knowing whether or not you mind, whether you think we can still be friends.*' Sylvie replied straight away to say it couldn't possibly be that bad and begging Connie to put her out of her misery, because she was imagining terrible things that were bound to be worse than the truth. Connie refused. '*I'll wait until I see you*', she said in her next letter. '*When can you come to London?*'

Sylvie was desperate to visit, but frivolous journeys were frowned upon for the waste of fuel and carriage space. Then, in a stroke of luck, she received notification of Lewis' interview. She wrote to tell Connie they would be travelling to London the following week and the response arrived practically panting for breath on the doormat. '*I shan't ever forgive you if you don't come and see me*', the letter stated, and gave Sylvie a detailed account of the ways in which she might cross London.

The CORB interview meant that when she talked about her trip to London she didn't have to mention visiting Connie to her mother, or anyone else for that matter. She wasn't sure how her mother would react. Her mother wasn't a snob, not much of one at any rate, but she did seem to get nervous about the effect other people might have on Sylvie. It was almost as if she sensed the marital tightrope on which Sylvie was balancing, and worried the slightest breath of fresh air might topple her off. It had been laughably, blackly ironic, Sylvie thought, that her mother had been the one to send her to Kennie after he came back from Dunkirk. Not that it made a difference any more, of course. Every time she thought of him a toxic swell of emotion swept through her. Mostly it was grief, and a twisting, shameful guilt that pressed her eyes together in dismay, but recently she had begun to feel the first shoots of something else, something calmer, and she realised, to her astonishment, that it was an exhausted kind of relief. When the bus arrived they climbed up to the top floor. Sylvie let Lewis into the seat first and he buried into the corner, forehead flat against the glass. The experience at Grosvenor House, the undeniable reality of his evacuation, seemed to have stunned them both to silence. They sat without speaking as they trundled towards Holborn and Cheapside and then east, beyond the grimy mass of Liverpool Street to Bishopsgate. At one point Sylvie went to take Lewis' hand again, but on this occasion he dragged it back and tucked his fist into his trouser pocket.

Once they reached Bethnal Green Road, Sylvie watched for landmarks following Connie's instructions – a barber, a public house called the Earl Grey and then a shop with different-sized birdcages dangling across the window and from the doorframe. As soon as she spied Kelly's Eel and Pies, Sylvie rang the bell and the vehicle juddered to a halt and spilled them out. Immediately an unbridled cloud of noise enveloped them – shouting, laughter, the ringing clatter of iron wheels and hooves – that was entirely different from the measured hum of Oxford Street.

For a moment they stood and got their bearings. The signage painted on Kelly's architrave promised STEWED EELS, JELLIED EELS, MEAT PIES AND MASHED POTATOES. 'Do they really eat stewed eels?' Lewis asked.

'I suppose they must do.'

Lewis made a disgusted face.

The eel and pie shop was wedged between a grocer's displaying tins of condensed milk, fish paste and a baker's called Levy Bros that had flatbreads and rolls with holes in the middle, stacked in the window. Traffic teemed in front of them; not just motorcars and buses but carts drawn by horses and weaving bicycles. They crossed the thoroughfare, heading north. They were searching for a park described by Connie as being shaped like a triangle. She had written that she would stay there all afternoon, until Sylvie and Lewis arrived: '*Whatever time you get there, I'll be waiting.*'

As they walked, Sylvie glanced down alleyways that ran back from the road like the teeth of a comb. They were flocked with children of all ages, climbing on each other's backs, kicking balls and swinging on ropes that had been thrown around lamp posts and looped under their armpits. Some, she saw, were barefoot and wearing garments that looked more like sacking than proper clothes. A number of women in crossover aprons were talking together with folded arms, another, she noticed was on her knees, scrubbing a doorstep. The smell of beer and coal dust clung to the air, with other more pungent odours, like onions and garlic and, every so often, the stink of sewerage. They passed a public house called The White Heart, where someone had stuck a notice saying, NO GAS, NO WATER, BUT GOOD SPIRITS! From inside she could hear singing, a man's voice, bold and melodic, and although she was thirsty, and guessed Lewis was too, Sylvie daren't go in to ask for even a glass of water.

When they reached the end of the street a piece of green was facing them, not much bigger than her parents' garden. A figure in front of the entrance gates waved her arm, tentatively at first and then with increasing abandon. Sylvie began to hurry, pulling Lewis to make him keep up. At the junction she hopped impatiently from foot to foot until there was a gap that allowed them to cross.

Connie came running towards them. She looked as if she was about to hug Sylvie, but then appeared to think better of it and stopped about a foot away. 'I thought you'd never arrive!' She seemed glazed with anxiety; Sylvie couldn't tell if it was because of the waiting or the business Connie had mentioned in her letter.

'We came as soon as we could.'

'I know,' – Connie bit her lip – 'but I've been here since just gone eleven. I couldn't risk missing you.' She stretched out her hand to tousle Lewis' hair and as she did Sylvie glimpsed the wedding band, and felt again that instant of giddy disbelief when she had found it in the sand. She reached for Connie's wrist. 'It's so good to see you again,' she said quietly.

Connie broke into a smile and for a moment her face emptied of worry. 'Isn't it just!' she said, and stepped forward to crush Sylvie in an embrace.

After they disentangled themselves, beaming and slightly embarrassed, Connie picked up a wicker basket at her feet. 'Charlie's in the park somewhere,' she said, leading them through a pair of wrought-iron gates. 'I left him playing.' She pulled a flask and a brown-paper package out of the basket and gave them to Lewis. 'Lemonade and sandwiches,' she said. 'Go and find him. I think he's down the other end.'

Lewis took them, glanced quickly at Sylvie as if for approbation, and then darted away. She had the sensation of a bird being released from a cage. She watched him jog the length of the lawn and saw a ginger-haired figure emerge from a group of boys and come towards him. A second later they had vanished behind some bushes.

'Come and sit down.' Connie had positioned herself under a tree and she patted the ground next to her. 'I've got tea and sandwiches for us too.' She fished out another flask and poured out a cup for Sylvie into a tin mug. The taste of it was strong and very sweet. Sylvie hadn't put sugar in her tea for months, and now even the tea was rationed too. She had to make an effort not to guzzle.

'However much of your allowance did you use in this?'

'I thought you could do with the energy. Coming all the way to London and then out here to the back of beyond.' Connie laughed rather self-consciously. 'I bet you've never been anywhere like it before.'

Sylvie dipped her head as images of the seething passageways and the half-naked children swam before her eyes. She hadn't seen anything like it before, but she didn't want to say so. The people she knew at home might moan about the price of a new pair of curtains or need to save up to go away on a holiday, but there was enough money to buy food and clothes. Nobody went hungry, or at least they hadn't done before the war adjusted everyone's appetites.

Connie seemed to tell what she was thinking. 'We're all right, you know…'

'I didn't think—'

'I know you didn't.' Connie interrupted her lightly. 'But Dad has a business, a good business. He makes gramophone cabinets. They're ever so smart. He sells them to Fullotones, up in Camden. I do all the bookkeeping and they fetch nearly ten pounds a piece, or at any rate they did until recently.' Her voice had started confident and proud, but all at once it faded. She shifted a little further back from Sylvie.

Sylvie had never heard of Fullotones. 'Well, that sounds marvellous…' she began, but Connie's face had acquired the same sheen of distracted worry Sylvie had noticed earlier. 'What's happened?' she asked. 'What's gone wrong?'

Connie met her eyes, but looked down again almost immediately. She had drawn up her knees, tight under her skirt. She began to tear at the lawn in sharp bursts. 'It's Dad,' she froze for a moment and then took a breath. 'He's in prison. Pentonville Prison.' She gave a little hiccup, as if saying it out loud had rekindled the trauma.

'Prison?' Sylvie repeated. She rested her cup on the ground. 'What did he…? I mean how did he…?' She couldn't find a way of articulating the obvious question.

Connie gulped; Sylvie saw the skin on her throat tremble and settle again. 'There was a march, a protest, at the end of June. It got a bit out of hand. People started to throw bricks and milk bottles at the police…' Sylvie's expression must have changed, hardened even, because Connie said quickly, 'Dad didn't do that. He was trying to stop a lad chucking some stones at a copper, a female copper. Only the kid scarpered and Dad was the one who was left holding onto them.' A downy heap was accumulating beneath her fingers as she continued to tug at the grass.

Sylvie nodded, slowly. She didn't trust herself to speak. Was that the truth, she wondered, or was that what Connie's father had told Connie? Eventually she said, rather thickly, 'What was the protest about?'

'Rent. About rents being too high and families being evicted.' Connie sighed, 'Something that's been going on for years.'

'Your dad thinks he's paying too much rent?'

'No.' Connie shook her head a touch impatiently. 'It's much more complicated than that. It's not our rent he's bothered about. It's other people's rent. He's got involved with this group, I suppose they're… they're…' – glancing behind them her voice dipped to a whisper – 'communists. Well some of them are. They formed a sort of league.'

Sylvie rocked backwards. She was staring, she knew. Connie's eyes darted to Sylvie's face and flicked away again. 'We've been having our own little war here for years: the Commies against the Fascists.' Her tone had lifted, as if to make light of what she was saying, but now it became more defensive. 'My dad's lot, they've done some good things; some brave things. They even got an agreement about the rent in the end. Only problem is,' – she shuddered – 'Dad's been put away for it!'

The details of Connie's story were impossible to digest; each piece of information seemed alien and shocking, like something Sylvie would read about in the newspaper. Her thoughts reverted to the practical. 'How long is it for?'

'Five years.'

'*Five years*? For throwing a stone?'

Connie shivered miserably. 'The policewoman was hit on the head. She got knocked unconscious and needed stitches. The judge told my dad he was lucky not to get more.'

'Oh, but that's awful,' Sylvie said. She wasn't entirely sure whether she was referring to the policewoman's injury or the prison sentence. 'What about the gramophones, the business? What will happen to it?'

'We're managing, there's a couple of lads that come in and lend a hand. And Ted does too, he's been very good.'

'They don't mind,' Sylvie asked, 'that your dad is in prison?'

'They're Jewish,' Connie said simply. When Sylvie didn't react, she added. 'The Commies helped the Jews fight the Fascists. To them Dad's a bit of a hero. And as for Ted, well I think Dad could have thrown a thousand stones and it wouldn't stop him wanting to help me.'

Sylvie was still grappling with this information when two shadows fell over them. Lewis and Charlie were standing beside them. Charlie looked older than Sylvie remembered. His shins were elongated and bony, and his features were heavier, less childlike. Then she registered with a start that Lewis was almost the same height; Lewis must have grown a lot too, without her noticing it.

'Lewis is still hungry,' Charlie said. 'Have you got anything else?'

'I'm not!' Lewis flooded crimson. 'It was you that wanted...' He was hushed by a glare from Charlie.

Connie rummaged in the basket and produced another parcel of sandwiches. 'These were for Sylvie, only I forgot about them.'

'I'm not hungry,' Sylvie said, hurriedly. 'Really I'm not.' In fact the mention of food had triggered a hollow growl in her stomach but the boys were already eyeing the package in Connie's hand and she remembered that in her haste to get to Bethnal Green she had forgotten to think about lunch.

'Well, if you're certain.' As soon as the paper packet was proffered the boys dived on it and disappeared. 'I was nervous,' Connie said, twisting back to face Sylvie, 'to tell you about Dad. I worried you'd think I was a bad influence and not want to know me.'

'Well, it's not you that's in prison, is it?' She had barely followed Connie's account of the politics but the pleasure at being with her again had already eclipsed her sense of shock. She leaned forwards to squeeze Connie's hand, and Connie pressed hers in return.

When they let go, Connie sat back on her heels and tilted her head. 'It's your turn now. Tell me about the interview.'

Sylvie felt the air around her grow suddenly still. 'There isn't much to say.'

'Well, did Lewis get a place or not?'

Sylvie nodded. She picked up the tin mug again, although she knew it was empty. Any minute Connie would be bound to comment how lucky she was, or try to cheer her up by saying that anyone nowadays would give an arm or a leg to have a slot on one of the boats. For a moment Connie didn't speak, then she said, 'Do you remember the conversation we had on the beach? About how we couldn't bear for them to go?'

Sylvie nodded again.

Connie was watching her closely. 'I suppose it's different now,' she said, carefully.

There was a silence.

At last Sylvie said, 'It's not different for me.' She could feel an ache expanding through her throat. 'It's only Howard that wants Lewis evacuated.' In the intimate slant of afternoon sunlight she could feel herself close – perilously close – to telling Connie the truth. Quietly, she added, 'I think Howard hopes Lewis will stay in Canada.'

Connie's eyes shot wide open. 'His own son? Why ever would he want that?'

Sylvie stared at the ground for a long while, but when she lifted her head Connie was still frowning at her, expectant. Eventually, thick on her tongue, the words struggled out. 'Because Lewis is not his son. At least, I don't think he is, and neither does Howard.'

A second passed. And another. Connie didn't say anything.

To break the quiet Sylvie murmured, 'And you worried *I* might find *you* a bad influence.' The little joke rose and died in the same breath.

Connie looked around, as if checking the boys were still out of earshot. 'Who…?' she began.

'Kennie,' Sylvie said. 'His name was Kennie.' She was determined not to cry. 'We were courting, only… only he went away, he left me when I wasn't expecting it. By the time he came back I was married to Howard, but one day he was there, just standing on the step, like he'd never been gone.' She stopped. 'He wanted… I wanted…' Her voice tailed to a whisper. 'I couldn't…' The wonder of the long-ago kitchen, Kennie in the doorway, the texture of his coat, the tug and release of her apron string, felt more vivid than the clamour of east London, more real than the faded, scrubby grass they were sitting on.

'But what about Howard, how did he find out? You surely didn't tell him?' Connie seemed dazed but her expression was soft.

'He knew all about Kennie; he knew that Kennie and I had been courting just before we met. I even told Howard I couldn't marry him because I was still in love with Kennie, but he kept on wanting to see me, not taking no for an answer, and in the end I couldn't think of a reason *not* to marry him, since I'd lost Kennie. Anyway, somebody told him Kennie had come home and Howard asked if I'd seen him. I said I hadn't. His face went completely white and he said that was funny because that same person was sure they had spotted Kennie leaving our house. I should have said yes, that Kennie had popped round and made it sound quite normal. But it was awful the way it happened. I can't tell you how awful it was. He knew I'd lied to him and that it meant I had something to hide.' Sylvie shuddered. It had been like ice cracking, a shearing of something solid into separate pieces. Howard had walked out without another word, and returned late reeking of whisky.

She paused to gather herself. 'After… after Lewis was born, there was a nice period when he seemed almost to have forgotten. Maybe he made himself believe nothing had happened after all. But then I couldn't get pregnant again. Every time I got my monthlies Howard grew more distant, like he knew all over again that Lewis couldn't be his.'

'Are you quite certain he isn't?' Connie asked gently.

Sylvie's face flamed. 'Not completely. There's no way of telling.'

'And then you had Esther,' Connie prompted.

'Six years later, Connie! Not a flicker until then. And Lewis, he has this air sometimes. A deep sort of look. As if he's staring right inside himself. And that's like Kennie, not Howard.'

'Did Howard ever ask you what happened with Kennie?'

'No.' Sylvie was whispering. 'Not exactly. I don't think he could bring himself to. Though once, after Esther was born, one of our neighbours came round to admire her and said she had Howard's nose and chin, a right little Daddy's girl is what she called her. And Howard' – Sylvie took a breath – 'Howard replied, like he was passing the time of day, how nice it was he could be sure at least one of the children was his own. I didn't know where to put myself, but our neighbour just laughed. Of course she assumed Howard was joking – only he wasn't.'

'But you don't know about Lewis, not for certain. And neither does Howard. Remember, he brought Lewis up. He's more his father than anyone else. I expect he just wants Lewis to be evacuated to keep him safe, that's all.' Then she added in a firmer tone, 'He must love you an awful lot to have kept quiet about something like that all these years.'

Sylvie bowed her head. She didn't know, suddenly, what to think. She felt a tear quiver on her cheek, and fall. After that there was no stopping them. Presently she became aware of Connie's arm around her shoulder, her voice in her ear. 'Lewis will come back again. After this horrid war is over. You'll see.' There was a space before Connie added casually, 'Did you see him – Kennie – again, after…?'

Somewhere high above, the gnat-like drone of an engine started. 'Once,' Sylvie said, 'but only recently. He had been injured in France and was convalescing with his mother.' She closed her eyes, willing Connie not to probe the terrible truth of it.

'He didn't check… you know that everything was *all right*?' Connie was still referring to the first time, in the sun-streaked kitchen.

Sylvie shook her head. 'He went away again. I was married and it was too late. There was nothing to be done.' She didn't mention to Connie how for weeks afterwards she had hoped Kennie would reappear on the doorstep and beg her to come with him. How, when he hadn't, she almost left Howard of her own accord but drew back at the last instant; how she stood outside Mrs Baxter's house and heard Kennie whistling, behaving as if he didn't have a care in the world.

They sat for a while without speaking. The plane had disappeared but the rumble of traffic in the surrounding streets was quite audible, so too the squeals of children and once a raw crash of dustbins. Presently Connie asked quietly, 'Where is Kennie now, Sylvie?'

'He's dead,' Sylvie said flatly. 'He was killed by a bomb in Norwich, just a few weeks ago.' She could sense Connie absorbing this, collecting her thoughts.

Then Connie said, very gently, 'You know that might be for the best. He sounds like bad news to me.' A second later she pulled abruptly away and Sylvie heard her say in a bright tone over Sylvie's shoulder. 'Have you finished playing, boys? Do you want to go home now? Well just run back first and check you haven't left anything behind.' There was a scuffling, a protest from Charlie that was cut short by Connie, and then a sense of privacy again.

Sylvie took a handkerchief from her handbag and rubbed her eyes and nose. She climbed shakily to her feet. Connie got up too, brushing her skirt. Sylvie regarded her for a long, thankful moment, and then she hugged her tightly, 'I've never told anyone before.'

'Well, that's what friends are for, isn't it? Telling them things you can't say to anyone else.' After they separated, Connie picked up her basket. 'What happens next?' she said. 'About the evacuation, I mean.'

Sylvie swallowed. Her pangs of hunger had passed completely. 'We'll get word when the ship is about to sail and then I shall take him to Euston station. He'll travel by train to Liverpool with the rest of the children.'

'The day before he goes,' Connie said, 'come and stay with us. It's hardly a palace but we can manage for one night. That way you won't have to do it all on your own.'

Before Sylvie could reply the boys returned. Their knees were inked with grass stains and flakes of bark spattered the back of Lewis' shirt. 'Whatever have you been doing?' she asked, starting to pick off the fragments, but she was pleased to see him out of breath and smiling.

As they approached the park gates, Connie grabbed Sylvie's forearm. 'Look!' she said. 'Look up there!' She had dropped her basket and was pointing at the sky to the south of London. At first Sylvie couldn't see anything, but then two black dots emerged from a cloud. They resembled birds, crows or ravens, lonely and vulnerable. Only of course they were nothing of the kind. One plane was diving downwards, turning small circles and emitting puffs of tracer fire. It seemed about to crash but then it levelled out and began to climb back towards the other. For long minutes the two aircraft ducked and rolled, pitching and plunging. It was like a courtship, or a dance, the twisting white vapour trails weaving patterns in the sky.

From nowhere a knot of people had gathered. Somebody said, 'I thought the fighting was over the Channel. That's what I heard on the radio.'

'Well by the size of it this Jerry scum-dog hasn't been listening to the radio!' It was a fat woman with a baby on her hip who had spoken. She unwound an arm from the child and shook her fist at the heavens. Sylvie wanted to ask if she could tell the fighters apart, they were so far away, but the woman was too distracted, yelling, 'You give him what for, love. You show Hitler where he can stick it.'

Sylvie murmured to Connie, 'Which one is the Spitfire?' But Connie shook her head.

They watched on, appalled and mesmerised. Finally, one of the squiggles tipped nose downwards, trailing a column of black smoke until it disappeared from view. The fat woman cheered, but Sylvie was engulfed by a sense of dread. She screwed up her eyes, straining to locate a parachute, but the harder she searched, the emptier the sky seemed to be.

CHAPTER FIFTEEN

Norfolk, recently

'Well, hello!' Henry says. For a fleeting second Martha is back at his side crossing the ink-black sand, watching his bicycle lights dissolve into the night. Or facing him in the train, the unexpected warmth of his hand burning a path through her skin. He must be surprised to see her, she thinks, but his voice is even and relaxed; to somebody watching it would look like any normal visit. He moves to one side, making space in the doorway. 'Do you want to come in?'

Dumbstruck, she nods and steps over the threshold. Henry threads his arm around her waist, pulls shut the door and turns down the hallway. Martha follows, trotting uncomfortably behind him. Her head is spinning. Naturally he must assume she has come to see *him*.

They come into a low-ceilinged space that is two rooms made one. At the farthest end a couple of sofas are set at right angles to a yawning fireplace while the part nearest to the door contains the kitchen with a table and chairs painted delicate dove-grey. A pair of French windows opens onto wooden decking and the distant drift of something sweet, like honeysuckle or jasmine.

Henry picks up a kettle and pads over to the sink. He is barefoot, wearing shorts and a baggy T-shirt, both of which are faded to the same indiscriminate shade of fawn. When he reaches for the tap Martha sees the hairs on his arms are bleached a pale, downy gold. 'Tea?' he says, over the stream of the water. 'Or would you prefer something cold?'

'Tea is fine,' Martha says. She's not sure where to stand, whether to move deeper into the room, or stay where she is, close to the door. And she doesn't know where to look; there's an awkward intensity to simply watching Henry. She fingers the collar of her cotton dress. 'I expect you're wondering what I'm doing here?'

Henry turns off the faucet. The question hovers, birdlike, for an instant but oddly, as he busies himself with the lid and a plug, appears to evaporate. After a moment Henry says in an easy kind of way, 'How did you find my address?'

'Well,' Martha says, 'the thing is, I…' She pauses. 'Actually I used the online phonebook, but…' She stops.

'The online phonebook.' It's not so much a question as a statement of reflection. For a split second their gaze meets and then Henry gestures at the French doors. 'Let's sit in the garden. You go outside and I'll bring the tea.'

The lawn near the decking resembles the baize of a pool table but the garden beyond the grass is a spontaneous sprawl of poppies, campions and a bushel of other wildflowers Martha has no hope of identifying. She drops into a chair, listening to the drone of a worker bee compete with the mechanical buzz of a neighbour's mower. She ought to be disappointed her search has been fruitless but all she feels is an unmistakable glow of pleasure. She watches Henry put down the tray boasting a milk jug, sugar bowl and even a saucer of lemon slices and then fill a china mug in the same unhurried way that seems to characterise all his actions.

'I take milk, but no sugar,' Martha directs. 'But Henry…' Something about her tone must have changed because he freezes midway through handing her a cup and waits. She fiddles with her collar again. 'I did use the online phonebook to get your address, but it wasn't your address I was trying to find.'

'It wasn't?'

'No. I was searching for the address of someone called Esther O'Neil. But the website came up with this one.' She takes the china mug from Henry and sets it on the ground. 'Maybe the online directory isn't up to date.'

Henry begins to pour a second cup. His head is bent over the teapot and Martha can't see his expression. 'Why do you want to find Esther O'Neil?' he asks levelly.

'Because it turns out she's my aunt. My father's sister. Only I don't think she knows about me. I certainly didn't know about her. She might not still be alive.'

To her astonishment, Henry's posture stiffens in a way she hasn't seen before and she senses an atmospheric shift, a blossoming of tension or expectation. Henry sits up and looks at her with a new kind of intensity. Eventually, he says, 'Well I can tell you she's alive. She's in bed right now having an afternoon nap. Today isn't one of her best days.'

Martha stares at him.

'Esther O'Neil is my mother.' Henry's voice is laced with suppressed, unidentifiable emotion.

'Your mother?' Martha leans back, absorbing the news. Esther O'Neil is here. Right *here*. Henry is Esther's son. This makes Henry her first cousin. All of this information should have been positive, even exciting news. Yet there's something terribly wrong about it, like a mistimed strike of a ball or a discordant note in the middle of a lullaby. She glances at Henry, who is stirring his tea with a deeply preoccupied expression. Then she says, because it seems worth spelling out her position, to avoid any possible misunderstanding. 'You see my father was Lewis Rodwell.'

'Right.' Henry's concentration appears to be directed on his teaspoon. After a second he rouses himself. 'What do you mean, he *was*…?'

'Well, he, Lewis – my father – well, he recently passed away.' Martha takes a quick breath. 'That's partly why I came to England. Because my father had booked the rental of the beach hut before he died and I thought I'd use it instead.'

'What a terrible shock.' Henry leans forward a little. 'I had no idea at all.'

'No,' Martha says. 'I guess you wouldn't have done. I don't imagine you ever knew him?'

'I didn't know him well, I suppose, since he lived so far away. Although I used to see something of him as a kid.' The sentence fades away.

'Did you? Did you really?' Martha tries to think how this could possibly be true. Her father used to take business trips, and she can recall him going abroad. She has no recollection of him ever going to England, but maybe he did…

'I didn't realise that he had a daughter.' Henry snags her thoughts.

'You didn't know…? Wait,' – the tug of Elizabeth's shadow – 'not *a* daughter! Two daughters! There are two of us! I don't understand. Why wouldn't he tell his nephew about his own children, or mention his family in Norfolk to us?'

Henry doesn't answer. Instead he says in a tone that is bright but in a brittle, plastic sort of a way, 'Well, I suppose whatever his reasons, this means we're related.'

Martha bites her lip and turns away.

The neighbour's lawnmower has come close to Henry's fence. Martha only appreciates that fact when the frenzied whine of the motor terminates abruptly. In the razor-sharp hush that follows a shale-thin voice can be heard, calling from the house.

'Henry! Henry! Where are you?'

Henry jumps out of his chair. 'I'm coming, Mum,' he shouts. He hurries towards the French windows, but then stops and takes a pace back towards Martha. 'Look' – he hesitates – 'I'll try to explain who you are but it won't be easy. Don't…' – he passes his hand across his forehead – 'don't expect too much.'

He returns fifteen minutes later. 'She's waiting inside. I've said that her niece from Canada has come to visit. There didn't seem any point making it more complicated than that. Even if she had known you before she wouldn't remember you now anyway.'

Martha regards him with dismay. 'Oh my Lord! Are you her full-time carer?'

'I live with her now, but normally a woman from town comes in every day. She had to rush away last week because her daughter's baby arrived early. It's why I haven't called you. I really can't leave Mum on her own, but,' – his tone is hollow – 'I would have done as soon as I could.'

They trade unhappy glances. After a while, Martha leans across and lightly pokes his shoulder. She takes a deep breath. 'Come on, Henry.'

'All right,' – he gets to his feet with a grimace of concern – 'but please don't mention to Mum that her brother has died. I'll try to tell her another time.'

'Of course,' Martha says. 'I understand completely.'

Inside the house a cartoon cat is cavorting across a TV screen against a faint jingle of music. Martha makes out a diminutive person sitting on the couch wearing a cotton dress that balloons around her body like a flour sack.

'Mum, this is Martha. Do you remember I said Martha had come to visit?'

The figure turns slowly around. Her features must have once been pretty but they now have an anxious, shrivelled quality. Martha searches for some resemblance to her father, but there's nothing at all familiar in the pouched and crumpled face, or the vulnerable hunch of the shoulders. Walking slowly forwards, she reminds herself this is the same woman who used to control a classroom of children, whom Gretchen saw beaming with happiness on her wedding day.

'Hello, Mrs O'Neil. Esther. Is it okay if I call you Esther?'

There's no reply.

'I'm Martha. I've come all the way from Canada to meet you!'

Esther stares straight past Martha towards Henry, who is rinsing out the teapot in the kitchen.

'Is it Helen?' she asks. 'Has Helen come to see me?'

'No Mum, it's not Helen. This is Martha.'

The elderly figure turns her gaze back to Martha. 'I can't remember what he said.' A panicked look sweeps across her face. She begins to tug at a bracelet on her wrist. 'Are you Helen?'

Martha drops onto the sofa. Esther is sunk within her dress, a missing button accentuates the gape of the fabric, but her hair is still elegant, Martha sees, swept back and coiled in a bun. She thinks of Henry struggling with his mother's grips, juggling the pins and combs, and tenderness for them both impales her like a laser beam. 'I'm not Helen. My name is Martha and I'm here from Canada.'

Esther's eyes light up in comprehension. 'Where is Helen? Why doesn't Helen visit me?'

Martha turns helplessly to Henry, who comes towards them drying his hands on a towel. 'Helen does visit you sometimes, Mum. She came last week remember? But Helen and I aren't married any longer, Mum. You know that. Helen still lives in London and I live here, with you. It's been four years now.' Although Henry is talking to his mother, there's something about the projection of his voice, the detail of the explanation that gives Martha the impression the words are intended for her ears as well.

'You live with me?'

'Yes, Mum.'

'Then where's Helen? Where does Helen live?'

'She lives in London, Mum. We're not married anymore.' He flips the towel onto his shoulder.

'Oh.' Esther's eyes fill with consternation.

Martha squeezes her hand; it feels ridiculously thin, like bird bones. *Did this woman share her father's childhood? What would he say to her, if he were here now?*

Esther is studying Martha's face. 'I can't remember who you are.'

'That's okay,' Martha says. 'It doesn't matter.' In the corner of her vision the cartoon cat is sleeping in a basket and credits are bowling over the screen. Esther's fingers start to agitate in her lap. Gently,

Martha presses them still. 'Do you remember somebody called Lewis?' she asks quietly.

'Lewis?' Esther's focus sharpens, her hands relax and she seems to hold herself a little straighter. 'I have a brother called Lewis.'

'That's right!' Martha says. She nods encouragingly. 'Do you remember him?'

'I haven't seen him for a long time, have I?'

'No,' Martha says softly, 'you haven't.'

'Mum…' Henry begins, but Esther ignores him.

'Will he come and see me?' She shakes Martha's arm. 'He never comes to see me.'

'Mum…' Henry moves a step closer, but Esther twists her head away and pulls at Martha.

'Tell him to come and see me!'

'Oh…' Martha says, 'Well…' She should have anticipated this; of course she should have done. She wants to meet Esther's eyes but the appeal in them is unbearable. 'Okay,' she says at last. 'I'll do that.'

The next instant Esther breaks contact, her attention switching to the TV screen. Some kind of quiz show is starting, a male and a female contestant are poised in front of an electronic board peppered with letters. Esther seems enraptured. Martha rises to her feet and goes to stand next to Henry. 'It's one of her favourites,' he says with weary affection.

'Shall I turn up the volume?' Martha can barely hear what the contestants are saying.

Henry shakes his head. 'Loud noises tend to upset her.' He peers more closely at Martha. 'Is everything okay?'

Martha peeks at the couch, her throat swollen with sadness. Confusion too. She feels more detached from her father than ever, as if even his memory is swimming away from her. Swallowing the ache, she says quickly, partly to change the subject and partly because she really does want to know more, 'I was sorry to hear about your split from Helen.'

Henry flinches. 'Oh,' he says. 'It was a while ago now.'

'You said four years,' Martha prompts as they move into the kitchen. She pulls a piece of kitchen paper from a roll jostling for space alongside a Bruce Springsteen calendar and a stack of *Drumbeat* magazines, and blows her nose.

Henry looks away. 'It's not a very interesting tale. Or an unusual one.'

'I'm interested' – she flashes him a glance – 'if you don't mind talking about it.'

'Right. Okay.' Henry picks up a publication from the pile and puts it down again. There's a small silence before he says, 'It started to go wrong a long time before I knew about it. It seems Helen met someone on a work trip abroad. She told me afterwards she didn't expect it to last.'

Martha nods, although in a distracted sort of a way. An entry on the calendar for the coming week has caught her notice. Digesting its meaning – its *possible* meaning – in a blink, she diverts her gaze.

'I guess it did?' she prompts, getting back on point.

'Apparently he got transferred to the London office.'

'Oh! Well, I bet he arranged that!' Martha hesitates. 'How did you find out?'

'The usual way: phone bills, emails…' Henry shifts uncomfortably. 'Although by then it was pretty clear something was going on.' He folds the hand towel neatly in two and places it by the sink. 'Helen had stopped being careful. I think she probably wanted me to find out.'

'Emails, Facebook, they leave such a trail, don't they?' Martha says, her thoughts drawn to her father and the files Elizabeth found on his computer. 'Not,' she adds hastily, 'that it wasn't a good thing you found out. It sounds to me like she messed you about long enough.' She can't help but have another peek at the calendar – at the scribbled note, at the *AA* meeting, 5pm on Tuesday afternoon, at those two little letters that might explain Henry's haggard demeanour, his lived-in, *suffered-in*, features – and, to her relief, Martha finds the explanation doesn't trouble her at all. Realising he has followed her line of sight, she colours slightly. 'I—' she begins, but Henry interrupts her.

'I had some difficulties coming to terms with it. The break-up with Helen, I mean.' He is staring directly into her face, the creases on his own more thickly scored than ever.

Martha holds his gaze. There's a steady, thoughtful interval before she says, 'I know how bad a break-up can feel.'

Henry clears his throat. 'Really?'

'I got through it a different way,' Martha says, the truth dawning, as the words speak themselves – 'Janey. My daughter.' In response to Henry's quizzical expression, she adds, 'I split with her father years ago. He's remarried now and has eight-year-old twins, would you believe!' She's surprised how pleasantly neutral she sounds. 'Janey is studying in Cambridge. I plan to see her, of course, that's the other reason for coming to Norfolk.' She pauses. 'The first one being the beach hut and my father.' She seems to have come full circle, the same question presenting itself. 'Henry,' she says, glad to move away from the business of the calendar, 'do you happen to know anyone who goes by the name of Catkins?'

'Catkins?' He looks nonplussed. 'No, why do you ask?'

'I think she might be someone my father knew. Somebody he wrote to for a very long time.' Martha tries to retain the same untroubled tone she used about Clem, but already she can hear the tightness in her throat. 'It's just that we – my sister and I – can't think of anyone at all called Catkins. In actual fact, her name might not be Catkins at all. It may be Catherine. Or something else entirely, Catkins could be a nickname. But I've been wondering if my father was writing to somebody over here. In England.'

'Why wouldn't your father be writing to someone in England?'

'Well, no reason, I guess, just that naturally most of his friends didn't live here.'

Henry nods thoughtfully. 'Yes, I suppose that's true.' He opens his mouth again but swings away suddenly. 'What are you trying to do, Mum?' Esther is doubled over, struggling with a pair of thick-strapped sandals poking out from underneath the skirt of the couch. 'There's no need to put your shoes on. We're not going out.' Esther looks up at him, her hands hover uncertainly, but then she uncurls herself and resumes her sitting position.

After an appropriate pause Martha says, 'So you don't know anyone called Catkins?'

'I probably know a *Catherine* somewhere, but nobody I can imagine your father might have known or wanted to contact. And definitely not anyone who calls herself Catkins...' Henry breaks off. 'Mum!' Then, his mouth softens and he says more mildly, 'Well, I suppose if you want to wear your shoes, there's no reason why you shouldn't.' He walks over to his mother and crouches down. Martha follows. Esther's feet are encased in opaque brown nylon and bulge with onion shaped lumps. Henry manoeuvres them into the sandals, tightens the buckles with a theatrical flourish and falls back on his heels. 'There! Now you're good to go!'

Obediently, Esther stands up.

'Hey, Mum, I was only joking! You can sit down. We're not going anywhere.' When Esther doesn't move, Henry props his arm under his mother's elbow and ushers her down onto the cushion. 'I forgot where I wanted to go,' she tells Martha.

'It doesn't matter,' Martha says. 'You can stay right here.' She smiles brightly but Esther stares straight past her and a second later struggles to her feet again. Without another word she begins to shuffle across the room, her steps precarious and slow but filled, somehow, with purpose.

'Mum!' Henry calls, 'Where are you going?'

Esther retreats through a doorway.

'What is she doing?' Martha asks; she feels a strange compulsion to whisper.

Henry takes a few steps forward and peers after his mother. 'I've no idea. That's her bedroom, but I don't know why she set off like that.' He's speaking quietly too, Martha notes.

'Should you go with her?'

Henry rubs his forehead again; somehow the gesture already seems deeply familiar. 'I don't know.'

When Esther returns a few minutes later, it's obvious that she's carrying a container of some kind, but Martha can't tell what it is, even after Esther has reclaimed her place on the couch and placed the item in the well of her lap. 'What have you got there, Esther?' she asks.

Esther tightens her grip on the chest. Her eyes are fixed on the ivorine coating, which is tarnished with spots of grubby ochre.

'It's my grandmother's jewellery case,' Henry says. 'It was given to Mum after my grandmother died.' Then, he asks, 'Why do you want the jewellery box, Mum?' Getting no response, he touches Esther's knee. 'Why did you get the box out, Mum?'

Esther lifts her head. 'Are you Helen?'

'No,' Martha says. 'I'm Martha. I'm visiting from Canada.' Esther examines her for a long second and then thrusts the chest at Martha's ribcage.

'You want me to take it?' Martha's eyes dart to Henry, who makes a perplexed, shrugging sort of a gesture. 'Well, okay.' Dubiously, she places her hands on either side of the ivory. 'I'm not sure about this,' she says to nobody in particular, but when neither Henry nor Esther reacts, she prises the chest from Esther's grasp. The box is heavier than she expects and the coating is worn at the corners, exposing metal edging. 'Should I look inside?' she asks Henry.

'I suppose so,' he says. 'I've really no idea.'

Martha takes another peek at Esther and squeezes the metallic clasp.

As the top opens her own face appears: the alive, bright, midnight-blue of her irises and the freckled hue of her cheeks flash briefly in the mirror set beneath the lid and then vanish as the glass swings upwards. Inside, a few small boxes are tucked against the velvet lining. There are loose items too, folded within compartment trays: a three-string pearl necklace, a choker formed of tiny gold rose leaves, a wooden brooch in the shape of a rose and a pair of long jade earrings. A faint trace of almonds and rosewater lingers on the velvet. She wonders how many times Esther has opened the chest to savour its treasured smell, or the ghost of her mother's fingers sifting through the pieces, searching for the one that would best show off a dress or blouse. 'Esther's mother was killed in the war, right?'

Henry nods. 'My mother was still quite small at the time.'

'How sad.' Martha lifts the brooch to examine the intricate carved petals arranged around a darker, central stigma. It's only as she's putting it back that she sees the plain gold wedding band and the square of newspaper that was lodged underneath it. 'I guess this was your grandmother's ring?'

Henry frowns and peers into the box. 'I don't think so,' he says. 'My mother wears my grandmother's ring. She always has done.' Instinctively they both look at Esther, and register a metallic glow on the third finger of her left hand.

Martha takes the gold band out of the chest. 'In that case I wonder who this belonged to?' She turns the tiny hoop over on the palm of her hand. All at once she stops, and draws it close to her eyes. 'Henry,' she says, 'there's something written here, on the inner edge. I can't make it out. Can you see it?' She passes the ring to Henry who squints and tilts it up to the light.'

'Names,' he says at last. 'Edna and Frank. Edna could be Emma, but the other name is definitely Frank.' He lowers his arm.

'Who were Edna and Frank?'

'Nobody I know.'

'Well…' Martha says. 'Wait… This might be a clue.' She fishes the yellowed scrap of newspaper out of the box and smooths it flat on her knee nearest to Henry.

There's a photograph of two women standing in bathers before a beach hut. The taller, fair one is hanging onto the arm of the younger, dark one whose fist is thrust towards the camera. They are both laughing, cheeks flushed, eyes crooked from the sunlight, and wedged into the sand behind them Martha can spot something that looks like a bottle. Beside the picture a column reads:

Constance Atkins of Quilter Street, Bethnal Green, celebrates after Sylvia Rodwell, of Chestnut Place, Norwich, finds her mother's wedding band. Miss Atkins despaired after she lost her deceased mother's ring in the sand during a holiday at Wells beach, but Norfolk mother, Mrs Rodwell, came to her aid, saving the day with an extraordinary feat of luck and determination.

'How amazing,' Martha begins, 'finding a ring in the sand.' Her voice falls away, her concentration locked onto the newspaper. 'Henry,' she says, tremulously. 'Look!'

'What?'

'Look!' Martha grabs his arm and indicates the caption immediately beneath the picture: S. RODWELL AND C. ATKINS, ON WELLS BEACH. 'C. Atkins,' she reads out loud. 'C. Atkins,' she says again, more slowly. 'Catkins. *Catkins!* This could be the person my father was writing to!'

'Do you think so?' Henry says doubtfully. 'It's probably just a coincidence.'

'I'm certain of it! C. Atkins – written as an email address or file name, it could easily be *Catkins*, right?'

'Well, yes, but…'

'Wait!' Martha goes in search of her purse, abandoned, at some point, on the kitchen table. She retrieves her mobile and hastily scrolls through her WhatsApp messages from Elizabeth. 'See!' she says triumphantly, displaying the photograph of the woman on the beach to Henry. 'I'm certain this is the same person. But' – her voice drops, a hundred thoughts dizzy in her head – 'how can that be? I mean why would my father be writing to Constance? And if this is the lost ring, why is it in the jewellery case? Sylvia found it, didn't she? And gave it back.'

'I can't help you, I'm afraid. I don't know anything about the ring or the newspaper.'

'That's why your mother fetched the box, isn't it' – Martha is quivering – 'because she wanted me to find them?'

The question seems to freeze the conversation. From the television comes a low ripple of laughter and applause. Tentatively, Henry picks up the cutting. 'Mum…' Esther turns her head. 'See this photograph? It was in the jewellery case, do you remember it?'

For a long time Esther gapes at it, her face impassive. Martha exchanges a despairing glance with Henry, but then, all of a sudden, Esther says, 'I was there. We both were,' and Martha lets out a long breath.

'Who were you with, Mum?'

'Lewis, of course.' Esther sounds almost snappy. 'But he went away. He went away during the war.' She pushes the newspaper away, and looks at Martha as if at the haziest outline, a glimmer of land from the bow of a boat. 'Are you Helen?'

Martha swallows. 'No,' she says. 'I'm not.'

'Then where is Helen?'

'She's in London, Mum.'

'Oh.'

Esther reverts to the television.

For a second, Henry closes his eyes. Then holding up the picture he says to Martha in a determinedly normal tone, 'So that's my… our… grandmother, Sylvia Rodwell. Doesn't she look young?'

'She was very beautiful, wasn't she?' Martha says, wistfully. 'And Constance too, in a different kind of a way.' She points at the beach hut, 'Is that the hut you were in the other night?'

'It's had a couple of makeovers over the years, but it's still the same patch of sand. It's been in the family as long as I know.'

'And did you ever meet Constance? She seems to be very friendly with Sylvie.'

'Not that I can remember. Anyhow, she was on holiday remember' – Henry checks the newspaper – 'it says she came from Bethnal Green.'

'Where's that?'

'London. East London.'

'Then maybe they never saw each other again.' Martha sighs. 'That would be sad too.'

'But the ring is here,' Henry points out. 'There must be a reason for that.' He looks to his mother and his face fogs with hopelessness.

Immediately Martha knows what she wants to do. Her expression must change because she sees Henry's eyes widen in understanding.

'I'd come with you,' he says, 'if I wasn't needed here.'

Standing on the doorstep, Henry slips something small into her hand. 'You should take this with you.' When Martha opens her palm the ring sparks needles of afternoon sunlight.

'I may not find her – Constance, *Catkins* – or she might not be alive.'

'In that case you can bring it back again.'

'How do you know I won't keep it?'

'Will you keep it?'

'Of course not!'

'Well then.'

Neither of them appears to know how to say goodbye. In the end, Martha presses herself briefly against the wall of Henry's chest and leaves with a deliberately jaunty wave of her hand and a promise to tell him the moment she has any news.

Walking past the school railings, Martha's mobile rings.

'Janey! Hello sweetie!' The line is silent. Martha stops and double-checks the caller display. 'I can't hear you, sweetie,' she says more loudly. 'I don't think the signal is strong enough.' But without the beat of her footsteps Martha *can* hear something; a barely audible whimper and then all at once a choking intake of breath.

'Mom!' The word breaks into a thousand fragments.

'Janey, darling, what's happened?' A surge of panic blooms in Martha's stomach, and then abates; her daughter is alive and able to call her, nothing else matters as much as that.

'Mom!'

'What is it, Janey? Tell me what's wrong.'

There's a pause, in which Martha can sense a bunching of effort, a moment of commitment.

'Mom,' Janey's voice is faint. She sounds, she sounds... *petrified*. 'Mom, don't be mad—'

'I won't—'

'You mean that?'

'What? Of course I mean it! I—'

Janey interrupts her. 'I was pregnant.' She's crying now, softly down the line. 'But... but, I'm not anymore.'

'Oh Janey—'

'Mom—'

'I'm coming to find you. I'm on my way.' Still clutching the phone, Martha breaks into a jog, and then, as if her own feet might propel her all the way to Cambridge, she starts to run.

CHAPTER SIXTEEN

Norfolk, August 1940

Sylvie's mother, blouse gaping and forehead shiny, was wedged against the sink while Sylvie was standing in the daily help's usual spot. Both of them were folding clean wet bedclothes surrounded by the daisy-white fug of the laundry. Stooping low to gather up another sheet, her mother grimaced. Sylvie assumed it was because of her back, or the amount of work they still had ahead of them, but then she said, 'I can't stop myself from thinking about poor Mrs Baxter.'

Sylvie bit her lip; she didn't trust herself to reply. The previous weekend her mother had made a point of telling her about the bomb that had fallen on Kennie's house in Norwich, passing on the news while Sylvie was still taking off her coat as if she couldn't keep it to herself a second longer. Sylvie had to pretend she didn't know already. Worse than that, she had to keep her feelings under control and not let them run away with her. It was horrible having to act out just the right amount of emotion, showing some upset, but in a measured way, and afterwards she wondered if she had kept herself too buttoned up because once or twice she caught her mother gazing at her with a queer expression. She didn't think she could bear to revisit the conversation, trapped in the kitchen with the washing, but her mother kept frowning and before Sylvie could change the subject her mother gave her head another worried shake. 'She's taken it very badly, of course. But what can you expect? Kennie was the apple of her eye. If something had happened to him when he was younger I expect the neighbours would have rallied round more, but nowadays everyone's got their own heartache to cope with. She hasn't even had the comfort of a funeral yet. I imagine there will be one, but nobody's said anything to me about it.'

'Can't Mary help?' Sylvie spoke quietly. She was standing right in front of her mother, close enough to spot the turmoil behind her eyes if her mother knew to look for it.

'She only came home for a couple of days, it was all the leave she could get. They can't spare nurses for long at the moment.' Her mother sighed, but gradually her face acquired a purposeful air that Sylvie knew well. 'I know what to do,' she said. 'When I get the dinner tonight, I'll make some extra and take it round to Mrs Baxter in the morning. It will do for a Sunday lunch and show we haven't forgotten her.'

That night the house was unpleasantly warm. At the top of the back stairs, Sylvie's bedroom seemed to suck the heat into it with the efficiency of a greenhouse. Tossing under the sheets, Sylvie counted the long chime of midnight from the grandfather clock and after an eternity of more twisting and pillow plumping the solitary strike that marked the passing of another hour. Unable to bear it any longer she swung her legs out of bed and tweaked aside the blackout curtain. A pool of milky moonshine gushed over the floorboards. She rummaged in her handbag for the packet of Chesterfields and box of matches lurking beneath her purse and then crept out of the room. Despite the absolute dark she could navigate instinctively. Her hand reached at just the right moment for the smooth slide of the bannister. Her legs counted the exact number of paces from the foot of the stairs to the kitchen. The soles of her feet anticipated the cat's-tongue surface of the pamment tiles, followed by the rough scullery matting. Finally, she eased back the bolts of the yard door, taking care to make as little noise as possible, and pushed it open. The night flared brazenly before her; the sky shot with stars, the moon a fat, silver hunting horn over the roof of the outhouse.

Tucking her nightdress under her thighs she sat down on the back step and lit a cigarette. It was the first one she'd had since arriving with the children on Friday evening and it was a relief to feel the slimness of it between her fingers. Her mother never liked to see her smoking and would be upset to know Sylvie had taken it up again. Whenever she caught anyone with a cigarette she had a tendency to wrinkle her nose and throw open the nearest window, complaining about the smell and issuing dire health warnings that seemed to have no authority but her own. Not that Sylvie had smoked much before Victoria Terrace was bombed, but these days everyone she knew did – even if it ought to be a luxury it felt increasingly like a necessity, something to steady the nerves and the slow the mind. She pressed back against the doorpost and inhaled deeply.

Kennie was gone.

The brutality of it was never out of her thoughts for long. And yet, almost imperceptibly, the shock was beginning to lessen. She supposed her emotions had become numbed – during the past few months the flimsiness of life, including her own, had never been so obvious or felt so true – but to her surprise she was starting to find the space to think beyond her grief. Staring at the pale threads of smoke rising and melting into the dark she could see how the comfort she had gained from knowing that Kennie was out there, somewhere in the world, had been her undoing too. How it had unsettled her, how she had always believed that she could – should – have been living a different life. How she had feared her susceptibility, were he to return. Well, now she had no choice, she had to make the best of things with Howard. In a way, Sylvie reflected, she had been saved from herself – made to stop before she destroyed her marriage entirely.

She bent down and tapped the tail of glowing ash into a heap beside her ankle. Perhaps Connie was right; it was not inconceivable that Lewis was Howard's child. There was a chance after the war

Howard might even believe that possibility, if Sylvie would let him. She drew again on the cigarette, a sense of clarity blooming. She wouldn't evacuate Lewis. But when the time came she would take him to London, just as if he was really going, so she wouldn't have to confront her mother, or anyone else, about her decision. They would stay the night with Connie and only come home once the ship had sailed. Afterwards, she would tell Howard and her parents she had simply mixed up the date, or arrived at the train station too late. They might not believe her but there would be nothing Howard could do about it, and when the war was over she would work to make things better for them all.

After another minute or two Sylvie ground out the cigarette stub and stood up. The sense of decisiveness was emboldening. With her hand on the scullery door she cast a last glance at the mackerel-bright heavens. In Howard's last letter he had written about the marvellous skies in the African desert, how they reminded him of Norfolk. He sounded wistful and quite sad. She wondered if he was gazing at them now, thinking of home.

The next morning, as Sylvie was searching out breakfast for the children, her mother appeared wearing a floor-length ivory night-gown. She looked wan, with her hair long and startlingly grey about her shoulders. When Sylvie asked if anything was the matter she complained of a headache. Sitting at the table while Sylvie filled the kettle, she kept taking her hand to her forehead. 'It's no good,' she said, eventually, 'I shall have to go back to bed.' At the doorway she turned. 'Be a dear and run that pie over to Mrs Baxter for me, I'd like to get it there in time for her Sunday dinner. Besides, she'll probably be glad of the opportunity to see one of Kennie's old friends.'

Waiting on Mrs Baxter's doorstep, Sylvie couldn't help but worry whether the pie was such a kind idea after all. Of course her mother meant well, but the meagre size of it, encased within a small Pyrex dish, seemed to shout out loud that it was intended for only one person sitting entirely alone at her kitchen table. Sylvie regarded it unhappily and then swung the lion-head knocker quickly, before thoughts about Kennie and the memories of Victoria Terrace – the smoking piles of rubble and the charred smell of cordite – destroyed her composure.

When the door opened it seemed, for a disorientating instant, that the figure bowed over a cane was not Mrs Baxter but an older sister or aunt. Although spidery veins reddened the woman's cheeks, the pallor underneath them was winter-sky white and there was a glassy sheen to her eyes.

While Sylvie was still struggling to adjust, Mrs Baxter broke the silence. 'Sylvia,' – her voice had a peculiar edge to it, thick and unpractised sounding – 'what have you got there?'

Sylvie fought the urge to thrust the golden-crusted pastry into her hands and bolt. 'My mother thought you might be glad of this,' she said, holding out the dish, 'To save you the trouble of cooking on a Sunday. She would have brought it herself only she woke this morning with a terrible head and had to go back to bed.'

Mrs Baxter didn't take the pot as Sylvie had hoped. Instead she gestured at Sylvie to come inside and headed down the hallway with her stick knocking dully against the tiles. After a second's hesitation Sylvie followed, shutting the door behind her. As soon as it closed she became aware of a vinegary, out-of-place smell emanating from the back of the house. More than ever she wished she could leave, but Mrs Baxter was already disappearing into the parlour and obviously expected Sylvie to join her. It was the last place on earth that Sylvie wanted to go.

'Shall I take the dish to the larder?' she called.

'No!' Mrs Baxter's voice was unaccountably firm. 'Come in here. I'll put it away in a minute.'

The window of the small room was sealed tight against the summer's day with the curtains only half pulled back. A selection of dirty crockery sprawled over the table while by one of the legs a knitting bag had tipped on its side, spilling the needles and a confusion of wool over the carpet. Mrs Baxter lowered herself into the armchair. Sylvie pulled out an upright dining chair and perched on the edge of it; she was still holding the pie.

She had barely sat down when Mrs Baxter leaned forwards and said in a fierce whisper, 'He wasn't meant to die, you know. Not blown to smithereens by a bomb.' She spoke as though they were in the middle of a conversation rather than at the beginning of one. 'He'd got back safe from France. Injured, but safe. He'd done his bit and he didn't need to fight again.'

It felt like a scene from a terrible drama, as if they were acting out something that wasn't real and as long as they both played along for a minute or two it must all revert to normal. Sylvie found she was holding her breath and let it out unevenly. 'I'm very sorry,' she said, 'for your loss.'

Mrs Baxter's eyes snagged unexpectedly on her own. The anguish in them was so intense Sylvie had to look away.

'We don't even live in Norwich. He was only stopping up there a week or two. He wasn't supposed to be in that house.'

'I'm so sorry,' Sylvie said again.

Mrs Baxter fell silent and her face acquired a mask-like stillness. Sylvie couldn't think what to say. The unpleasant odour she'd noticed before was stronger and seemed to come from the door that linked to the kitchen. Outside someone was bouncing a ball on the pavement. She could hear the repetitive thwack and then, as the rhythm broke, a cry of annoyance, before it started again. She put the dish on the table and cleared her throat, ready to make her departure, but just as she did Mrs Baxter heaved herself to her feet. 'I expect you'd like some tea before you go. I'll make us both a cup.' She shuffled away before Sylvie could respond.

Alone in the room, Sylvie's gaze was drawn to the spot next to the fireplace where she and Kennie had lain together only weeks earlier. The memory of it danced in front of her eyes and filled her with such a disturbing mixture of longing and horror that it was a relief when her thoughts were pierced by the whistle of the kettle. Soon afterwards Mrs Baxter returned carrying two white china teacups that rattled on their saucers as she shuffled across the carpet. As the deadening silence began to slide back, Sylvie asked in desperation about the garden, whether Mrs Baxter was managing to keep her vegetables going and what she might grow during the summer? Lettuces, for instance, they were easy to manage and a nice green salad, she found, was practically a meal in itself when the weather was hot. Sipping the bitter tea Sylvie felt her words hang hopelessly between them while she rushed from one inanity to another.

The moment she saw both the cups were drained, she sprang up. 'I'll run the pie into the kitchen and put it somewhere cool,' she said.

Mrs Baxter's expression grew more pinched. 'Sit down,' she said. 'I'll do it later.'

'It's quite all right.' Now Sylvie was standing, escape felt within reach. If she didn't take the chance she sensed she might be stuck with Mrs Baxter the whole of the afternoon. 'I'm halfway there already.'

She walked with purpose and determined cheeriness through the connecting door but when she entered the kitchen it was all she could do not to shout out in surprise. The wooden rocker was barely visible beneath a snarled mass of wet laundry. Saucepans and dishes tottered in the sink, while a thicket of cardboard boxes and empty beer bottles blocked the exit to the yard. Sylvie realised the smell was the same one that drifted from the back of public houses in hot weather.

'I'll take that from you, shall I?' Mrs Baxter was standing behind her, a defiant sort of embarrassment etched on her mouth.

'I'm sorry,' Sylvie stammered. 'I didn't meant to intrude.' She pushed the pie dish at Mrs Baxter.

'I suppose you can see yourself out?'

'Of course.' Sylvie backed a few steps, hesitated and stopped. She wasn't sure how to take her leave. In the end she raised her hand in a shy kind of wave and, with a rush of relief, turned for the front door. As it closed on her heels she was hit by the premonition she would never in her life go back there again.

*

The notification of the sailing date came in the post exactly one week beforehand. Lewis had to be taken to the meeting point at Euston station for eight o'clock in the morning on Friday, 6 September; the SS *Nerissa* would sail from the Liverpool docks the following day. The official black typing gave Sylvie an electric-like jolt and she had to remind herself it didn't matter what the letter said, because Lewis wouldn't actually be going anywhere. Steadying her breathing, she folded the pages away. Later she wrote to tell Connie that she and Lewis would arrive in London sometime on Thursday afternoon. She didn't explain her plan – it would be easier face-to-face, she thought – and, after some hesitancy, she decided not to say anything to Lewis, either. Better to tell him once they were on their way and there was no chance of him blurting it out to Elsie, or her mother, who was bound to telephone before they left.

On the Tuesday she was kneeling beside an old trunk that belonged to Howard, going through the motion of packing Lewis' clothes, when Elsie appeared in the doorway. Elsie gazed down at the muddle of shirts and trousers, underclothes and socks, which Sylvie had accumulated on the floor beside her. 'Hasn't he got anything else?' she said after a moment. 'Canada can get very cold. Won't he need some heavier jumpers and a coat with a good, thick lining?'

Sylvie shook out a vest and folded it in half. 'His winter clothes from last year are too small for him now.' This was true but there had also seemed no earthly point in making the trunk heavier than it needed to be for its journey down to London and back.

'In that case perhaps you need to buy him some pullovers. The crossing itself is bound to be chilly and you don't want him arriving with a nasty cold or none of the Canadian families will want to have him.' Elsie's whine of concern was out of character and it made Sylvie stop what she was doing and look at her properly. A copy of the *Daily Express* was wedged under Elsie's arm in a way that suddenly struck Sylvie as not quite casual enough. She gestured towards it.

'Is there bad news?'

'Oh!' Elsie considered the newspaper with affected surprise. Then she sighed and said, 'Well, I suppose you ought to see it.' As Sylvie scrambled to her feet Elsie opened it out to one of the middle pages.

At first Sylvie couldn't see what Elsie wanted to show her, but soon she saw the headline halfway down the middle column: BRITISH EVACUEE SHIP TORPEDOED. She gasped and took the paper, drawing it close to her face.

'Everyone was saved,' Elsie said hurriedly. 'They were all saved.'

Sylvie nodded slowly. She was reading for herself about the attack and how the passengers were taken to Scotland. The report insisted the children had found it a great adventure. More like a nightmare, Sylvie wondered in disbelief. It had happened in the early hours of the morning, apparently. She imagined the precarious, panicked climb down to the lifeboats, the journey over the dark, choppy seas in nothing but pyjamas and a blanket thrown around the shoulders. She felt the remaining doubts about her plan for Lewis blasted away as surely as this ship had been. Thank God it wasn't too late to stop him from going.

Letting the page drop, she became aware Elsie was watching her. 'Do you think they'll carry on with the evacuation programme now that this has happened?' Elsie asked. There was a childlike note of hope in her voice.

It hadn't occurred to Sylvie that they might not and her heart jumped at the thought of the project being abandoned, how it would solve everything for her. But almost immediately she realised it wouldn't happen. 'They're bound to say the Germans wouldn't get through the convoy a second time,' she said slowly. 'And that even if they did, there's no reason to think the children wouldn't be rescued again. Look at the way it's written' – she glanced at the passage again – 'almost as if being attacked made it all the more exciting.'

Elsie shook her head, either in disbelief or disapproval. She must have grown fond of Lewis during the last six weeks, Sylvie realised, because her face was grey with worry. Sylvie badly wanted to tell her there was no need to be, that Lewis would be staying at home with them. Instead, she closed up the newspaper in a businesslike fashion and handed it back. 'I'd better get on with the packing. We leave for London the day after tomorrow and there's still a great deal left to do.'

Elsie blinked, as if Sylvie's reaction was different from the one she had anticipated, and with laboured effort she turned her attention back to the trunk. 'What about his clothes, then?' she said brusquely. 'These itty-bitty things you've got here don't look nearly warm enough to me. And you'll have to sew on some name tapes, otherwise he'll lose half of them before the ship has left Liverpool.'

'Where on earth am I going to find winter woollies in the middle of the summer?' Sylvie protested. 'Especially when there's a war on.' But half an hour later she had allowed herself to be bundled into the hallway, shopping bag in hand.

She noticed the man loitering in the alley out of the corner of her eye, without making anything of it. Despite the sunshine he was wearing a coat – a pale beige trench – and a fedora hat. His back was facing the street and he appeared to be consulting something like a notebook. She was hurrying onward, keen to get home, when she thought she heard somebody call her name. She stopped.

'Sylvie! Sylvia!'

Sylvie's stomach flipped. A second later she felt a hand on her sleeve, pulling her sideways into the shadows. It happened too quickly for her to resist, and besides, somehow, deep in her subconscious, she knew what was happening.

The man pushed back the hat from his face. He was smiling but his expression had a strange, manic intensity to it. Sylvie could only stare. The emotion flooding through her made it impossible to either move or think. Slowly, the fact of him there in front of her acquired a reality.

'Kennie!' she said at last. 'My God, you're alive!' In disbelief, she reached up to touch his cheek.

'Shh.' He peered over Sylvie's shoulder towards the road. 'Keep your voice down.'

'Why?' She twisted around to follow his gaze, but nobody was there, nobody, at any rate, who appeared to have the slightest interest in them. She turned back to Kennie. 'Where have you been? What happened to—'

'Be quiet, Sylvia.' Still gripping her arm, he dragged her further away from the street and didn't let go, even when they were stationary again. 'Nobody must know you've seen me.'

She shook her head. 'I don't understand. What do you—'

'It's an operation. A secret one. It's better everyone thinks I'm dead, for the next few months at least.'

It took a while for the impact of what he was saying to register and then Sylvie felt a hot-cold clash of passion swell within her like rising floodwaters. 'That *everyone* thinks you're dead? Everyone? Me? Your own mother, driven half crazy because she thinks she lost you to a bomb?' Her voice was rising, out of control, but she couldn't have cared less.

Kennie glanced at the traffic again. 'She'll find out in due course. When I've done what I have to do.' His whisper had a hissing, pantomime quality and the empty black of his pupils gleamed feral in the borrowed light. It was impossible to tell if he was deluding himself, if France or the bomb had affected his head, or if he really was doing something important. 'I've come back for you, Sylvia, haven't I? You thought I was gone, but I'm not, I'm here.' His fingertip ran down the side of her neck and she let him bring her closer. His hand moved to her hair and gradually she found herself with her head on his coat, inhaling the smog of cigarettes and the intoxicating smell of him that she had thought was lost forever. The stroking of her scalp was hypnotising.

All at once it stopped. 'I want to talk about Lewis.' Kennie's tone was calm, almost gentle, but Sylvie felt an immediate pinch of fear. 'I remembered what you told me, how old he is. And so I checked his birthday.' He pushed her away from his chest and held her at a distance. 'He's mine, isn't he?'

Sylvie's heart froze, and then it began to race. 'How did you find out about his birthday?'

'I telephoned your mother. I pretended to be a friend of Howard's. I said he was too embarrassed to write and ask himself, but he couldn't for the life of him remember the date of the little chap's birthday.' He broke off, as if expecting Sylvie to applaud his cleverness. When she didn't speak he said in a colder voice, 'He is mine, isn't he?'

'I don't know,' Sylvie stammered. 'It's impossible to be certain.'

'I've been watching him—'

'Watching him! Where?'

'When he's outside playing. Or running errands. He's a proper good boy like that – and I'd say he looks like me.'

Sylvie could sense her terror dilating, spreading like an ink stain. 'Everyone says he looks like me!'

Kennie ignored her. 'You should have told me I have a son.'

She didn't reply and he shook her shoulder. 'Why didn't you tell me?'

'How could I?' Sylvie burst out. 'I was married to Howard. I *am* married to Howard.'

'You should have told me! I had a right to know!'

The memories of standing on Kennie's doorstep – of hearing his cheery, oblivious whistling – and then her pathetic return to Howard, combined within her like a chemical reaction. 'You kept leaving me!' she cried. 'First you want me, next you go away to Ireland. You don't come back until it's too late, and then you disappear again. You must have known I could be pregnant but you never even bothered to find out. All you did was use me when it suited you!' She saw now with absolute clarity how true this was.

Kennie started to fondle her hair again. She flicked away his hand, but he put it back. 'It wasn't like that, Sylvia.' His voice had become low and warm, crooning. 'I love you, Sylvia. I always have.' After a moment his hand stopped moving and he said, 'I want you to bring Lewis and live with me.'

Sylvie wondered if he really was demented. 'But everyone thinks you're dead, Kennie!'

'As soon as this is over, I mean. It won't be long. We can be together then.'

'*This*? You mean your special operation, do you? This mission that's so terribly important it's made you half kill your mother with grief.' She couldn't keep the contempt out of her voice, but she regretted it when she saw the fixed, dark expression that came over his face. In a more appeasing tone she added, 'But what about Esther? I can't leave Esther.'

'Bring her too.'

'Howard would never let me. Not in a million years.' An image came to her of Howard tossing Esther in his arms, Esther laughing, both of them framed by the laurel in the garden. 'And besides, Esther loves Howard!'

'Then leave her with Howard.'

'I can't do that! I can't just leave her!' She was beginning to shake. She took hold of Kennie's lapel. 'Wait, Kennie. Wait until the end of the war. It might… Howard might…' She hesitated. 'Howard may not come back.' The words sounded horribly callous, immediately she added to herself, *I only said it. I didn't wish it – I don't wish it.*

Kennie appeared to consider the proposal, but after a second he shook his head. 'Lewis is my son, Sylvia. He should come to me. I have rights. You can stay with Howard if you want, but Lewis must live with me.' He looked straight at her and smiled, as if this was perfectly reasonable. Sylvie thought, I don't want him; for the first time in my life, I don't want him. And then she thought, I'm afraid of him.

He began to caress her neck again. 'Meet me here tomorrow, Sylvia. At the same time. We can talk some more, but you mustn't keep me from my son any longer.'

Seconds passed. Very slowly, Sylvie put down her shopping basket. Then, standing upright, she leaned forwards, cupped Kennie's face between her hands and kissed him on the lips. For a moment he seemed too surprised to respond, but soon he pressed himself against her, his tongue searching her mouth, and she felt his body harden. When they drew back Sylvie said, 'I have to visit my mother tomorrow, Kennie. I'll come the day after.' She made herself smile into his eyes.

'All right.' Kennie nodded his approval. He was panting slightly. 'But don't be late.'

*

Wednesday evening was a miserable affair. As Lewis was due to leave for London the following day Sylvie cooked his favourite meal of toad-in-the-hole. She had hoped to turn it into something of a send-off, baking a honey cake for dessert and digging out a couple of the Christmas streamers to brighten the place up, but they were all too unhappy to carry off the sham for long. Nobody had an appetite and soon they were wrapped in a jittery silence, punctured only by scraps of conversation spoken in unnaturally buoyant tones. In the end, defeated, Sylvie suggested that Lewis have an early night. To her surprise he agreed and immediately scrambled down from the table but as he reached the door there was a peculiar whimpering noise and it took Sylvie a moment to realise that Esther was crying.

'Oh darling!' Sylvie rushed to her side, but Esther threw down her knife and fork and ran to stand by Lewis.

'Go away!' she screamed as Sylvie stepped towards them. 'I want Lewis!'

'Darling…' Sylvie watched her, aghast.

'Why do you have to go to Canada?' Esther's arms were wrapped around her brother's waist, her face buried against his stomach, her chest heaving. 'Why can't you stay here?'

Nobody spoke.

Lewis gazed at his mother over the top of Esther's head. Eventually he said, 'Do I really have to go?'

Sylvie started to tremble. The question was a knife blade, slicing her open. She heard Kennie, '*You can stay with Howard if you want, but Lewis must live with me.*' At last she was able to make her tongue and mouth move again, although the words were like boulders, rough and dry and almost impossible to get out. 'Yes,' she said. 'It's all arranged now.' Her jaw braced. 'We must think of it as an opportunity. You'll be safely out of harm's way during this horrible war and home again before we know it.'

Lewis left the room, Esther following behind. Sylvie started after them, but Elsie caught her arm. 'I would leave them be a few minutes,' she said gently.

When Sylvie went upstairs a little later, she found them both in Lewis' bed. They were asleep – or pretending to be – Esther nestled beneath her brother's shoulder, the eiderdown obscuring her face completely and pulled halfway over Lewis' head. For a while Sylvie stood beside the bed, watching the rise and fall of the covers and fighting the urge to shake them awake. Eventually, she kissed the tips of her fingers, pressed them lightly on Lewis' forehead and tiptoed from the room.

In the kitchen she found Elsie scraping the leftover food onto one of the plates. 'All that waste,' Sylvie said, coming beside her. She couldn't summon up much interest in it, but she prodded a soggy piece of batter pudding with a fork. 'Whatever would Lord Woolton say? Shouldn't we save it for pig food or something?'

Elsie lifted her head and contemplated Sylvie. 'Just this once,' she said. 'I'm not going to worry about Lord Woolton, or the pigs.' Then she added, 'You look exhausted, my dear. Go and sit down. I don't mind clearing up in here.'

Sylvie scanned the cluttered sink and stove. She had a sudden, horrible memory of Mrs Baxter's kitchen, the beer bottles stacked like skittles by the back door, and the awful sour smell. It made her feel quite ill. She touched Elsie's arm. 'I think I might go to bed,' she said. 'If you're certain you can manage on your own.' But on her way upstairs she extracted a fountain pen and a sheet of Basildon Bond from the bureau in the drawing room.

Settling at her dressing table she swept the pots and jars to one side. She flattened out the paper with the heel of her hand and studied herself in the mirror. The face staring back at her was tired and sad, but also resolved. A lock of hair had fallen into her eyes. Sylvie twisted it around her forefinger until the tip throbbed red, then all at once she let it spiral loose, picked up the pen and began to write. Once it was finished she sat for a long time without moving, watching the sky outside the bedroom window change indiscernibly from blue to plum black.

Out on the landing a thin glow was seeping from the entrance to Elsie's room but as Sylvie gazed at it, clutching an envelope, it flickered and died. Quickly Sylvie tapped on the door. The bead of light reappeared and there was a heavy creaking of bedsprings. Shortly afterwards Elsie appeared in the doorway, knotting the cord of her dressing gown.

'Is everything all right?' She peered over Sylvie's shoulder, as if some calamitous event might be unfolding in the stairwell. 'Is it Lewis? Is he upset?'

'No. No, it's not Lewis or Esther.' Sylvie tried to keep her tone matter of fact, as much for her own sake as Elsie's. 'It's only that I have a favour to ask of you. I should have spoken to you about it earlier. I'm sorry, but I…' Her voice died.

'What kind of favour is it?'

'Do you know the passageway at the back of the Lamb Inn?'

Elsie stopped fussing with her dressing gown. 'I think so…'

'I have a letter' – Sylvie made a little gesturing motion – 'that I'd like you to give to somebody for me. It shouldn't take very long and I'm sure Evelyn would be happy to mind Esther.' She paused. Elsie was watching her uncertainly. 'Tomorrow afternoon, if you go to the alley at three o'clock, he'll be waiting. I think he'll be wearing a beige coat, but you'll spot him easily because he'll be watching out for me. Please… please give him this.' She swallowed and thrust the envelope at Elsie. 'Tell him I couldn't come because I'm on a train to London. With Lewis. He's not' – she added – 'anyone you know.'

As soon as she stopped talking the house seemed intensely quiet. The phrase 'brazen it out' came to mind; Sylvie didn't feel at all brazen but she did have a curious sense of composure, of taking control.

After a moment Elsie's expression cleared. She took the letter and tucked it into her dressing gown pocket. 'I shall be glad to repay some of your kindness,' she said. 'I don't know what I would have done without you these past few weeks.' She too sounded businesslike, almost brisk, as if they were discussing a shopping list, or the wool raffle. 'Now, if there's nothing else…?'

Sylvie shook her head.

Fleetingly, their eyes met before the door softly closed.

CHAPTER SEVENTEEN

Norfolk, recently

The road out of Norfolk cuts through tracts of purple-green woods interspersed with towns of mellow-stoned hotels, market squares and assorted charity shops. Imperceptibly the sky retreats and the sense of sea, of edge and space, lessens and then dissipates completely. At one point they pass an American airbase. Catching a glint of movement, Martha points to a fighter jet purring behind a perimeter fence topped with barbed wire and searchlights. Janey allows herself a transitory stab of interest before her face snaps shut again.

It's been like this for the past twenty-four hours, since almost the second Janey disembarked at King's Lynn railway station with an ink-stained tote containing only a toothbrush, some thick black mascara and a serious-looking tome entitled *Transformative Art of the Twentieth Century*. At least, this is what Martha surmises from the fact that Janey is today wearing the same long cotton skirt and T-shirt she arrived in, the constant heavy-lidded state of Janey's eyes and the shield-like status the book acquires whenever Janey suspects Martha is about to attempt a conversation.

Some way through Janey's call, the one Martha took on the way back from Henry's house, it occurred to Martha it made more sense for Janey to come to Wells than for her to go to Janey; she envisaged enveloping Janey into the bosom of the hotel, a long, possibly tearful, walk along the sand and, a gentle, healing evening filled with good food and wine.

Naturally, it didn't happen like that.

'You're in England?' Janey said in a shocked tone when Martha admitted she was not on the other side of the Atlantic but less than two hours away. 'When exactly were you planning on telling me? Or did you not want to see me?'

'Of course I want to see you. I can't wait to see you!' Martha cried, 'I was only waiting until I'd been here a while in case… in case you thought I couldn't bear to let you go and have adventures on your own.' She swallowed. Janey stayed silent. 'The truth is,' Martha continued, 'I had other reasons for coming to England. Reasons to do with your grandad.' She explained a little about the beach hut, although she didn't, at that point, complicate matters by mentioning Constance. Besides, Janey didn't seem terribly interested.

That same evening Martha collected Janey from the train. She watched her daughter emerge from the mass of strangers on the platform and then, for a second or two, she held Janey close, inhaling, like a nicotine addict, the achingly familiar scent of skin and hair. But after that Janey pulled away. She didn't want to talk about the pregnancy, about the end of the pregnancy, about, for heaven's sake, even the train ride. Not in the car on the journey to Wells. Not in her room, when Martha slipped a tentative arm around Janey's shoulders. Not during dinner, as unasked questions hovered like extra guests around the table while Janey pushed eggplant *parmigiana* back and forth across her plate. Coming out of the dining room the young receptionist asked Janey how long she would be staying. The enquiry was met with a curt, almost insolent shrug, and then, appallingly, Janey's eyes filled with tears and she looked away.

'About a week,' Martha said hurriedly, and ushered Janey upstairs, where Janey announced she wanted to take a bath and promptly disappeared behind a locked door.

During the night Martha stared for hours into the shape-shifting black. By the time Janey appeared at Martha's bedroom door the following morning, hanging onto the frame as if it were holding her up,

Martha had been dressed for some time and her car keys and denim jacket were lying on the bed beside her purse and airplane rucksack.

Janey eyed them warily. 'Where are you going?' she asked.

'*We…*' Martha said, '*we* are going to Bethnal Green. In London.'

'Why?'

'I'll tell you over breakfast.'

'Why can't you tell me now?' Janey let go of the door and the cloudy blue of her irises glimmered like stirred paint.

'Breakfast,' Martha said firmly, steering her along the corridor. And she made the mysterious files called Catkins, the tale of finding Esther, and the discovery of the wedding ring and the newspaper last the time it took Janey to divide her toast into ever smaller pieces until she had no option left other than to put them in her mouth, and after that two soft-boiled eggs and a sliced peach. But Martha didn't, as it happened, say much about Henry.

Now, in the passenger seat, Janey is dozing, neck crooked, lashes curled against the mauve-coloured pigment of her eye sockets. The spell of fine weather has faltered; a veil of high cloud has given the day a filtered, blank appearance and occasional bursts of wind tug at the steering. Martha grips the wheel more tightly. It's an effort to concentrate on driving, rather than take the opportunity to scrutinise Janey. Her hairstyle is the most obvious difference, cut close to the back of Janey's neck but long on top, in a shape Martha supposes is meant to look sophisticated but to Martha's eyes makes her daughter seem younger, more unprotected, than ever. And Janey has lost weight too, her cheeks are hollow and her limbs slender as broom handles. Yet some parts of her appearance are touchingly unchanged, the gemstone bracelet she has worn since the day Clem brought it back from Mexico, the dusky rose T-shirt – Janey's all-time favourite shade since she was six years old. What would Martha give to be folding tiny pink beach shorts and Minnie-Mouse T-shirts into Janey's bureau now? She glances at Janey's bare arms, reaches across and flicks the heater into action.

A minute later, Janey shifts position. 'For God's sake, Mom, it's stifling in here.' She opens the window several inches, causing a candy wrapper to fly straight out of it, and immediately settles back to sleep. Martha sighs and glues her eyes to the road.

In time the single-lane highway expands into two, and soon three, lanes of traffic. It pours from all directions, sweeping them past retail parks and under motorway bridges, through tunnels and over concrete intersections. It pulls them on like swarming insects, gathering exhaust fumes and noise. There's no sense of being anywhere in particular, only of movement, travelling forwards, until eventually the skyline erupts into a geometry of towers and shortly afterwards Martha is directed off the motorway, plunging into the teeming, stuttering, cobweb of Greater London.

Thirty minutes later she switches off the engine. Janey rubs a hand across her face. 'Where are we?'

'Bethnal Green.' They are parked opposite a halal supermarket and outside a pub called the Dog and Duck, the name inscribed in gold curly letters on a racing-green background. A man dressed in bikers' leathers is sitting on the pavement with his back against the wall, sipping a pint.

Janey struggles upright. 'What are we going to do now?'

'Well,' Martha says cautiously, 'I suppose I'll go to Quilter Street and see if anyone has heard of Constance Atkins.'

'You're just going to knock on people's doors? That's the only plan you have?' Janey is awake now, staring at her mother with naked astonishment.

'I guess.' Martha opens the door before the thinness of the strategy sends her scurrying back to Norfolk. She isn't sure whether Janey will even get out of the car but after a moment Janey clambers from the passenger seat and comes to stand beside her. Martha is careful not to acknowledge this small triumph. 'Okay, so it's up here and then left.' She's reading from a map on her cell phone.

'Wow. This would be such a cool place to live.' Janey is looking around with a brightened expression. In addition to the pub and the supermarket, there's a vegetarian cafe, an outlet for vinyl records and another unit selling silk and cotton saris. They walk past a French bakery, a spice emporium and a window full of shimmering tropical fish. Janey hangs back to read some details posted in the window of an estate agent. 'Oh my God!' She jogs to catch up with Martha, 'I could never afford to come here!'

Martha stops in surprise. 'Really?'

'No way.' Janey's voice is tight with shock. 'The tiniest place is like half a million pounds.'

Two minutes later they come to a park shaped like a triangle. A group of long-legged, twenty-something women are sitting in a circle talking in a foreign language while a gaggle of toddlers potter aimlessly around them. Martha consults her phone and turns into a street lined with terraced cottages. 'This,' she says, 'is Quilter Street.'

The houses manage to look both old and new, as if recently constructed for a movie or TV program set many years ago. Grey brick facades are scrubbed to raw silver and most of the sash windows contain boxes of trailing geraniums positioned exactly in the middle of the sill. Martha hoped there might be people in the street, people she could speak to; old people, even, who would know immediately about Constance Atkins. But there doesn't seem to be anyone about at all. The only small sign of life is a cat stretched motionless along a low brick wall.

'What are you going to do?' Janey asks. 'Just go and ring a doorbell?'

By way of answer Martha hoiks her purse strap further up her shoulder, strides towards the closest door and presses the buzzer. The sound ricochets around the interior long after she takes away her hand, but nobody comes in response. Stepping sideways, she cups her face in her hands, and peers through the glass above the geraniums. She can see stripped-pine floorboards and a red sofa, but the room has a flat, deserted air.

'Mom! For God's sake!' Janey is hopping from foot to foot and gazing up and down the street. 'Someone might come. They'll think you're about to burgle the place.'

There's no reply at the neighbour's house either. Nor at the house after that. On her following attempt, Martha encounters a girl with iron-straight hair and bare feet who looks very much like the women in the park. The girl flicks her wrist in a dismissive gesture and re-shuts the door before Martha can open her mouth. Martha tries to send Janey an exasperated look, but Janey is busy with her phone.

There are no flowers in the window of the next cottage and the paintwork has animal-like scratch marks that may or may not belong to the sleeping cat. Unable to find a bell she raps the knocker, dropping it against the wood with more force than she intended. Immediately she hears the slap of approaching footsteps and the door opens. A woman regards her from beneath a helmet of grey hair. 'Yes?'

'Excuse me,' Martha says, 'I was wondering if you could help? I'm looking for someone called Constance Atkins.'

'Never heard of her.' Tucked into her skirt the woman is wearing a white blouse with the kind of neck frill that looks like it belongs on a bone of roast meat. Thin, stockinged legs disappear into enormous sheepskin slippers. 'Is she a runaway? One of them druggies?'

'No! I think she used to live in this street. A long time ago, before the war.'

'Well, she won't be here now. They're all immigrants round here. Australian, or worse. Some of them don't even speak English. Makes you wonder why we bothered fighting a war at all!' Martha inches backwards. 'What do you want her for, anyway?'

'Well, I…'

'Are you the government?'

'No!' Martha says. 'It's nothing official, just a family matter.' A strong smell of air freshener wafts over the doorstep.

'Hmm…' The woman's eyes ripple over Martha and then settle on Martha's face. 'I suppose you could ask my father-in-law. Dad!'

she shouts, twisting her neck but keeping her shoulders square to the door. 'He's half deaf,' she tells Martha, as if by way of complaint. 'Never seems to hear a thing I say and about as much use to anyone as a chocolate teapot. Dad! Royston! Come here. You're needed at the door.' Her voice spurts down the hallway. Eventually there's a chafing sound and an old man shuffles into view. 'You took your time! This lady if trying to find... Who was it again?'

'Constance,' Martha says. 'Constance Atkins.'

The old man sucks through his teeth. His body is bent in the shape of a banana, his skull spattered with age spots and single white hairs while the angle of his back directs his gaze onto the squares of carpet at his feet.

When he doesn't answer, his daughter-in-law puts her hands on her hips. 'Well, do you remember her, or don't you, Royston? Don't keep us stood here all day!'

Eventually the old man shakes his head. 'I don't know that name.'

'There! What did I say!' His daughter-in-law narrows the door, as if about to shut it.

'Wait!' Royston tips back his head to reveal dulled, rheumy eyes but they hook onto Martha with surprising decisiveness. 'Ted Rossiter. That's who you should speak to. He grew up round here. He's the one to ask.'

Martha becomes aware of Janey hovering somewhere behind her left shoulder. 'Ted Rossiter? Where does he live?'

'Somewhere around the corner.' A hand, knarled like tree-bark, flaps beyond the far end of Quilter Street.

'I don't suppose,' Martha says, 'you can remember the address?'

'No, of course he can't,' the daughter-in-law snaps. 'He doesn't know whether it's Tuesday or last Christmas. He hasn't been out of the house all year and he's not able to remember names and numbers like a walking telephone book.' She begins to close the door, but stops, as if struck by something. She blinks at Martha as if she's just opened the fridge and discovered something mouldy lurking at the back of it. 'Here, you've got a funny accent an' all! Are you a foreigner as well?'

Martha's mouth opens. She's about to say something reasonable and placatory, something about being on vacation from Canada with no intention of overstaying her welcome, but the curdled expression on the woman's face ignites a little flame of fury that takes hold before Martha can stamp it down. 'Actually,' she says, 'I come from a place called Shag Rock.'

The woman blanches. 'Shag Rock?'

From out of nowhere Royston explodes with a cackle.

His daughter-in-law rounds on him. 'You disgusting old man! I know just what you're thinking!' She turns back to Martha, cheeks flooding crimson. 'You're having me on, there's no such place!'

Before Martha is conscious of formulating any further contribution at all the words fall out like a pre-recorded message, like somebody else talking, someone sitting beside her drinking brandy on an airplane. 'Yes there is,' she says conversationally. 'It's part of a place called Downderry, but Downderry doesn't sound like nearly so much of a good time!'

The door slams shut.

Martha freezes. From behind the still-trembling wood she can hear waves of throaty guffaws. Slowly, she turns around. Janey is gaping at her. 'Why did you say that? What on earth were you thinking?'

Martha stares back, equally shocked. 'I couldn't help it. She was just so awful. I wanted…'

But Janey isn't listening to her. 'It's part of a place called Downderry. But Downderry doesn't sound like nearly so much of a good time?' Janey repeats in horrified tones. 'How *old* are you?'

Martha says nothing.

'It's part of a place called Downderry…' Janey starts for a second time. 'But Downderry doesn't sound…' She stops. 'Doesn't sound…' She seems unable to continue. Finally, in a high, quavery voice,

'…doesn't sound like nearly so much of a good time!' To Martha's amazement, Janey doubles over and begins to take deep, shuddering breaths. It takes her a second to realise that Janey is laughing. And then Martha is laughing too. Janey clutches Martha's forearm. There are tears streaming down her face. Neither of them can speak properly. They stagger to the side of the pavement and lean weakly against each other. Every so often, Janey splutters, 'Her face! Did you see her face?' And it starts them both off again.

Eventually, they are able to walk again. Without anything being said, they both set off in the same direction, towards the corner of Quilter Street where Royston pointed. For nearly two hours Janey works her way down one side of each pavement and Martha the other, progressing steadily from one row of terraces to the next. Neither of them mentions the possibility of giving up, of going back to the car.

Eventually a door is opened by a large woman dressed in a dark green cotton dress that appears to be some kind of uniform. Around her neck is a lanyard threaded through a photograph with an employee number stamped across it.

'Mr Edward Rossiter?' It takes Martha a fraction of a second to extract the Ted from the Edward, slowed by the lowness of her expectations that dimmed an extra notch each time she and Janey moved one road further distant from Quilter Street. 'You won't be long will you? I've only got twenty minutes to give him his bath and get some dinner sorted out.' As the woman is speaking a man in a wheelchair appears behind her, sparse white hair combed sideways over his pate.

'I'm sorry to bother you, when,' – Martha glances at the uniformed woman, now pressed against the wall to make room for the wheelchair – 'when you're so busy. I'm looking for somebody called Constance Atkins. I think she used to live on Quilter Street before the war.'

'Constance Atkins? Connie Atkins, did you say?' The man looks like he has just been smacked in the face by a blast of sea-spray. And then, 'She's not in any trouble is she?'

'No, it's nothing like that. I…' Martha hesitates and stops because Ted is watching her face with an intense, fixed expression, almost as if there's something familiar about it, about *her*.

'Have you come about the boy?'

Martha stares at him. 'What boy?'

Ted doesn't speak, neither of them do. At last he clears his throat and says, 'Connie went to live in Norfolk. A few years after the war she got married and they moved to a place called Binham.'

'Norfolk?' Martha feels as though she ought to understand what's happening, but she doesn't. None of it makes any sense at all. 'Are you sure?'

'I'm quite certain. There's nothing at all I ever forgot about Connie Atkins. Now if you'll excuse me' – Ted inclines his head – 'I must go and have my bath.' He propels himself backwards down the hallway.

Martha and Janey walk to the car arm in arm. Martha starts the ignition. The atmosphere feels lighter, like sunshine after rain, or a cloudburst after days of heat.

'Do you know this village in Norfolk?' Janey asks, as the traffic crowds around them again.

Martha nods slowly. 'I think so.' The name Binham is vaguely familiar from her day trips along the North Norfolk coast. She remembers stumbling across a ruined priory and a pub with walls as thick as her forearm and pitted, sagging beams. She adds, hearing the marvel in her own voice, 'I don't think it's very far from Wells.'

'So we're going back to where we started?'

The question doesn't seem to require a reply.

For a while they drive in silence. Janey starts to pick at a thread on her skirt, in a distracted sort of a way. Eventually she raises her head, considering her mother through narrowed eyes. 'How come you know about Shag Rock?'

'Oh,' Martha says. 'I've just heard the name mentioned, that's all.' She leans forwards and switches on the radio.

They've been back on the motorway a while when Martha senses a draining, a diminishing, of energy within the car. She looks over to Janey and sees that she's crying. Properly crying. Every so often she wipes the back of her hand across her eyes or nose, but it makes no impact on the ribbons of snot and water emptying down her face.

'Oh, *sweetie…*' Martha lifts her left hand from the steering wheel and reaches across. Janey grabs hold and clutches it tightly.

At the next opportunity Martha draws into the parking bay of a service station. She pulls Janey towards her and wraps her arms around Janey's storm-stricken ribcage. Over Janey's hair she can see people returning to their vehicles, carrying bags of drinks and snacks, bickering, yawning, strapping children into seats, anxious to be leaving, wanting to be headed someplace else, but the space inside the car feels secure and timeless.

After a while Janey's weight shifts and she swallows. 'We'd already broken up,' she whispers. 'He never even knew I was pregnant.'

'Did you…?' Martha begins. 'Was it…?'

Janey's head moves against Martha's collarbone. 'It just happened.' And then, 'I was eleven weeks.' Her voice is muffled by Martha's denim jacket, but Martha can still detect the test; the challenge, the dare, to suggest it might have been for the best. But with Janey warm and breathing in her arms and the last twenty years a priceless mosaic of Janey memories, how could she possibly ever say that?

Finally, Janey gives one last hiccup and sits up. Her eyes appear surrounded by tyre tracks and a crease runs down her right cheek where it has been pressed against Martha's zip. Martha leaves her to tidy up with the help of a tissue and the mirror stuck on the sun visor and goes to fetch coffee and sandwiches from the service station.

The shelf by the pay desk has a stack of faded road maps and it occurs to her that now she has a reader it might be an idea to purchase one. When Martha picks out one that covers East Anglia the young cashier examines it with interest, as if the idea of a printed map is a novel one she hasn't encountered before. 'They're still the best thing when you want to see all of your journey at once,' Martha tells her, a trifle smugly, shoving it in her purse.

Her enthusiasm dims when she unfolds the map and finds the only way to cope with the volume of paper is to pin it on top of the car bonnet and use her elbow and coffee cup as paperweights. After scouring Norfolk for several minutes, she eventually finds the tiny dot that is Binham, about five miles from Wells. The spidery lines of the A roads make it painfully apparent just how many steps they have to retrace. Yet England is small, she reasons, and when she calculates the total return mileage, it turns out to be less distance than the route from central Toronto to Clem's house. And she has never considered Clem as living particularly far away from her at all.

Thinking of Clem makes her wonder whether she should put him in the picture about Janey, but how can she construct a text that uses words like 'pregnancy' and 'miscarriage' without sounding alarmist? Ten seconds after receiving the message, Clem would be sure to call and, to her surprise, Martha finds that she doesn't much want to speak to him. After a brief tussle with her conscience, she writes simply, '*Janey fine. Taking a road trip with me across England!*'– which, she reasons, is more or less the truth.

By the time the expanse of deepening sky tells them they are nearly home, Martha knows the final part of the journey will have to wait until the following day. She pulls up outside the hotel in Wells and cuts the engine. Janey takes Martha's wallet to fetch some take-out food – both of them are too tired for the restaurant or bar – and by the time Janey returns Martha is napping. She rests with her eyes closed, taking pleasure in the sounds of Janey moving about the room: the rain-like rattle of a paper carrier opening, the potent aroma of fried chicken, a whispered, 'Mom, are you hungry?' Before more rustling as the bag is stowed, the clunk of Janey's shoes falling onto the floor, the zip of her tote, and then watery bathroom sounds. Finally, to Martha's surprise, she feels the mattress beside her sink a little, as Janey, instead of leaving for her own room, climbs under the duvet. An instant later, darkness engulfs them and then a second after that, Martha opens her eyes. The room isn't as black as she was expecting, Janey hasn't drawn the curtains and the window is glowing mercurial grey as the last echoes of light depart. Martha strains her ears for sounds of crying, but Janey's breathing quickly settles into a steady, percussive rhythm. It's Martha who can't sleep. For Janey's sake she keeps as still as she can, though her mind churns back and forth like a lap swimmer.

The following morning, as they head east from Wells, Janey by turns consults the map and watches out the window with a vigilant expression. As if to make up for the blandness of the day before, the sunshine has a clear, lemon-squeezy quality and cotton puffballs are chasing each other across bright blue racetrack. The ink-stained tote has produced a clean T-shirt and some less dramatic eye make-up, while *Transformative Art of the Twentieth Century* is languishing on the back seat under an empty box of Oreos. Janey must have found the Reader's Ticket from the National Archives in Martha's purse because every so often she makes a little quip about the unsightly photograph. She seems to find it very amusing, but after a while Martha snaps, 'Okay! So I look terrible! What's new about that?'

Janey cocks her head in surprise. 'Hey Mom, the reason it's a bad photograph, the reason it's *funny*, is because it doesn't look like you at all!'

The rest of the journey takes place in a thoughtful silence. When they pull up beside the Binham village store, Janey says, 'Of course, she won't be Constance Atkins any more. Not if she's married.'

'No.' The same thought had already occurred to Martha at around 4 a.m. 'I guess we'll just have to ask around.'

'For someone called Constance?'

'Right.'

As Martha locks the car – although there's barely a soul about – Janey exhales an exasperated guff of air. 'In that case, I'll go and ask someone in the pub. They're bound to know most people who live here.' She flounces off, and returns barely four minutes later brandishing a piece of notepaper and radiating success. 'He thinks her name is Constance Matthews and this is the address.' Janey thrusts the piece of paper into Martha's hand. 'It's five minutes at most. Just on top of the hill.' She points at the lane that winds steeply upwards, away from the village centre.

'Right.' Martha looks down at the writing and then, pointlessly, along the deserted road. From nowhere a sense of foreboding creeps around the corner and taps her shoulder. She wonders if she could simply drive Janey and herself to London, to the airport, whether it's ever been in her psyche to be able to walk away at the eleventh hour and whether, sometimes, it might be better if she could.

Janey tweaks the note from Martha's grasp. 'Too late to back out now,' she says. Her skirt swishes around her legs as she struts away from the car. After a second, Martha follows. As they climb the slope, the wind picks up, and Martha becomes aware of an eerie, hollow clinking, like halliards in a harbour. At the crest of a hill is a flagpole standing outside the village hall, the rope rattling against the mast. The view from there to the sharp-edged horizon, over the flint remains of the priory and the dazzling sweep of green and yellow, is entirely unobstructed; no pennant is flying but it's clear that any flag would be visible across the miles and out towards the North Sea itself.

'Connie?' The elderly man who opens the door is wearing trousers with braces and a maroon flannel shirt. His face is deeply aged, but he seems quite spry. 'She's just out the back. I'll go and get her. Come inside if you like.' He doesn't seem surprised to see them. Martha imagines he's used to dealing with female visitors. The cottage is opposite the church and it's easy to envisage a steady flow of activity to do with summer fetes and village socials being conducted within its whitewashed walls.

Martha and Janey wait beside a half-moon table that bears several framed photographs and a fluted dish containing car keys. The hallway leads straight to the rear of the house. Flower beds and the pale green kite tails of a weeping willow are visible through the glass of a patio door. As the man reaches it, he turns back to them. 'Will she know what it's about?'

'No,' Martha begins, 'we—'

Janey cuts across her. 'Yes,' she says. There's a peculiar tension to her voice. 'I think she will.'

As the man disappears into the garden, Martha looks at Janey. 'What did you tell him that for?'

Janey gestures at the half-moon table.

For a moment Martha can't see anything of significance. And then she does. Nestled amongst the frames, between the wedding and the baby pictures, is one of Janey, a black-and-white snap taken when Janey was learning to walk. Martha is crouched behind her looking absurdly young in torn jeans and a vest top. In front of them both, a short distance away, is Martha's father. He's squatting down on his heels, his face ablaze with love, encouraging Janey to step right into his open arms.

CHAPTER EIGHTEEN

London, August 1940

The carriage door opened to a sea of bodies. Immediately, Sylvie sensed a difference from before. Like a shift in season, signalled by birds lining the telegraph wires or the first sharp frost, something in the air had changed. The pensive mood of earlier weeks had been replaced by one of grey, steely urgency. As they clambered down into the melee of shouts and curses that coiled around the engine blasts and slamming doors, a porter miraculously appeared out of the crowd. With puffs of exertion he manoeuvred the trunk onto a trolley and secured it with a leather strap. The case was heavier now. The night before, after she had delivered her letter to Elsie, Sylvie had added the meagre fruits of her shopping trip and those of Lewis' old winter clothes she hoped might still fit him. Then, after a moment's thought, she went to fetch an old navy overcoat belonging to Howard, sewed a name tape into the collar, and threw that in too.

The porter cut a path along the platform, shouting, 'Make way!' and 'Move along!' although nobody took any notice of him until the trolley was pushing against their legs. The central concourse had the appearance of a military encampment, packed wall to wall with service personnel wearing a kaleidoscope of uniforms, while the steam and smoke swirling towards the galleries and soot-smeared windows created a timeless, twilight gloom. The porter stopped next to a set of steps that led to one of the exits. A taproom was tucked into the stairwell, almost out of sight. Soldiers were spilling out of the doorway, beer glasses in hand and boots flecked with sawdust from the floor inside. Other drinkers packed the interior, their laughter plainly audible.

The porter pulled a handkerchief from his top pocket and wiped his forehead. He was quite old, Sylvie realised; she supposed most of the young ones had joined the forces. 'Is somebody coming to meet you?' he asked.

Sylvie shook her head. 'We need a taxicab.' The porter gestured towards the far end of the station, picked up the handle, and plunged into the crowds again.

They finally exited through an archway, trolley wheels grumbling over the cobblestone approach, and drew to a halt at the end of a queue. Despite the traffic and stream of pedestrians it felt altogether quieter and more airy. In front of them a young woman was carrying something the shape of a picture frame wrapped in brown paper. She was standing with her eyes half closed, but as the trunk was dragged from the trolley they flew open. Sylvie fished in her purse for a sixpence, and then remembering the porter's age, added another penny. He touched his cap and disappeared into the throng.

'That's quite a suitcase you've got there.' The young woman was regarding them in a friendly sort of way. 'Have you come far?'

'My son is being evacuated abroad. He leaves from Euston tomorrow.' Sylvie glanced across at Lewis, but he turned his head away.

'Oh, that's good luck!' The girl's gaze switched from Sylvie to Lewis and back again. 'Or bad luck…' The momentum ran out of her voice and she put down her package with a theatrical sigh. 'You'll have to excuse me; I'm practically dead on my feet. What with the siren getting us up three times a night, the only chance I've had to sleep is a catnap in the park during my lunch hour. The trouble is, everyone else does the same thing – soon we shall all have to book a tree to sit under three days in advance!'

Sylvie scanned the line of shops that faced the taxi rank. In the middle of the row a public house called Dirty Dicks promised a pie and a pint for a shilling and sixpence. Although the grimy facade suggested the place lived up to its name there was no sign of bomb damage. 'But it doesn't look like much has happened around here?'

'No,' the girl agreed. 'That's the funny thing. So far it's all been further west. Yet go a mile or two in that direction' – she took a hand from her parcel and waved it towards the tallest roofline – 'and it's a different story. About a week ago the Germans dropped a screaming bomb at London Wall and you've never seen so many fire engines in the whole of your life. And just the other day my bus stopped outside a cafe where the front had been blown off. Two blokes in bartenders' aprons were sitting at a table talking business, as if it was perfectly normal not to have any bricks or windows between them and the pavement!' She sounded so gay and animated Sylvie couldn't help but smile and the girl beamed back at her. 'That's the attitude isn't it? We've just got to get on with things the best we can. Though if I can't get one night soon without Wailing Willie waking me up, I might just go completely bonkers and run amok through… Oh' – she broke off – 'here's my cab.' She opened the door, slid the picture frame inside and slipped easily in behind it. 'Goodbye,' she called, as she pulled the door shut, and then, glancing at the trunk, 'Bon voyage!'

With her departure the day lost its buoyancy. Gazing around, Sylvie noticed everyone had an exhausted, lifeless look, as if fighting fatigue rather than fear had become the priority. She supposed that was the effect of Wailing Willie or Winnie, or whatever the girl had called it. Better though, to be woken by a siren, than the sound of crumpling walls, of shattered bricks and glass. She shivered.

They didn't have to wait for long before another taxi drew up. Letting the engine run, the driver got out and came to stand beside them. He rubbed his chin as he eyed first the trunk and next Lewis. Then he said to Lewis, 'Now young man, you'll have to give me a hand with this.' Sylvie was about to protest that Lewis was only a boy and the driver would have to ask one of the other cabbies for help, but as she opened her mouth Lewis bent down to grab one of the handles, the driver took hold of the other and they swung it into the motor with no trouble at all. He wasn't a baby any more, she realised, and when he came home – if he came home – his childhood might be over entirely. She became aware the driver was watching her, waiting, no doubt, to be told where they wanted to go. She busied herself, searching her handbag for Connie's address, and by the time she found the right piece of notepaper she had smoothed the thought from her face.

The cab set off northwards but soon turned east, away from the main thoroughfare. They passed a brewery, its name emblazoned down the spine of a chimney, and a large covered market. Next a white church with pillars that made the building look almost Roman or Greek. Gradually the surroundings became shabbier and more crowded. Down an alley she glimpsed the hustle of a football game: a goalpost chalked on a wall and a tangle of barefoot players, and then, from somewhere close, she heard a clock strike three.

Elsie would be meeting Kennie this very moment. She hoped Elsie would simply give him the letter and walk away, rather than linger and wait for Kennie to finish it. Perhaps she should have said as much to Elsie, but she couldn't help that now. She imagined Kennie studying the careful sentences, his expression blackening when he read that Lewis was on his way to Canada. She had kept the letter short and unemotional, partly to make it less painful to write, but partly because her feelings towards Kennie, even the angry and frightened ones, seemed to be evaporating, as if there was an exhaustible amount of energy you might devote to any one person and, as far as Kennie was concerned, she had used all of hers up. Of course Kennie was bound to be furious. She supposed he might search for her when she came back from London, but she found she didn't even care much about that. Once he saw she was telling the truth about Lewis, that he had really gone to Canada, she doubted Kennie would trouble her for very long at all.

Out of the window the buildings started to become familiar. She recognised the public house with the chalked wit, NO GAS, NO WATER, BUT GOOD SPIRITS! Next the triangular park where she had sat with Connie. A moment later they pulled up in front of a row of terraced houses directly abutting the road. A little further along a young girl squatted onto her heels and threw a stone into a hopscotch square while her friend watched, chewing the end of a plait. Leaving Lewis and the driver to manage the trunk, Sylvie went to the door, but as she raised her hand Connie opened it. She was wearing lipstick and her chestnut hair had a freshly brushed gloss. She looked flushed and a little self-conscious. 'Come in,' she said, sounding almost shy.

Lewis and the cabman dragged the trunk inside where it occupied most of the hallway. Seeing Lewis and Sylvie edge past it, Connie said apologetically, 'You'll find it a bit of a squeeze in here, after what you're used to.'

'It doesn't matter,' Sylvie said. 'It's only because this trunk is so stupidly big.' She was following Connie, who was heading towards the back of the house, but Connie stopped and gestured at a doorway by the staircase.

'Wait in here with Lewis,' she said. 'I'll bring you something to drink, you must be parched.'

The room had an untouched feel to it, like an extra special dress only worn on rare occasions. It was carpeted in blue and the walls were papered in a cream-and-gold rose print. Uncertainly, Sylvie perched on the edge of a sofa with a lace-trim chair-back and crossed her ankles. She wished they were back on the steps of the beach hut, swigging gin from tin cups, or even sitting on the blanket in the park. In one corner there was an upright piano with its lid open and some sheet music in a neat pile. Lewis wandered over to it and before Sylvie could stop him, he pressed down a key. He smiled at Sylvie with impish delight as the note chimed. She shook her head and patted the sofa cushion, but he turned away and picked up a photograph of a woman with a baby on her knee and a wistful-looking girl in a pinafore dress standing beside them.

Sylvie was hissing at him to put it down when Connie appeared carrying a tray with glasses and a china jug. She had tied an apron over her skirt. 'Would you like…' she began.

'Is this your mother?' Lewis asked. 'And is that you and Charlie?'

'Lewis!' Sylvie said. 'Come and sit down!'

'It's all right,' Connie said. 'Yes it is,' she said to Lewis. 'It's the last photograph we took of her before she got ill.' She paused, and then added. 'She died from pneumonia when I was eight years old. She'd lost two babies between Charlie and me, and I think it made her weak.'

'How awful for you.' Sylvie thought of her own mother, grey and harassed, and wonderfully annoying and alive.

'It changed things, that's for certain. We not only lost her but it turned Dad angry. Not with us, but with the world, like he was searching for somebody to blame. The only good thing is it brought Charlie and me close, there are times when I feel more like his mother than his sister.'

Lewis put the frame down, carefully. After a moment he said, 'Where is Charlie?'

'He's at the workshop.' Connie looked at Sylvie as she put down the tray. 'What with Dad being…' – she hesitated – 'being away. It helps to have another pair of hands. Not that Charlie's hands are much use to anyone. He's too impatient. He wants to get it over soon as he can and get back outside. Still' – she shrugged her shoulders – 'what can you do? He's better than nobody.' She seemed to notice that Lewis was listening and her forehead wrinkled. 'Would you like to see what he's doing, Lewis? When we've all had some barley water.'

Lewis nodded.

'Would you mind?' Connie turned to Sylvie. 'It's only round the corner. Lewis could stay with Charlie for a bit and then' – she brought Lewis into the sweep of her gaze and smiled – 'you and me might get five minutes of peace and quiet.'

At that moment there was a rapping at the front door. Connie went to answer it and Sylvie could hear her talking to a man, sounding quite insistent about something that Sylvie couldn't make out. When Connie came back her mouth was fixed in a straight line. 'That was Ted. He wanted to come in but I told him we were about to go to the workshop.'

'Oh!' Sylvie said. 'I would have liked to meet him.'

'Well, I expect you will one day,' Connie said. 'If Ted has anything to do with it.' She didn't sound terribly pleased about it.

Sylvie looked at her quizzically but Connie made a half-gesture at Lewis and shook her head.

Twenty minutes later they were all standing in a yard bordered by small units, each with a double door and windows built into the roof. Barrows parked alongside the building were packed with the carcasses of half-made furniture while planks and cuts of timbers were propped against every spare inch of wall. The jagged rip of sawing came at them from all directions and the sap laced the air like rum or whisky in a cellar.

Connie led them to the furthest workshop and pushed open a barn-wide door. The noise inside was even louder, the floor littered with sprawling mounds of slats and staves and pieces of board. Two heavy sheets were hanging from the ceiling joists, gathering shards of dust and woodchips, and between them Sylvie could see a ladder leading to a platform where a number of tidily stacked items resembled gramophone cabinets.

Two men were bent over machines, wearing caps and with their sleeves rolled up. Connie went to speak to one of them who pointed to the higher level. A moment later Sylvie saw Charlie peering down over the platform railing. He beckoned at Lewis, shouted something Sylvie didn't catch and, before she could stop him, Lewis had begun to scale the ladder. She opened her mouth to say, 'Wait!' or 'Be

Careful!' but then concerned she might distract him, held her tongue. She watched him clamber safely from the top rung but just as that relief registered he and Charlie disappeared out of sight towards the back of the building.

Connie read her thoughts. 'Don't worry, Charlie will take care of him.'

Sylvie gave herself a little shake. 'It's so silly, isn't it? Tomorrow he'll be getting on a ship to cross the Atlantic and I'm worrying about him running around a workshop.' She turned her back on the ladder and the machines. 'Come on, let's go back and have a cup of tea while we've got the chance.'

*

They heard the front door open and close with a crash. Sylvie expected the boys' chatter to follow but oddly there was silence. Connie must have been anticipating the same thing because she met Sylvie's gaze with raised eyebrows. A moment later Charlie came into the kitchen, Lewis close behind him.

'Now where have you two been?' Connie asked Charlie. She was laying the table and paused her arrangement of the knives and forks. 'It's nearly half past six. We were about to send out a search party.'

'At the workshop.'

'You were at the workshop all this time?'

Charlie nodded. 'Lewis liked it. Eric showed him how to plane down a cabinet.' There was a faraway tone to his voice.

'Did he now?' Connie gave him a quizzical look.

'Lewis come here!' Sylvie was staring at his chest. 'What have you got all down your front? It had better not be paint!' When he stepped up to her she saw it wasn't paint at all but a thick coat of wood shavings. She raised a hand to brush them off, but thinking better of it steered him by the shoulder out of the back door and into the yard. As they passed Charlie she thought she saw the boys trade glances, but it happened too quickly to be certain.

She stopped a few feet from the washing line. 'Whatever were you doing?' she said, holding his pullover away from his chest.

'I was only helping.'

'Well, it's made a real mess of your clothes.' She tried to catch his eye to soften her scolding but he kept his head twisted towards the house while she slapped a storm of yellow flecks from the wool and picked off the stubborn ones with her fingers. Just beyond where they were standing the corrugated hump of an Anderson shelter jutted out of the ground. It had been well dug in, the roof covered with dirt and a ridge of sandbags; better protection, she thought grimly, than the cupboard under the stairs had been.

'All finished!' she said at last. Lewis didn't say a word. Sylvie realised he was watching Charlie and Connie through the kitchen window and pivoted round to follow his gaze. They were facing each other, Charlie gesticulating and Connie standing with her hands on her hips. They had the appearance of people heated or even angry about something. Sylvie wondered whether she and Lewis should stay outside for a minute, but Lewis had already begun to run ahead.

As she stepped into the kitchen she heard Connie say. 'It's a barmy idea, Charlie! I won't hear another word about it!' Charlie looked at Lewis and then at Connie. He opened his mouth, but Connie cut across him. 'That's enough! Go upstairs and check the back bedroom is tidy enough for Sylvie and Lewis.' When Charlie didn't move Connie clapped her hands in front of his face. 'Go! Now!'

After he left, Connie took a shuddering breath. She lifted a stack of plates from the dresser and laid the first in one of the place settings. Her complexion was white and shocked.

'Is everything all right?' Sylvie was standing very still by the door. Connie nodded, but the next plate nearly slipped from her grasp and she had to catch the edge of it to stop it from falling. After a second or two, Sylvie said, 'What was it? What was the barmy idea?'

'It was nothing.' Connie put down the final two dishes before she lifted her head. 'It's not even worth speaking about.' She moved back to the stove and began to stir the pot.

Sylvie looked questioningly at Lewis. She wasn't expecting a response but all of a sudden he said in a loud voice. 'Charlie says he'll to go to Canada instead of me and I can stop here.'

Sylvie walked towards him. 'What on earth do you mean? Charlie can't go to Canada.'

'I said it was nonsense.' Connie spoke without turning round. She dipped a teaspoon into the casserole dish and tasted it. Her movements seemed very deliberate and precise, like actions she had rehearsed but needed to think about.

'Why is it nonsense?' Lewis said. 'Charlie wants to go and I want to stay here. He—'

'Be quiet!' Sylvie's voice came out somewhere between a hiss and a cry. 'It's bad enough,' she began and stopped. She tried again. 'It's bad enough as it is,' she said to him shakily, 'Don't, please, make it any worse.'

'Supper's ready!' Connie turned to Lewis. 'Go and fetch Charlie, would you?' Once they were alone she touched Sylvie's shoulder. 'Take no notice of them,' she said. 'They don't know what they're talking about.'

Over dinner they stumbled from one topic to another. It seemed nobody dared to mention the following day, or the days that would come afterwards, but all the time Sylvie couldn't stop thinking about what Lewis had said. That he would rather stay here with Connie – whom he hardly knew – than go to Canada, broke her heart. Yet was it so surprising? The idea of spending weeks at sea and then being dispatched to live with strangers must be a terrifying one. More astonishing, perhaps, was the fact that Charlie wanted to go. But looking at him now, elbows splayed, spooning up his gravy with gusto, she didn't doubt for a second he meant what he said. She saw that Connie was watching Charlie too. Her expression had become more thoughtful and less stricken. Sylvie's own eyes begin to film. She blinked rapidly and made herself concentrate on the stew. Connie had used potatoes and onions to bulk it out and added herbs – thyme and rosemary, she guessed – to give it flavour.

'Did you enjoy seeing the workshop?' she asked Lewis, when she had regained control. The question seemed unnaturally polite but to her surprise his eyes lit up.

'They let me use a backsaw.'

'Well I guessed you must have used something like that. I saw your jumper, remember?' She managed a smile.

Lewis put down his spoon with a clatter. 'That was from the plane saw. The backsaw is for making dovetail joints. You have to cut one piece of wood into pins and the other into tails to they can lock together. Like this' – he held up both hands with the fingers spread wide and interlaced them – 'but it only works if you get the angles right.'

'Well I never, you're a fast learner,' Connie said.

'I told you,' Charlie put in. 'I told you Lewis liked it.'

'What about you, Charlie?' Sylvie asked. 'Do you like it too?'

'Not much.' He peeked sideways at Connie before adding, 'I think it's boring.' Picking up his plate, he tipped it to his mouth.

Connie made a grab for his arm. 'Charlie Atkins! Not when we've got company!' She raised despairing eyebrows at Sylvie and the solid ordinariness of the moment felt like a life raft in a storm-tossed sea.

*

'Fifteen-two, fifteen-four, and one for his nob is five. I can't see any more than that, can you?' Sylvie frowned at her cards, which were fanned over the kitchen table.

'It's enough, though,' Connie said. 'You've won.'

'Have I?'

'See!' Connie moved Sylvie's matchstick five holes along the cribbage board – it was a heavy, brick-shaped block that looked like the sort of thing you might keep under your bed in case of burglars.

'I'm not at the finish yet. I'm one mark short.'

'Well you're bound to get that on the following go. And I'll never catch you. You've as good as won.' Connie had been preoccupied throughout most of the game. She couldn't seem to focus on the counting and Sylvie had to keep correcting her score.

'You might get a marvellous hand next time. You haven't had much luck with the cards so far.'

'No, I'm quite certain I won't. Let's call it a day.'

The matchsticks were stuck lopsidedly into the board, like two drunken men on a running track. Connie pulled them out and began to gather up the cards. Once she had a complete pile she knocked the deck into shape against the table and looped a rubber band around it.

Sylvie wondered if this was the cue for them both to go to bed. It was late, nearly eleven o'clock, and she supposed Connie must be tired. The boys had gone up hours earlier. Sylvie and Lewis were sharing the bed that Connie's father used to occupy. Lewis was supposed to be asleep in it now but Sylvie was certain a few minutes earlier she had heard somebody creep along the landing, and she guessed he and Charlie were together, whispering by torchlight, in Charlie's room.

She summoned herself to stand up and bid Connie goodnight, but the kitchen held a sense of sanctuary she was loath to relinquish. Once she went upstairs there would be nothing to shield her from Lewis's departure, only the slow, inexorable, roll towards the morning. She gazed around the room. It was plain but comfortable. The red-checked curtain beneath the earthenware sink matched the ones at the window and a wooden coal scuttle stood at the ready in front of the stove. A shelf beside the table contained a tidy stack of ledgers; Sylvie supposed they were to do with Connie's bookkeeping for the gramophone business. Connie had suggested moving to the front room to play cards, but Sylvie insisted they stay where they were.

'Do you fancy a taste of this?' Connie was standing in the doorway of a pantry cupboard, holding a bottle of something that had the appearance of custard.

'Whatever is it?'

'It's eggnog. Similar anyway. Dad bought it at Christmas. Do you want to try a splash?'

'Well, I suppose it might help me to sleep.' Anything, she reasoned, to tease out the day a little longer.

Connie poured them both a generous tumbler and sat back down. Sylvie took a sip. Thick and sweet, it was strong with whisky or brandy. She pulled a face. 'I think I might be sick if I had too much of this.'

'It'll do you good. I think you need a drop of something to get some colour in your cheeks.'

A heartbeat or two passed before Sylvie suddenly said, 'I saw Kennie again.'

'Kennie?' Connie echoed. She froze. 'But you said…'

'I know.' Sylvie looked at her glass. 'It turns out he wasn't killed by the bomb. Only he wants everyone to believe he was. He says he's doing some secret mission and it's better that people think he's dead.' She tried to keep her voice neutral. She wanted to see if Connie's reaction would be the same as her own had been.

'What kind of a secret mission?'

Sylvie shrugged. 'I don't even know that there is one. Nothing official anyway.'

'You think he's making it up!'

'It wouldn't surprise me. The war… it seems to have done something funny, something strange to his head.'

Connie stared at her. 'What do his family say?'

'They think he died. His mother is in a real state.'

'But he told you about it?'

'Two days ago, when I was shopping, he pulled me into an alleyway. I got the shock of my life…'

'Sylvie' – Connie's voice had become low and serious – 'it's wonderful he's still alive and you must be over the moon, but,' – she hesitated – 'well, to be honest I think you need to be careful.' She rested a hand on Sylvie's forearm.

'I know.' The words came out more curtly than Sylvie intended. 'The reason he came to find me' – she tried to keep her voice from shaking – 'was not because he wants me, but because he wants Lewis.'

'Lewis!' Connie rocked back in her chair. 'What on earth do you mean, he wants Lewis?'

'He's worked out Lewis is his son.'

'How did he do that?'

'I told him how old Lewis is,' Sylvie said, bitterly. 'I wasn't thinking. And then he found out the date of Lewis' birthday and, well…'

'But he doesn't know for sure.'

'He says that Lewis looks like him.'

'And does he?'

'I don't know.' Sylvie put her hand to her forehead. 'I think he might…' her voice fell away. She had always managed to convince herself that Lewis resembled her, but ever since the encounter with Kennie she had begun to see more of Kennie in Lewis' expressions: the set of Lewis' chin when he was concentrating, or the shape of his bottom lip when he smiled. She took a gulp of eggnog. 'Kennie told me that Lewis must go and live with him. He did say,' she added with a kind of sarcastic levity, 'that he wanted both of us to go, but when I pointed out I couldn't leave Esther he said that Lewis on his own would do just fine.'

Connie seemed to stop breathing. After a while she whispered, 'He must have gone mad. Completely bonkers.'

'It's a dangerous kind of mad though, isn't it? Because he's got every right to claim that Lewis is his son.'

'He wouldn't get custody of him, surely? He's a complete stranger to Lewis. And you could say he was lying. That you wouldn't think of doing' – she paused – 'you know what, with him.'

'Who knows what would happen?!' Sylvie cried. 'And what would Howard say? God knows it's been hard enough for us as it is, but if Kennie started to go around and tell people that he… that we… that he was Lewis' father, well I don't think Howard could take that.' At some point she had closed her eyes, but now she opened them again and her voice grew hollow. 'Anyway, I've told him – Kennie – there's no point in bothering me anymore. I've sent him a letter to say that Lewis is being evacuated.'

Connie nodded slowly. 'I suppose it's lucky really.' She gave Sylvie a worried glance. 'I mean lucky it was all arranged. I know…' – she took hold of Sylvie's arm again – 'I know you hate the thought of him going.'

Sylvie looked at her helplessly, shaking her head. 'I'd made up my mind,' she said. 'I'd decided we would come to London but then I'd take Lewis home again. I'd tell Howard that I'd got the wrong date. He'd have been angry, but he wouldn't have been able to do anything about it. And we'd have muddled through somehow, I know we would. I had it all planned out in my mind. But now…' She bit on her lip to try to halt the tears that were blurring her vision. Eventually she added, 'At the station I had to buy us both single tickets. I couldn't bear to get a return for me and only a single one for Lewis.'

A silence grew between them.

Presently, Connie cleared her throat. 'Did you mean it?' she said. 'That you wouldn't have sent Lewis to Canada? Do you really hate the thought that much?'

Sylvie nodded emphatically; for a moment she didn't trust herself to speak.

'Even though he'd be safer in Canada?'

'He's got to get there first! The last ship they sent got torpedoed and the children had to be rescued.'

'Really?' Connie's face paled. 'But still,' she persisted, 'they must think it's safer than staying here, or they wouldn't send them.'

Sylvie groaned. 'Nowhere is safe. Not any more. If Lewis goes…' – she steadied her voice – '*when* Lewis goes, I shall be scared about the journey. I shall be scared of what will happen when he gets there. And most of all I shall be scared Howard will decide it's better for all of us that Lewis stays in Canada.'

'But you could insist he comes home.'

'How?' Sylvie looked her straight in the eye. 'How can I be completely certain of making it happen?'

There was another silence. Ordinary at first but then, as if an invisible dog had slunk into the room and was waiting, head on paws, by the stove, it changed. Holding Sylvie's gaze, Connie said quietly. 'If you're certain you don't want Lewis to go, what if Charlie were to take his place and Lewis were to stay here? With me.'

Sylvie's hand began to tremble. She could see the eggnog ruffling yellow against the glass. 'That was Charlie's idea,' she said finally.

'Yes.'

'You said it was nonsense.'

'I thought it was nonsense. It probably *is* nonsense. Only… only Charlie wants to go and Lewis doesn't. If Lewis stays at home, you'll have trouble from Kennie, but if Lewis comes here then Kennie will believe Lewis has been evacuated and you can come and see him whenever you like. You can even fetch him home whenever you like.'

The kitchen seemed colder suddenly. Sylvie shivered. She drank some more of the alcohol although the sugary richness was making her head swim. 'The place is reserved for Lewis Rodwell,' she said slowly. 'They won't transfer it to anyone else.'

For a minute neither of them spoke, then Connie said, 'Charlie could pretend to be Lewis. If he had Lewis' identity card, nobody would know that he wasn't Lewis.'

'What about Lewis?'

'He can use Charlie's card.'

'But everyone here will know he isn't Charlie.'

'Anyone official, anyone interested in the card, won't know he isn't Charlie. And when you get him back home you can say his card got lost. There must be a way of getting a new one.'

Sylvie's pulse was beating in her stomach. At the same time the seconds seemed to have slowed almost to a standstill. 'It's a crime to give your identity card to somebody else,' she said thickly, 'and if anyone should find out Charlie isn't Lewis, they'll know it was deliberate, to get him on the ship…'

'They won't find out. Charlie won't tell anyone.'

Sylvie stared into her friend's face. The idea was so big, so barmy and yet the way Connie spoke it sounded so easy. For a while they listened to the quiet of the kitchen. Connie topped up their glasses, though Sylvie knew she would be sick if she drank any more of the stuff. 'Why are you so keen for Charlie to go to Canada?' she asked at last.

'There's not much for him here, is there? His father in prison, branded a communist. This could be Charlie's opportunity. He's a bright boy. Not much good with a hammer or a chisel,' – Connie pulled a face – 'I think your Lewis would make a better carpenter. But Charlie's got something about him, and stuck here I don't see how he'll ever make it show.'

'And you wouldn't mind?'

For an instant Connie's face took on the same wretched look Sylvie had seen earlier. 'I'd hate it,' Connie whispered. 'I'd bloody hate it. But if there's a chance for him then I want him to have it.' She squared her jaw. 'And it's not like I'd be on my own, would I? I'd have Lewis to keep me company.'

'There are bound to be bombs here.' Sylvie gazed vaguely around the kitchen, as if it was marked territory. 'Everyone says the East End will get it bad.'

'We've got a shelter. A good one. You must have seen it when you went outside. Anyway,' Connie added, steadily, 'you can always come and get Lewis, anytime you want.'

Sylvie didn't say anything.

After a long, stretched-out moment, Connie began to twist the ring on her finger. She finally worked it loose and held it out to Sylvie.

'What are you doing?'

'I'll take good care of him.' Connie's eyes were blazing. 'The ring is to show that I mean it…'

'You don't have to do that…' Sylvie pushed Connie's hand away, but Connie put the ring down next to Sylvie's glass.

'I know I don't. But I want to give it to you, to prove I'll look after Lewis as good as I would Charlie. When you fetch him home you can give it me back.'

Sylvie remembered the first time she had seen Connie, the shimmering heat, the stillness of the sand and the pine trees.

Her handbag was on the floor by the kitchen door. She got up stiffly and brought it back to the table. She rummaged inside and drew out both Lewis' identity card and her own. 'They said not to bother with passports, but you'd better take my card with you tomorrow in case anyone wants to see that instead. I'll wait here with Lewis until you get back. And Charlie must take the trunk – the clothes in there have got Lewis' name on, and some of them at least are warm.' She dug into the bag again and held out a buff-coloured luggage label.

'What's that for?'

'I think Charlie will have to wear it tomorrow. It's got Lewis' evacuation number on it.'

Their eyes met. For a second they were both clutching the small piece of card, and then Sylvie let go. She extracted her purse, dropped the ring inside, and snapped it shut. She was about to put it away when she thought of something else. Opening the clasp again, she took out most of the notes and shoved them across the table at Connie. 'You'll need to buy some clothes for Lewis, as Charlie is taking the trunk. I can send you some more when I get home.'

'But I can't take your money.'

'Please. You must have it. It would make me feel better. Lewis might need shoes, or a doctor…'

She was trying to pick a way through the brume of guilt swirling about the kitchen, even if, rationally, she couldn't have explained why what they were doing was wrong.

'All right.' Slowly, Connie picked up the small wedge of paper. 'If you change your mind in the morning—'

Sylvie cut across her. 'I won't,' she said. 'This is the best I can do. It's too late for anything else.'

*

By eleven o'clock the following morning Sylvie was starting to wonder if their plan had gone wrong already. She didn't know what would be involved aside from putting Charlie on the train, but she didn't see how it could take very long. By lunchtime, she was pacing the kitchen and by three o'clock in the afternoon it felt as though the knot of worry that had lodged in her stomach was scrabbling away her insides. She became convinced Charlie had been found out, that he had said something to give the game away or somebody had been able to tell from the paperwork that he wasn't Lewis. She envisioned Connie and Charlie sitting in a police station, possibly in handcuffs, and even now being questioned in a room with just a bare table and chair inside it. Any minute she thought, there would be knock at the door and another policeman would be waiting there for her and Lewis.

Earlier Lewis had asked to go to the workshop and when Sylvie had refused – she wasn't sure he would be allowed on his own – he had spent the day curled on Charlie's bed flicking through a pile of *Beano* comics that were lying in a pile beside it. Every so often he came downstairs to ask where Connie was. 'I expect it's taken longer than we realised,' was all Sylvie could say, trying not to let her panic show.

When at nearly five o'clock she heard the front door opening, she rushed towards it in relief. 'Thank heavens,' she began, 'I couldn't think what had happened…' But she stopped when she saw Connie's face.

Connie came down the hallway with the stiff, unseeing, gait of someone walking in their sleep. There was a bloodless translucency to her complexion and she didn't say a word to either Sylvie or Lewis. Once in the kitchen she dropped onto one of the chairs beside the table. 'Connie?' Sylvie said tentatively, but before she could say any more, Connie buried her face in her arms and began to make anguished animal howls that shook her shoulders and forced her to take great, hacking breaths.

Shooing Lewis from the kitchen, Sylvie drew up a chair beside her. She placed her arm across Connie's back and prised her away from the rigidity of the tabletop, pulling her close so she could feel the racking of Connie's ribcage, jagged and uneven, against her own chest. They stayed like that for a while, long enough for the light to lower and shadows to lengthen across the kitchen floor, but eventually Connie sat up and drew her forearm across her face.

'I walked from Euston station.'

'You walked all the way back?'

'I don't know where I walked at first. It could have been anywhere. I couldn't think of anything except that Charlie had gone.'

'And Charlie... How was Charlie?' Sylvie hardly dared ask.

'I don't know. It happened so quick. One minute we were in a queue, holding the label and Lewis' identity card, the next thing a lady came over and whisked him away. There was hardly time to say goodbye. I think that's how they wanted it.' Connie began to sob again. 'I had to pretend to myself it wasn't real, that we were playing a game, otherwise I could never have done it.'

Sylvie watched in horror. This would have been me, she thought, if Lewis had gone to Canada, I would be thinking right now that I might never see him again. She laid her hand over Connie's forearm, as if she could siphon off some of the pain.

After another minute or two, Connie whispered, 'You must go to the station.'

'I can't leave you like this.'

'You have to, otherwise you'll have no chance of getting a train to Norwich tonight.'

Sylvie glanced at the kitchen clock; its hands seemed to be moving faster and faster. 'What about Ted?' she asked in desperation. 'Shall I ask him to come over? I don't suppose his house is very far away?'

'No, it's only a couple of streets from here, but—'

Sylvie interrupted her. 'You need someone to keep you company this evening. Tell me where he lives and I'll run and fetch him.'

'All right.' Connie's face was swollen and raw.

At the door Sylvie hesitated and looked back towards the table. 'Ted – he won't tell anyone what we've done, will he?'

Connie shook her head. 'He won't if I ask him not to.'

*

It was still light as Sylvie walked to Liverpool Street but it seemed like she was journeying at night, a black, lampless night, with no stars or moon or map or landmarks by which to navigate. Saying goodbye to Lewis had been terrible, but in the moment itself she had been cowed, almost, by the intensity of Connie's grief, as if she had no right to feel unhappy when Lewis was only a train ride away, when she was able to visit him and even, she told herself, fetch him back again if it all became unbearable. She thought Lewis must have felt the same way because he didn't cry and she didn't allow herself to cry either, not until she had rounded the corner, when the ache in her throat burst like an ulcer and she could hardly see to put one foot in front of the other. It was only when she finally stepped up and into the heaving train, thick with the smell of smoke and grease and the din of a dozen different voices, that the assault on her senses brought her back to herself.

Since she had given most of her money to Connie she'd only been able to afford a third-class ticket, but she managed, somehow, to find a carriage with a vacant seat by the door. She sank down with relief next to a curly haired Wren. Two airmen were positioned either side of the window playing cards, and an elderly husband and wife were sitting on the bench opposite. The airman adjacent to the Wren kept catching the Wren's eye. A minute or two later he poked her arm and gestured through the glass at an advertisement for Woodbine cigarettes. He took some Woodbines out of his top pocket, angling the packet in the exact same way as the image in the picture, and the Wren laughed out loud.

The shrillness of it shattered Sylvie's composure and she leapt to her feet. Even as she thought she ought to go back the carriage lurched forwards and she staggered, clutching at the luggage rack to keep her balance. At that moment a woman appeared in the doorway. 'I say,' the woman said, pointing at the empty cushion, 'are you using that seat?'

Sylvie watched the blue-and-white enamel of the Woodbine advertisement disappear behind the edge of the window frame. Outside the station, above the ragged line of tenement buildings and dirty backyards, the sky was becoming a luminous mauve. The train began to gather speed. Nodding, she sat down again slowly.

'Oh!' The woman looked a little put out. 'Well, in that case would you mind budging up for me? I don't fancy standing and there's no room to sit down anywhere else.' Without waiting for a reply the woman wedged herself onto the bench, settled her shopping bag on her lap and took out some knitting.

Sylvie closed her eyes. The airmen had begun to play cards. She could hear the gentle slap and shuffle of a hand being dealt. In time a shout, like the passing of a baton, came looping through the train. 'Blackout! Blackout!' She looked up as a light attendant put her head round the door and one of the airmen reached above the window and pulled down the blind. The carriage was instantly drenched in darkness. A second later somebody switched on the overhead bulb, faint and blue it made ghosts out of all of them. The indigo of the airmen's uniforms became lost against the wood of the carriage, their faces floating in the dimness, pale and insubstantial; the elderly couple became grey, stony shapes under the ebony ropes of the luggage rack, and even the Wren and the knitting woman seemed no more real or solid than twilight shadows.

A short while later the train stopped. There was the sound of voices and doors slamming further down the corridor, then footsteps on concrete fading into nothing. Nobody moved or spoke and soon the train jolted forwards again. Cigarette smoke swirled about their heads like trailing muslin, the light bulb giving it a violet hue.

She gazed around. The carriage seemed ethereal and otherworldly. The sense of powerlessness seemed to empty her out, but it was also strangely numbing; she'd done what she could and now she had no alternative but to live with the consequences.

When the train reached Norwich it was past nine o'clock. She walked towards the silhouette of the cathedral tower, following the trace of moonshine on the river. The night was overcast but from time to time the clouds shifted to unveil puddles of stars; fat diamonds that seemed within touching distance and barely visible pinpricks of light. She crossed the medieval span of Bishop Bridge and continued past the Great Hospital until she reached the end of her road and finally her own front door. As the key turned she could hear the wireless, low and indistinct, wafting from the drawing room where Elsie must be.

She went straight upstairs and into the bedroom. She opened the top drawer of her bedside table, lifted out her ivorine jewellery chest and placed it on the counterpane. Then she reached into her handbag and extracted the wedding ring. She held it for a moment or two, before positioning it carefully inside the box on top of the photograph of herself and Connie she had cut from the newspaper. After she had shut the box back in the drawer she sat down on the bed and listened; the house seemed newly alien, thick with longing – her longing – as though the walls were emitting a constant high-pitched moan.

Downstairs, Elsie was waiting in the hallway. She hurried up and hugged Sylvie hard, then stood back to scrutinise her face. 'I'll put on the kettle, shall I? I expect you're dying for a cup of something.' Sylvie nodded. If Elsie were to start asking questions about Lewis, about Euston and the evacuation, she didn't trust herself not to tell her the truth and confess what she had done, what she *and* Connie had done. She extracted herself from Elsie's gaze by turning to unbutton her coat and drape it over the bannisters, aware of Elsie hesitating but stepping away. After a moment Sylvie followed her into the kitchen.

Watching Elsie spoon a small amount of tea into the pot, she remembered the favour Elsie had carried out for her the previous day; already it felt like a lifetime ago. She cleared her throat. 'Did you... did you find the man to give my letter to?'

Elsie didn't turn around. 'He was standing just where you said he would be.' She reached for the kettle and poured the boiling water.

'And did you wait while he read the letter?'

Elsie nodded.

Sylvie's pulse jumped. 'Did he... did he say anything?'

Elsie took a minute to reply, still busy, somehow, with the teapot. Then she said, her voice almost, but not quite, normal, 'He asked me if I knew that he was Lewis' father.'

There was an acute silence. Sylvie rocked back on her heels, staring at the back of Elsie's head. She opened her mouth but no words came out.

'Of course I told him I didn't for one moment believe him. And that neither would anyone else if he went around saying such nonsense. I said I'd seen plenty of photographs of Howard around the house and it was obvious to me that Lewis was quite the spitting image of him.'

'What did he say to that?' Sylvie whispered.

'Oh, he swore a bit, the way that those kind of men do. And then just as he was leaving he said you weren't worth the bother anyway.' Elsie finally turned around and looked squarely at Sylvie. 'I told him he was wrong about that too.'

CHAPTER NINETEEN

Norfolk, recently

When Connie ushered them into the sitting room the afternoon sunshine was burnishing the walls. Now the light has emptied and the tones are the grainy, monochrome ones of black-and-white photographs. Martha can still see Connie, sitting in an armchair on the far side of the fireplace, but her profile is cast in shadow, age-lines melted into the past. At some point in Connie's story Martha must have reached for Janey because her daughter's fingers are woven between her own, their combined fist resting on Martha's lap. Unless, of course, it was Janey who took her mother's hand.

'So,' Martha says, because they have arrived at the point where it is clearly her turn to speak. 'My father wasn't called Lewis at all? He was your brother Charlie?' Although the words edge forward as a question she's not really posing one, merely taking the opportunity to hear the facts forming, however awkwardly, on her lips, to give herself a chance to adjust, as if to a change in temperature, like inching into the swimming baths one step at a time.

For a moment Connie watches Martha carefully. Then she says, 'It doesn't change the person he was, it's only his name that was different.'

Martha considers this, but a name seems to her a significant thing, too important to dismiss so easily. She tucks the problem away for closer examination another time and moves to less complicated territory. 'Catkins…' she begins, 'Catkins is the name of a folder on his computer. We – my sister Elizabeth and I…' – she's not sure how much she has to explain, how familiar this is to Connie already, but Connie is nodding, she plainly does know, as obviously she would, about Elizabeth too – 'we thought it sounded like a woman's name, like somebody my father might be having a relationship with. And because there are letters from before my mother died, we worried it meant he had an affair. But the folder, and the file names, I guess they were referring to you – Connie Atkins – *Catkins*?'

Connie doesn't reply immediately. Eventually, to Martha's surprise, she shrugs uncertainly. 'Yes, I suppose that's possible. But it might be that Catkins was short for *Charlie* Atkins – his own name – maybe the folder also contains the letters and photos I sent him by email, or maybe it was just his way of remembering the past when he wrote to me. The only time he could sign his real name was in those letters. Catkins could be me, but if I had to guess I'd say it was probably him.'

'At least Catkins wasn't a girlfriend, a lover.' The relief of that certainty is the first emotion to extricate itself from the messy swirl of all the others, but almost instantly Martha is pierced by a different, no less powerful, jab of betrayal. Her next sentence is louder, practically an accusation. 'But why didn't he tell his family? His own daughters! He lived his whole life pretending to us he was somebody else!'

'Mum…' Martha turns towards the tug of Janey's hand. Janey is wearing an expression Martha hasn't seen before, serious but kind: adult, Martha realises. The set of her daughter's features is the version she will carry forward until she becomes as old as her mother is now, and then as old as Connie, a face that people still to be encountered and children not yet born will cherish almost as much as Martha does. 'It was just a name, a label. Grandad could never have been anyone else but himself.' Janey's smile is mildly, affectionately, chastising. 'You should know that already!'

'Before I took Charlie to the station,' Connie interjects, 'I told him, we both told him, that he had to keep pretending to be Lewis or he might get sent home again. We said we would all get into trouble with the police if anyone found out we'd swapped him with Lewis, and I could end up in prison alongside his dad.'

Martha swings her gaze from Janey to Connie. 'That was when the war was on, when he was still a child…'

'But after that came the Cold War …

'The Cold War?' Crumbly news footage of Russian presidents and bullet-shaped cruise missiles, of Cuban tanks and peace rallies, floods Martha's mind. 'I don't see what that has got to do with my father!'

'Anyone suspected of being a communist in America and Canada had a terrible time. People lost their jobs, got blacklisted. If Charlie had said who he really was they would have discovered his dad was a communist, a communist who had been to prison. They would have assumed Charlie was a communist too. They might even have thought he had been switched with Lewis because of it, that Charlie was some kind of spy.'

'He was only eleven at the time!'

'I can tell you,' – Connie's voice is sombre – 'in those days it would have been bad news for him to be linked with his dad. And then, well, his whole life is up and running, and the longer it goes on, the more successful he gets, the harder it becomes to say something.'

'Still…' Martha isn't prepared to let her father off the hook, not completely, not yet, although the soreness is already blunter, hurting very slightly less than only the minute before.

'I think that's why he wanted to write his book, his memoirs, to set the record straight before he died.'

'Only he did die!' A shard of grief scatters all of Martha's other feelings like a bowling ball. 'Before he had the chance to come back and finish it.' She searches her sleeve for a Kleenex. A second later Janey produces one and Martha blows her nose, but it doesn't halt the tears sliding down her cheeks. 'I guess,' she says to Connie, 'you would have seen him, when he came to England. It must be hard for you as well. Very hard' – she lifts away the piece of damp tissue to consider Connie properly – 'that he never made it.'

'Yes, it is hard.' Connie begins to wring her hands, but then they fall still. 'Though I don't regret any of it. And' – her face lights with memory – 'I did see him once. He came to my wedding. He just turned up at the church. I didn't know until we came out, and there he was waiting for us, like magic, like all my wishes turning into gold at once.'

Martha feels the moment radiate across years like a beacon pulsing from deep in space. Another piece of mosaic lodges into place. 'Did you plan to meet at the beach hut in Wells?'

'Charlie wanted to go back. He said that was where it started. If I hadn't lost my mother's wedding band on that beach, I never would have met Sylvie, not properly, and none of it would ever have happened. I've lived that day a hundred times over, before that dreadful war, before my dad got sent to prison. Sylvie kneeling on the sand, holding out the ring as if she'd found the Crown Jewels themselves...' She stops and there's a gap like a missing word before her voice drops almost to a whisper. 'It never tasted so good again as it did that afternoon.'

Martha and Janey glance at each other.

'What didn't?' Martha says.

'Gin! We drank it out of tin cups with a drop of lemonade that had been sitting in the sun all day. By rights it should have been awful, but it was wonderful. I shall never forget it. I can taste it now. And I can see Sylvie, that lovely figure, that pretty face. At first I thought she was haughty and stuck-up. But she wasn't like that at all. She wanted to do the right thing for Lewis, only she didn't know, we neither of us had any idea, what the right thing was. And even after we'd done it, we couldn't ever be certain if it was right or not, because we never knew what would have happened instead. We had to make the best of it, turn it into the right thing, however long it took.' Connie's focus has softened and swung to a point over Martha's right shoulder, almost as though she's speaking to somebody else, someone standing near the door.

Ridiculously, Martha peeks behind her, but of course the only other person in the room is Janey, her newly grown-up face emanating a rapt expression.

Martha swivels back to Connie. 'What happened to Lewis?' She pauses. 'The real Lewis, I mean.'

'When I stopped hearing from Sylvie I guessed something had happened. It was the Baedeker raids – at the end of April 1942 the Nazis attacked Norwich out of the blue. It was all over the news. I wrote to her, of course, but I didn't hear back, and the longer it went on the more I feared the worst. One day in June I went to Norwich. When I saw her house was standing, all intact, I had this hope, this sudden hope, she was all right after all, that there was another reason she had stopped writing. But then,' – Connie's voice begins to shake, and her hands twist in her lap again – 'but then she told me…'

'Who told you?'

'The old lady who answered the door. When I said I was a friend of Sylvie's from London the lady said Sylvie had been killed. By a wall.' Connie's lips clamp hard. 'She was helping in the streets that had been bombed, making the rescue men tea and sausages, and a building collapsed on top of her. I know they tried to make it safe as quick as they could, but it didn't work, not that time… Two of them died, Sylvie and one of the other women. I still can't bear to think…' The sentence disintegrates.

Janey squeezes Martha's hand and they watch helplessly.

Eventually, Connie starts again. 'After the war ended I wrote to Howard. I thought if he didn't want Lewis, Lewis could stay with me, but I decided Howard should be told, that he should have the chance of putting his family together again – what was left of it. For months there was no word from him at all, not a peep, and I assumed that was that. But it turned out Howard had moved closer to Sylvie's parents, and it took a long while for my letter to find him.'

'And he wrote back?' Martha and Janey speak simultaneously.

'No! He just arrived on my doorstep one February night, his hat in one hand and my best notepaper in the other, saying he wanted to see his son. I got the impression the letter had arrived that very same morning.'

Janey leans forwards. 'And he took Lewis with him?'

'Not quite.' Connie sighs. 'At first it wasn't easy. You have to remember Howard hadn't seen Lewis for a long while. And a lot had happened. Still, Howard came each Sunday, every week, to London without fail, until one Sunday when Lewis found me to say he was going home with his dad. I thought I might never see Lewis again either, but I did. He became a furniture designer, a good one. Although it took him all over the world he always called on me whenever he came to Norfolk to see his dad. Being near Wells made that easy of course, nobody but us needed to know. Eventually, he married a Danish girl and settled in Copenhagen. Jim – that's my husband – and I have been to visit him. Once after Lewis' son was born, and once nine years ago to celebrate our golden wedding anniversary. Both times Lewis arranged everything; he says he can never repay me for taking care of him during the war. I don't see it like that, of course. I came to love Lewis like he was my own family.'

'Is that why you moved to Norfolk, because of Lewis?' This time Martha asks the question.

'When I got married I wanted to leave Quilter Street. The business got sold and there was a person… someone who found it hard to see me being with another man.' Connie pauses and Martha knows she is remembering Ted Rossiter. Before Martha can decide whether to mention the carer or the wheelchair, Connie moves on. 'Besides,' she says, and her expression deepens, becomes more preoccupied, 'being here made me feel closer to Sylvie. Sometimes I would sit on that beach and it seemed like she was sitting right beside me. I would tell her things, about Lewis, about me, and as long as I kept looking at the sea I'd know that she was listening.'

They fall quiet for a moment. The room has acquired a silvery hue that is neither light nor dark. Finally Janey voices what Martha is thinking. 'Do you think Howard really did plan for Lewis to stay in Canada? Is that why he wanted him to be evacuated?'

The silence in the room tenses, as if it, too, is waiting for the answer.

'I don't know,' Connie says after a minute. 'I could never decide, however much I thought about it afterwards and in the end I gave up trying. Howard never liked Lewis to talk about what had happened during the war. Esther knew of course, but I think Howard didn't want other people finding out because he felt guilty, ashamed even, that Sylvie had been driven to do such a thing. And he never married again, I suppose he realised he could never replace her, that the best he could do was to treasure Esther and Lewis. I never met Howard until the day he arrived on my doorstep, but whenever Sylvie spoke about him it sounded to me like he loved her, even if she couldn't see it herself and even if he couldn't see it either. But the war changed us all and I don't suppose he realised what he had lost until it was too late. Nearly too late – my letter must have given him the shock of his life.'

Martha thinks about Howard pulling the sheet from the envelope, coat over his arm, his mind on his work. Reading. Stopping. Staring at the page.

Another minute passes.

'Oh!'

She untangles her hand from Janey's grasp and starts to root around in a pocket of her purse. At last she finds what she's searching for. She crosses the room towards Connie, squats onto her heels and displays the item in her outstretched palm.

At first Connie doesn't move. Then she reaches forwards, her hand trembling. 'Oh my word! I never thought I'd see this again! Wherever did you get it from?'

'It was in Sylvie's jewellery box. I found Sylvie's grandson. I thought he was my cousin but it turns out he's no relation to me at all.' As she speaks Martha's feels a lifting, a smoothing of her spirits, like a knot unravelling with a single, correct tug.

Connie brings the ring close to her face, angling it, running her finger over the glow of the metal and murmuring the inscription. For several minutes she seems to forget that anyone else is there, lost on a tide of memories that spill unstaunched tears onto her cheeks. Eventually she lowers her arm. 'All these years and it hasn't changed, it's just the same as when I dropped it in the sand.' She rests the knuckles of her free hand against Martha's cheek, her touch is dry and papery but now a fierce blaze has appeared in her eyes. 'This is such a lucky ring! First it brought me Sylvie, and now it's brought me Janey and you.'

CHAPTER TWENTY

London, April 1942

'Where is he then?' Sylvie gazed up the staircase as she followed Connie along the hallway, Connie glanced over her shoulder.

'He'll be here any minute. He's at the workshop, of course. He spends as much time there as possible, sometimes I can't even make him stop for breakfast.'

They came into the kitchen. Connie filled a kettle and set it on the stove. Sylvie collapsed onto a kitchen chair, kicked off her shoes and bent down to massage her toes.

'Did you walk all the way from Liverpool Street?'

Sylvie nodded. 'I waited half an hour for a bus and then gave it up as a lost cause.' Her impatience had been too great, although she knew in the end it would probably be quicker to wait she found she couldn't stand still any longer, once the chance to see Lewis became a reality, something that was actually about to happen, she couldn't contain herself and had to channel the fever into action, even if it meant ruining her shoes. She picked them up now, frowning as she examined the dust-clouded leather.

'I expect the streets still look pretty bad?'

'They look ghastly.' Sylvie lifted her gaze. 'I don't suppose very much has changed since I was here last, but for some reason a part of me always assumes it will be like normal and then the journey from the station to your house… it's… it's like crossing a building site.'

It was worse than a building site, of course. The wreckage of bombed houses, the slag heaps of bricks and broken glass that extended mile after mile, conveyed no sense of construction or purpose but only a grim monument to suffering and tenacity. Although the scene ought to have become familiar, the fact of it – in England, in London – struck Sylvie afresh each time she saw it. She couldn't conceive how the damage might be made whole, how anyone who lived there could ever find the will to begin to put it together again. Today she had seen a girl and a boy of about six or seven clambering over a mountain of rubble. The day was fine with a sharp wind and the children framed by a blue curtain of sky. The boy was carrying a tin pail and every so often one of them would bend down to extract something from the debris, the girl's skirt and hair flapping untidily in the breeze. Sylvie called at them to come down, worrying there might be unexploded bombs, but they ignored her and after a moment she hurried on.

She felt a hand on her knee and realised Connie was squatting beside her holding out a duster, for the shoes Sylvie supposed, although she suddenly couldn't have cared less about them. 'It's been very quiet recently, you know. We've hardly had to use the shelter at all. Everyone has stopped talking about London and is worrying about Singapore instead. I'll make the tea, you'll feel better then.'

Sylvie nodded and took the cloth. It was ridiculous, she thought, that Connie should be the one to do the reassuring, when it was Sylvie who was living in a city where you could still walk down most of the streets and pretend, if you tried hard enough, there wasn't a war happening at all. Yet Connie had been like that from almost the moment Sylvie first left Lewis and London erupted into flames so quickly it seemed her own departing heels had lit the touchpaper.

The raids had started barely a week after that first awful journey home. From the stories in the paper and on the wireless it was clear the East End was taking the brunt; entire districts razed to the ground and rows of homes turned into a charred, burning shambles. The news first came through as Sylvie was having breakfast with Elsie and Esther, all of them carefully ignoring the empty place at the table.

She was hit by such a sick and overwhelming fear that afterwards she was quite unable to focus on anything at all. In desperation she asked Elsie to take Esther to the park, and as soon as the front door closed she gathered up her coat and handbag and headed to the railway station. There was no choice in the matter, she told herself, she would have to fetch Lewis home. Yet once on the platform she dithered, pacing back and forth, unable to bring herself to get on the train that loomed alongside her. Charlie was still on board the ship, not yet in Canada. What would happen if someone official were to find out that he wasn't Lewis before he arrived? Would they let him into Canada or send him home again? And what would happen to Connie and herself? She realised she had no idea how seriously they had broken the law. An image of them both standing in a dock came to mind, Charlie and Lewis frightened and bewildered, having to give evidence. There was Kennie to think of as well. She couldn't guess what he might have made of Elsie's show of defiance, but if Lewis came back so soon he would understand that Sylvie had been bluffing in her letter, and his anger would be bound to make him more dangerous, more unpredictable than ever.

The porters began to stride the length of the carriages, slamming the doors. There were whistles and shouts of imminent departure, and still Sylvie couldn't move. Through a wetly smudged haze, she watched the train begin to roll imperceptibly forward and only turned around when it had quite disappeared from view and the thump of the pistons had faded to distant, tattered rags of noise.

That evening, while she and Elsie were together in the sitting room she pretended to tidy her handbag, lining up her purse and make-up bag and hairbrush on the sofa cushion. As she pulled out her identity card she turned it over with feigned nonchalance. 'I say,' she said, her voice bright with surprise, 'it says here you could be sent to prison for giving your identity card to somebody else, or having somebody else's card in your possession. That's sounds a bit steep, doesn't it?' She tried a little laugh.

Elsie gave her a queer look, her eyes sweeping from the card up to Sylvie's face. 'It doesn't sound at all steep to me. I should think these days anyone would take a dim view of something like that. Imagine what might happen if we could pass our identity cards around willy-nilly!' Elsie paused, and for a second it appeared she might say something else, but Sylvie started, busily, to pack her belongings away again, and thankfully the moment passed.

During the next few nights Sylvie lay awake, imagining what might be happening in Quilter Street. Sometimes those imaginings became dreams that swept the night of the Norwich raid, the burned-out shell of Victoria Terrace and the bombardment of London into one confused, horrific soup in which fiery walls fell about her as she searched frantically for Lewis. But one morning, shortly after Elsie had taken Esther to the shops, the telephone rang. It was Connie. 'I can't be long, I'm calling from a phone box.' Her voice came fast and breathless down the wire. 'I wanted to tell you that we're all right.'

'What's it like? Is it bad?' Sylvie was squeezing the receiver so tightly her knuckles were white.

There was a gap, long enough for Sylvie to anticipate Connie telling her that it wasn't nearly as awful as it must sound on the wireless, that the Bethnal Green part of London was quite untouched, before Connie replied. 'It is bad, yes. I can't say that it isn't... I've turned the front room into a bedroom and Lewis and I are both sleeping downstairs because they say it's more protected than being upstairs. But the siren goes off every night so we end up in the shelter in any case. It feels quite safe there and Quilter Street hasn't been hit at all.' She added more quietly, 'Lewis is being very brave.'

The import of her words made Sylvie's stomach plummet, the nausea flood back. 'Is he there? Let me speak to him!'

A shuffling, a few indecipherable words, and then, 'Mum!'

'Lewis!' Hearing him, it was all she could do not to start crying again. 'I haven't stopped thinking about you! Do you want to come home? I'll come to London straight away if—'

'No, it's all right.' His words cut through her emotion, like snipping the string of a balloon and causing it to float up and away; he sounded older, infinitely older than she remembered. 'I have to stay here now. Otherwise… otherwise everyone will get into trouble.' At that point Connie must have said something, because when he next spoke Lewis' voice wasn't directed at Sylvie. 'Yes, it does matter! I don't want to go to Canada and I promised Charlie that he could go instead of me.'

'Lewis! Talk to me, not to Connie!' Sylvie found she was shouting to get his attention. 'If you want to come back—'

'No!' His tone was almost cross. 'I told you, I'm all right.'

Connie's voice broke in. 'My money's about to run out. We shall have to go.' Even as she spoke the pips began to bleep and a few helpless seconds later the connection was lost. Afterwards, Sylvie couldn't tell if she felt better or worse for having spoken to them, but two days later she received a letter from Connie, and three days after that a second one, and then another. They were no more than a paragraph in length, simply to say that she and Charlie were still alive, unhurt even, surviving the onslaught, and '*getting on with it*', which was the phrase that seemed to be on everyone's lips, whether they were living in London or not. Nervous that Elsie – or Howard even, should he ever get home leave – might discover them, once she had read, several times over, Connie's latest writing, Sylvie would strike a match and lift the tiny orange orb to the corner of the page. Standing in the garden, watching the paper reduced to flakes of blackened ash, she couldn't help but liken the ease and hunger of the flame to the fires surging unencumbered through the tenements and alleys of the East End.

Then just when Sylvie thought her nerves couldn't possibly stand any more, Hitler seemed to swing his attention away from London and direct it instead towards the smaller cities. Each morning there were reports of bombings in the provincial towns, one after another. Norwich seemed to be holding its breath, braced for the rain of silver fire that would surely fall on the market square or the cathedral. The perceived wisdom of everyone from the butcher to the bank clerk was that having softened up London, it was now the turn of the rest of the country, in readiness for an invasion any day from the south or east coast. It was an odd kind of relief, believing the most terrible part might have passed for Lewis, but with fresh anxiety swelling for Esther and herself. Whenever they visited Wells, her mother seemed always to be glancing out of the window, her gaze lifted skywards, as if checking for flares or the sight of German paratroopers.

Shortly before Christmas, Sylvie managed to visit Lewis. The sight of the roads close to Quilter Street, the yawning, scorched spaces and seabed of bricks and timber, was appalling. And yet when she arrived, ashen and trembling, at Connie's door, she found Connie baking bread and Lewis full of talk about carpentry – grooves and joints and bead-boards. By the time the deep dark of February had slackened its hold a routine of sorts began to emerge; throughout the depressingly wet summer and into the following winter, while Germany was invading Russia and Japan attacked America, every six weeks or so Sylvie found her way to Bethnal Green, to visit – so she told Elsie – her friend in London.

This occasion, though, was the first time Lewis hadn't been there to greet her. Sylvie glanced at Connie, who was pouring water from the kettle into a sturdy brown teapot. The kitchen had barely changed since the evening she had sat here with Connie playing cribbage, the prospect of Lewis' evacuation the following morning hanging over her like an executioner's blade. The scuttle contained less coal, and the window was badly cracked and patched with paper, but Connie herself looked no different, the midday sun making her hair gleam with chestnut lights. Absurdly, Sylvie felt a dart of jealousy. Perhaps Lewis didn't care whether she visited him or not? Perhaps he was happier with Connie than he had been at home? She rubbed hard at the toes of her shoes with the duster until the nasty little moment passed and she had managed to wrench her thoughts back onto a sensible track.

'How is Charlie? Have you heard from him lately?'

'Oh, he sounds happy enough.' Connie's reports about Charlie were always rather guarded, as if she felt guilty he was now safely out of it, and had, as far as Sylvie could tell, landed on his feet – even though Sylvie had never once suggested, because she had never once thought it, that she wished Lewis had gone after all.

'And the reverend?'

'Reverend Simmons is just as reverend-like as ever!' They shared a smile. Charlie had written in his first letter home that his foster family made him study the Bible every night for half an hour, and pray for the war to end and for the good health and spiritual welfare of his parents. 'If the reverend knew where Charlie's father was,' Connie had quipped when she had first recounted this to Sylvie, 'I doubt he would think that half an hour was nearly long enough!'

'Has Charlie learned to shoot and fish?' Sylvie asked, suddenly recalling the question Lewis had been asked at his CORB interview.

'Shoot and fish! Good heavens! No, I don't think so, but he canoes a lot. He seems to go off every weekend into the wilderness with sandwiches and tents and the riverbank full of birds and otters. At least,' – Connie bit her lip, wistful all at once – 'that's how I like to imagine it.'

Sylvie's duster hand fell still. She worried so much about Lewis she often forgot how hard it must be for Connie. She waited for Connie to say something else, but Connie stayed quiet. 'What about Ted?' Sylvie prompted gently after a moment, abandoning both the duster and shoes by her chair. 'Is he still as besotted as ever? I imagine he must be!'

To her surprise Connie didn't reply immediately. She waited until she had carried the teapot over to the table, fetched cups and a small striped milk jug, and sat down again. Then she took a breath. 'I've said to him I don't want to see him again. At least, not in the way we were seeing each other.' Her mouth twisted in anguish. 'I feel terrible about it. He was so awfully upset.'

'When did you tell him that?'

'Yesterday. I was dreading it. I'd been meaning to say something for ages but every time I saw him he seemed to have something the matter with him that meant I couldn't make things even worse. But yesterday was my chance.'

Sylvie looked at her, not understanding.

'Because you were coming today,' Connie said simply, 'and that gave me the strength to do it.' She sighed, and poured the milk and tea. 'I like him very much. He's a good, kind man, but I don't have romantic feelings for him and I can't pretend any more that I do.' When Sylvie didn't say anything, Connie's gaze grew more intense. 'I thought you'd understand.'

'I do,' Sylvie said hastily. 'I do understand. I'm just not certain that I'm the best person to give you advice. After all my mistakes.'

'I don't mind about the mistakes! But I do care what you think. It matters more to me than anything!'

Sylvie touched Connie's arm. 'Well, in that case I think you've done the right thing, you couldn't have kept on pretending for the rest of your life. And even if you could, that wouldn't have been fair to you or to Ted.' She fell silent again.

'Is that what you have to do with Howard?' Connie asked softly. 'Pretend.'

Sylvie shook her head. 'I don't know,' she said. 'I haven't seen him in such a long time. It's hard even to remember what it was like living together. And these days when I read his letters they seem to be from a person different to the one I remember. In his last letter he said how much he missed me, how much he missed all of us, and that he wished that he'd sometimes been more understanding. I think he might have meant about Lewis. If...' – she corrected herself – '*when* he comes home I shall have to hope he still feels understanding about

Lewis and why I didn't send him to Canada, I shall have to hope for that more than anything in the world.' She stopped and swallowed hard. 'I must think of it like starting again. Only this time I won't be always wishing that Howard was somebody else, so we'll have a proper chance of making it work.'

'And Kennie?' Connie asked, after a moment. 'Still no sign?'

Sylvie shook her head again, more decisively this time. 'No,' she said. 'Thank heavens! I don't even know whether he's alive or dead. There's been no word from him since Elsie gave him my letter. He might have been recruited for some secret mission, but it wouldn't surprise me if he went back to Ireland again and is skulking around over there. He'll probably appear when the war is over and have his mother believe that he's been doing something terribly secret and heroic.' She sprung up suddenly. 'Was that the door?'

Connie put her cup on the table and glanced towards the hallway. 'I don't think so, though I'm certain Lewis will be here in a minute. There was something he wanted to do…'

But then the sound of the front latch reverberated unmistakably into the kitchen, and Sylvie felt a bolt of perfect happiness.

The moment he appeared in the doorway she let her teacup clatter to the table and rushed to embrace him. With a start of surprise she realised he was now at least an inch taller than her; she had to recalibrate where to wrap her arms, where to find his cheek, where to plant a kiss. His hair had been cut very short and looked less fine, less fair, than she remembered, but his dark blue eyes were just the same and they were burning now with pleasure and a shy sort of embarrassment.

'Look at you!' Sylvie said, beaming as she led him to the table. 'So grown-up! I want to know all about everything that you've been doing.'

'I've been helping in the workshop mainly.' Lewis was blushing slightly and his right hand was burrowed deep inside his trouser pocket.

'And what about school? Have you started yet? I've heard nothing at all about it!' Several months previously she had asked Connie to find Lewis a school and make sure he began to attend regularly again, particularly since there didn't seem to be much of an interest in where he had come from. Nobody appeared to give a second thought to Connie's story that she had sent Charlie to relatives in the country and used the spare room to take in a needy boy.

Lewis shifted awkwardly. 'Well…' He looked at Connie.

'They're all closed,' Connie said. 'I was still trying to find one when we last spoke about it and couldn't bring myself to tell you in a letter.' Her voice was very quiet, as though she didn't want to tell Sylvie about it now.

'Closed?'

'The government has shut down all the schools near here because they thought the children would be evacuated to the country. Now the rescue parties meet in them and sometimes they get turned into shelters for people who've been bombed out.'

'Have all the children been evacuated?' Sylvie remembered the boy and girl she had seem clambering over the rubble.

'Only about half of them.'

'So what do they do all day? What does Lewis do?'

'Most of them don't do much at all, from what I can see. Some of them make a proper nuisance of themselves, but Lewis spends all his time in the workshop. He's as good as any of the men now. To be honest I don't know how I'd manage without him. I think he must have a real knack for it.'

Sylvie didn't know what to say. It had never occurred to her that hiding Lewis in London would stop his education, but maybe she ought to have realised? So many of her choices seemed to have spiralled out of control and yet, looking at him now, he seemed quite content, happy even. She thought of the sense of purpose she had found with the WVS; it must be very satisfying for him, she saw, to have discovered a skill for creating beautiful things at a time when the world seemed intent on destroying so much.

At that moment Lewis took his hand out of his pocket and placed a small parcel on the table. It was wrapped in newspaper and tied up with a piece of string that had been wound round the paper several times but was still far too long.

'What's this?' Sylvie said, although she already knew, and the pleasure he had remembered was something physical, like the forgotten taste of chocolate or the fragrance from a bank of honeysuckle.

'I made you something, that's why I wasn't here when you arrived. Because I needed to finish it and find something to wrap it up with. Though' – he added apologetically – 'I couldn't find any proper present paper.'

'It doesn't matter,' Sylvie said. 'I think you've done a wonderful job.' She picked up the little packet. A label was threaded onto the string that looked like it had been cut out from a box of something like oatmeal. Lewis had written '*To Mummy, Happy Birthday, all my love from Lewis*', the writing getting smaller and more cramped as he ran out of space. The nub of jealousy Sylvie had felt earlier melted as easily as candle wax. She saw his eyes shine with anticipation as she fiddled with the knot and deliberately made the moment last. Finally she slipped free the string and drew back the newspaper. Nestled inside she found a wooden brooch; glowing with rich, dark lights, it had been carved into the shape of a flower with six smooth petals spaced evenly around the stigma.

'Oh Lewis! It's beautiful!' Her eyes were pricking. 'Did you make it?'

He nodded.

'You're so clever. It's quite the nicest piece of jewellery I've ever seen. Can I wear it now?'

'Of course. It's your birthday present.'

Her hands were shaking too much to undo the catch and Lewis had to do it for her, his breathing steady and self-conscious as he leaned close to pin it on her blouse. When he stepped back again, Sylvie's fingers flew to touch it. 'There! Does it look fabulous? I'm sure it must do!'

'It looks just marvellous.' Connie was standing beside her and holding, Sylvie realised, a cake.

'My goodness, where did this come from?'

'This is my present, though it doesn't nearly compare to Lewis' one. I used some pink blancmange powder to try and make it look pretty but I think it stopped the rise and now it looks solid enough to stand on!'

'It doesn't matter,' Sylvie said happily. 'It doesn't matter at all. How did you know it was my birthday?'

'Lewis, of course! When I told him you were coming today, he knew the date straight away.'

'It was my present to myself,' Sylvie said. 'Seeing both of you.'

Connie handed her a knife. 'You must cut the cake and make a wish.'

Smiling, Sylvie pressed the blade into the sponge. 'Well then… I wish—'

'No!' Lewis grabbed her hand. 'You mustn't say the wish out loud, Mummy!'

'Really?'

'No, or else it won't come true.'

It was impossible to tell whether or not he was being serious, but after a moment she straightened her face. 'All right.' There was so much to hope for that one wish didn't seem nearly enough. Then she remembered what she had said to Connie, about Howard when he came home after the war, and how she would have to hope he understood about Lewis. She closed her eyes and eased down the knife. When she opened them again Connie and Lewis had linked arms. Connie nudged Lewis and they began to sing 'Happy Birthday'. Lewis started off so quietly Sylvie thought he would never persevere with it, but he kept going right to the end, his voice getting louder and louder, and when they finished Sylvie reached for his arm. 'I can't remember ever having such a nice birthday as this one.'

Connie laughed. 'Well, that's a funny thing to say. What with a war on and just a bit of chalky old cake to eat!'

Sylvie gazed at her, and then at Lewis. 'It's true,' she said. 'It's perfectly true.'

*

Leaving them, however, was worse than ever. Sylvie had planned to start her journey home at four o'clock, but it was half past five before she could finally summon the will to go. They all stood together in a huddle on the doorstep, now the moment had come the air felt fraught with cold and uncertainty. She hated this more than anything, parting from Lewis and having to start the countdown to when she would next see him all over again. She had hoped it would get easier, but instead it seemed to get worse each time, as if the odds of making it to the next occasion were constantly stretching thinner and thinner, like crawling over a sheet of ice that couldn't be trusted to hold her weight.

Seeing Sylvie's expression, Connie hugged her tightly. 'The worst of it must be over by now.'

'I suppose so.'

They looked at each other.

'You'll take care of him, won't you?'

'You know I will.' Connie stepped out of the way to make room for Lewis.

'Well...' Sylvie put her hands on Lewis' shoulders and pushed the ache in her throat as deep as she could. 'Be good.' She kissed his forehead.

'I will.'

She tried not to notice now bright his eyes were. 'And help Connie as much as you can.' She kissed his forehead again.

'I will.'

'All right then.' She slackened her grip.

'Mum,' Lewis hesitated, 'when will I see you again?'

'I'm not certain, darling, but it won't be long, not very long.'

'How long? Can it be sooner than last time?'

He had never asked her that before. She felt a tremor in her fingertips, a sound wave rolling in from somewhere far, far away.

'Come here.' She circled her arms around his waist, found his eyes and smiled straight into them. 'I'll see you again just as soon as I can, I promise.'

He nodded.

She felt his breath, warm and full of life.

There was a long second that might have lasted forever.

And then she let him go.

CHAPTER TWENTY-ONE

Norfolk, recently

Wells beach is busy with the business of summer. There are queues at the snacks van and inside the cafe, while cars prowl, shark-like, through the congested parking lot. Martha, Henry and Janey have set up camp in front of the beach huts at an equal distance between numbers 23 and 25. When they arrived Henry insisted on buying them all ice creams, even persuading Janey – to Martha's astonishment – to tackle an enormous knickerbocker-type arrangement with flakes and strawberry sauce. Now Janey is lying on her back, cell phone cradled in the dip of her stomach, while Henry and Martha are sitting on deckchairs. Every so often Martha stands up to better scrutinise the length of sand that runs towards the harbour and the town, but there's no sign of her yet.

Two things of note have happened since Martha and Janey returned from their trip to Binham.

The first was an impromptu drum concert given by Henry to Martha and Janey in a shed-like structure at the bottom of his garden. On hearing that Henry played the drums Janey had pestered him to play until he eventually caved in and set them up with two garden chairs in what was described as a 'ringside position'. Afterwards, while Henry was packing his kit away and the walls of the shed were still vibrating, she turned to Martha. 'He's good, Mum, he's really good,' she whispered in tones of something approaching awe. Although Martha appreciates her daughter knows nothing about drumming or, for that matter, Henry's musical ability, Janey's appraisal filled her with joy, for the simple reason that it could only mean she liked him.

The second event was the telephone call Martha made to Elizabeth. When Martha had finished explaining at length – about the ring, about their father, Charlie Atkins – *Catkins* – evacuated to Canada under the name of Lewis Rodwell, about Connie, their father's sister left in England, and even about Henry, Sylvie's grandson and Lewis' nephew, but no relation to Charlie or, thankfully, to Martha or Elizabeth – there was a long silence. Finally, Elizabeth cleared her throat. 'Right,' she said, and fell quiet again. On this occasion the other words that might have been on the tip of Elizabeth's tongue were, for once, not obvious. Martha couldn't fathom what her sister might be thinking or what she might be wanting to say. 'Right,' didn't seem to be the apex to anything at all. Martha waited a moment, listening for the click of a keyboard or the rumble of a car engine, but the line was noiseless.

'Elizabeth? Are you still there?' Martha asked at last.

To her astonishment Elizabeth's voice whooshed down the line like a released greyhound. 'You always get the best stuff, Martha! How come I always miss out?'

Martha stared at the screen with incredulity. 'I get… What on earth? I mean why—'

'I have to go now,' Elizabeth said, slicing with dignity through Martha's incoherence. And she hung up.

Three days later Martha was still trying to make sense of this exchange when Elizabeth rang Martha. 'I'm at the airport,' she announced.

'Okay,' Martha said cautiously. She stepped out of the sandwich shop where she and Janey were in the process of ordering lunch to give the call her full attention. 'Is it another business trip? Where are you going this time?'

'No, Martha, you don't understand!' A familiar ring of impatience had re-inhabited her sister's voice. 'I've already gone. I'm here. At Heathrow.'

'Heathrow! But why…? I mean, wow! But…?' Again Martha fumbled to find a foothold in this topsy-turvy world.

'I guess I thought I needed a vacation too.'

'So how long…?'

'Ten days.'

'Ten days! And he… they… your boss was okay with that?'

'Not really, no. But I told them it was non-negotiable. They only thing they got to choose was whether I came back or not.'

'Wow,' Martha repeated, a little weakly. 'What *did* they choose?'

'Oh, they want me back.' And to Martha's relief – because there's only so much change a person can take at any one time – Elizabeth added with feeling, '*Thank God!*'

In the distance a woman is moving towards them. Martha has to shield her eyes from the glare of the sun, but she can see Elizabeth now, picking a way through pockets of children crouched over buckets, mothers and fathers in shorts and bathers. She must, Martha realises, have taken the first set of steps and walked the whole exhausting length of the beach. For a while her sister seems stuck in the distance like a scene from a postcard and then all at once she's nearly in front of them. She's wearing a floaty, expensive-looking dress and strappy sandals that are quite hopeless for the beach. A cardigan or jacket is tucked around her shoulders and an enormous straw basket is hooked over her elbow.

Martha opens her arms and wraps Elizabeth into a hug. 'You made it!' She's startled at the whiteness of Elizabeth's skin, which is practically transparent in the salt-rich sunshine; even Janey appears more robust than her sister. After the welcomes and introductions are over, Martha fetches another deckchair and blanket from the hut, so that there's room for all four of them – Janey, Elizabeth, Henry and herself.

They have been chatting a while when Henry says to Martha, 'You can get to know the real Lewis Rodwell if you like. He's coming to visit my mother in two weeks' time.'

'Oh! Well, maybe that would be nice…' Martha's voice drifts on a breeze of indecision. She's curious to meet Lewis, yet at the same time she knows it will be decidedly weird to come face-to-face with the person whose name both does and doesn't belong to her father. And it's not just her father's name that's in question. She isn't Martha Rodwell, it has occurred to her, but Martha Atkins. The day before she had tossed this difficult thought at Janey – since they found Connie it seems they haven't stopped talking, about Sylvie, about Sylvie's decision, even about the difficult, painful stuff of Janey's heartbreak. During the conversation about names they were in the hire car on their way to buy Janey a rucksack, not a small one like Martha's but a proper backpacking one with sufficient space to accommodate a six-week rail trip around Europe before the start of the Cambridge year. To Martha's annoyance, Janey gave the problem short shrift.

'Nobody needs to know, Mom. You can stick with Rodwell if you want to.'

'But,' Martha persisted, 'it isn't my real name.'

Janey gave her an exasperated look. 'Why does that even matter? You were Martha Barrington all the time you were married to Dad. It doesn't *mean* anything.' She closed her eyes, leaning back against the headrest. After a moment she said, 'I suppose if you're that vexed about it you could always marry Henry and get a whole new name that way.'

'Marry Henry!' Martha snapped upright over the steering wheel. 'How did a crazy notion like that arrive in your head?'

Janey opened her eyes. 'Calm down, Mom,' she said mildly. 'It was only a joke.'

Martha is remembering this conversation when she sees Elizabeth shaking her head.

'You can't meet Lewis,' Elizabeth says. 'Even if you want to.' She's busy rubbing factor 50 sun lotion on her arms.

'Why not?' Martha says, frowning.

'Because you will have left Norfolk by then. I timed my flights so we could go back together. I go home – we both go home – in ten days' time.'

'That can't be right!' Martha looks at Henry to confirm the flaw in Elizabeth's calculations. 'What date is it today?'

Elizabeth answers before Henry can open his mouth, '21 May.'

'21 May!' Another alarm sounds inside Martha's head. '21 May?' How have the days run away from her like this? 'How can it possibly be May 21 already?'

Janey stirs from her horizontal position on the rug. 'Mom' – propping herself onto her elbows she regards her mother with alarm – 'you didn't forget Dad's birthday, did you?'

'Well if today is 21 May' – Martha is still struggling to come to terms with this fact – 'then I guess I must have done.'

Janey's mouth twists in disapproval. 'Well, why don't you call him? If you do it now he won't have left for work already.' She sits up, arm extended, to proffer her cell phone.

Martha gently pushes the phone away. 'I don't think so. It's still very early in Canada. Your dad will be celebrating with Christie and the twins. He wouldn't want me to interrupt that.' She leans forward to brush a patch of beach from the side of Janey's nose. 'Next time we're in town we can choose a postcard and send him one from the both of us.'

Henry clears his throat. 'But you are leaving, in ten days' time?' His gaze locks on Martha's face.

'Well, I guess that's the plan. That's the *current* plan.' She holds the connection.

Somewhere behind them a wave rolls in and draws away.

'Tide is going out,' Henry says. 'Anyone want a walk?' He's still looking straight at Martha.

She nods and scrambles to her feet.

The weather is being unpredictable. One minute the sun is dipping into cloud and the next bursting clear, creating long shadows that expand and contract on the blank page of sand. Low above the sea hovers a faint, uncertain moon, the ghost of her nighttime sister, she seems barely real; but Martha knows the truth about the moon now. Although the days have passed so quickly, the strange flight to London, her arrival in the airport, both feel as if they could have happened years ago, perhaps even to someone else. The trick, it occurs to her, is being able to tell the difference between the trivial opportunities, the choices and chances that will barely ruffle the surface, and the ones that can change the whole direction of the current, the ones that need to be grabbed and held onto and fought for.

She waits for Henry to come and stand beside her and then, because there isn't another minute to lose, she takes his hand and interlaces her fingers securely between his own.

A LETTER FROM SARAH

Dear Reader,

I want to say a huge thank you for choosing to read *The Lost Letters*. If you did enjoy it, and want to keep up-to-date with all my latest releases, just sign up at the following link. Your email address will never be shared and you can unsubscribe at any time.

www.bookouture.com/sarah-mitchell

I gained so much from writing this book. In particular, learning about the wartime overseas evacuation programme was a very moving experience for me, as my mother would have been evacuated from her home in Suffolk to Canada had my grandparents not changed their minds at the very last minute. It must have been a truly agonising time for them, and parents all over the country, faced with the choice between sending their children to strangers on the other side of the world and keeping their family together but exposing them to the daily terror of bombs and likely invasion. In such dreadful circumstances, and with so many men away fighting, women had to rely on each other and I like to think of Sylvie's friendship with Connie as the beacon that got them both through their darkest days. My grandparents' decision not to evacuate my mother was lucky for me because it meant she later became a member of the Women's Royal Naval Service (a 'Wren') and met my father, an aircraft gunner, when they took shelter in a Nissan hut during a thunderstorm.

I have tried to base the story around real events that happened in Norwich, London and the wider world between 1939 and 1942.

The details about the evacuation programme and the dates of the bombing raids on Norwich are, I hope, accurate. As part of my research I came across the bomb map of my local city, Norwich, a place that was targeted even before London. Compiled as the war progressed, the map pinpoints every blast and the date the bomb fell. Now, when I walk around these familiar streets I see them with different eyes and am continually reminded of the strength and resilience shown by people like us in the face of such horror.

If you liked *The Lost Letters* I would be very grateful if you could write a review. I really appreciate hearing what you think, and it makes such a difference in helping new readers to discover one of my books for the first time. Also, I love to hear from my readers – you can get in touch through Twitter – whether you have any comments or thoughts about the book or would just like to say hello. It means a great deal to me to know I am not writing away in isolation and that somebody out there is actually reading and enjoying my work.

With thanks,
Sarah Mitchell

 @SarahM_writer

ACKNOWLEDGEMENTS

I have had so much help and encouragement writing this book it feels as though a whole list of names should be on the front cover. At the UEA both of my workshop leaders, Andrew Cowan and Helen Cross, provided me with invaluable feedback and self-belief, while all the participants of those workshops helped to make them constructive, illuminative and thoroughly wonderful experiences. Thank you too, Liz Hambrick, for your friendship from before day one and having faith in the book long before I did, and Henry Sutton, my supervisor, who has given me steadfast support from the moment of my first interview. Outside UEA, I am deeply grateful to my friend Clare Barter for reading numerous drafts of numerous chapters and always being hugely positive, even when my momentum flagged. I am also very grateful to my fantastic agent and editor, Veronique Baxter and Jenny Geras - the expertise and insight of them both has made the book far better than I could have made it on my own. Finally, I want to thank my family: my children, Oliver, Thomas and Laura, and, of course, my husband, Peter. Without their love and belief in me I would never have written the first word.

Made in the USA
San Bernardino, CA
13 November 2018